One Year at Ellsmere

One Year at Ellsmere

FAITH ERIN HICKS

COLOR BY SHELLI PAROLINE

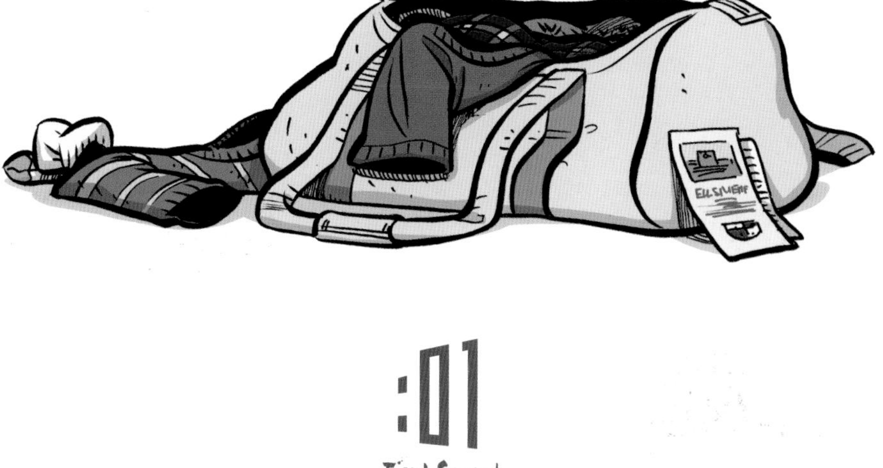
ELLSMERE

:01
First Second
New York

Chapter One

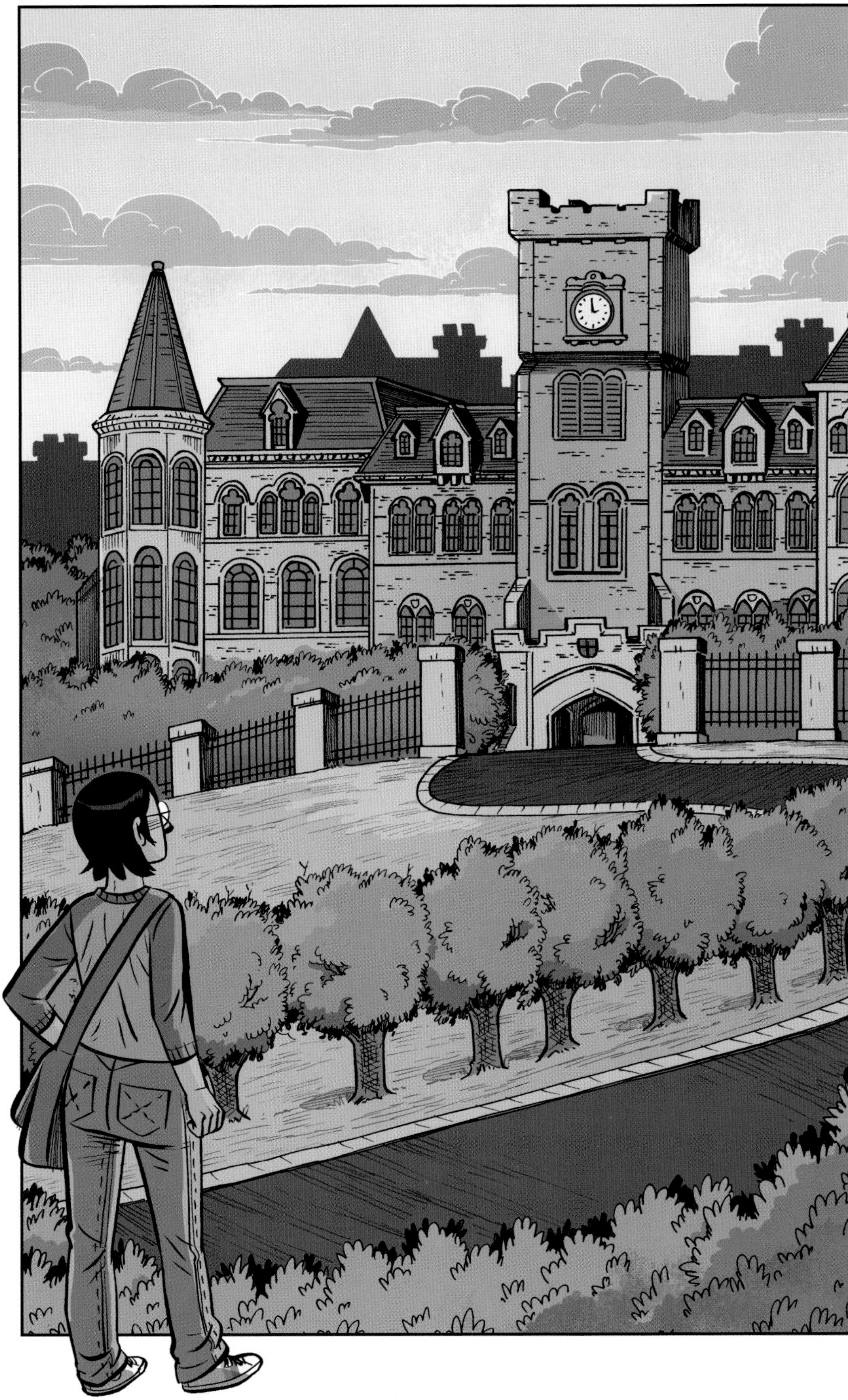

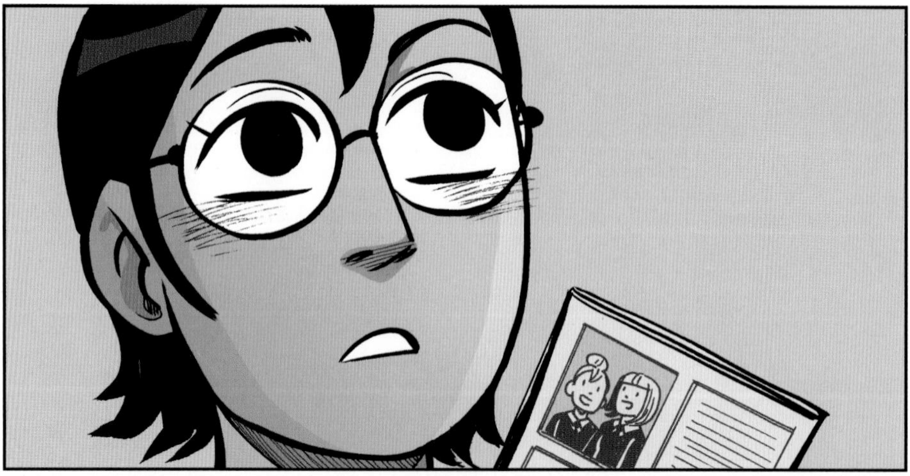

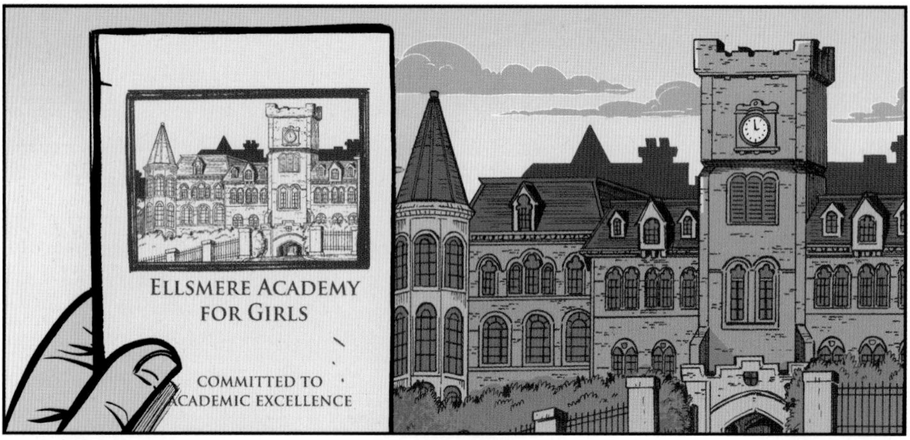
ELLSMERE ACADEMY FOR GIRLS
COMMITTED TO ACADEMIC EXCELLENCE

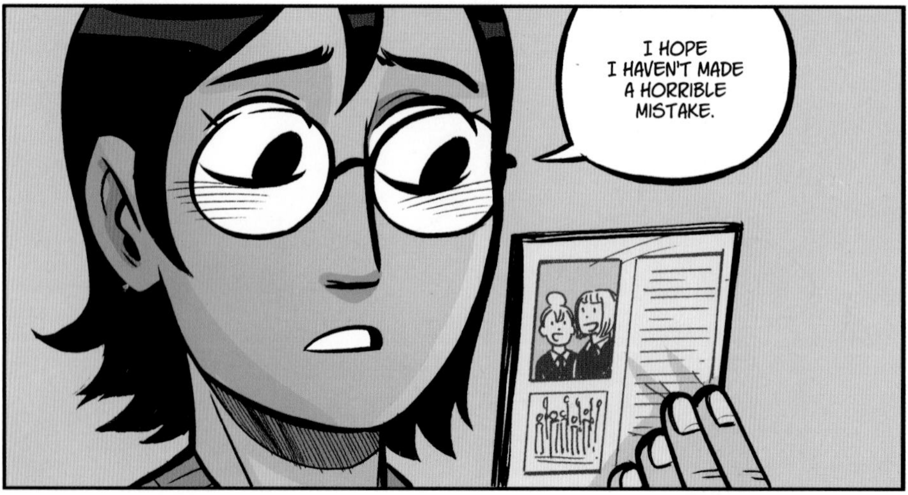
I HOPE I HAVEN'T MADE A HORRIBLE MISTAKE.

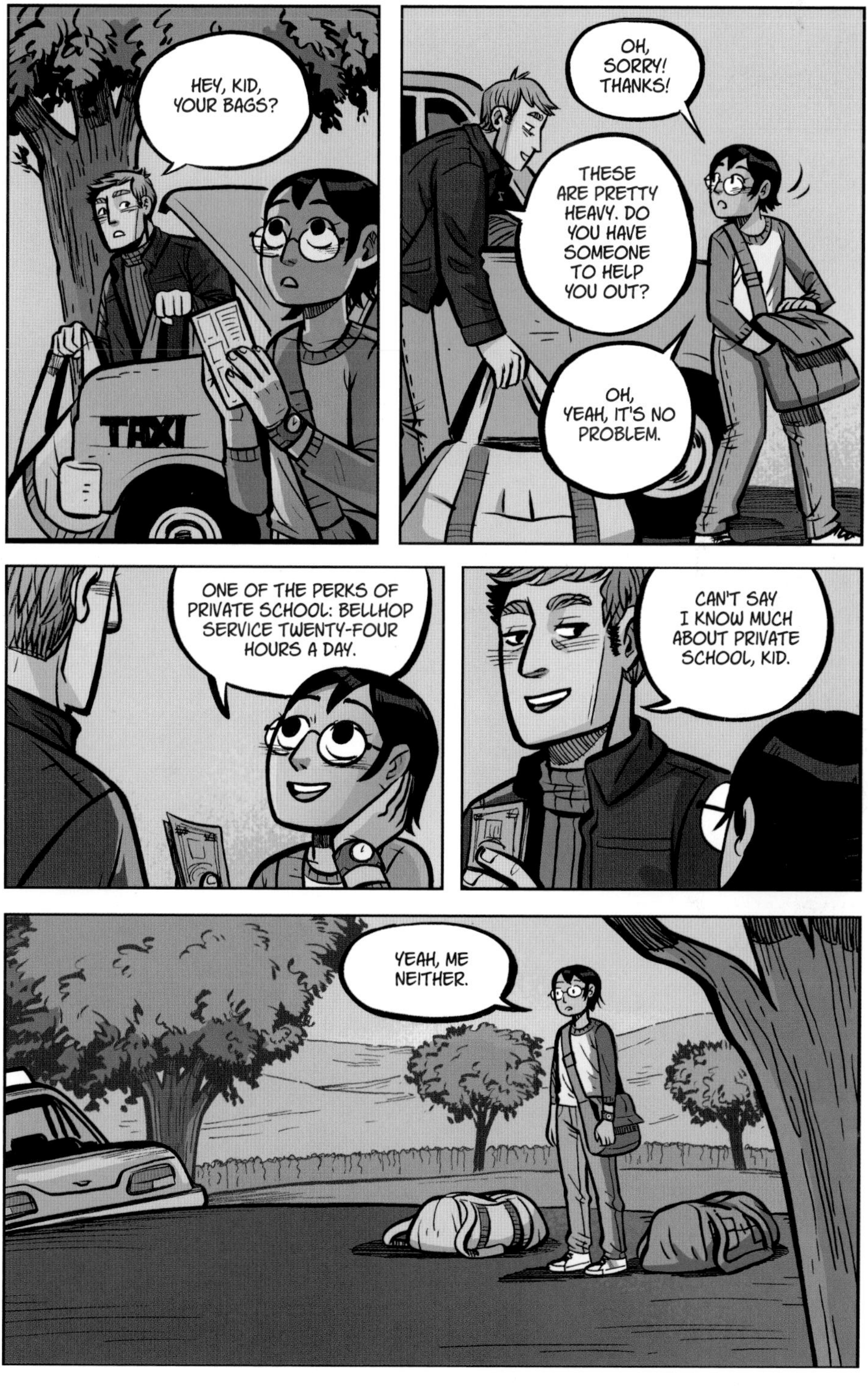
HEY, KID, YOUR BAGS?
OH, SORRY! THANKS!
THESE ARE PRETTY HEAVY. DO YOU HAVE SOMEONE TO HELP YOU OUT?
OH, YEAH, IT'S NO PROBLEM.
ONE OF THE PERKS OF PRIVATE SCHOOL: BELLHOP SERVICE TWENTY-FOUR HOURS A DAY.
CAN'T SAY I KNOW MUCH ABOUT PRIVATE SCHOOL, KID.
YEAH, ME NEITHER.
TAXI

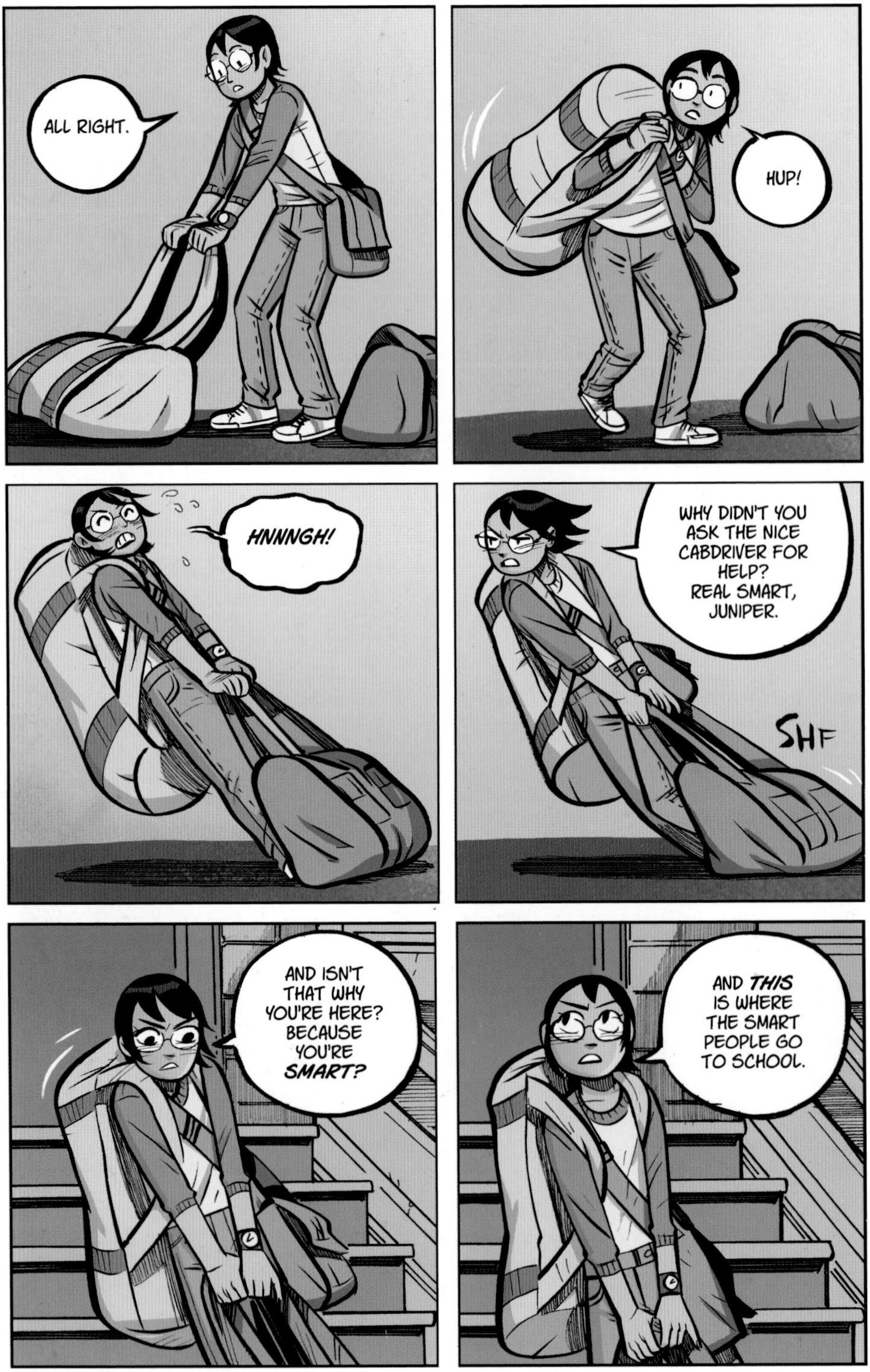

ALL RIGHT.
HUP!
HNNNGH!
WHY DIDN'T YOU ASK THE NICE CABDRIVER FOR HELP? REAL SMART, JUNIPER.
SHF
AND ISN'T THAT WHY YOU'RE HERE? BECAUSE YOU'RE SMART?
AND THIS IS WHERE THE SMART PEOPLE GO TO SCHOOL.

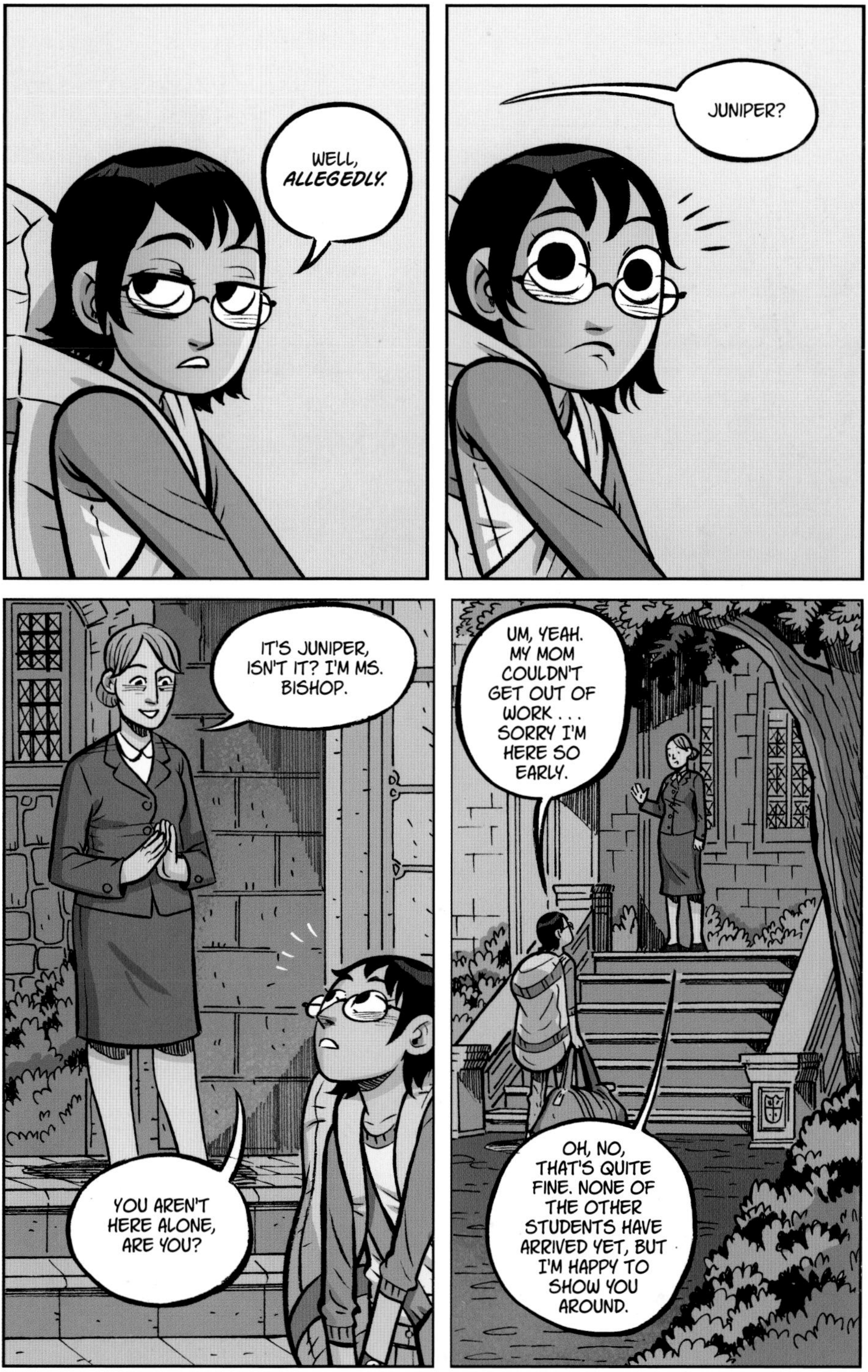
WELL, ALLEGEDLY.
JUNIPER?
IT'S JUNIPER, ISN'T IT? I'M MS. BISHOP.
YOU AREN'T HERE ALONE, ARE YOU?
UM, YEAH. MY MOM COULDN'T GET OUT OF WORK . . . SORRY I'M HERE SO EARLY.
OH, NO, THAT'S QUITE FINE. NONE OF THE OTHER STUDENTS HAVE ARRIVED YET, BUT I'M HAPPY TO SHOW YOU AROUND.

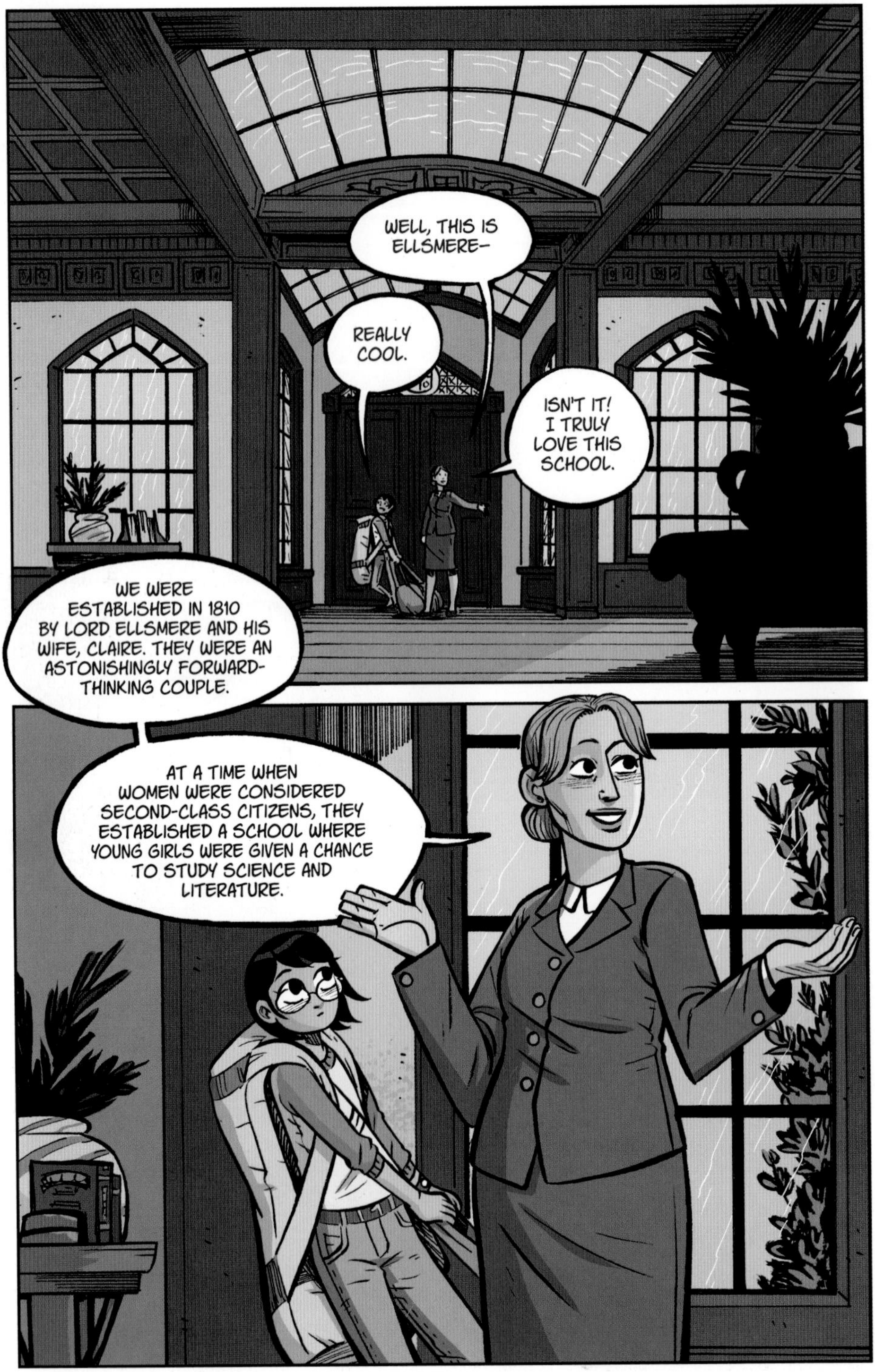
WELL, THIS IS ELLSMERE–
REALLY COOL.
ISN'T IT! I TRULY LOVE THIS SCHOOL.
WE WERE ESTABLISHED IN 1810 BY LORD ELLSMERE AND HIS WIFE, CLAIRE. THEY WERE AN ASTONISHINGLY FORWARD-THINKING COUPLE.
AT A TIME WHEN WOMEN WERE CONSIDERED SECOND-CLASS CITIZENS, THEY ESTABLISHED A SCHOOL WHERE YOUNG GIRLS WERE GIVEN A CHANCE TO STUDY SCIENCE AND LITERATURE.

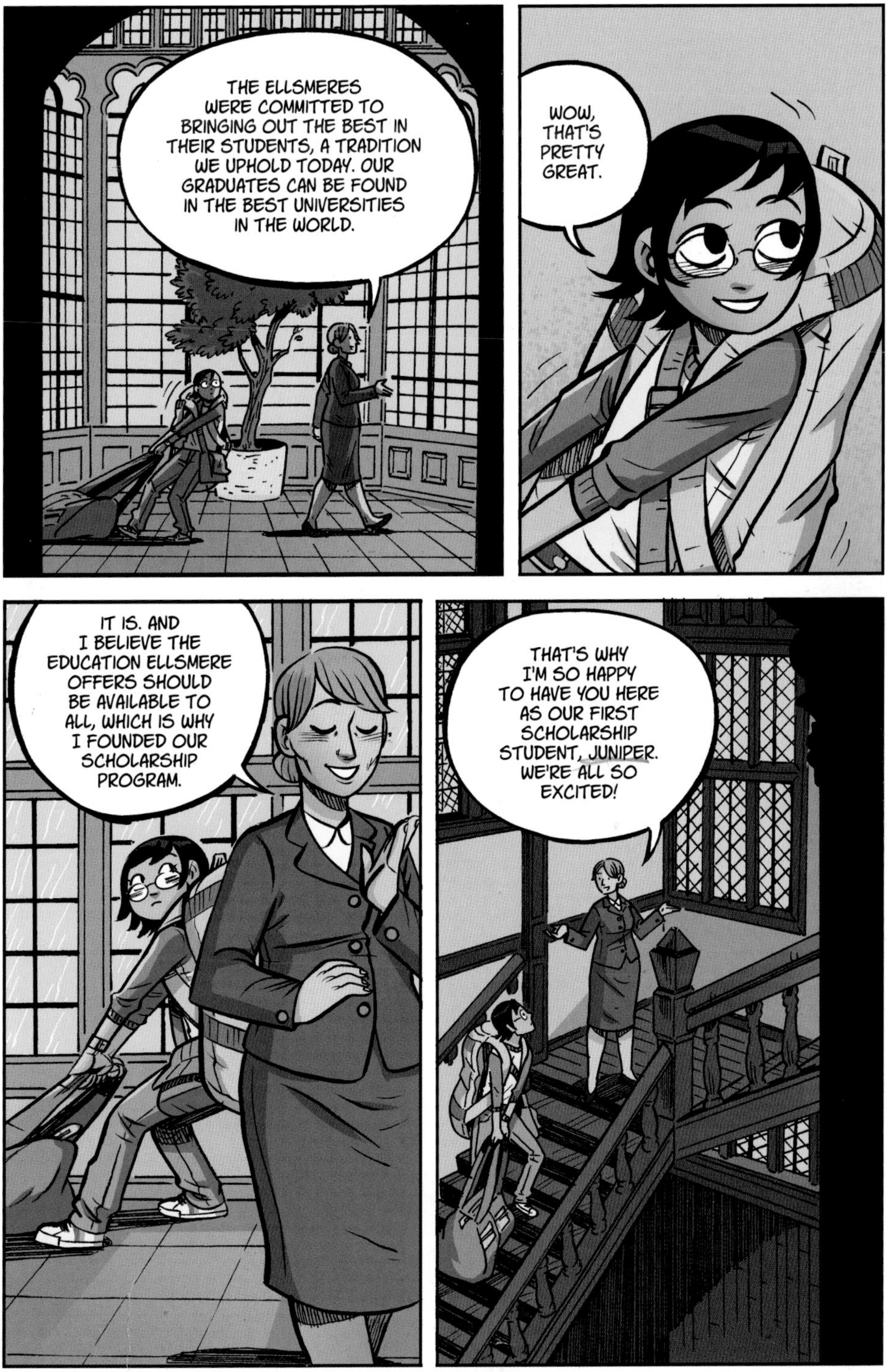
THE ELLSMERES WERE COMMITTED TO BRINGING OUT THE BEST IN THEIR STUDENTS, A TRADITION WE UPHOLD TODAY. OUR GRADUATES CAN BE FOUND IN THE BEST UNIVERSITIES IN THE WORLD.
WOW, THAT'S PRETTY GREAT.
IT IS. AND I BELIEVE THE EDUCATION ELLSMERE OFFERS SHOULD BE AVAILABLE TO ALL, WHICH IS WHY I FOUNDED OUR SCHOLARSHIP PROGRAM.
THAT'S WHY I'M SO HAPPY TO HAVE YOU HERE AS OUR FIRST SCHOLARSHIP STUDENT, JUNIPER. WE'RE ALL SO EXCITED!

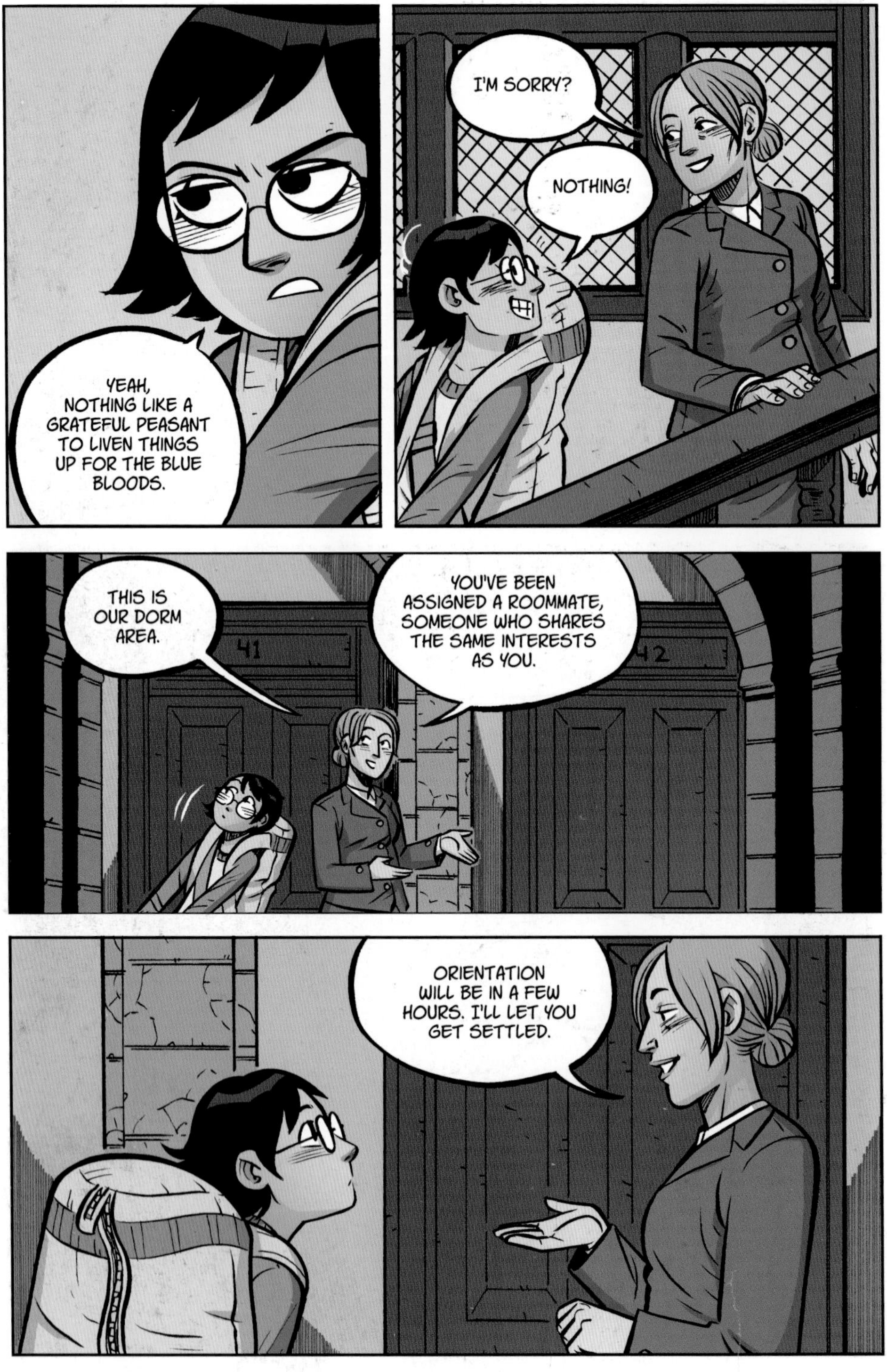
YEAH, NOTHING LIKE A GRATEFUL PEASANT TO LIVEN THINGS UP FOR THE BLUE BLOODS.
I'M SORRY?
NOTHING!
THIS IS OUR DORM AREA.
YOU'VE BEEN ASSIGNED A ROOMMATE, SOMEONE WHO SHARES THE SAME INTERESTS AS YOU.
ORIENTATION WILL BE IN A FEW HOURS. I'LL LET YOU GET SETTLED.

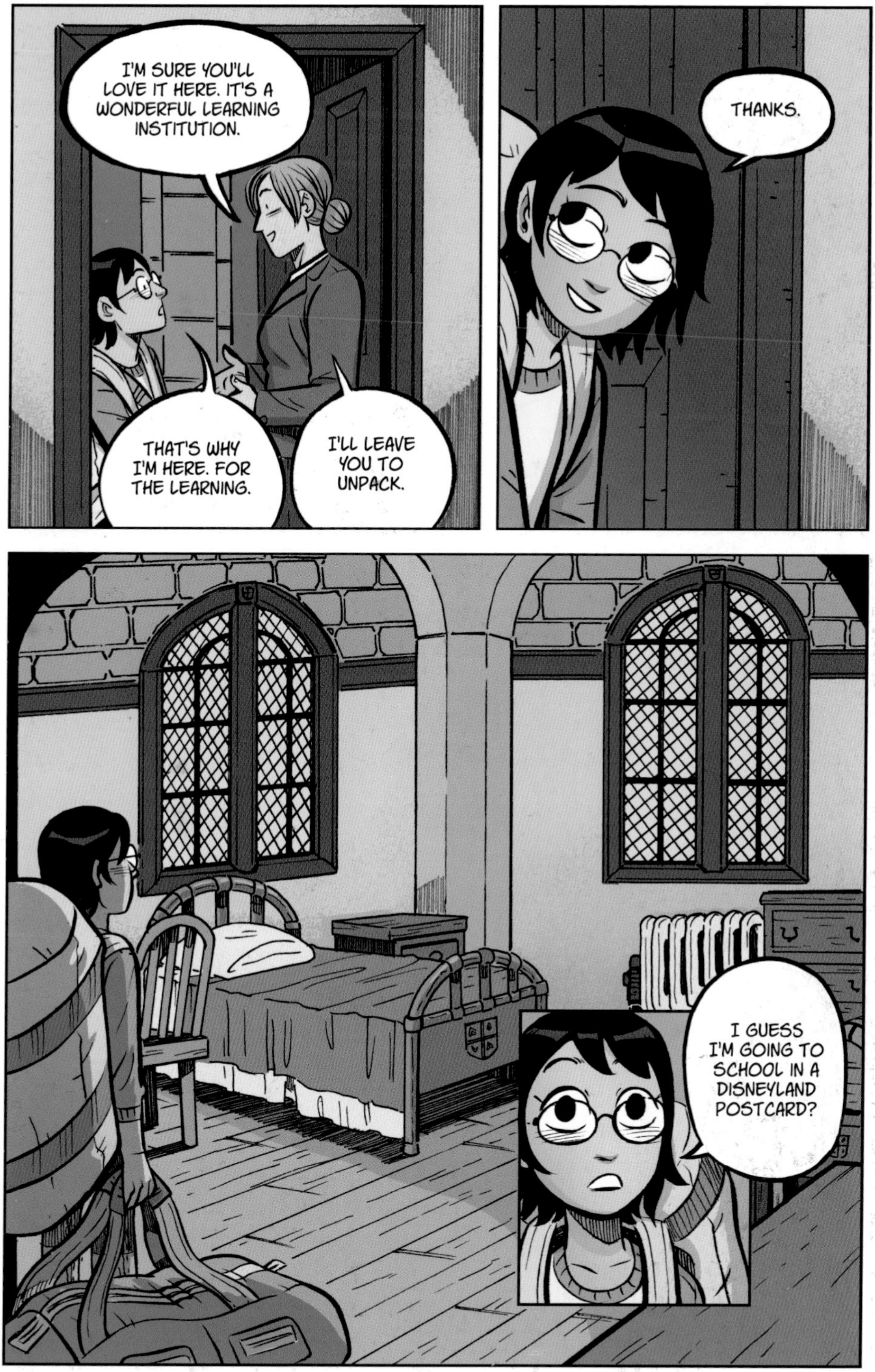
I'M SURE YOU'LL LOVE IT HERE. IT'S A WONDERFUL LEARNING INSTITUTION.
THAT'S WHY I'M HERE. FOR THE LEARNING.
I'LL LEAVE YOU TO UNPACK.
THANKS.
I GUESS I'M GOING TO SCHOOL IN A DISNEYLAND POSTCARD?

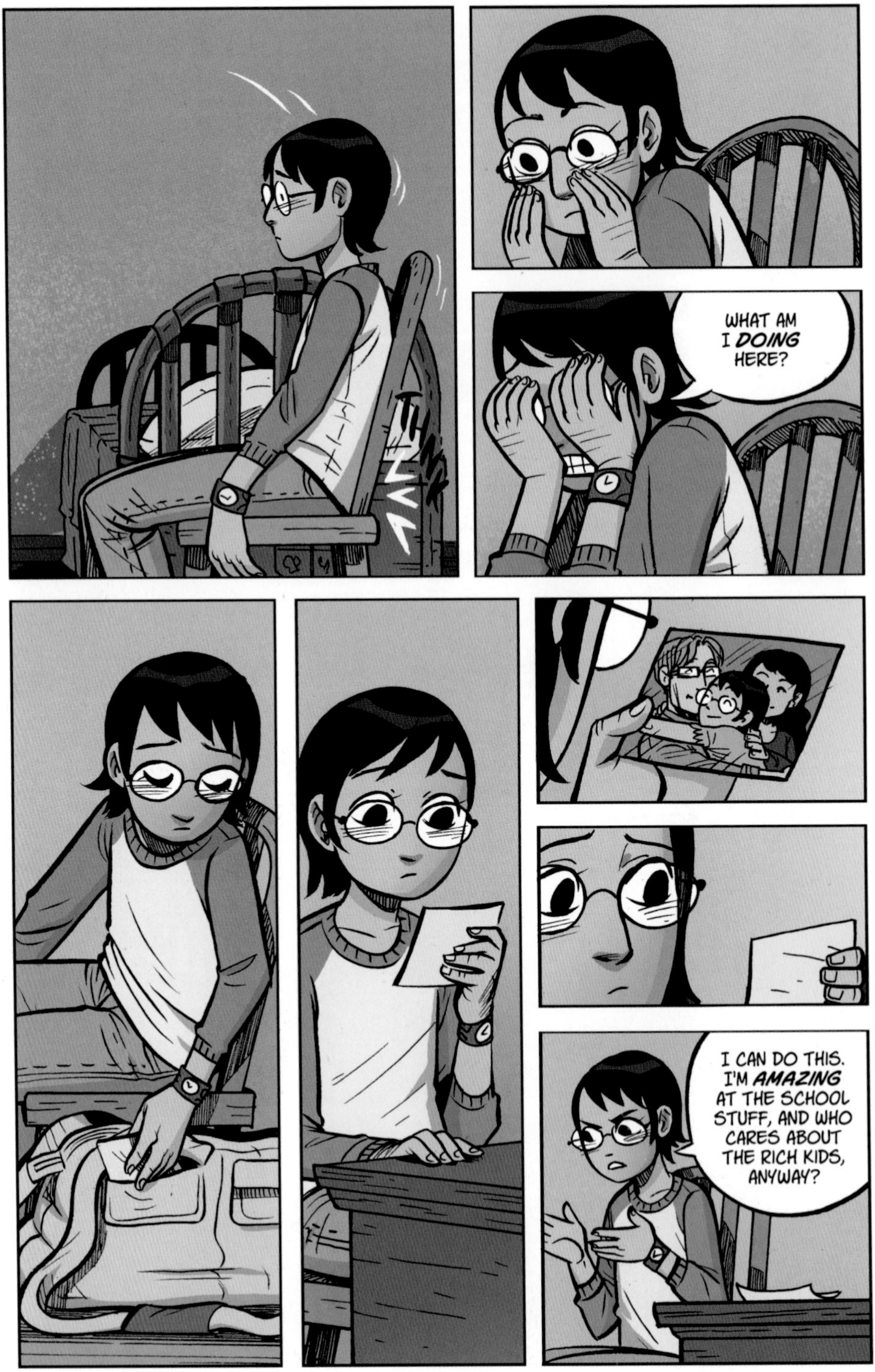
THUNK
WHAT AM I *DOING* HERE?
I CAN DO THIS. I'M *AMAZING* AT THE SCHOOL STUFF, AND WHO CARES ABOUT THE RICH KIDS, ANYWAY?

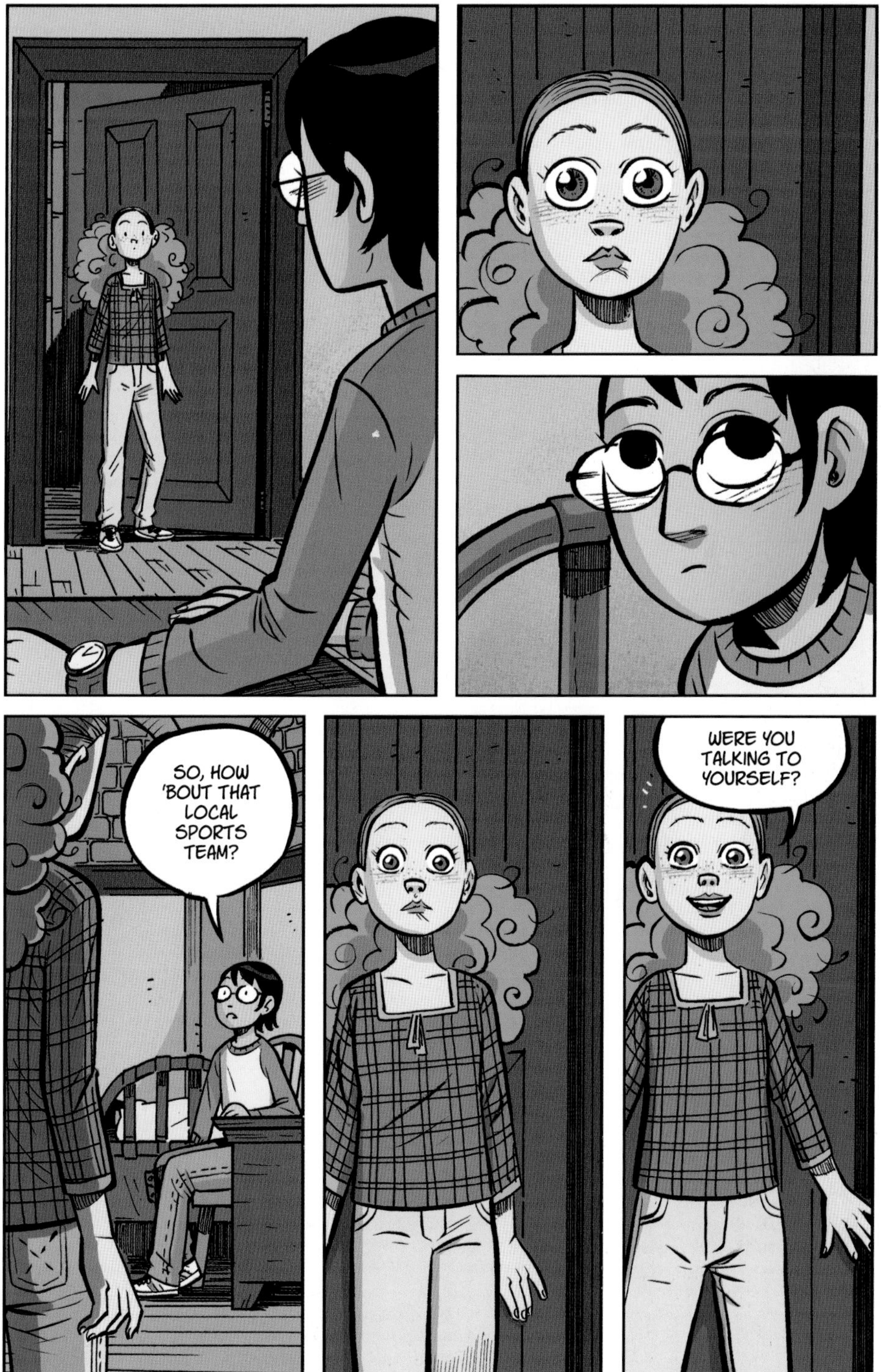
SO, HOW 'BOUT THAT LOCAL SPORTS TEAM?
WERE YOU TALKING TO YOURSELF?

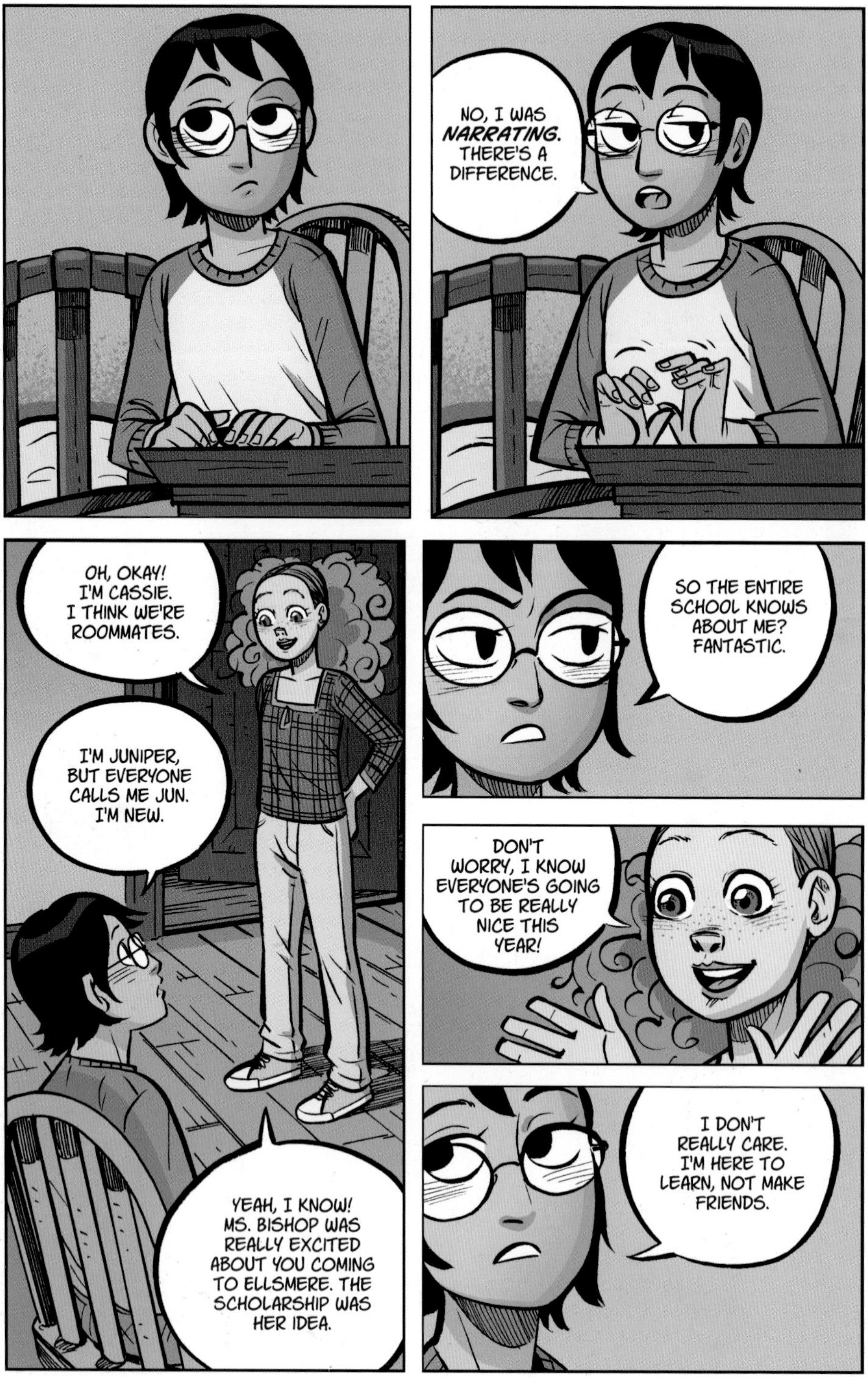
NO, I WAS **NARRATING.** THERE'S A DIFFERENCE.
OH, OKAY! I'M CASSIE. I THINK WE'RE ROOMMATES.
I'M JUNIPER, BUT EVERYONE CALLS ME JUN. I'M NEW.
YEAH, I KNOW! MS. BISHOP WAS REALLY EXCITED ABOUT YOU COMING TO ELLSMERE. THE SCHOLARSHIP WAS HER IDEA.
SO THE ENTIRE SCHOOL KNOWS ABOUT ME? FANTASTIC.
DON'T WORRY, I KNOW EVERYONE'S GOING TO BE REALLY NICE THIS YEAR!
I DON'T REALLY CARE. I'M HERE TO LEARN, NOT MAKE FRIENDS.

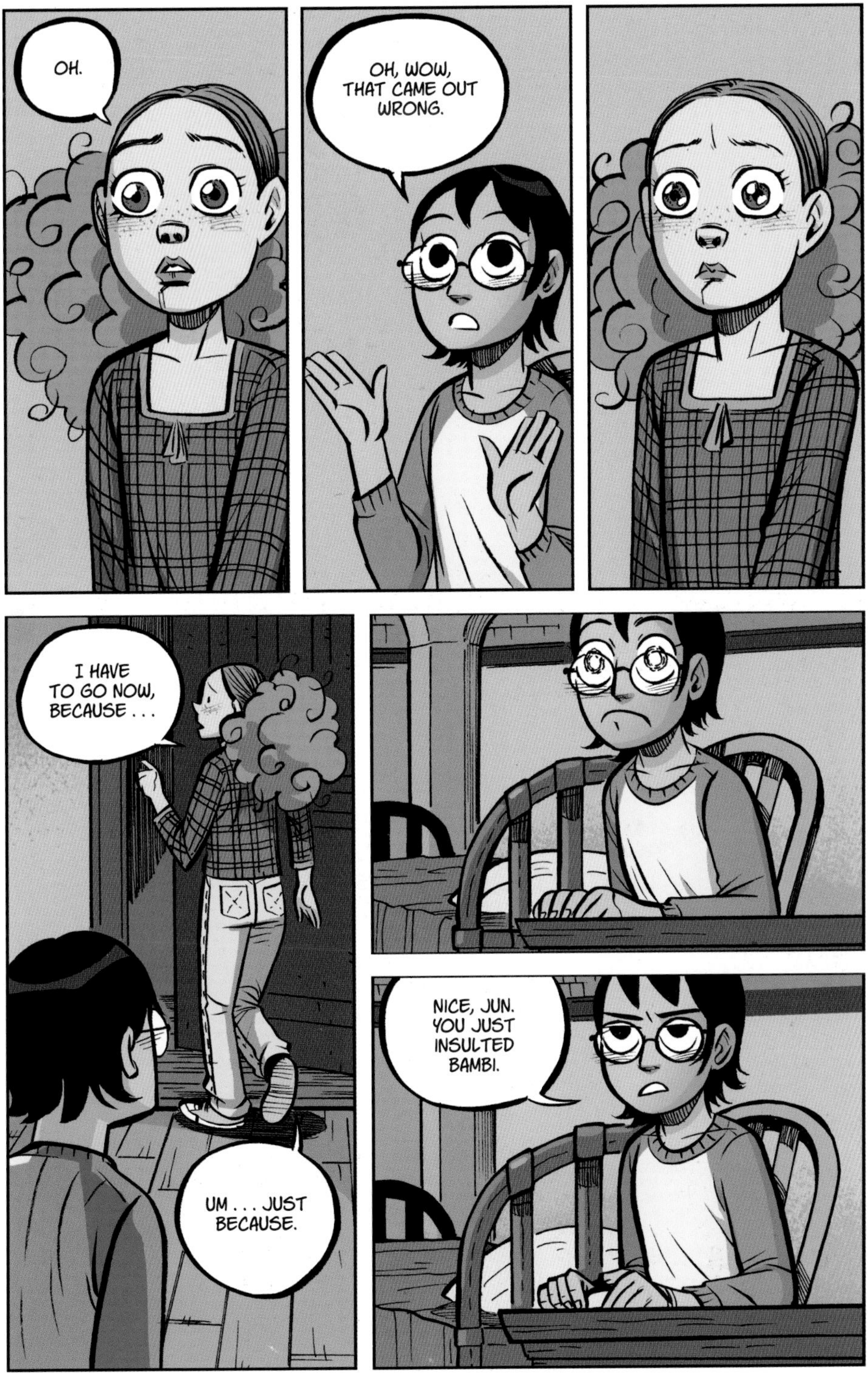
OH.
OH, WOW, THAT CAME OUT WRONG.
I HAVE TO GO NOW, BECAUSE . . .
UM . . . JUST BECAUSE.
NICE, JUN. YOU JUST INSULTED BAMBI.

Chapter Two

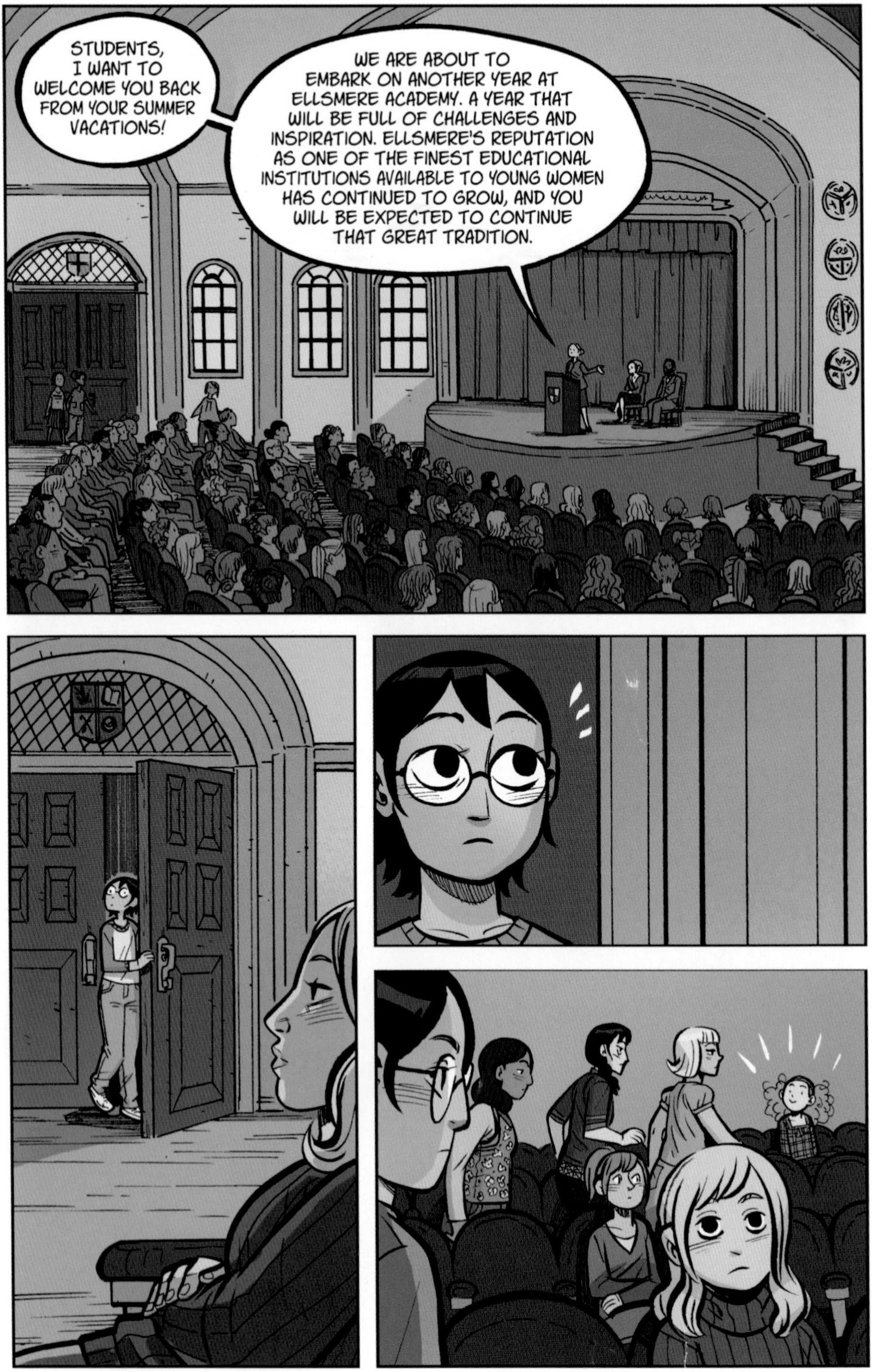
STUDENTS, I WANT TO WELCOME YOU BACK FROM YOUR SUMMER VACATIONS!
WE ARE ABOUT TO EMBARK ON ANOTHER YEAR AT ELLSMERE ACADEMY. A YEAR THAT WILL BE FULL OF CHALLENGES AND INSPIRATION. ELLSMERE'S REPUTATION AS ONE OF THE FINEST EDUCATIONAL INSTITUTIONS AVAILABLE TO YOUNG WOMEN HAS CONTINUED TO GROW, AND YOU WILL BE EXPECTED TO CONTINUE THAT GREAT TRADITION.

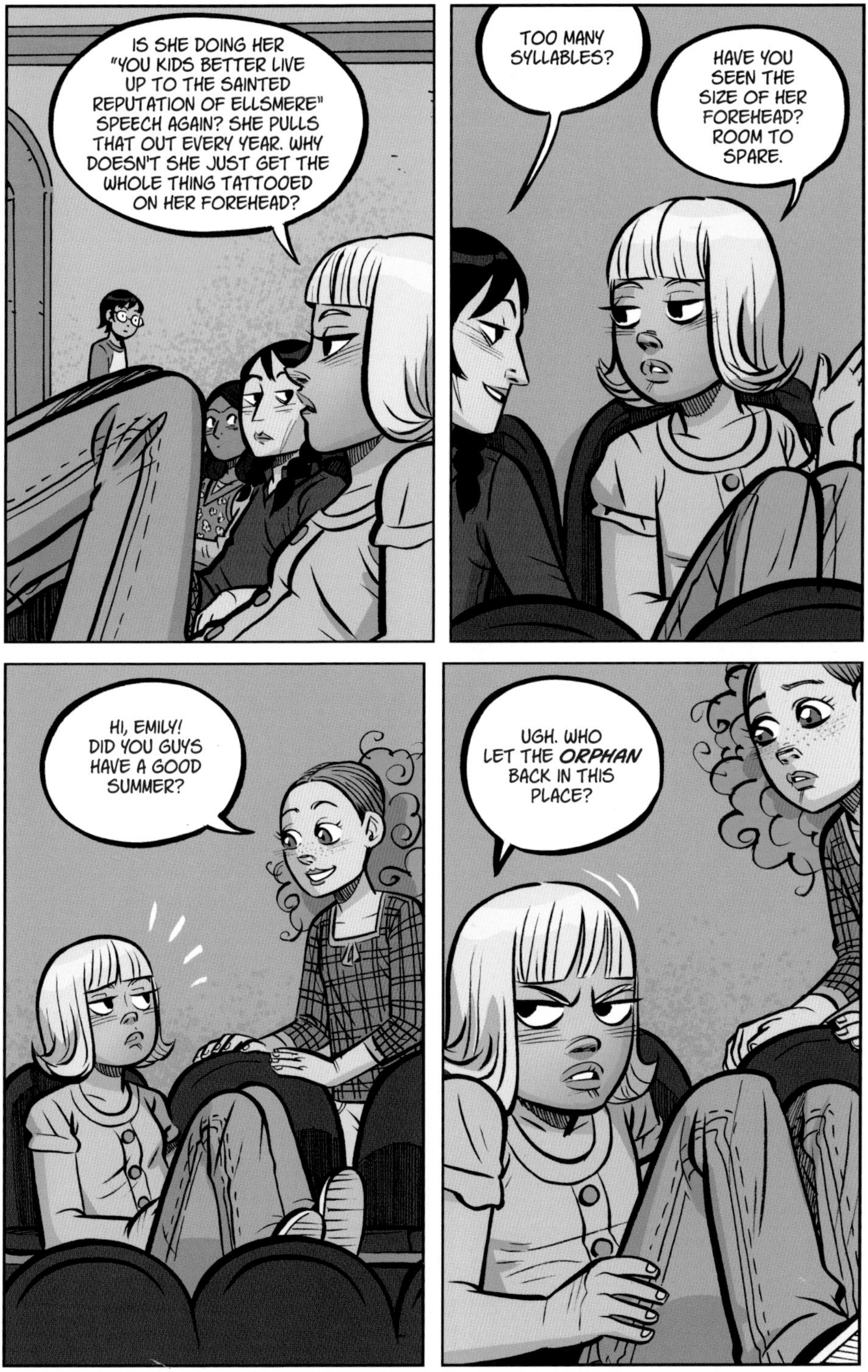
IS SHE DOING HER "YOU KIDS BETTER LIVE UP TO THE SAINTED REPUTATION OF ELLSMERE" SPEECH AGAIN? SHE PULLS THAT OUT EVERY YEAR. WHY DOESN'T SHE JUST GET THE WHOLE THING TATTOOED ON HER FOREHEAD?
TOO MANY SYLLABLES?
HAVE YOU SEEN THE SIZE OF HER FOREHEAD? ROOM TO SPARE.
HI, EMILY! DID YOU GUYS HAVE A GOOD SUMMER?
UGH. WHO LET THE *ORPHAN* BACK IN THIS PLACE?

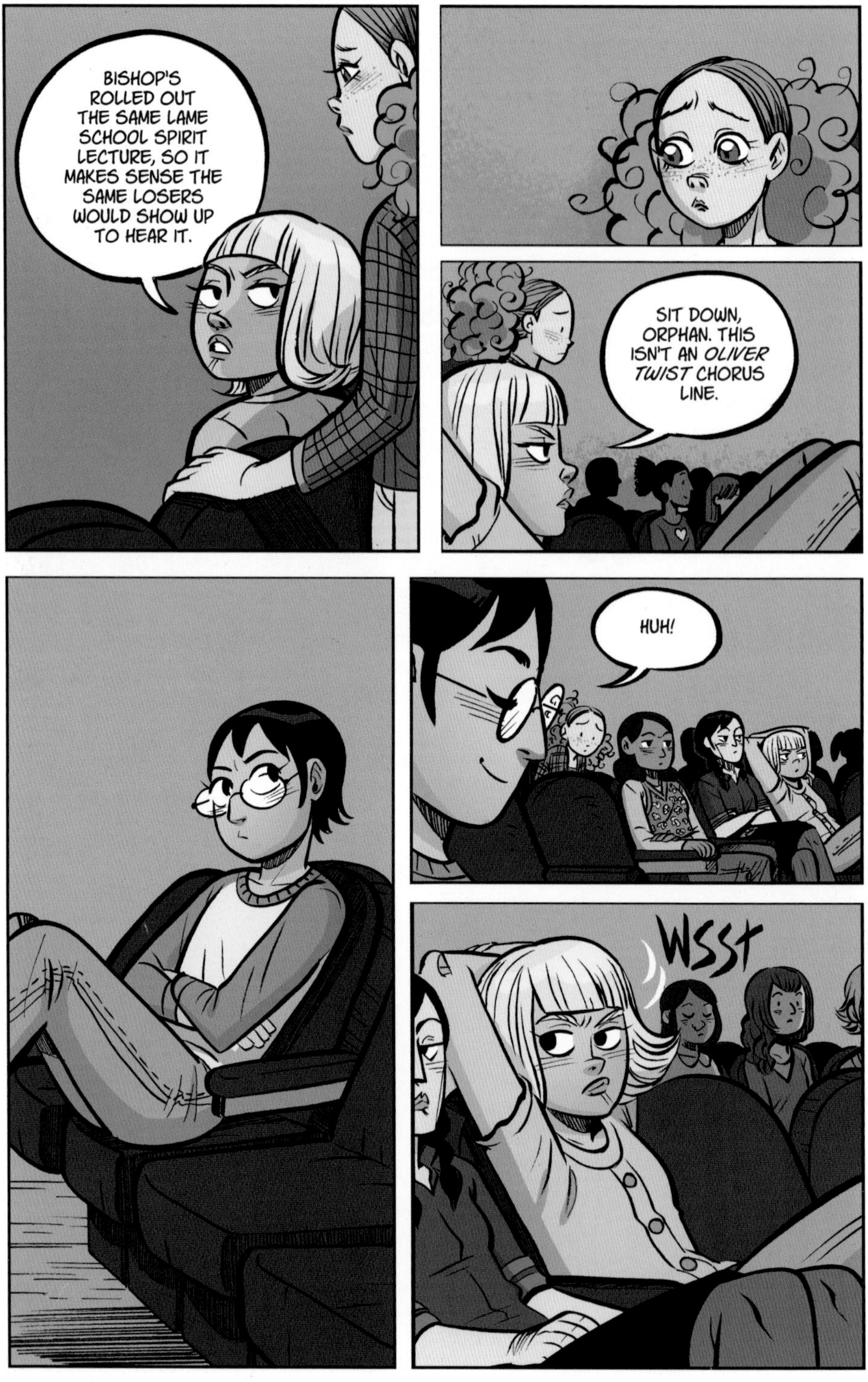
BISHOP'S ROLLED OUT THE SAME LAME SCHOOL SPIRIT LECTURE, SO IT MAKES SENSE THE SAME LOSERS WOULD SHOW UP TO HEAR IT.
SIT DOWN, ORPHAN. THIS ISN'T AN *OLIVER TWIST* CHORUS LINE.
HUH!
WSST

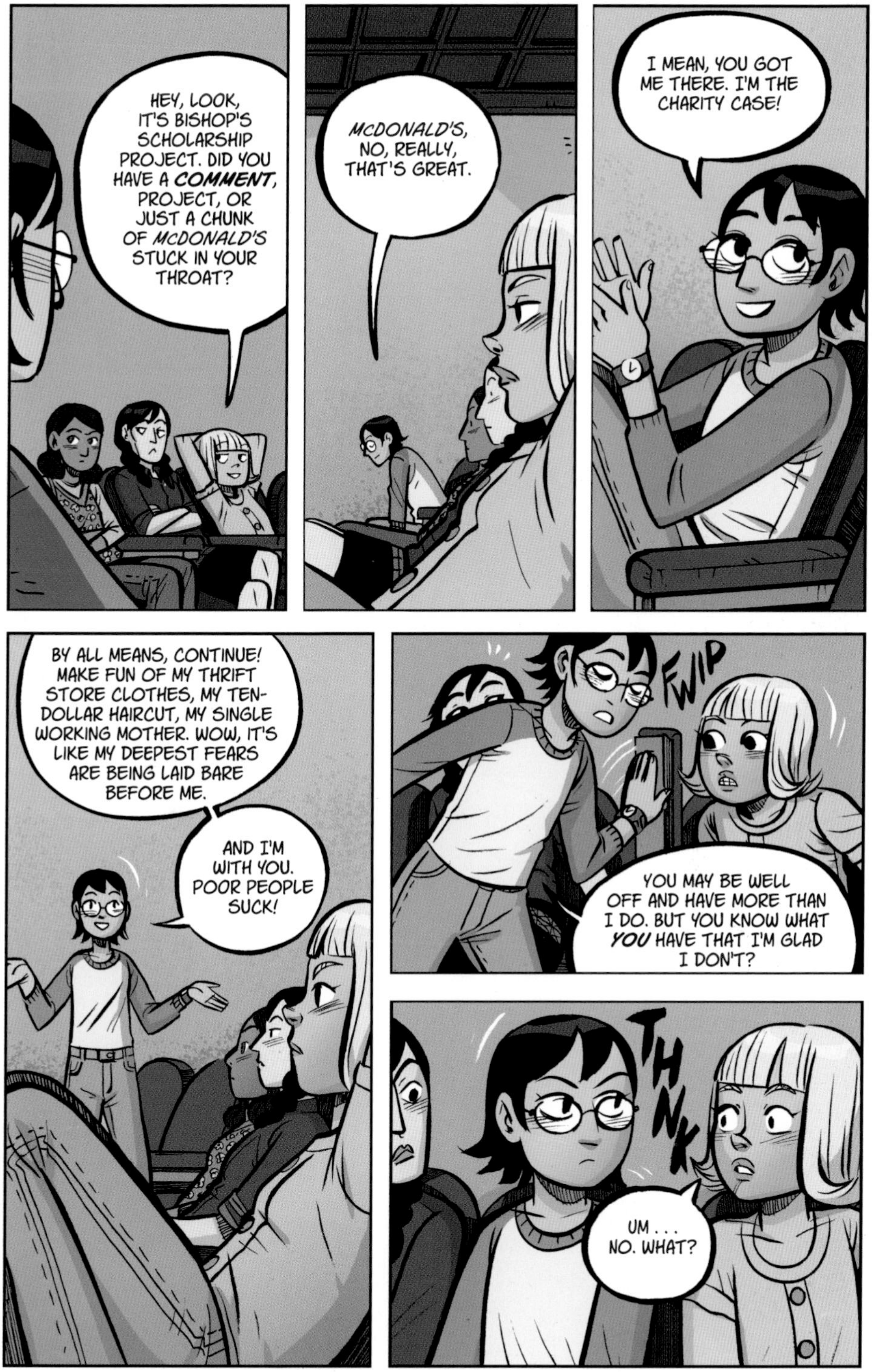
HEY, LOOK, IT'S BISHOP'S SCHOLARSHIP PROJECT. DID YOU HAVE A ***COMMENT***, PROJECT, OR JUST A CHUNK OF *MCDONALD'S* STUCK IN YOUR THROAT?
MCDONALD'S, NO, REALLY, THAT'S GREAT.
I MEAN, YOU GOT ME THERE. I'M THE CHARITY CASE!
BY ALL MEANS, CONTINUE! MAKE FUN OF MY THRIFT STORE CLOTHES, MY TEN-DOLLAR HAIRCUT, MY SINGLE WORKING MOTHER. WOW, IT'S LIKE MY DEEPEST FEARS ARE BEING LAID BARE BEFORE ME.
AND I'M WITH YOU. POOR PEOPLE SUCK!
FWIP
YOU MAY BE WELL OFF AND HAVE MORE THAN I DO. BUT YOU KNOW WHAT ***YOU*** HAVE THAT I'M GLAD I DON'T?
THNK
UM . . . NO. WHAT?

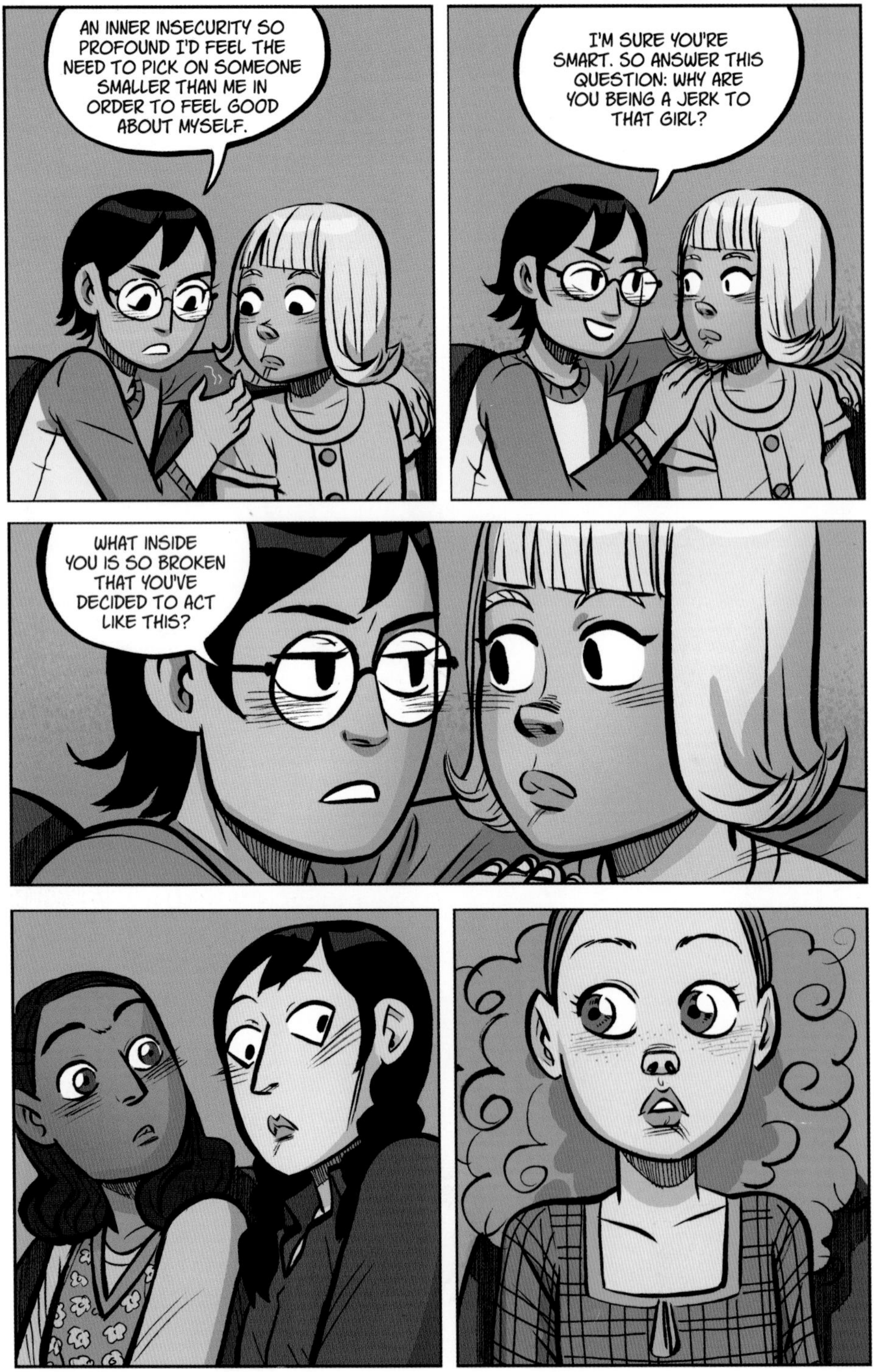
AN INNER INSECURITY SO PROFOUND I'D FEEL THE NEED TO PICK ON SOMEONE SMALLER THAN ME IN ORDER TO FEEL GOOD ABOUT MYSELF.
I'M SURE YOU'RE SMART. SO ANSWER THIS QUESTION: WHY ARE YOU BEING A JERK TO THAT GIRL?
WHAT INSIDE YOU IS SO BROKEN THAT YOU'VE DECIDED TO ACT LIKE THIS?

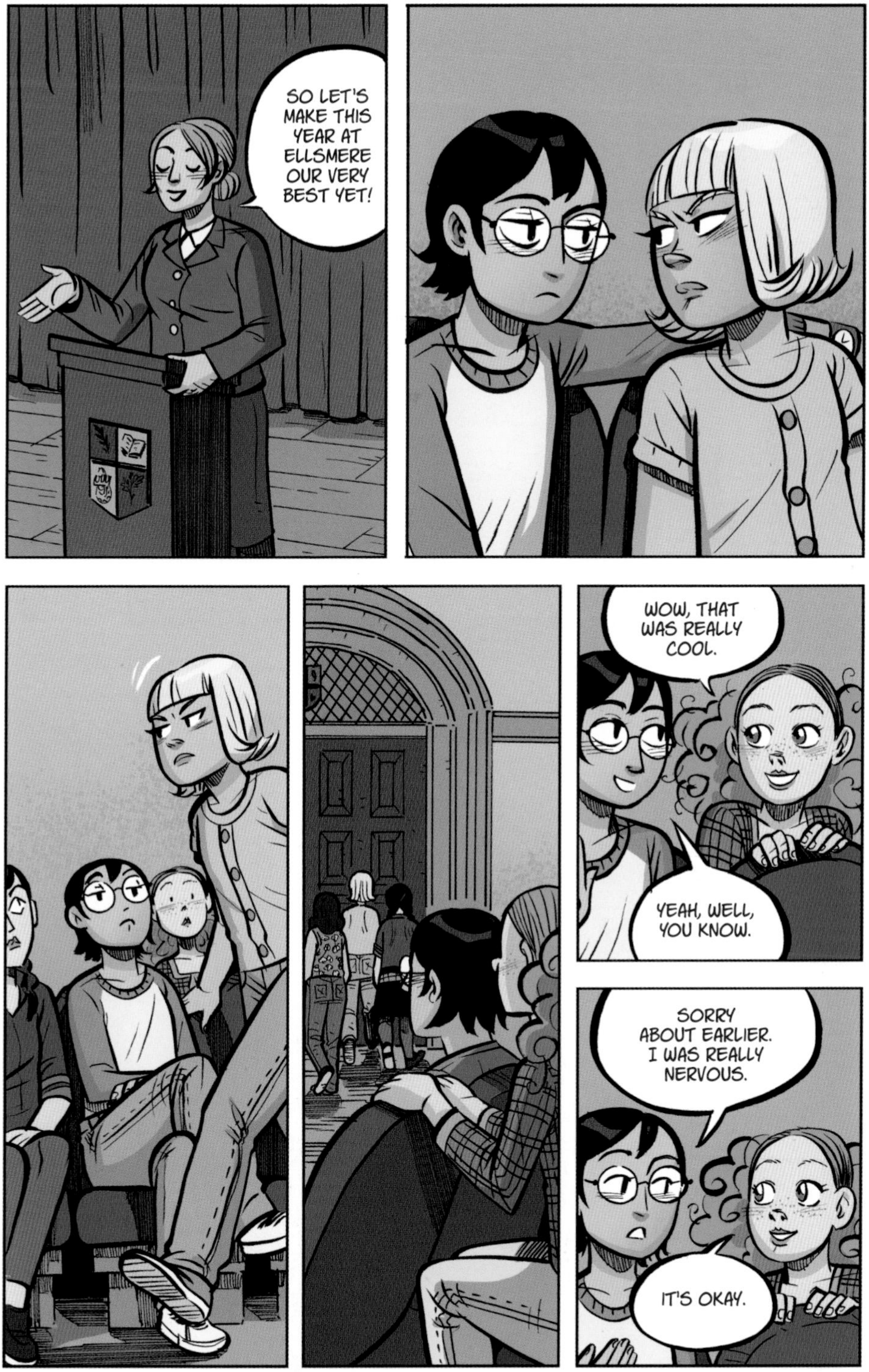
SO LET'S MAKE THIS YEAR AT ELLSMERE OUR VERY BEST YET!
WOW, THAT WAS REALLY COOL.
YEAH, WELL, YOU KNOW.
SORRY ABOUT EARLIER. I WAS REALLY NERVOUS.
IT'S OKAY.

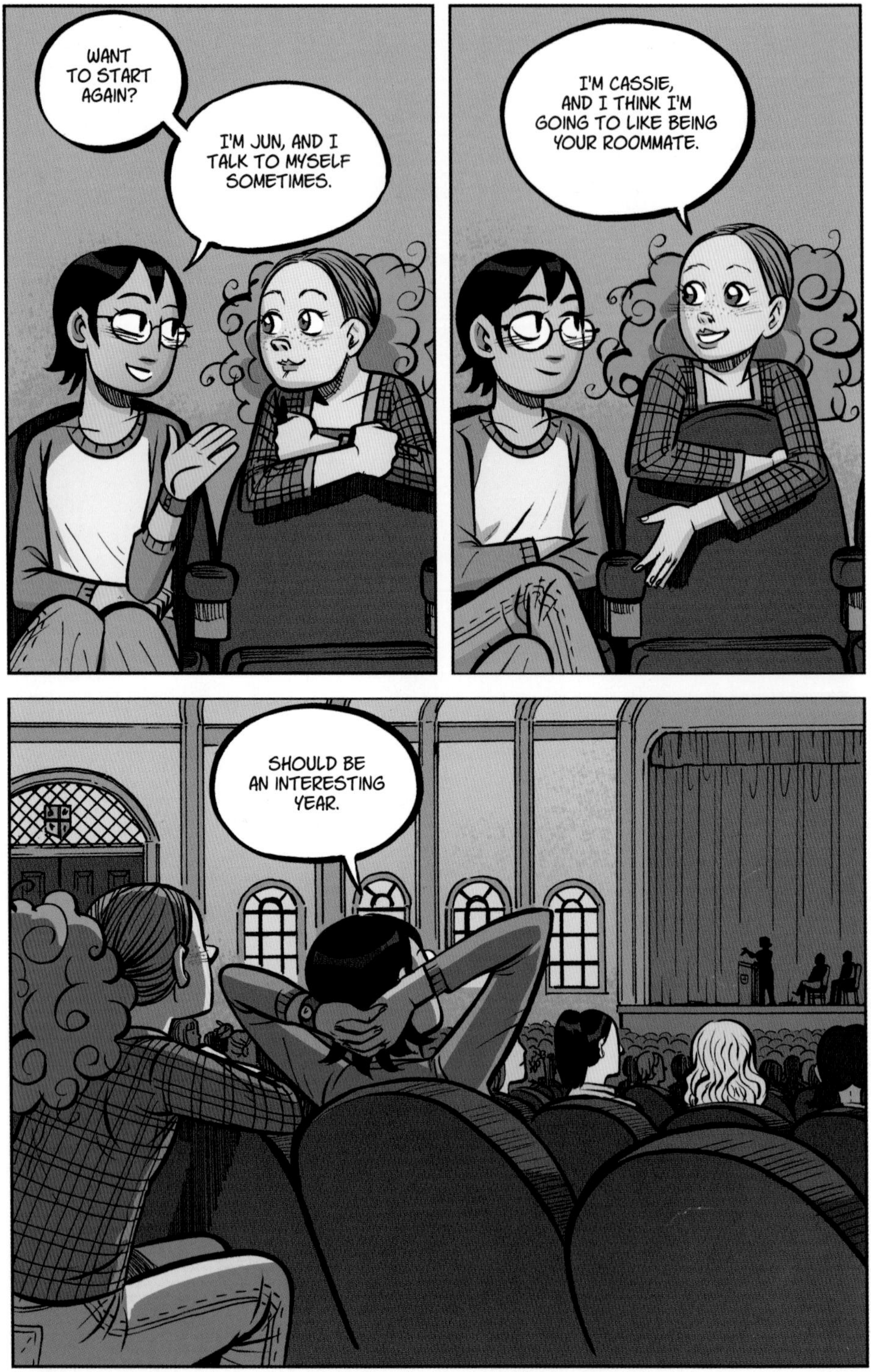
WANT TO START AGAIN?
I'M JUN, AND I TALK TO MYSELF SOMETIMES.
I'M CASSIE, AND I THINK I'M GOING TO LIKE BEING YOUR ROOMMATE.
SHOULD BE AN INTERESTING YEAR.

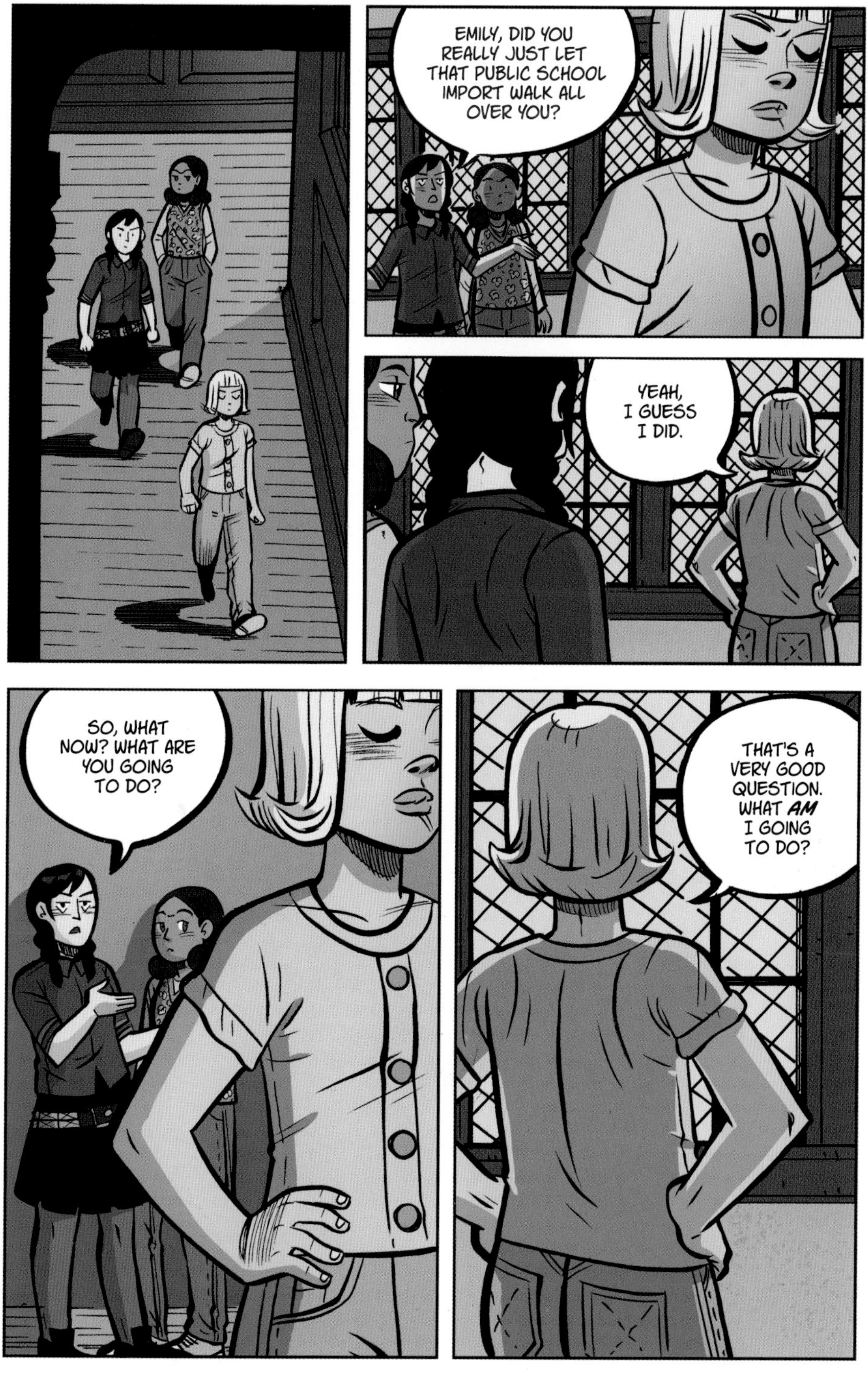
EMILY, DID YOU REALLY JUST LET THAT PUBLIC SCHOOL IMPORT WALK ALL OVER YOU?
YEAH, I GUESS I DID.
SO, WHAT NOW? WHAT ARE YOU GOING TO DO?
THAT'S A VERY GOOD QUESTION. WHAT *AM* I GOING TO DO?

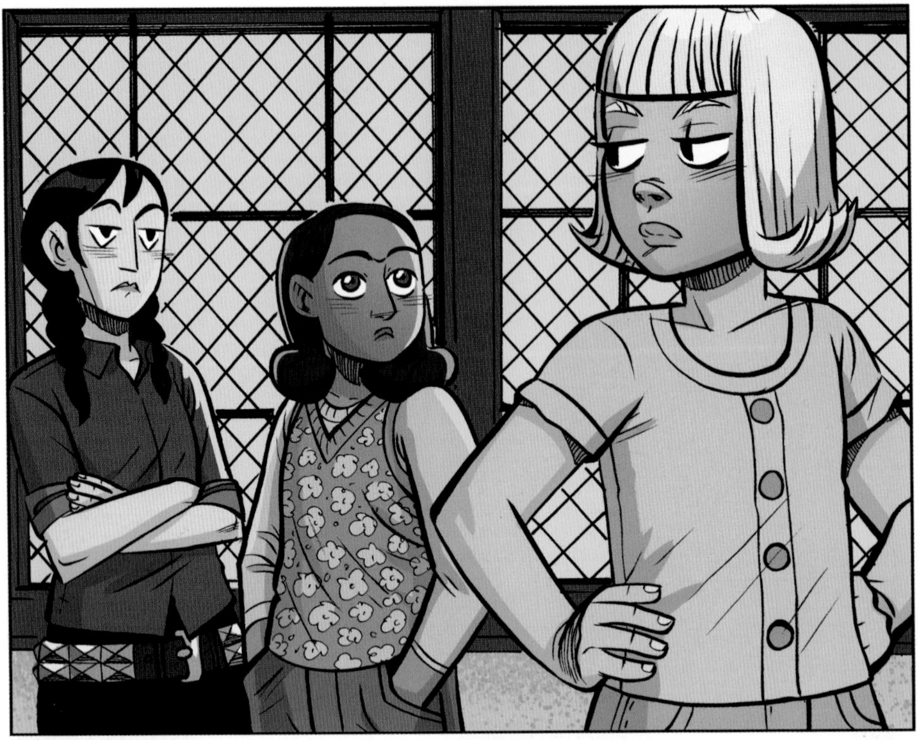

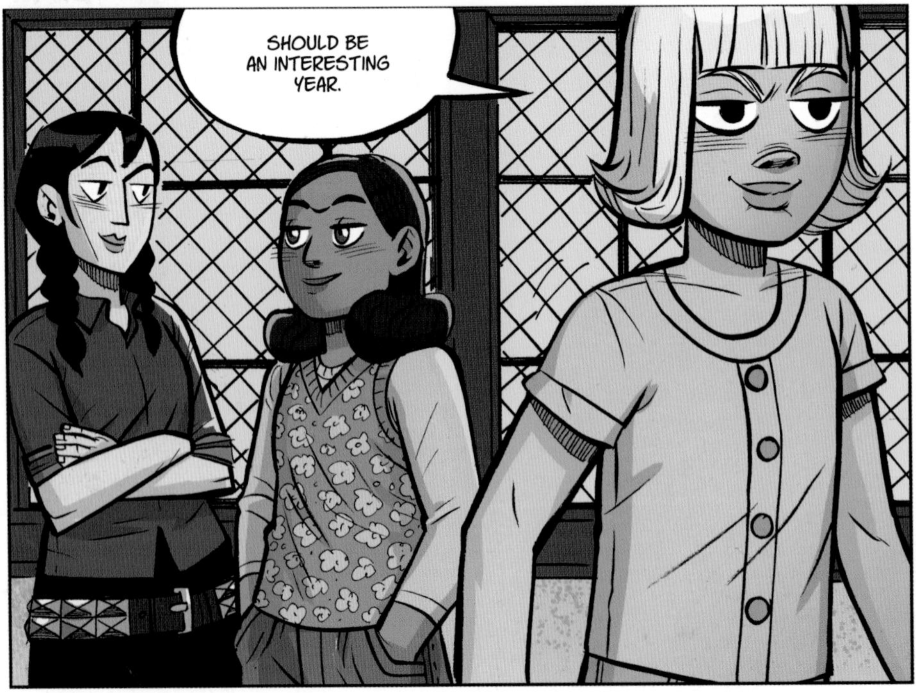
SHOULD BE AN INTERESTING YEAR.

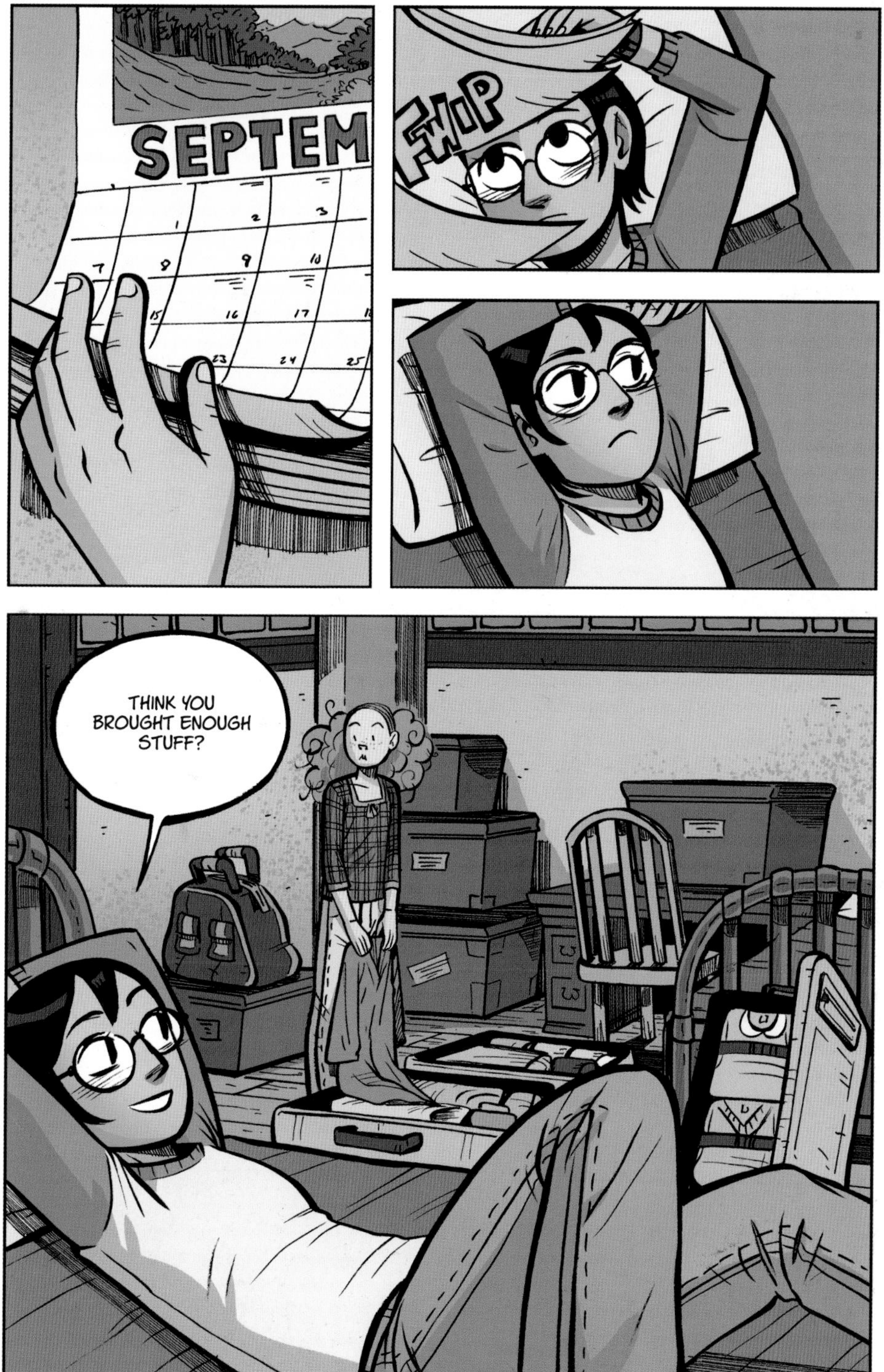
SEPTEM
FWIP
THINK YOU BROUGHT ENOUGH STUFF?

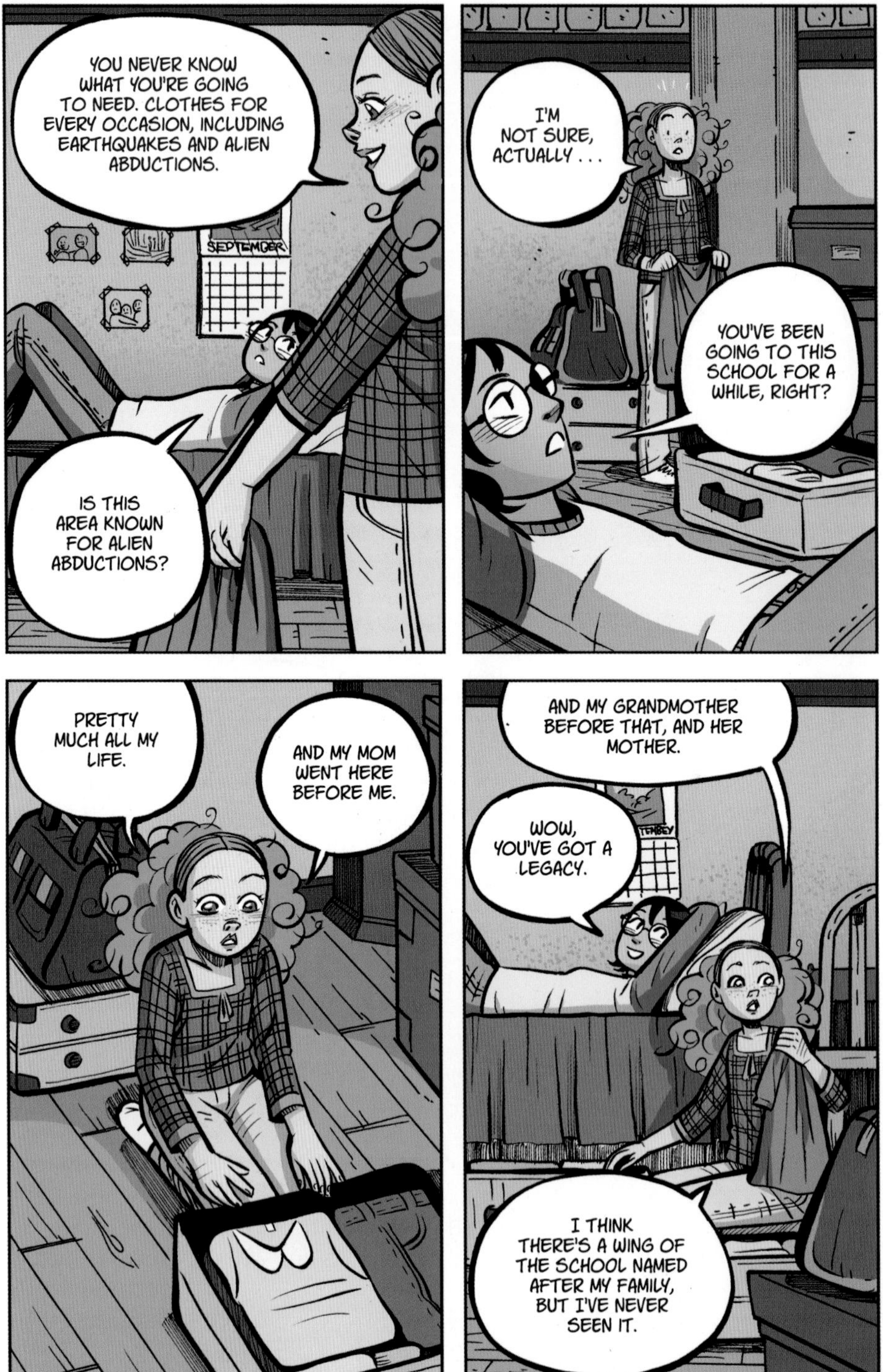
YOU NEVER KNOW WHAT YOU'RE GOING TO NEED. CLOTHES FOR EVERY OCCASION, INCLUDING EARTHQUAKES AND ALIEN ABDUCTIONS.
SEPTEMBER
IS THIS AREA KNOWN FOR ALIEN ABDUCTIONS?
I'M NOT SURE, ACTUALLY . . .
YOU'VE BEEN GOING TO THIS SCHOOL FOR A WHILE, RIGHT?
PRETTY MUCH ALL MY LIFE.
AND MY MOM WENT HERE BEFORE ME.
AND MY GRANDMOTHER BEFORE THAT, AND HER MOTHER.
WOW, YOU'VE GOT A LEGACY.
I THINK THERE'S A WING OF THE SCHOOL NAMED AFTER MY FAMILY, BUT I'VE NEVER SEEN IT.

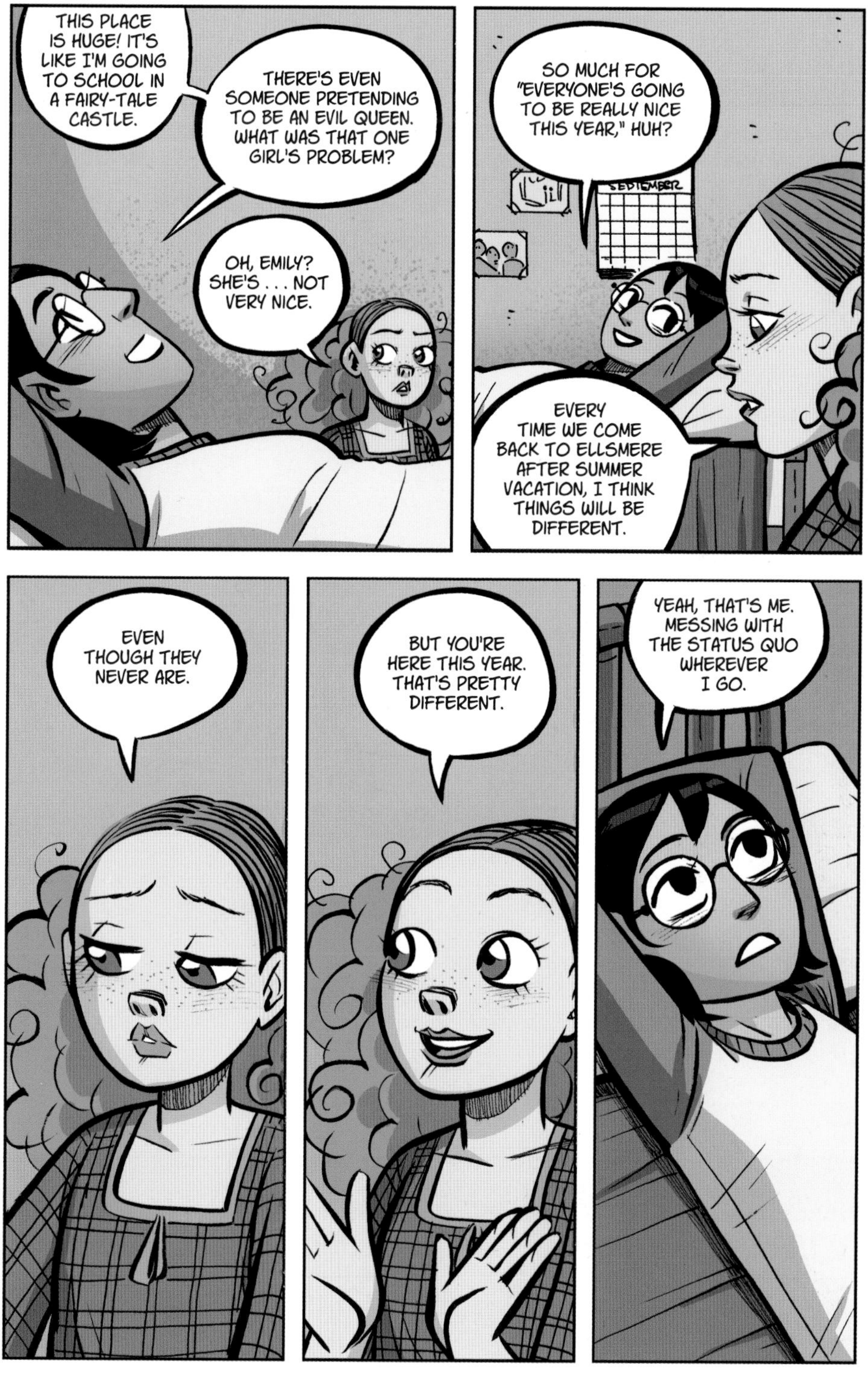
THIS PLACE IS HUGE! IT'S LIKE I'M GOING TO SCHOOL IN A FAIRY-TALE CASTLE.
THERE'S EVEN SOMEONE PRETENDING TO BE AN EVIL QUEEN. WHAT WAS THAT ONE GIRL'S PROBLEM?
OH, EMILY? SHE'S . . . NOT VERY NICE.
SO MUCH FOR "EVERYONE'S GOING TO BE REALLY NICE THIS YEAR," HUH?
SEPTEMBER
EVERY TIME WE COME BACK TO ELLSMERE AFTER SUMMER VACATION, I THINK THINGS WILL BE DIFFERENT.
EVEN THOUGH THEY NEVER ARE.
BUT YOU'RE HERE THIS YEAR. THAT'S PRETTY DIFFERENT.
YEAH, THAT'S ME. MESSING WITH THE STATUS QUO WHEREVER I GO.

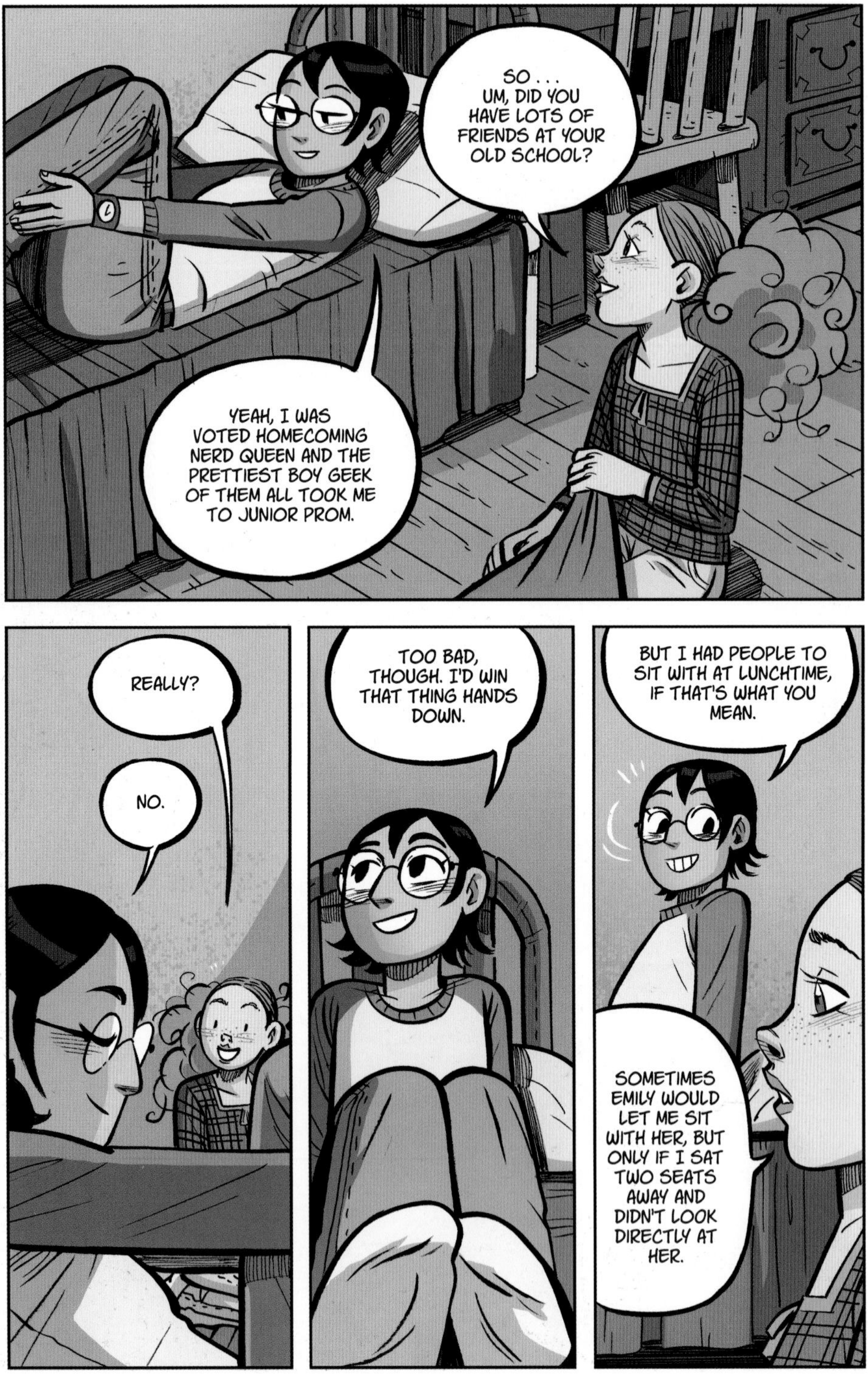
SO . . .
UM, DID YOU HAVE LOTS OF FRIENDS AT YOUR OLD SCHOOL?
YEAH, I WAS VOTED HOMECOMING NERD QUEEN AND THE PRETTIEST BOY GEEK OF THEM ALL TOOK ME TO JUNIOR PROM.
REALLY?
NO.
TOO BAD, THOUGH. I'D WIN THAT THING HANDS DOWN.
BUT I HAD PEOPLE TO SIT WITH AT LUNCHTIME, IF THAT'S WHAT YOU MEAN.
SOMETIMES EMILY WOULD LET ME SIT WITH HER, BUT ONLY IF I SAT TWO SEATS AWAY AND DIDN'T LOOK DIRECTLY AT HER.

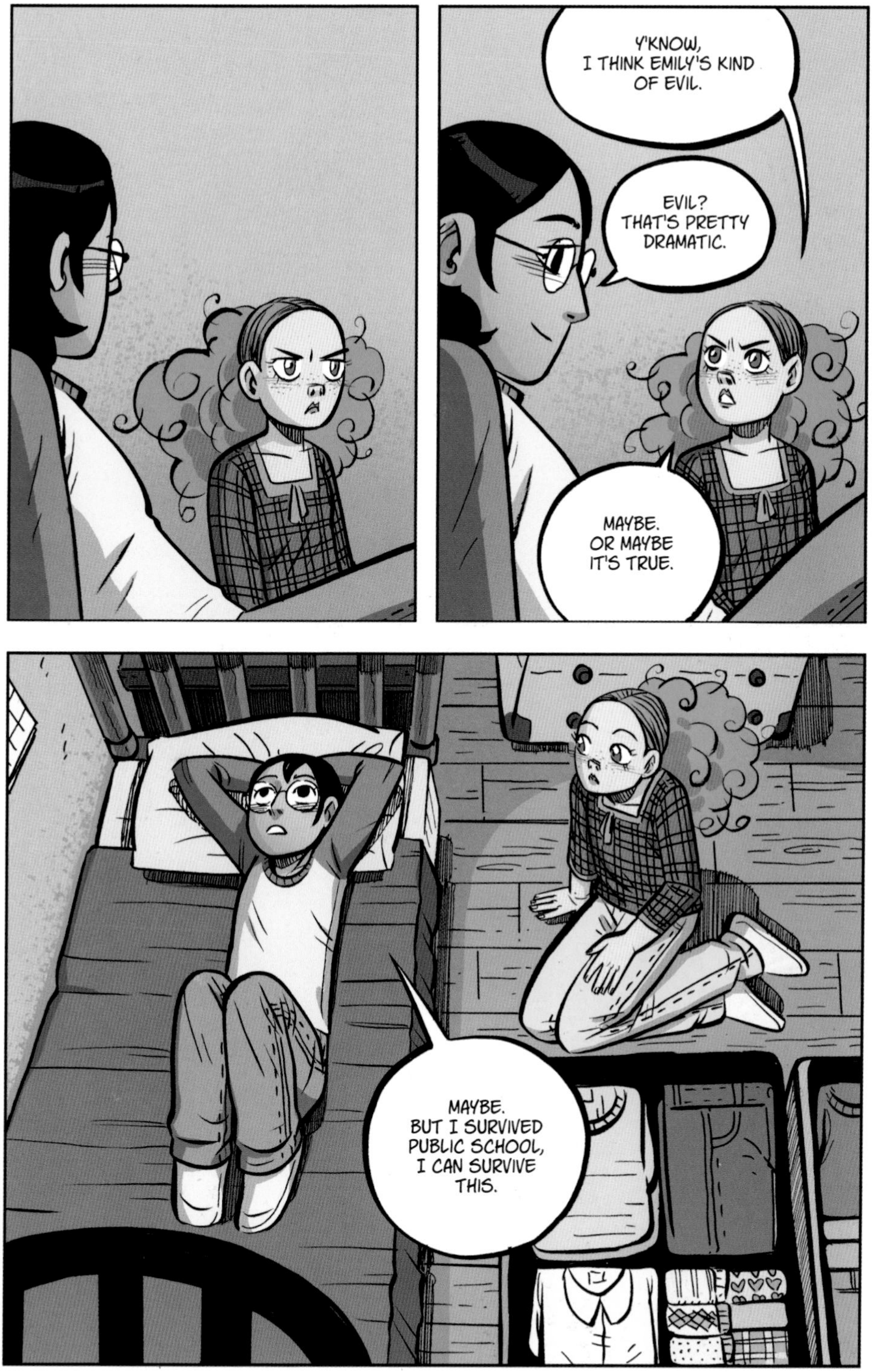
Y'KNOW, I THINK EMILY'S KIND OF EVIL.
EVIL? THAT'S PRETTY DRAMATIC.
MAYBE. OR MAYBE IT'S TRUE.
MAYBE. BUT I SURVIVED PUBLIC SCHOOL, I CAN SURVIVE THIS.

Chapter Three

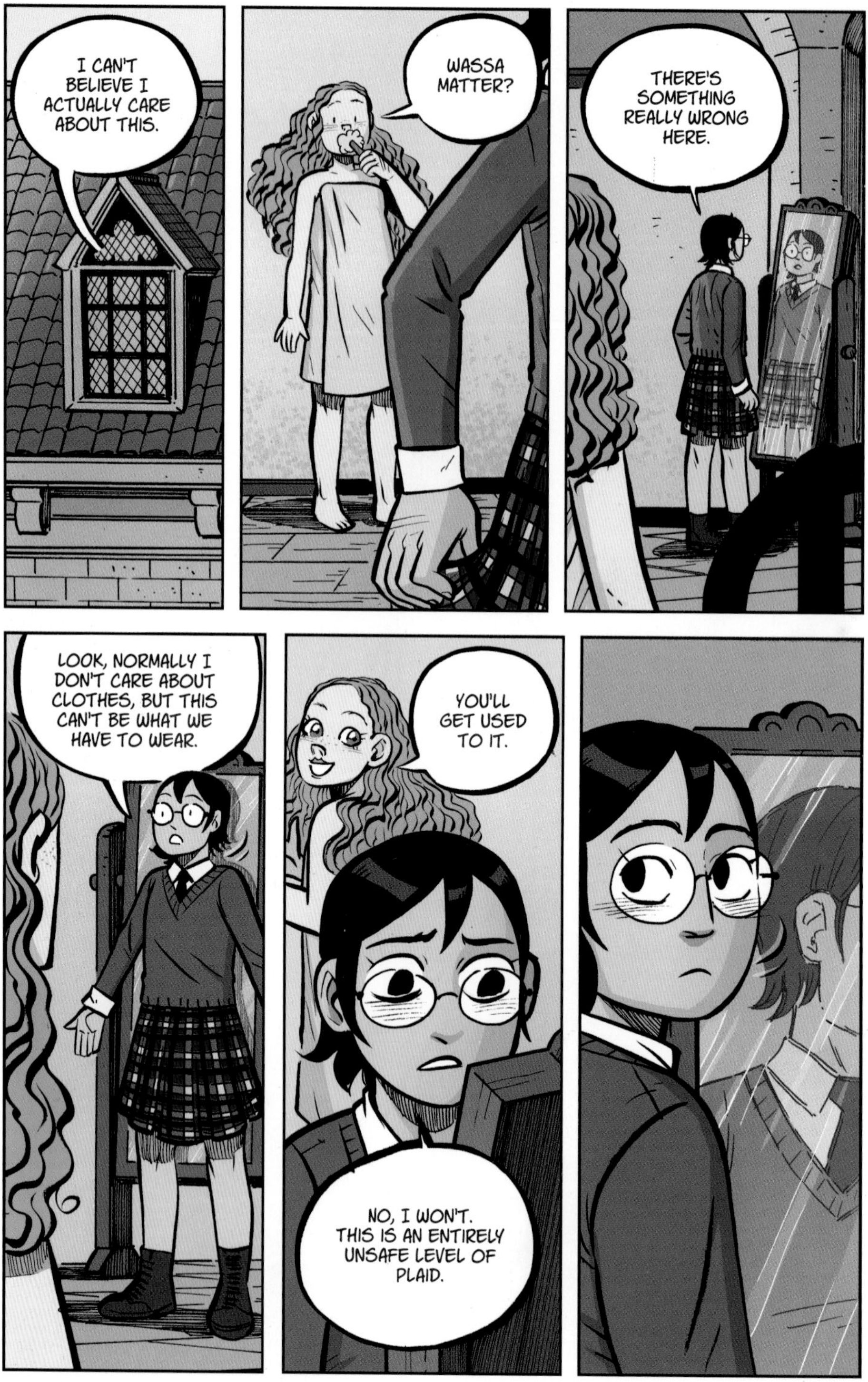
I CAN'T BELIEVE I ACTUALLY CARE ABOUT THIS.
WASSA MATTER?
THERE'S SOMETHING REALLY WRONG HERE.
LOOK, NORMALLY I DON'T CARE ABOUT CLOTHES, BUT THIS CAN'T BE WHAT WE HAVE TO WEAR.
YOU'LL GET USED TO IT.
NO, I WON'T. THIS IS AN ENTIRELY UNSAFE LEVEL OF PLAID.

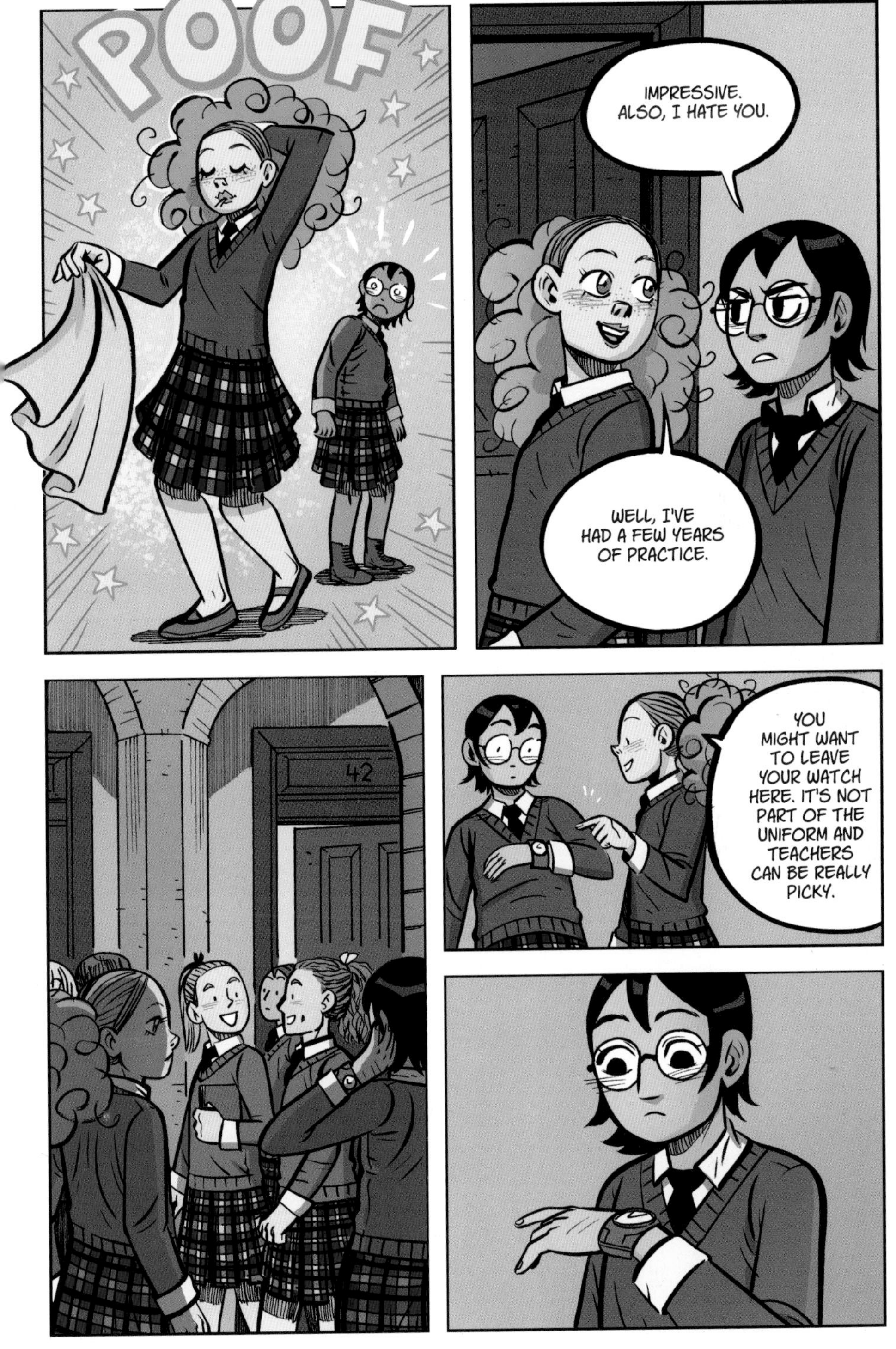
POOF
IMPRESSIVE. ALSO, I HATE YOU.
WELL, I'VE HAD A FEW YEARS OF PRACTICE.
42
YOU MIGHT WANT TO LEAVE YOUR WATCH HERE. IT'S NOT PART OF THE UNIFORM AND TEACHERS CAN BE REALLY PICKY.

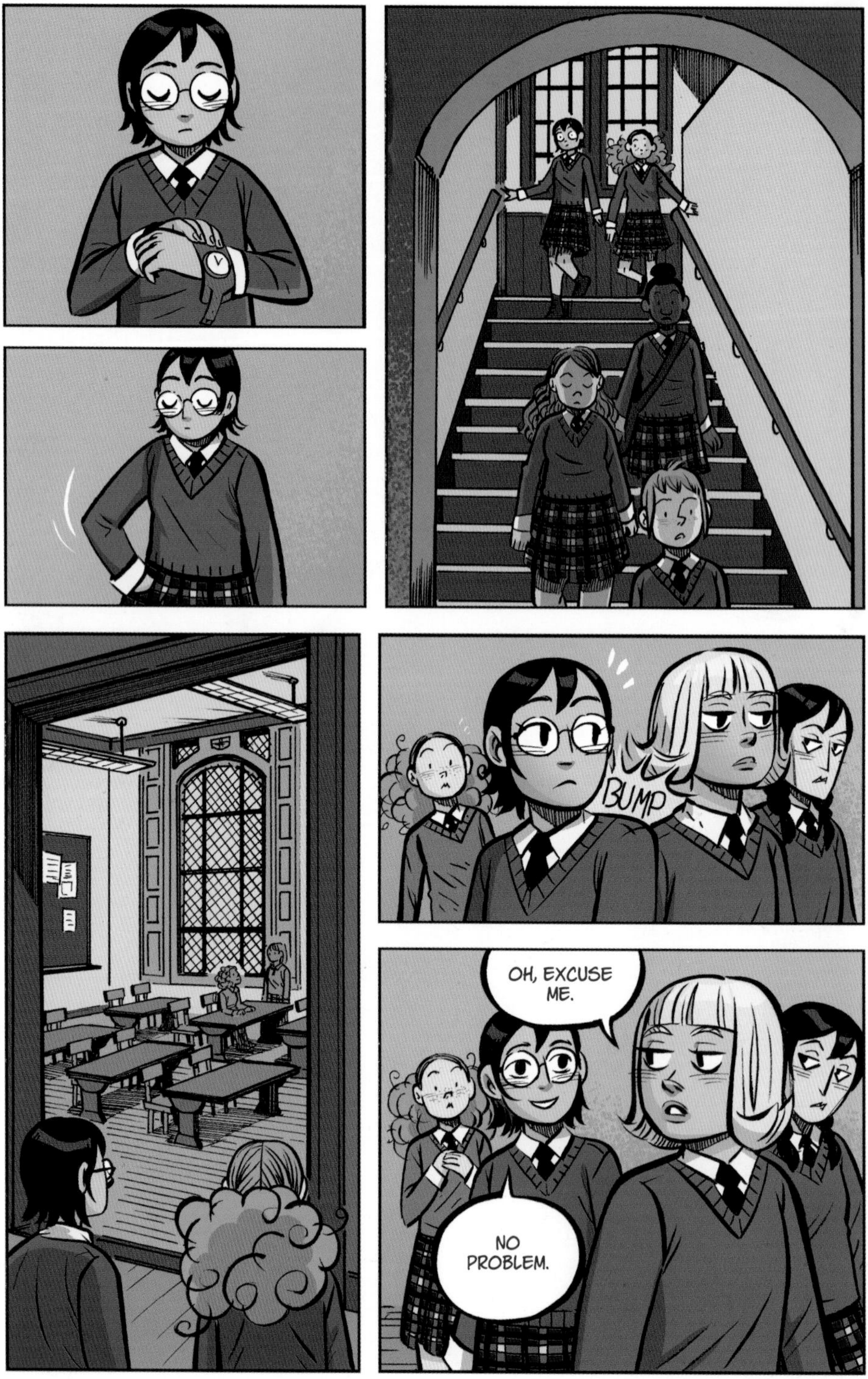
BUMP
OH, EXCUSE ME.
NO PROBLEM.

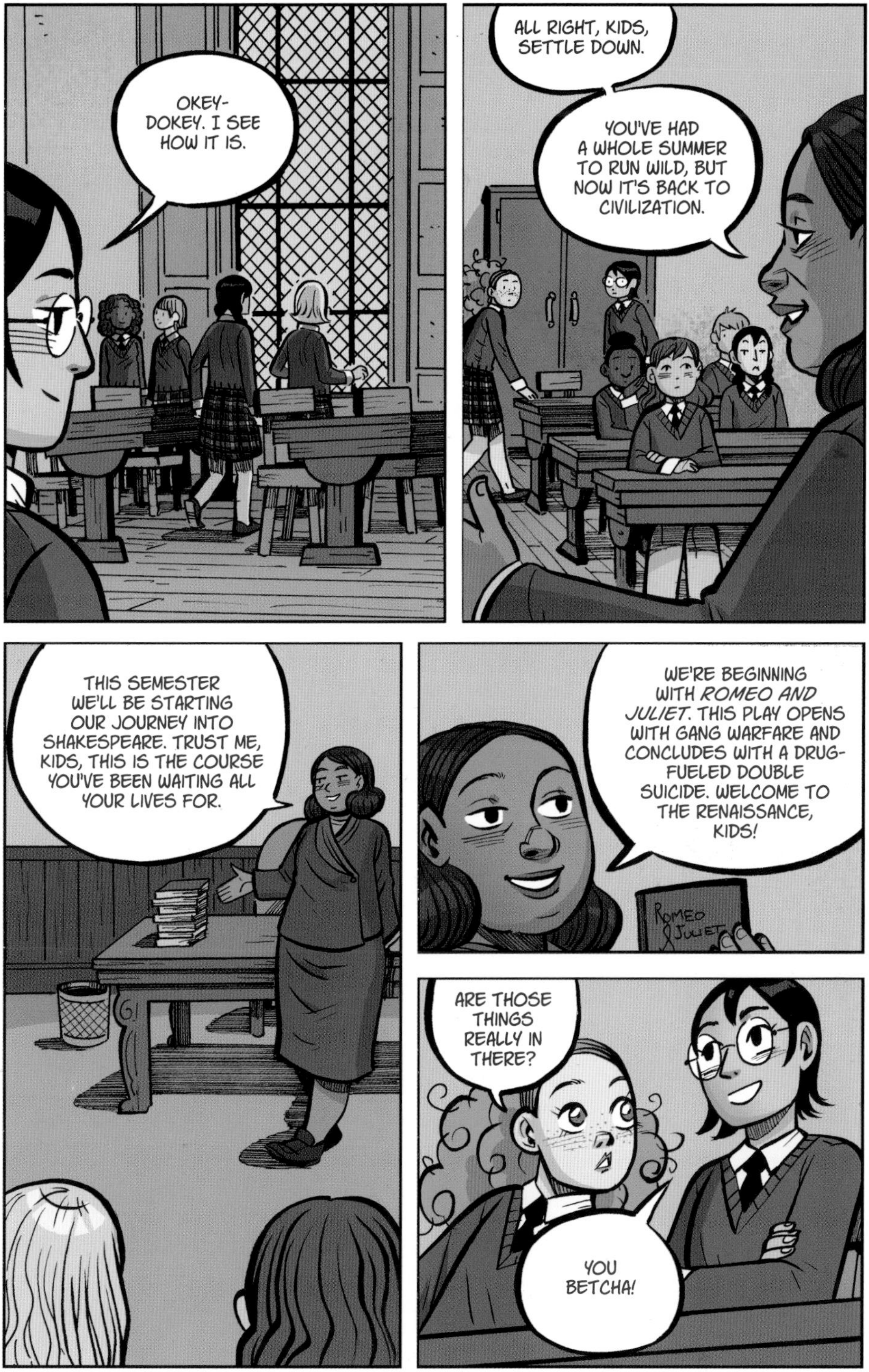
OKEY-DOKEY. I SEE HOW IT IS.
ALL RIGHT, KIDS, SETTLE DOWN.
YOU'VE HAD A WHOLE SUMMER TO RUN WILD, BUT NOW IT'S BACK TO CIVILIZATION.
THIS SEMESTER WE'LL BE STARTING OUR JOURNEY INTO SHAKESPEARE. TRUST ME, KIDS, THIS IS THE COURSE YOU'VE BEEN WAITING ALL YOUR LIVES FOR.
WE'RE BEGINNING WITH *ROMEO AND JULIET*. THIS PLAY OPENS WITH GANG WARFARE AND CONCLUDES WITH A DRUG-FUELED DOUBLE SUICIDE. WELCOME TO THE RENAISSANCE, KIDS!
ROMEO & JULIET
ARE THOSE THINGS REALLY IN THERE?
YOU BETCHA!

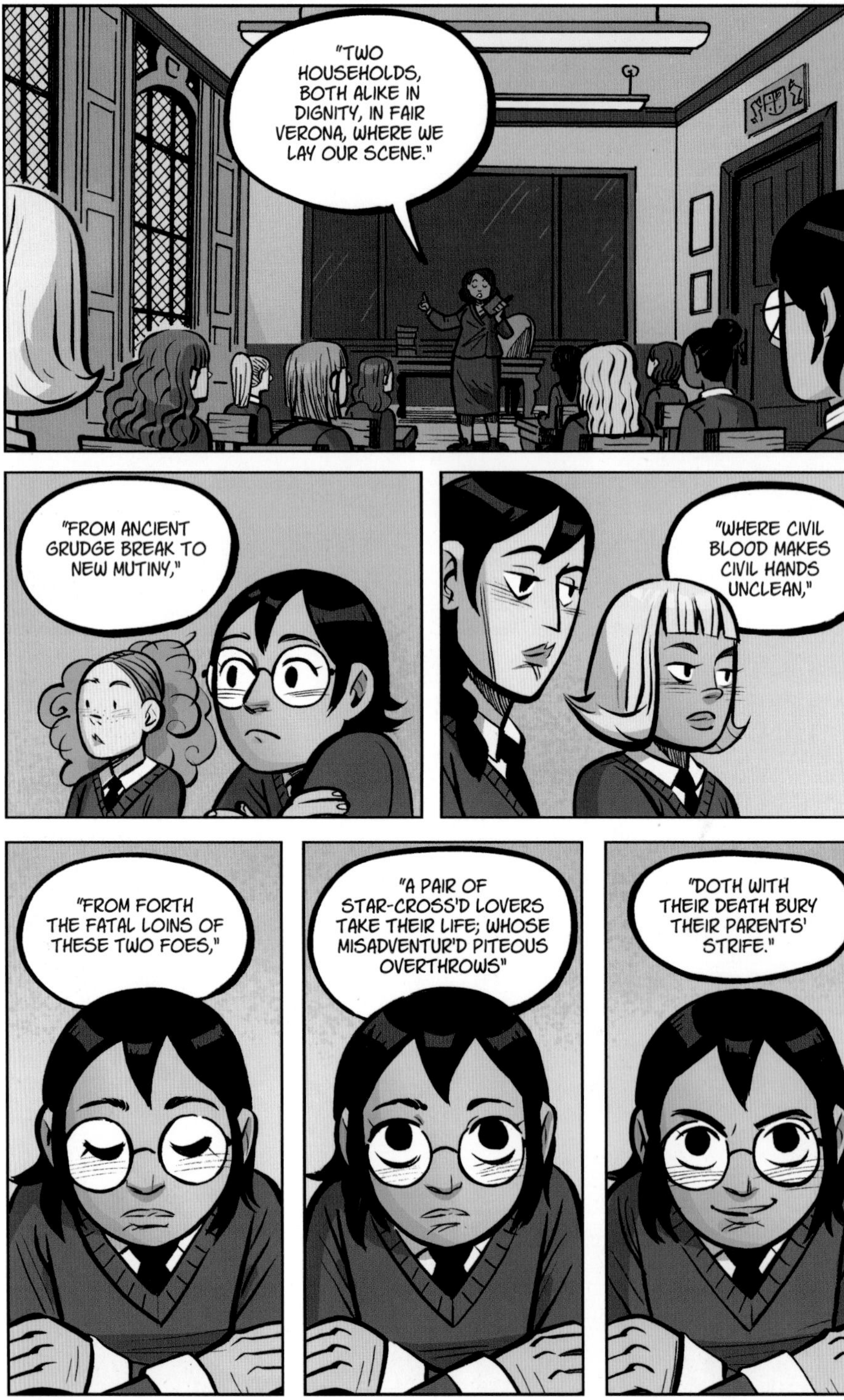
"TWO HOUSEHOLDS, BOTH ALIKE IN DIGNITY, IN FAIR VERONA, WHERE WE LAY OUR SCENE."
"FROM ANCIENT GRUDGE BREAK TO NEW MUTINY,"
"WHERE CIVIL BLOOD MAKES CIVIL HANDS UNCLEAN,"
"FROM FORTH THE FATAL LOINS OF THESE TWO FOES,"
"A PAIR OF STAR-CROSS'D LOVERS TAKE THEIR LIFE; WHOSE MISADVENTUR'D PITEOUS OVERTHROWS"
"DOTH WITH THEIR DEATH BURY THEIR PARENTS' STRIFE."

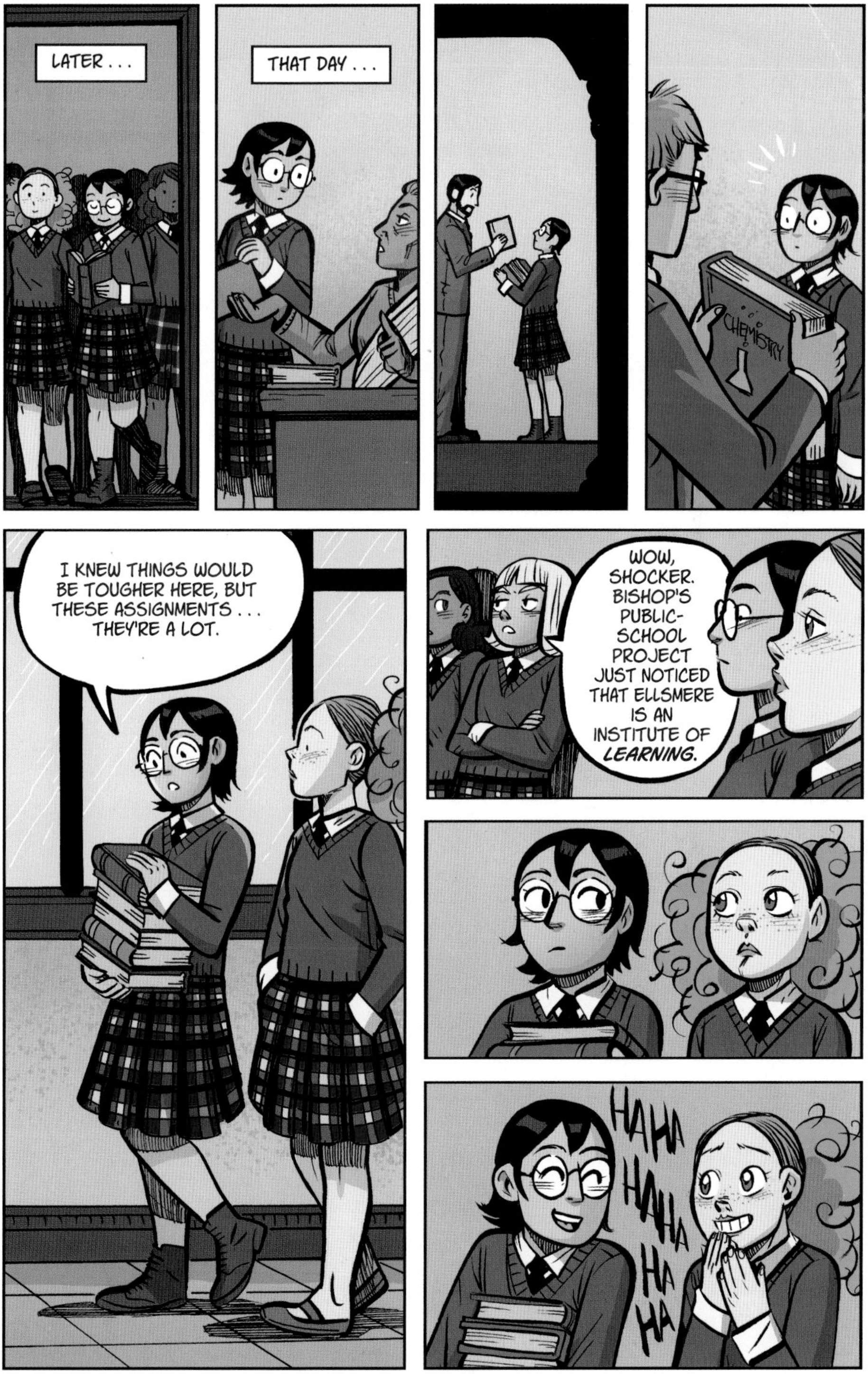
LATER . . .
THAT DAY . . .
CHEMISTRY
I KNEW THINGS WOULD BE TOUGHER HERE, BUT THESE ASSIGNMENTS . . . THEY'RE A LOT.
WOW, SHOCKER. BISHOP'S PUBLIC-SCHOOL PROJECT JUST NOTICED THAT ELLSMERE IS AN INSTITUTE OF *LEARNING*.
HAHA HAHA HAHA HA HA

MAYBE YOU WERE RIGHT ABOUT EMILY BEING EVIL. I CAN TOTALLY SEE HER SITTING IN AN UNDERGROUND LAIR, STROKING A WHITE CAT AND THINKING UP COMMENTS LIKE THAT.

IT'S VERY POSSIBLE.

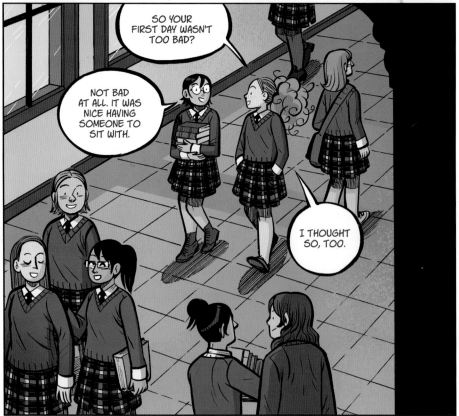

SO YOUR FIRST DAY WASN'T TOO BAD?

NOT BAD AT ALL. IT WAS NICE HAVING SOMEONE TO SIT WITH.

I THOUGHT SO, TOO.

Chapter Four

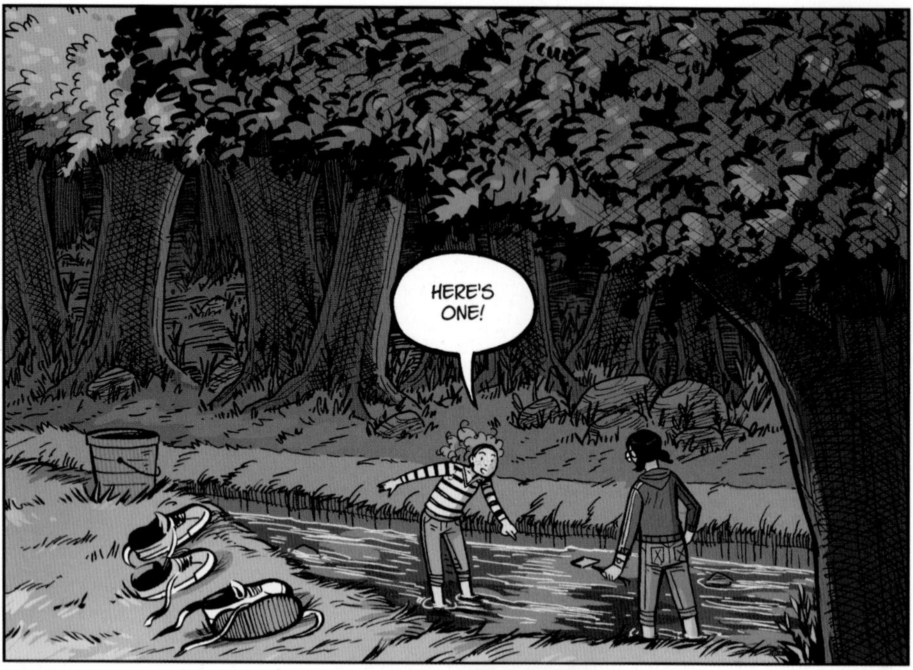
HERE'S ONE!

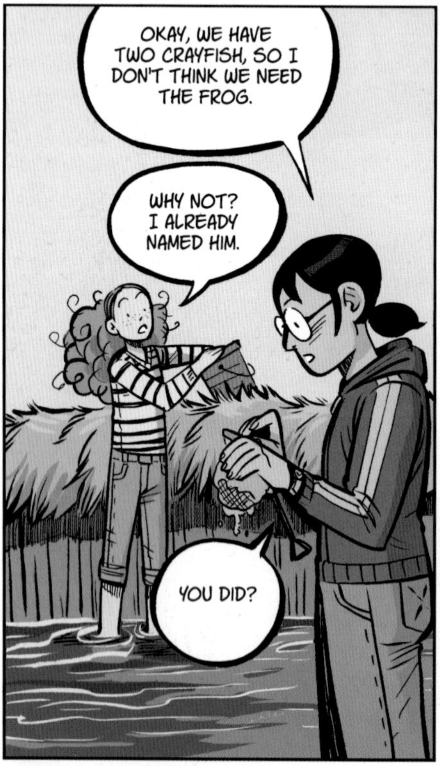
OKAY, WE HAVE TWO CRAYFISH, SO I DON'T THINK WE NEED THE FROG.
WHY NOT? I ALREADY NAMED HIM.
YOU DID?

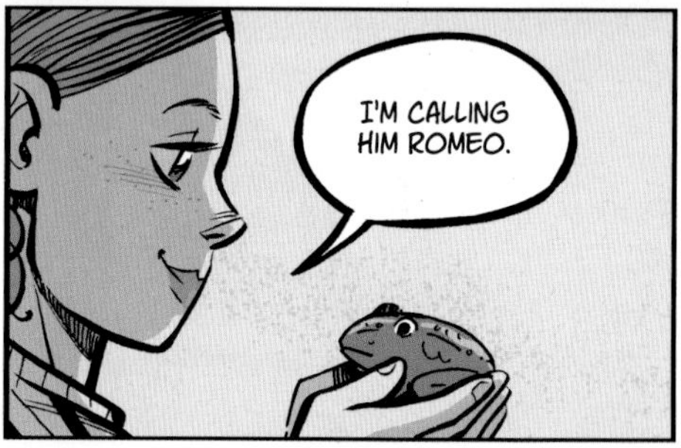
I'M CALLING HIM ROMEO.

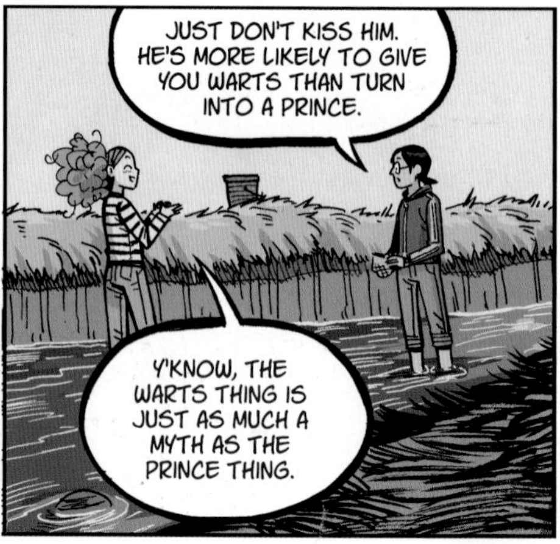
JUST DON'T KISS HIM. HE'S MORE LIKELY TO GIVE YOU WARTS THAN TURN INTO A PRINCE.
Y'KNOW, THE WARTS THING IS JUST AS MUCH A MYTH AS THE PRINCE THING.

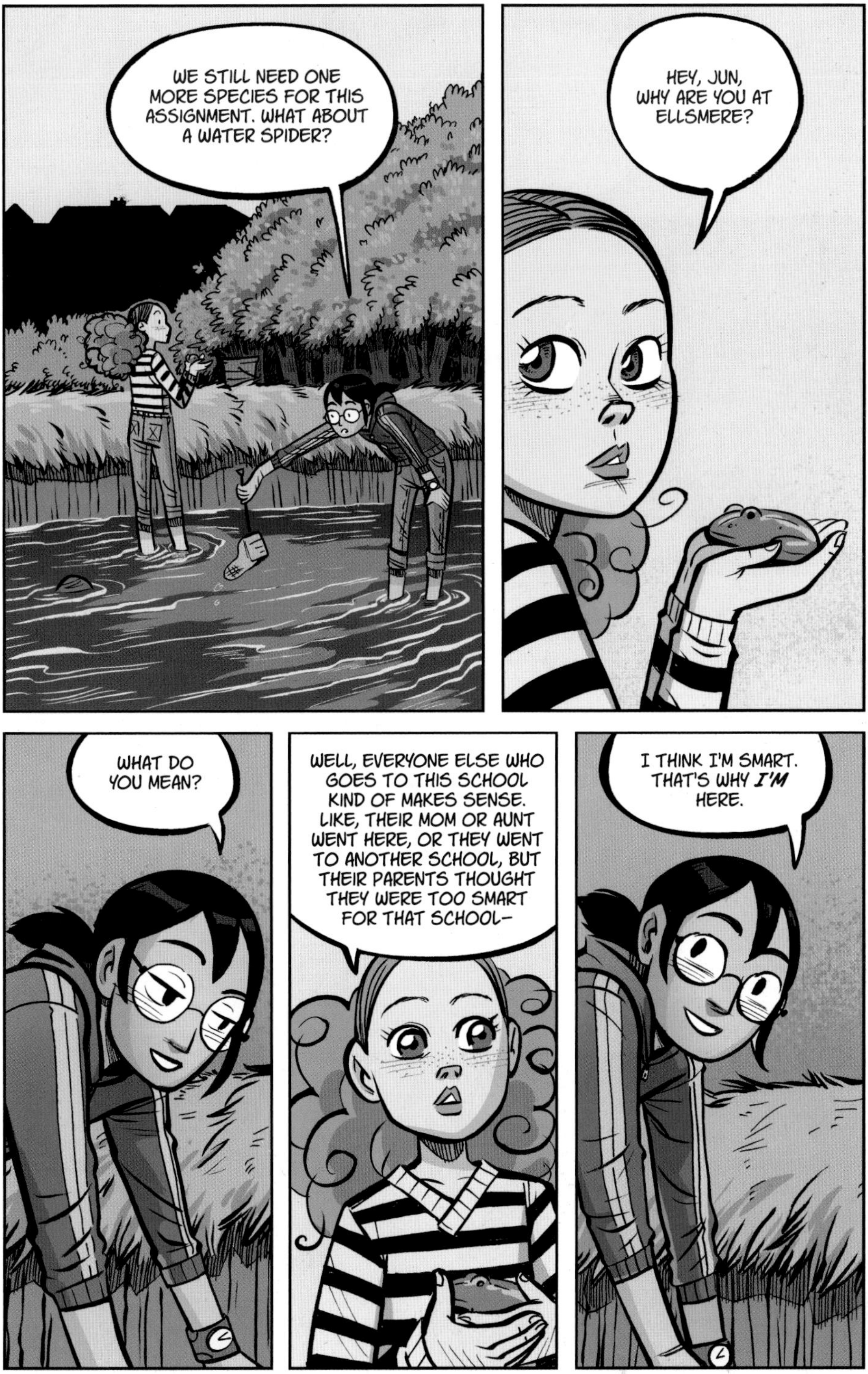
WE STILL NEED ONE MORE SPECIES FOR THIS ASSIGNMENT. WHAT ABOUT A WATER SPIDER?
HEY, JUN, WHY ARE YOU AT ELLSMERE?
WHAT DO YOU MEAN?
WELL, EVERYONE ELSE WHO GOES TO THIS SCHOOL KIND OF MAKES SENSE. LIKE, THEIR MOM OR AUNT WENT HERE, OR THEY WENT TO ANOTHER SCHOOL, BUT THEIR PARENTS THOUGHT THEY WERE TOO SMART FOR THAT SCHOOL–
I THINK I'M SMART. THAT'S WHY *I'M* HERE.

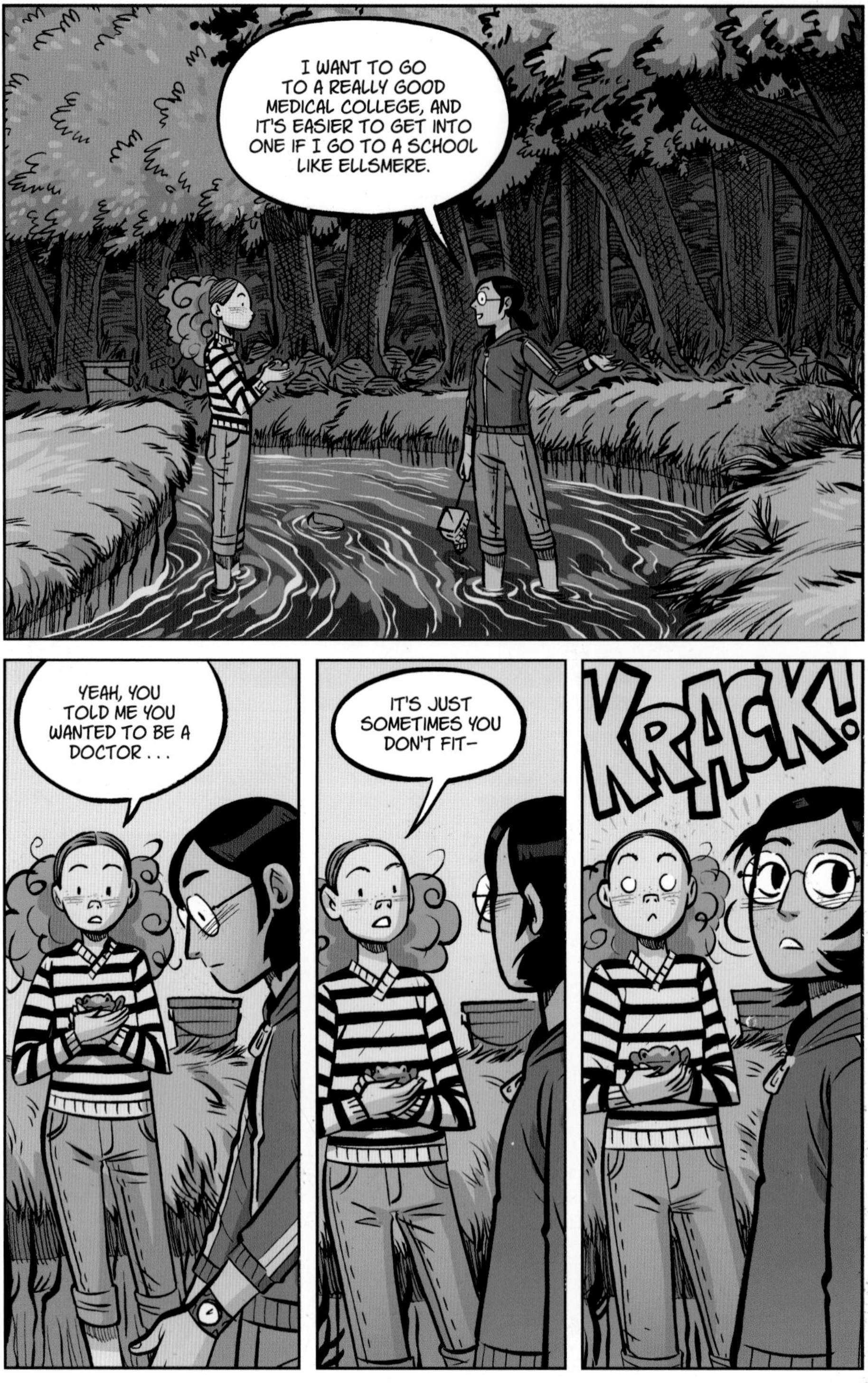
I WANT TO GO TO A REALLY GOOD MEDICAL COLLEGE, AND IT'S EASIER TO GET INTO ONE IF I GO TO A SCHOOL LIKE ELLSMERE.
YEAH, YOU TOLD ME YOU WANTED TO BE A DOCTOR . . .
IT'S JUST SOMETIMES YOU DON'T FIT–
KRACK!

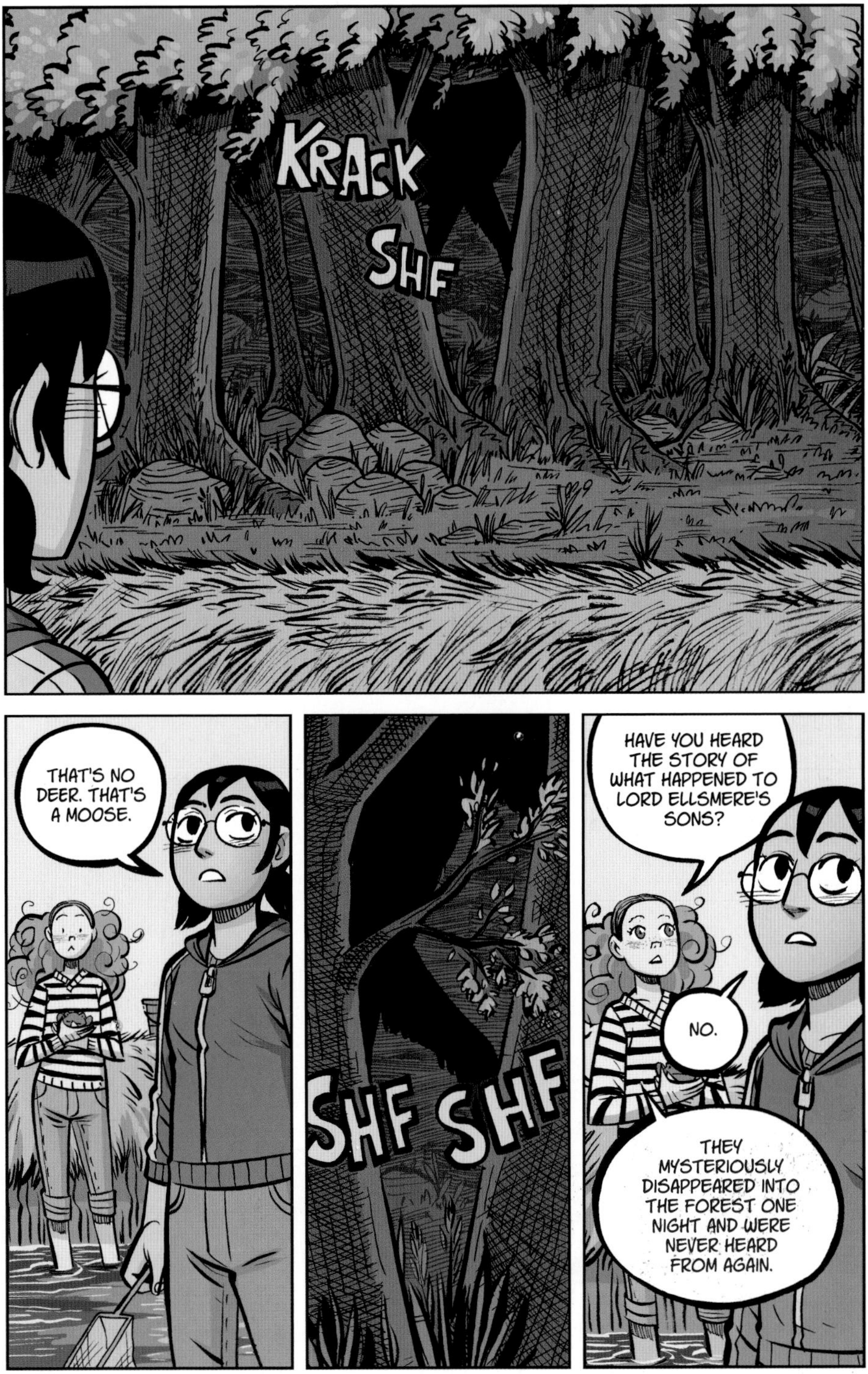
KRACK
SHF
THAT'S NO DEER. THAT'S A MOOSE.
SHF SHF
HAVE YOU HEARD THE STORY OF WHAT HAPPENED TO LORD ELLSMERE'S SONS?
NO.
THEY MYSTERIOUSLY DISAPPEARED INTO THE FOREST ONE NIGHT AND WERE NEVER HEARD FROM AGAIN.

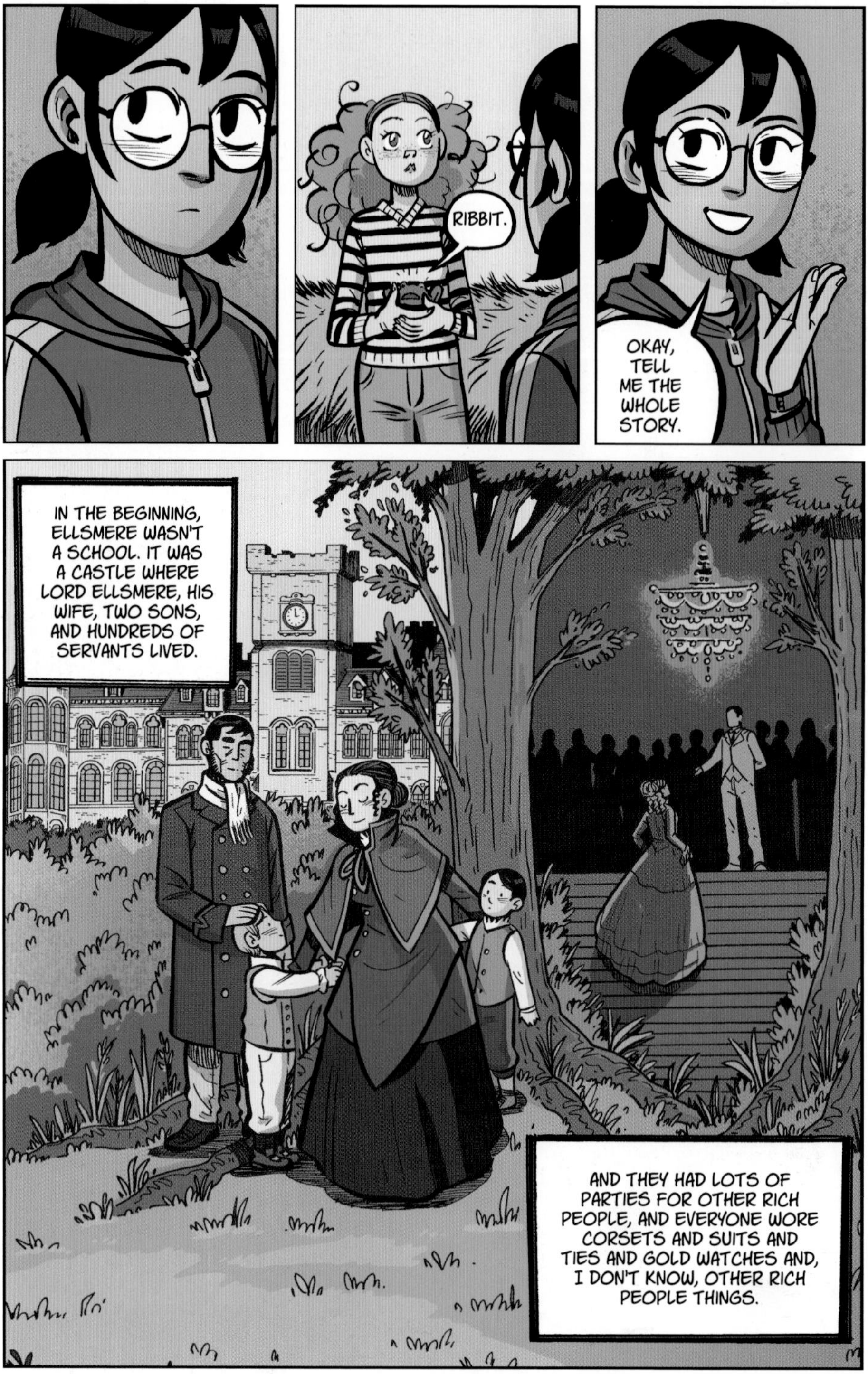
RIBBIT.
OKAY, TELL ME THE WHOLE STORY.
IN THE BEGINNING, ELLSMERE WASN'T A SCHOOL. IT WAS A CASTLE WHERE LORD ELLSMERE, HIS WIFE, TWO SONS, AND HUNDREDS OF SERVANTS LIVED.
AND THEY HAD LOTS OF PARTIES FOR OTHER RICH PEOPLE, AND EVERYONE WORE CORSETS AND SUITS AND TIES AND GOLD WATCHES AND, I DON'T KNOW, OTHER RICH PEOPLE THINGS.

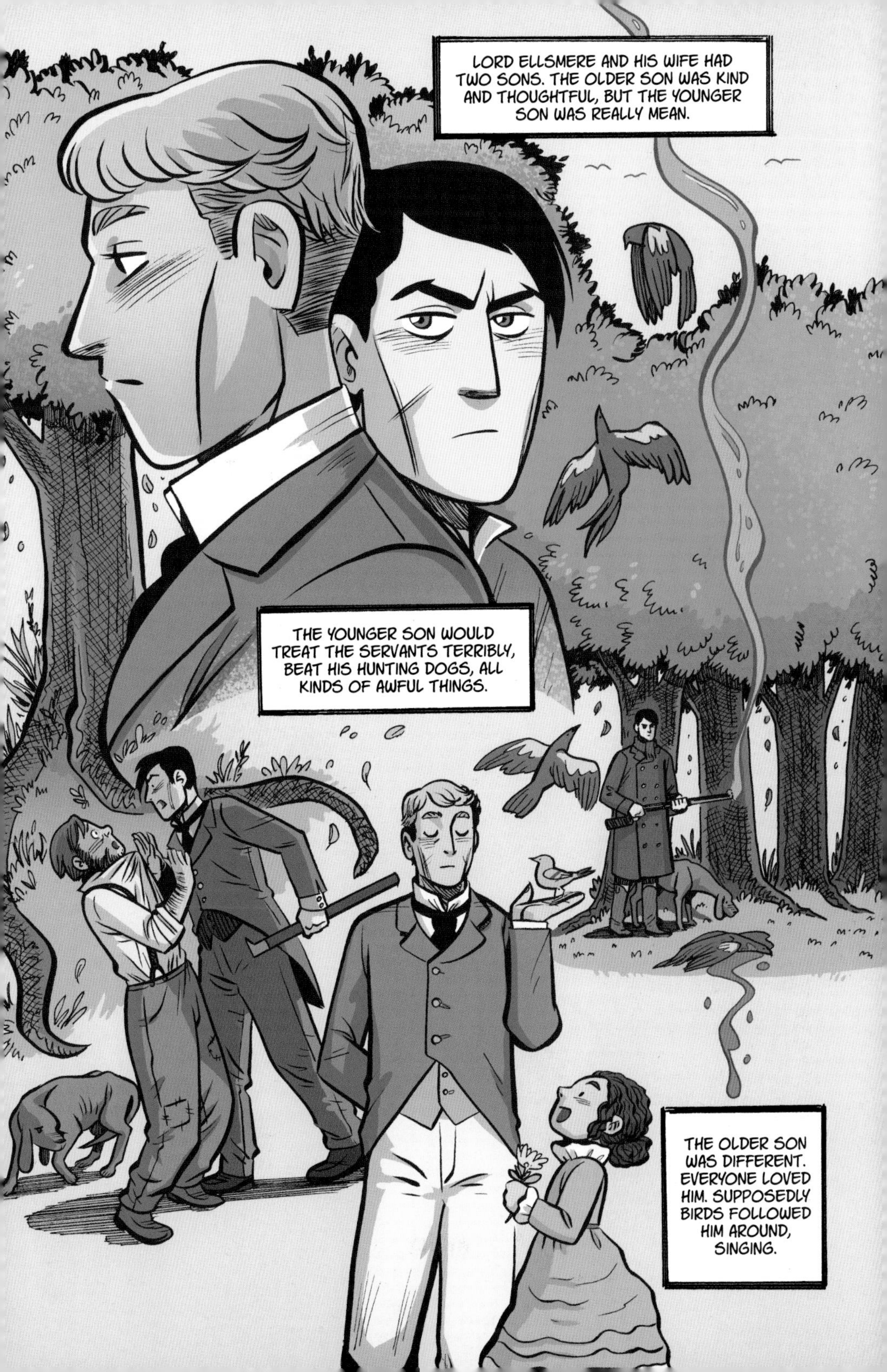
LORD ELLSMERE AND HIS WIFE HAD TWO SONS. THE OLDER SON WAS KIND AND THOUGHTFUL, BUT THE YOUNGER SON WAS REALLY MEAN.
THE YOUNGER SON WOULD TREAT THE SERVANTS TERRIBLY, BEAT HIS HUNTING DOGS, ALL KINDS OF AWFUL THINGS.
THE OLDER SON WAS DIFFERENT. EVERYONE LOVED HIM. SUPPOSEDLY BIRDS FOLLOWED HIM AROUND, SINGING.

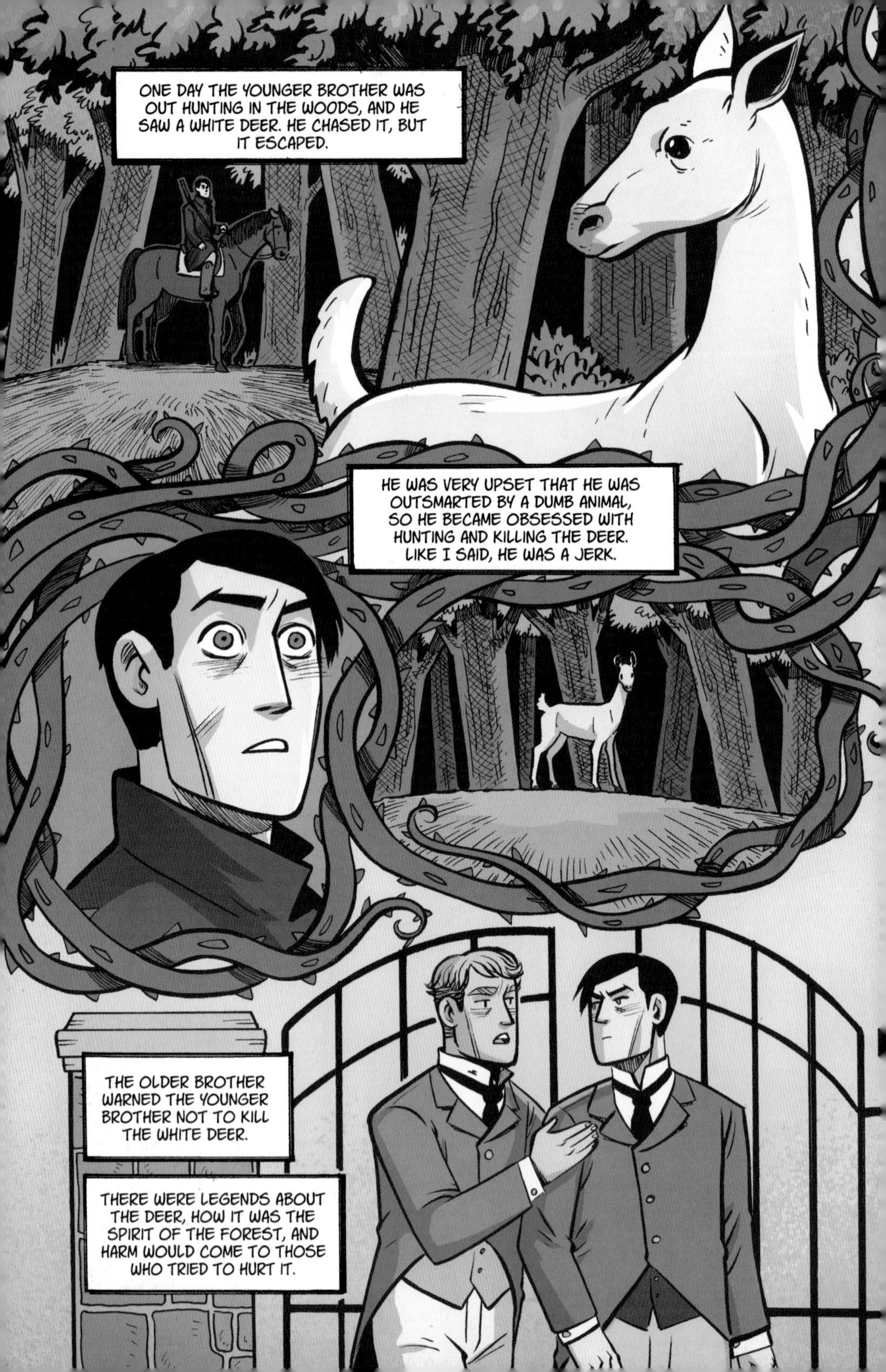
ONE DAY THE YOUNGER BROTHER WAS OUT HUNTING IN THE WOODS, AND HE SAW A WHITE DEER. HE CHASED IT, BUT IT ESCAPED.
HE WAS VERY UPSET THAT HE WAS OUTSMARTED BY A DUMB ANIMAL, SO HE BECAME OBSESSED WITH HUNTING AND KILLING THE DEER. LIKE I SAID, HE WAS A JERK.
THE OLDER BROTHER WARNED THE YOUNGER BROTHER NOT TO KILL THE WHITE DEER.
THERE WERE LEGENDS ABOUT THE DEER, HOW IT WAS THE SPIRIT OF THE FOREST, AND HARM WOULD COME TO THOSE WHO TRIED TO HURT IT.

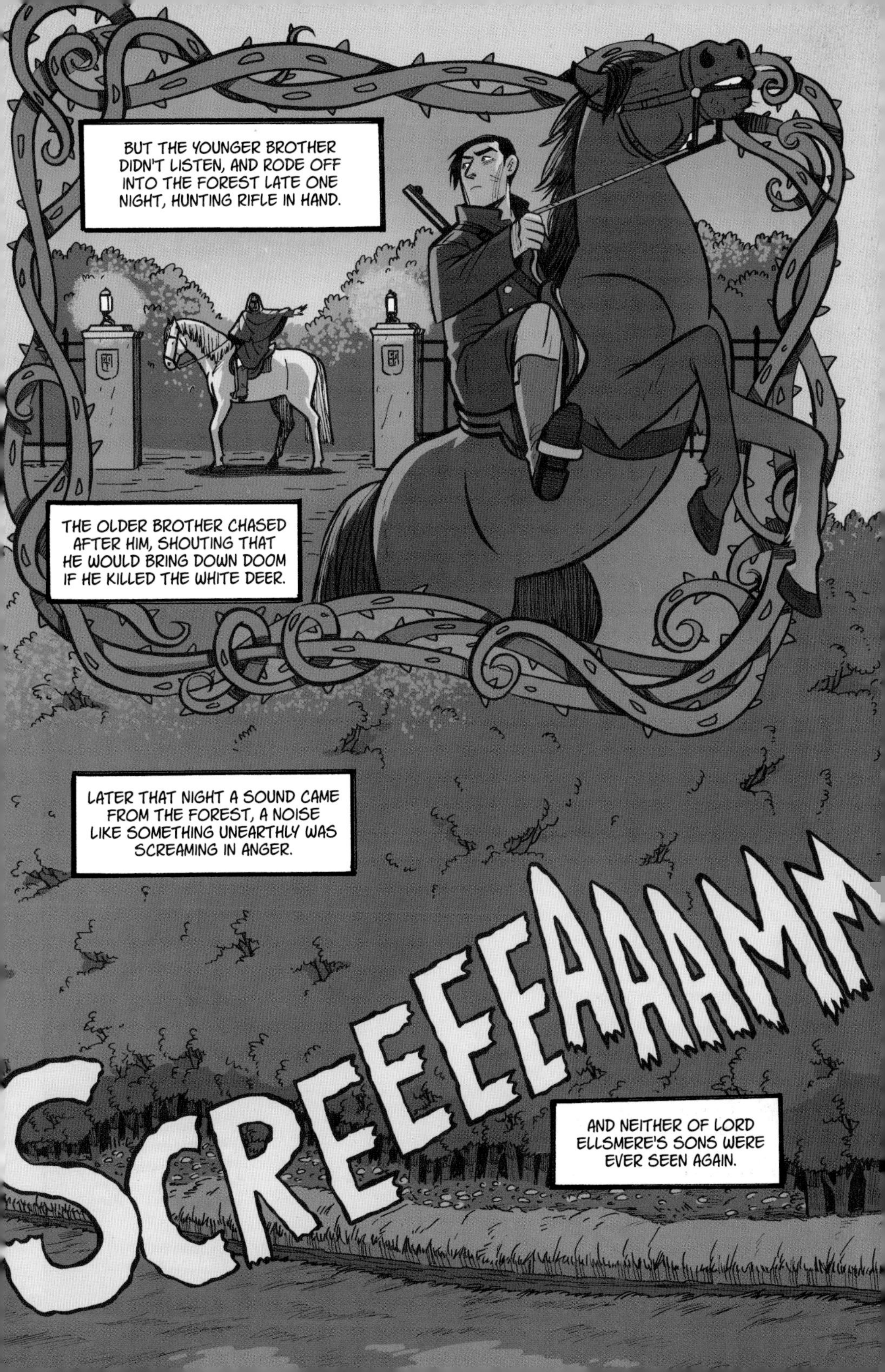

BUT THE YOUNGER BROTHER DIDN'T LISTEN, AND RODE OFF INTO THE FOREST LATE ONE NIGHT, HUNTING RIFLE IN HAND.
THE OLDER BROTHER CHASED AFTER HIM, SHOUTING THAT HE WOULD BRING DOWN DOOM IF HE KILLED THE WHITE DEER.
LATER THAT NIGHT A SOUND CAME FROM THE FOREST, A NOISE LIKE SOMETHING UNEARTHLY WAS SCREAMING IN ANGER.
SCREEEEAAAMM
AND NEITHER OF LORD ELLSMERE'S SONS WERE EVER SEEN AGAIN.

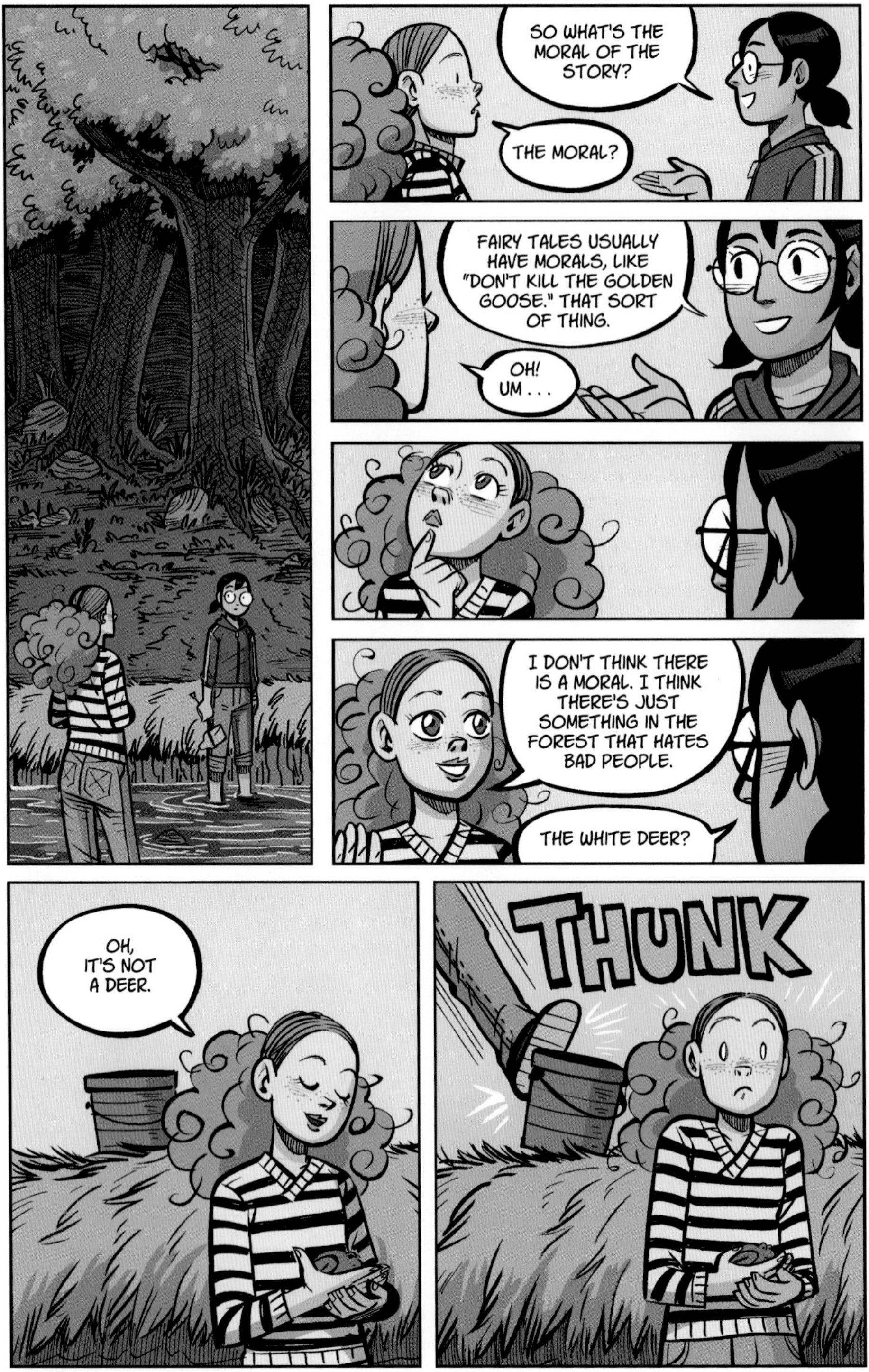
SO WHAT'S THE MORAL OF THE STORY?
THE MORAL?
FAIRY TALES USUALLY HAVE MORALS, LIKE "DON'T KILL THE GOLDEN GOOSE." THAT SORT OF THING.
OH! UM . . .
I DON'T THINK THERE IS A MORAL. I THINK THERE'S JUST SOMETHING IN THE FOREST THAT HATES BAD PEOPLE.
THE WHITE DEER?
OH, IT'S NOT A DEER.
THUNK

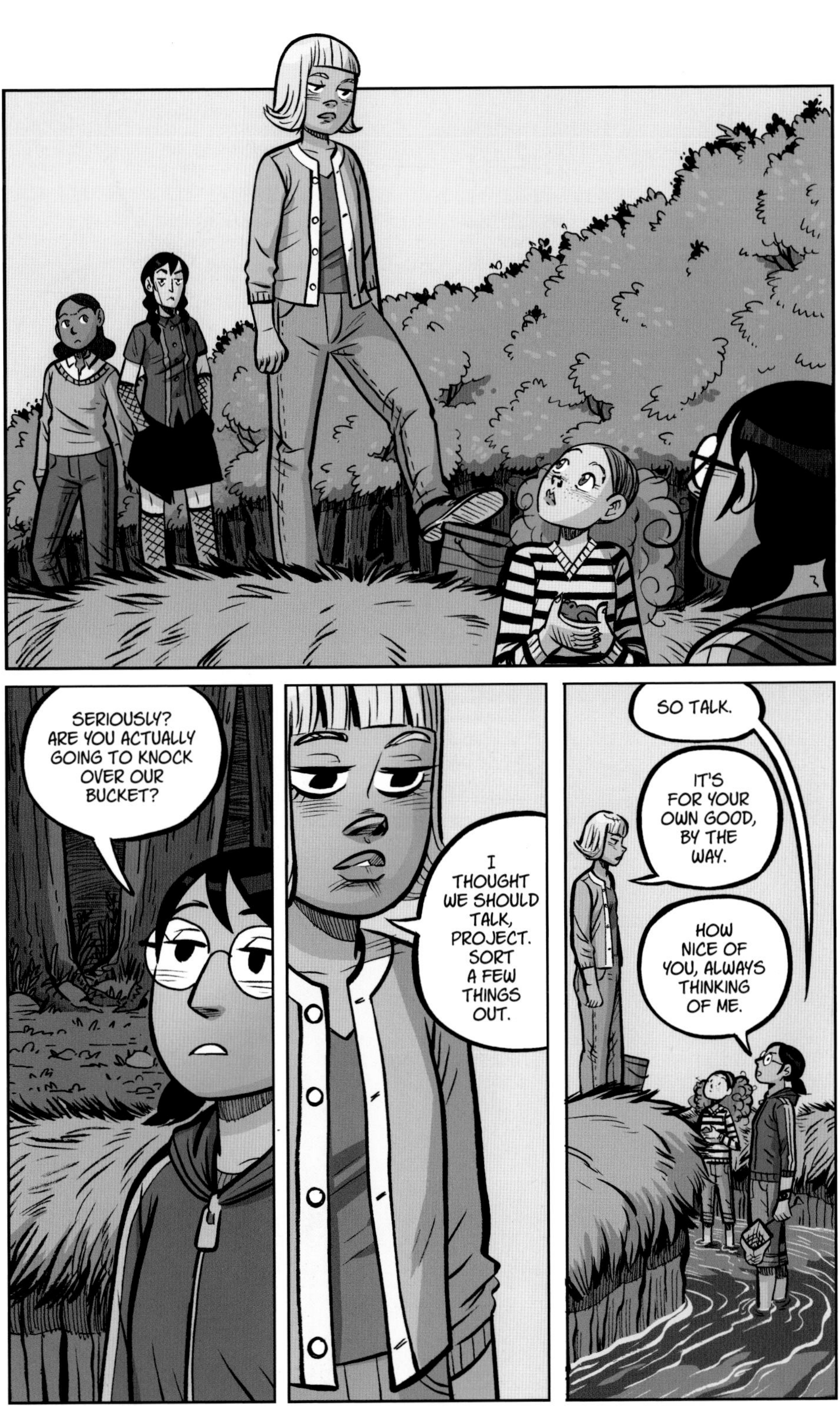
SERIOUSLY? ARE YOU ACTUALLY GOING TO KNOCK OVER OUR BUCKET?
I THOUGHT WE SHOULD TALK, PROJECT. SORT A FEW THINGS OUT.
SO TALK.
IT'S FOR YOUR OWN GOOD, BY THE WAY.
HOW NICE OF YOU, ALWAYS THINKING OF ME.

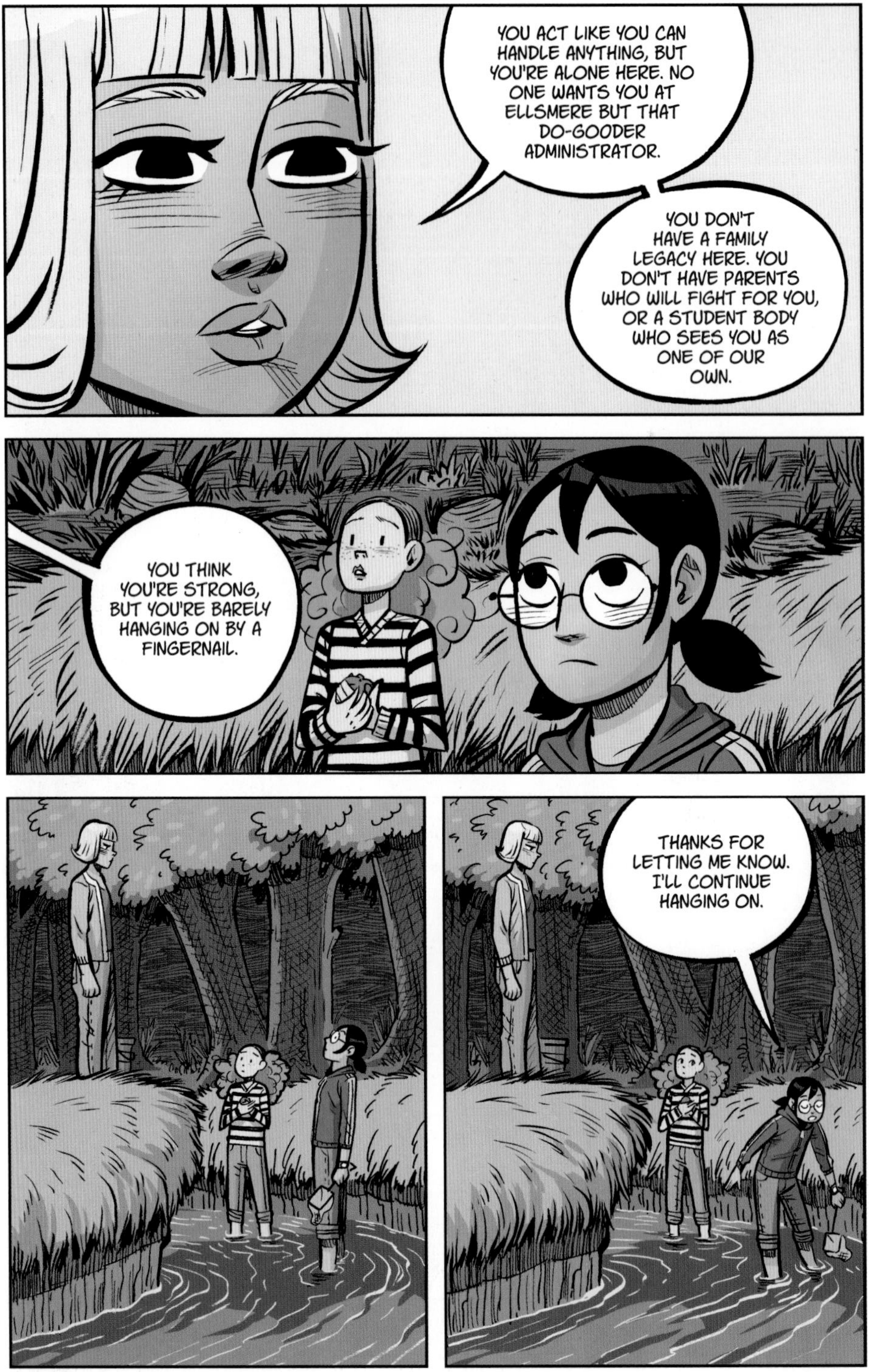
YOU ACT LIKE YOU CAN HANDLE ANYTHING, BUT YOU'RE ALONE HERE. NO ONE WANTS YOU AT ELLSMERE BUT THAT DO-GOODER ADMINISTRATOR.
YOU DON'T HAVE A FAMILY LEGACY HERE. YOU DON'T HAVE PARENTS WHO WILL FIGHT FOR YOU, OR A STUDENT BODY WHO SEES YOU AS ONE OF OUR OWN.
YOU THINK YOU'RE STRONG, BUT YOU'RE BARELY HANGING ON BY A FINGERNAIL.
THANKS FOR LETTING ME KNOW. I'LL CONTINUE HANGING ON.

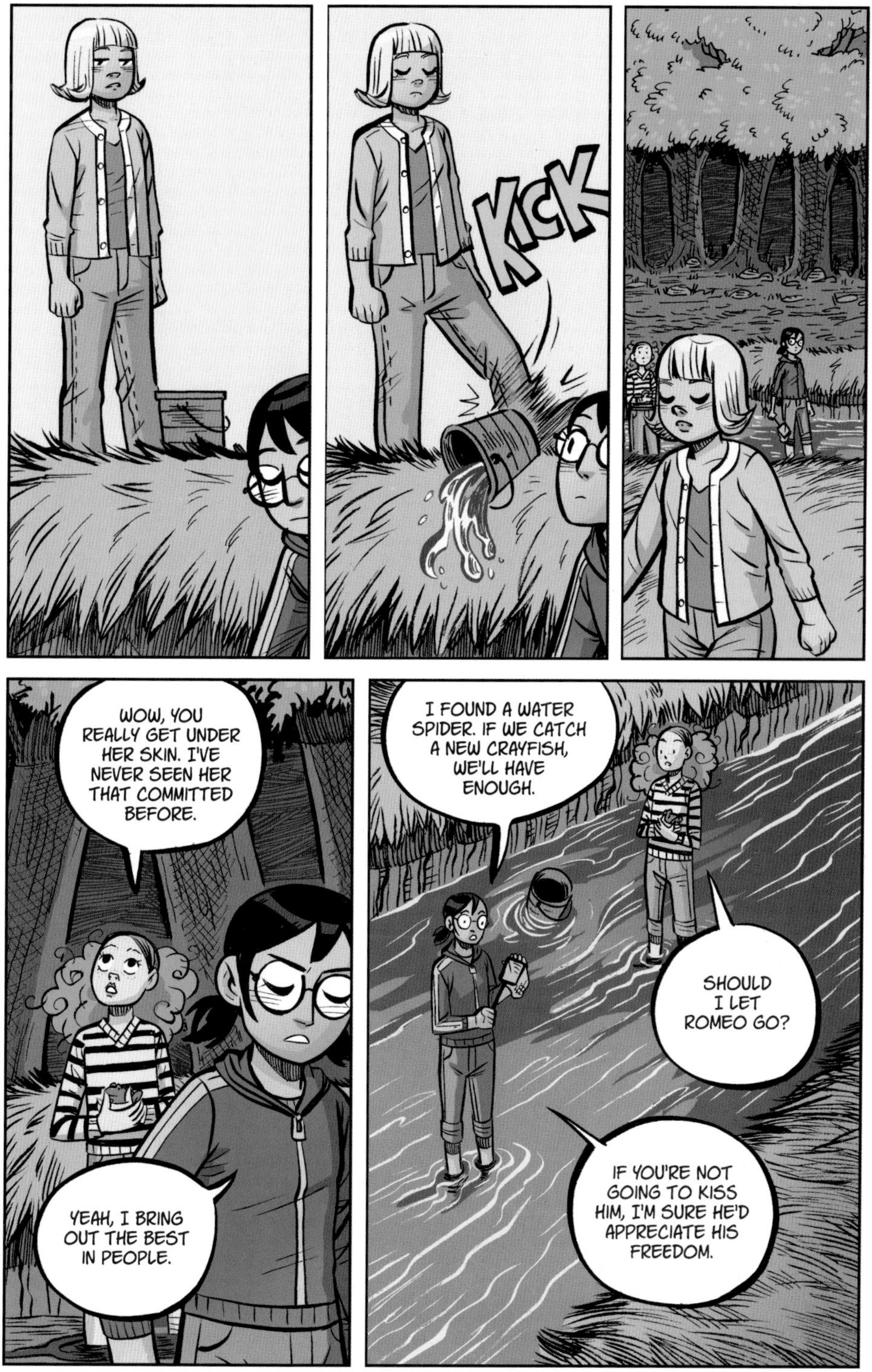
KICK
WOW, YOU REALLY GET UNDER HER SKIN. I'VE NEVER SEEN HER THAT COMMITTED BEFORE.
YEAH, I BRING OUT THE BEST IN PEOPLE.
I FOUND A WATER SPIDER. IF WE CATCH A NEW CRAYFISH, WE'LL HAVE ENOUGH.
SHOULD I LET ROMEO GO?
IF YOU'RE NOT GOING TO KISS HIM, I'M SURE HE'D APPRECIATE HIS FREEDOM.

Chapter Five

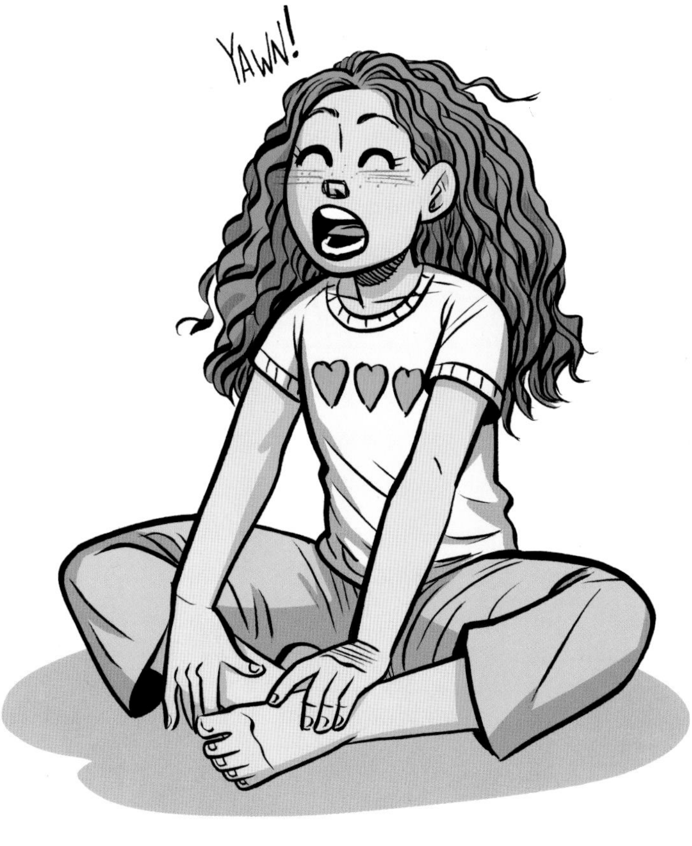
YAWN!

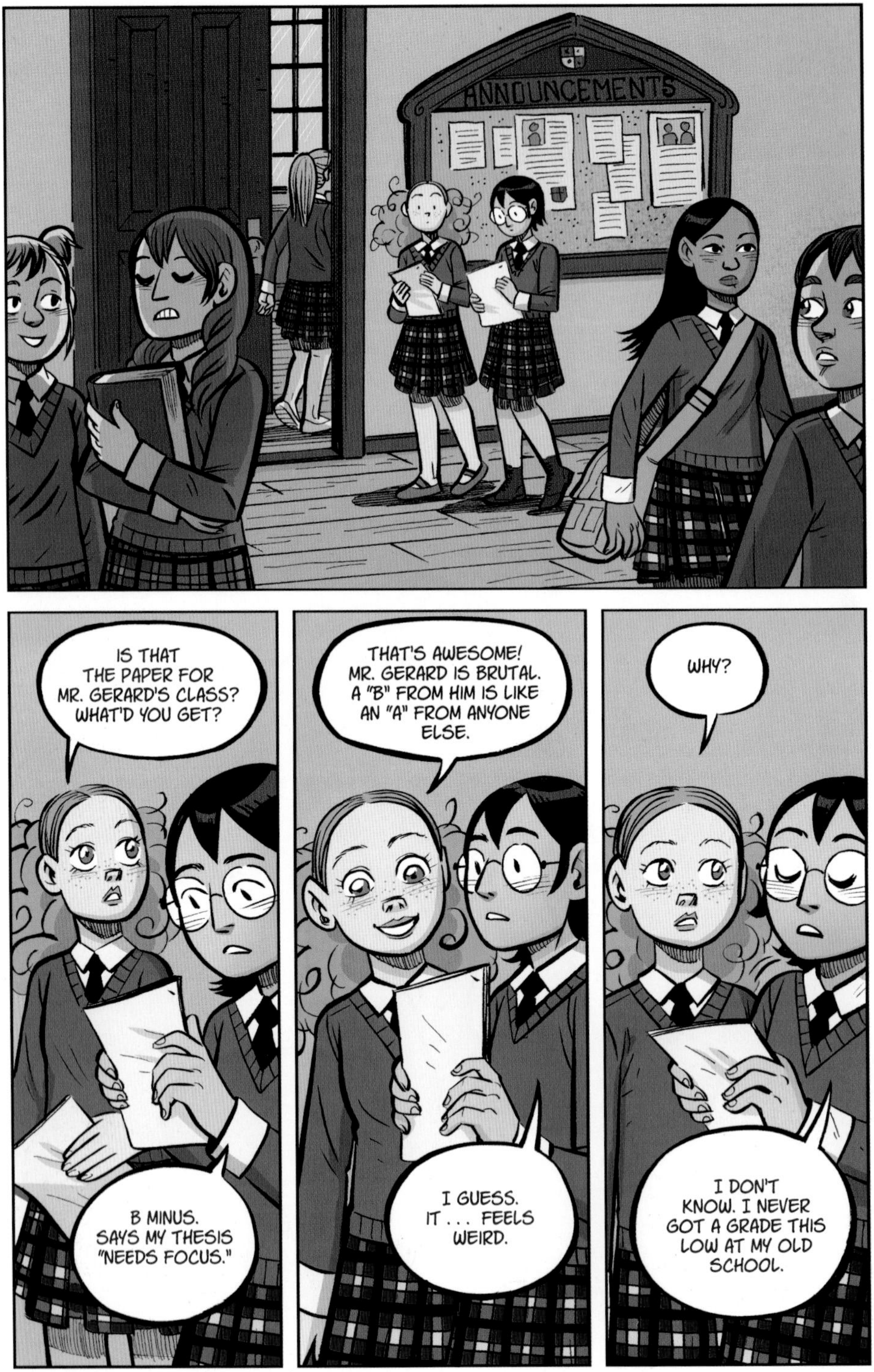
ANNOUNCEMENTS
IS THAT THE PAPER FOR MR. GERARD'S CLASS? WHAT'D YOU GET?
B MINUS. SAYS MY THESIS "NEEDS FOCUS."
THAT'S AWESOME! MR. GERARD IS BRUTAL. A "B" FROM HIM IS LIKE AN "A" FROM ANYONE ELSE.
I GUESS. IT . . . FEELS WEIRD.
WHY?
I DON'T KNOW. I NEVER GOT A GRADE THIS LOW AT MY OLD SCHOOL.

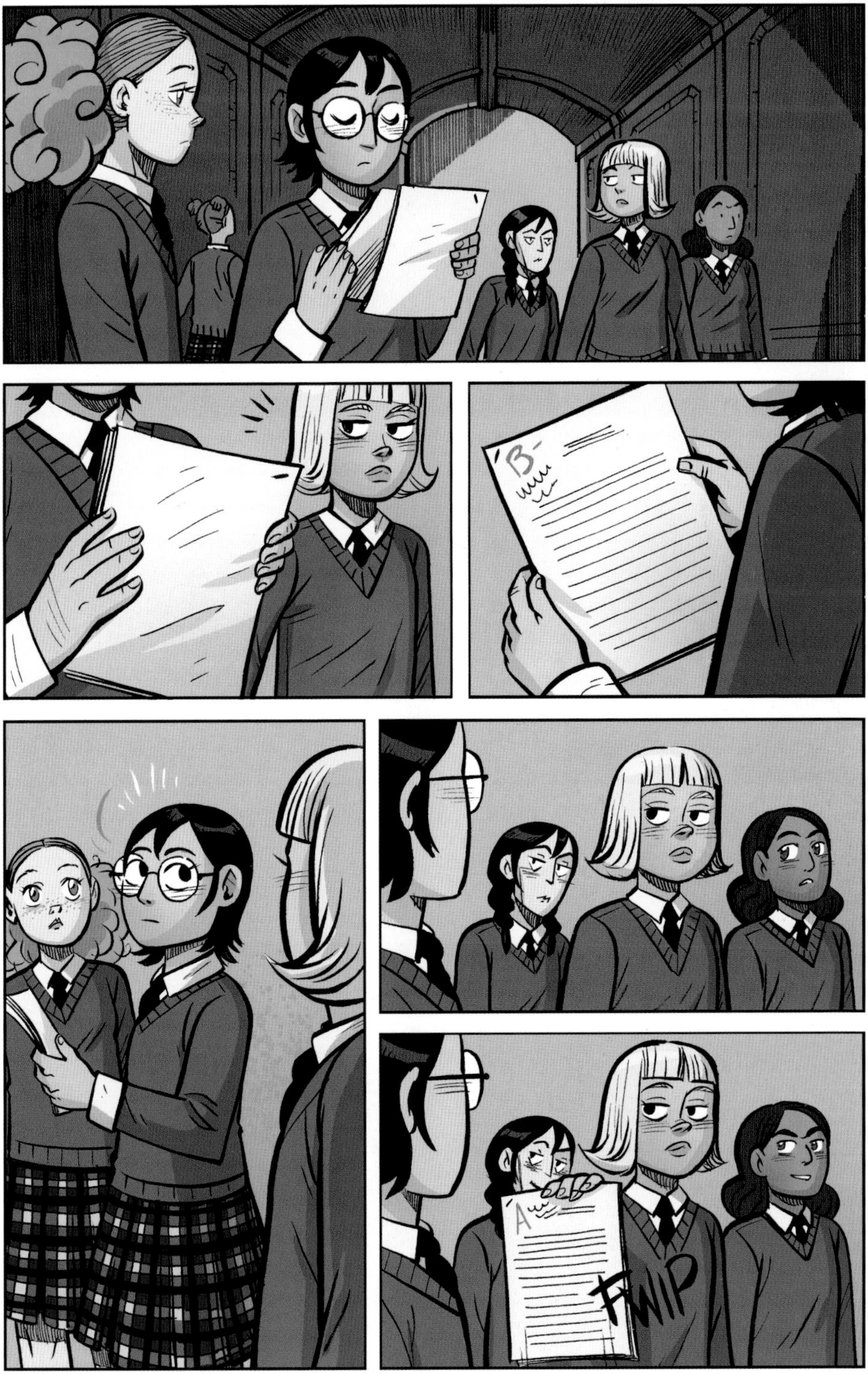
B-
A
FWIP

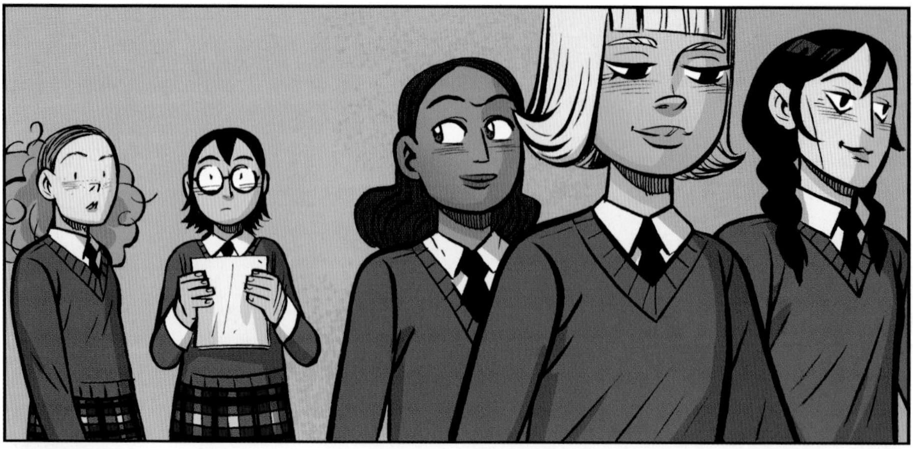

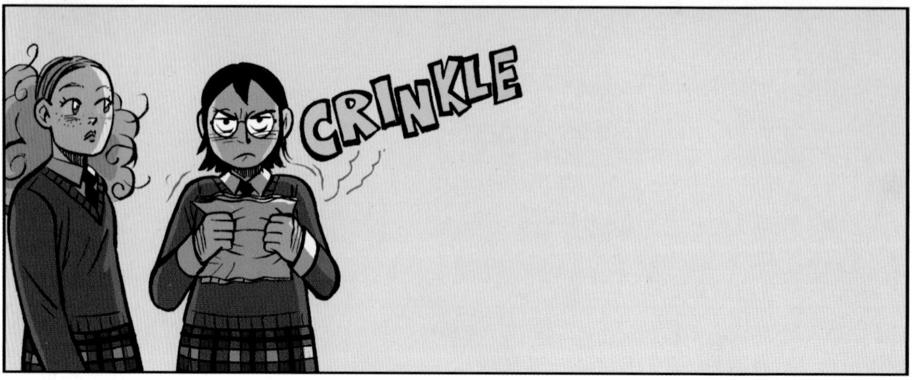
CRINKLE

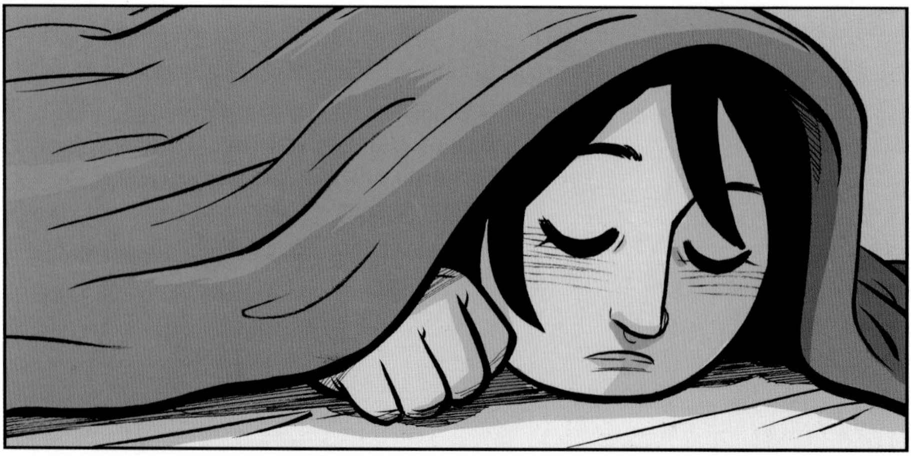

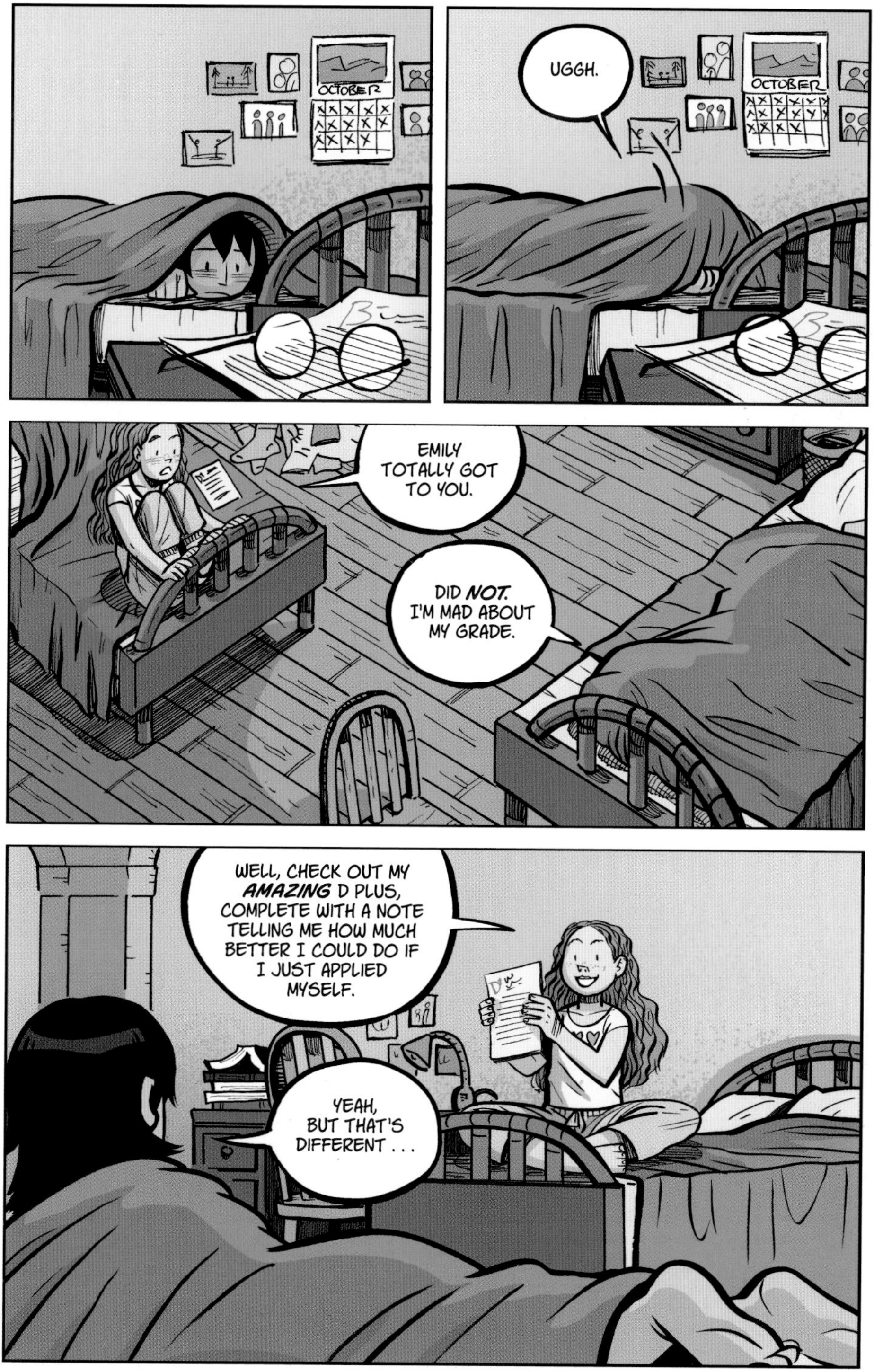
UGGH.
EMILY TOTALLY GOT TO YOU.
DID NOT. I'M MAD ABOUT MY GRADE.
WELL, CHECK OUT MY AMAZING D PLUS, COMPLETE WITH A NOTE TELLING ME HOW MUCH BETTER I COULD DO IF I JUST APPLIED MYSELF.
YEAH, BUT THAT'S DIFFERENT . . .

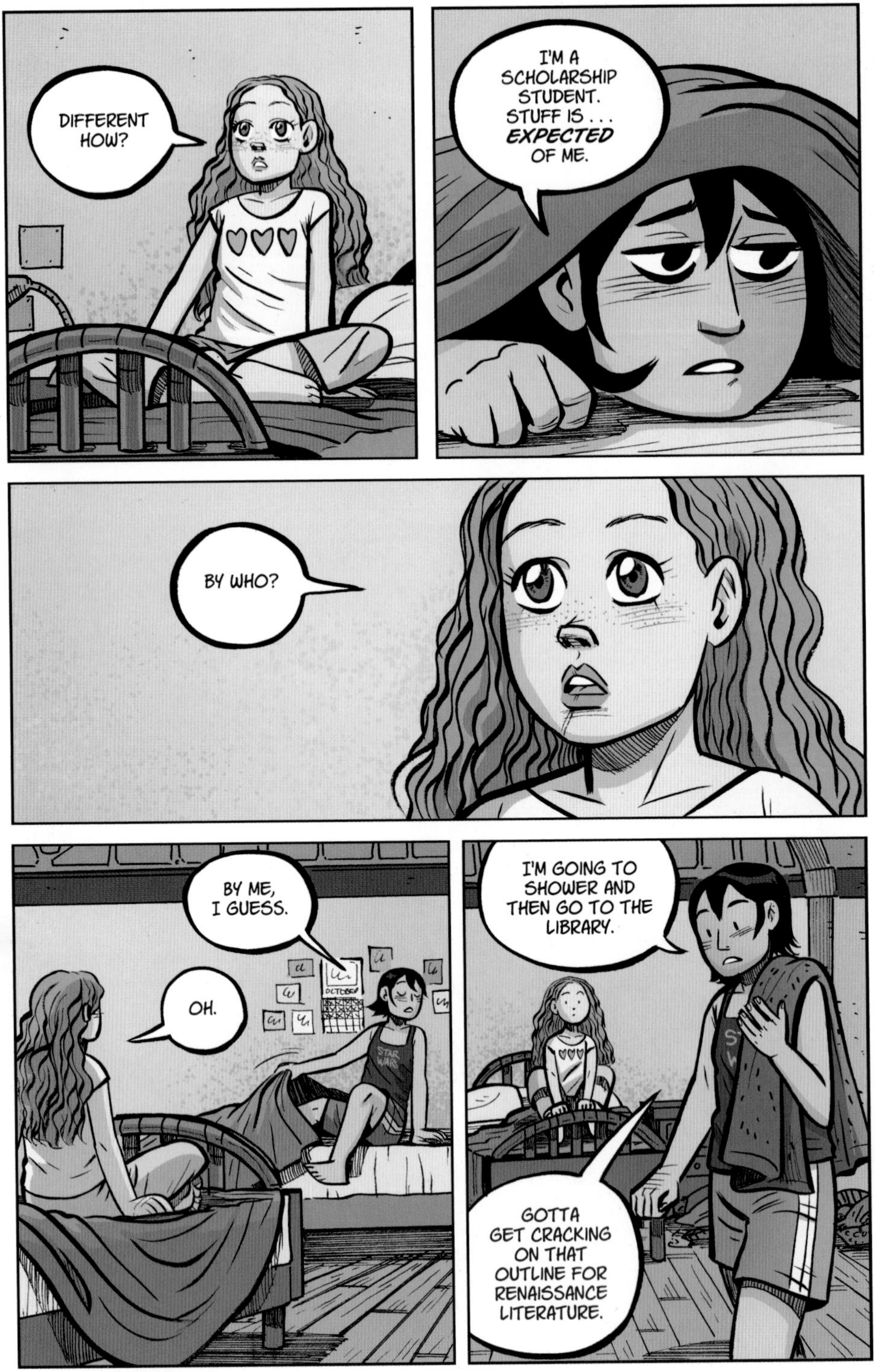
DIFFERENT HOW?
I'M A SCHOLARSHIP STUDENT. STUFF IS . . . EXPECTED OF ME.
BY WHO?
BY ME, I GUESS.
OH.
I'M GOING TO SHOWER AND THEN GO TO THE LIBRARY.
GOTTA GET CRACKING ON THAT OUTLINE FOR RENAISSANCE LITERATURE.

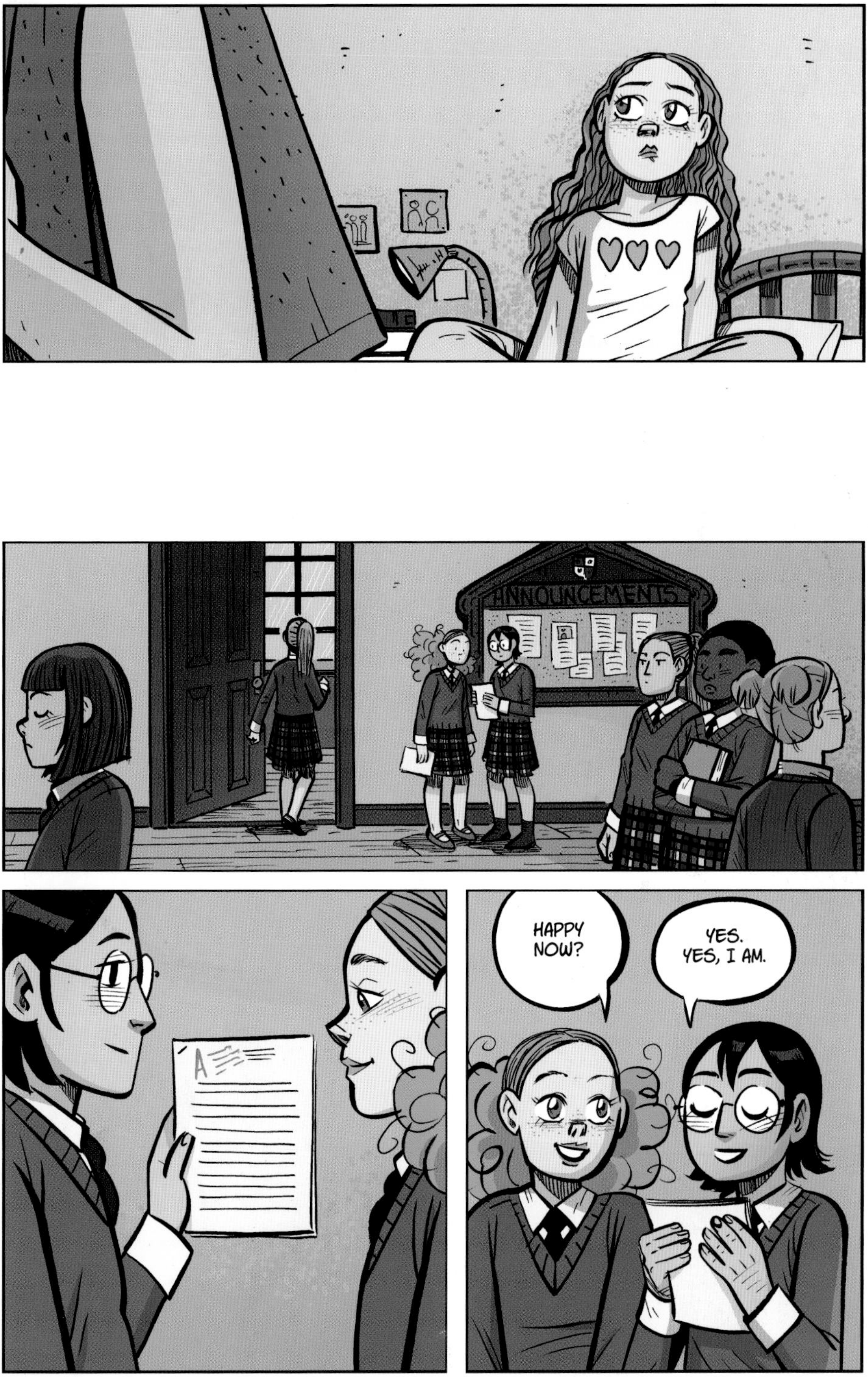
ANNOUNCEMENTS
HAPPY NOW?
YES. YES, I AM.

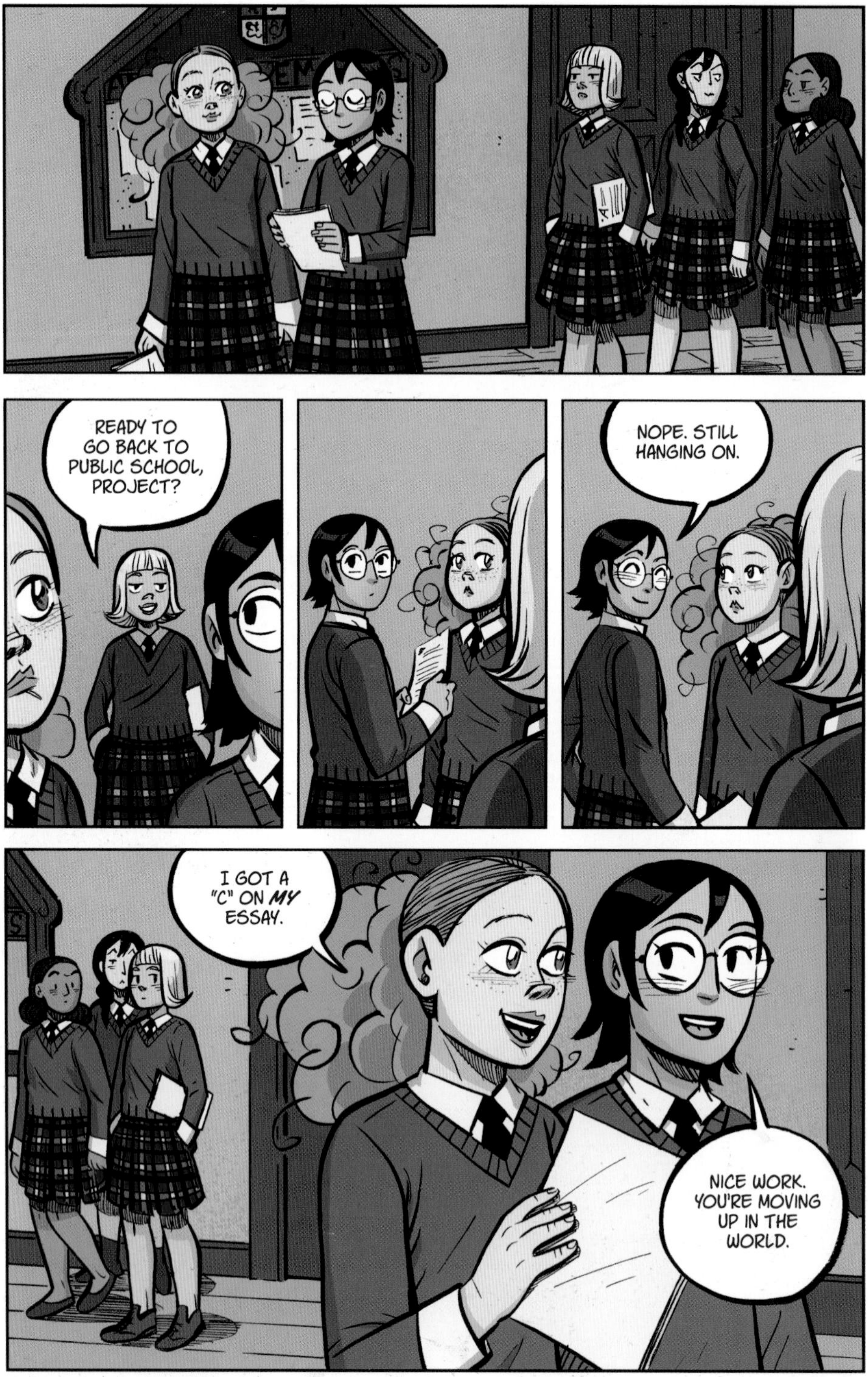
READY TO GO BACK TO PUBLIC SCHOOL, PROJECT?
NOPE. STILL HANGING ON.
I GOT A "C" ON *MY* ESSAY.
NICE WORK. YOU'RE MOVING UP IN THE WORLD.

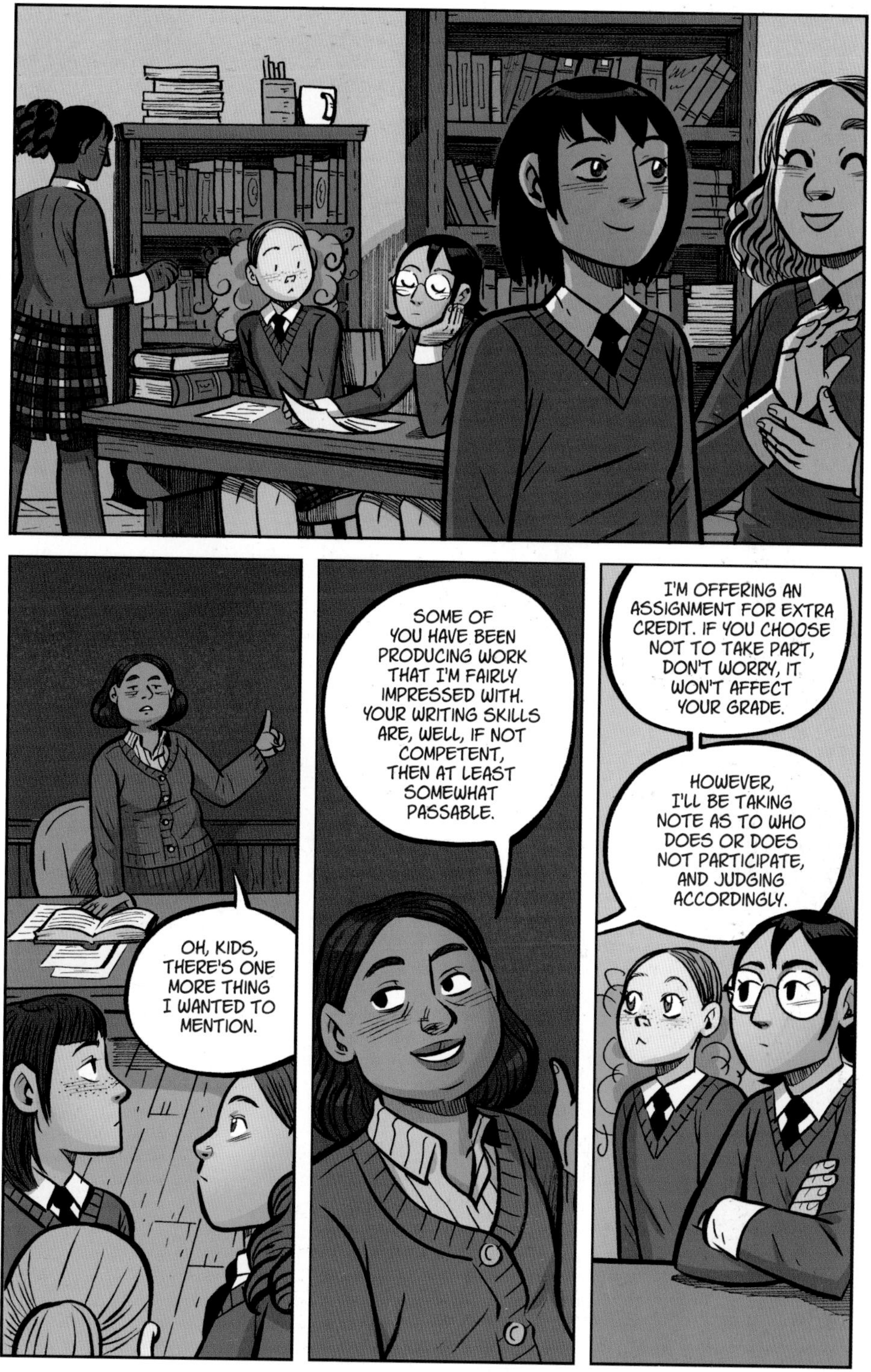
OH, KIDS, THERE'S ONE MORE THING I WANTED TO MENTION.
SOME OF YOU HAVE BEEN PRODUCING WORK THAT I'M FAIRLY IMPRESSED WITH. YOUR WRITING SKILLS ARE, WELL, IF NOT COMPETENT, THEN AT LEAST SOMEWHAT PASSABLE.
I'M OFFERING AN ASSIGNMENT FOR EXTRA CREDIT. IF YOU CHOOSE NOT TO TAKE PART, DON'T WORRY, IT WON'T AFFECT YOUR GRADE.
HOWEVER, I'LL BE TAKING NOTE AS TO WHO DOES OR DOES NOT PARTICIPATE, AND JUDGING ACCORDINGLY.

IT'S TIME FOR A CREATIVE WRITING EXERCISE.

SUBMIT A PERSONAL STORY TO ME. CALL IT A PRACTICE RUN FOR COLLEGE SUBMISSIONS.

THE STORY CAN BE ANY SUBJECT, NO MATTER HOW SMALL AND INSIGNIFICANT. IT'S YOUR JOB TO MAKE IT INTERESTING.

THE BEST STORY WILL BE CHOSEN BY ME AND SUBMITTED TO THE LOCAL LITERARY REVIEW FOR POSSIBLE PUBLICATION.

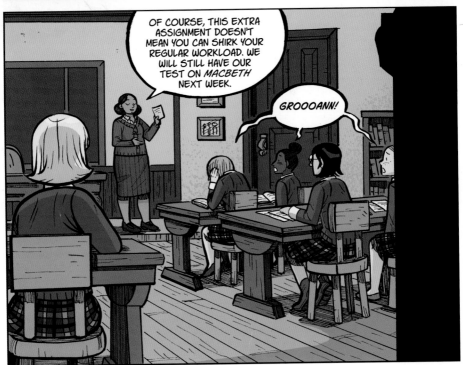

OF COURSE, THIS EXTRA ASSIGNMENT DOESN'T MEAN YOU CAN SHIRK YOUR REGULAR WORKLOAD. WE WILL STILL HAVE OUR TEST ON *MACBETH* NEXT WEEK.

GROOOANN!

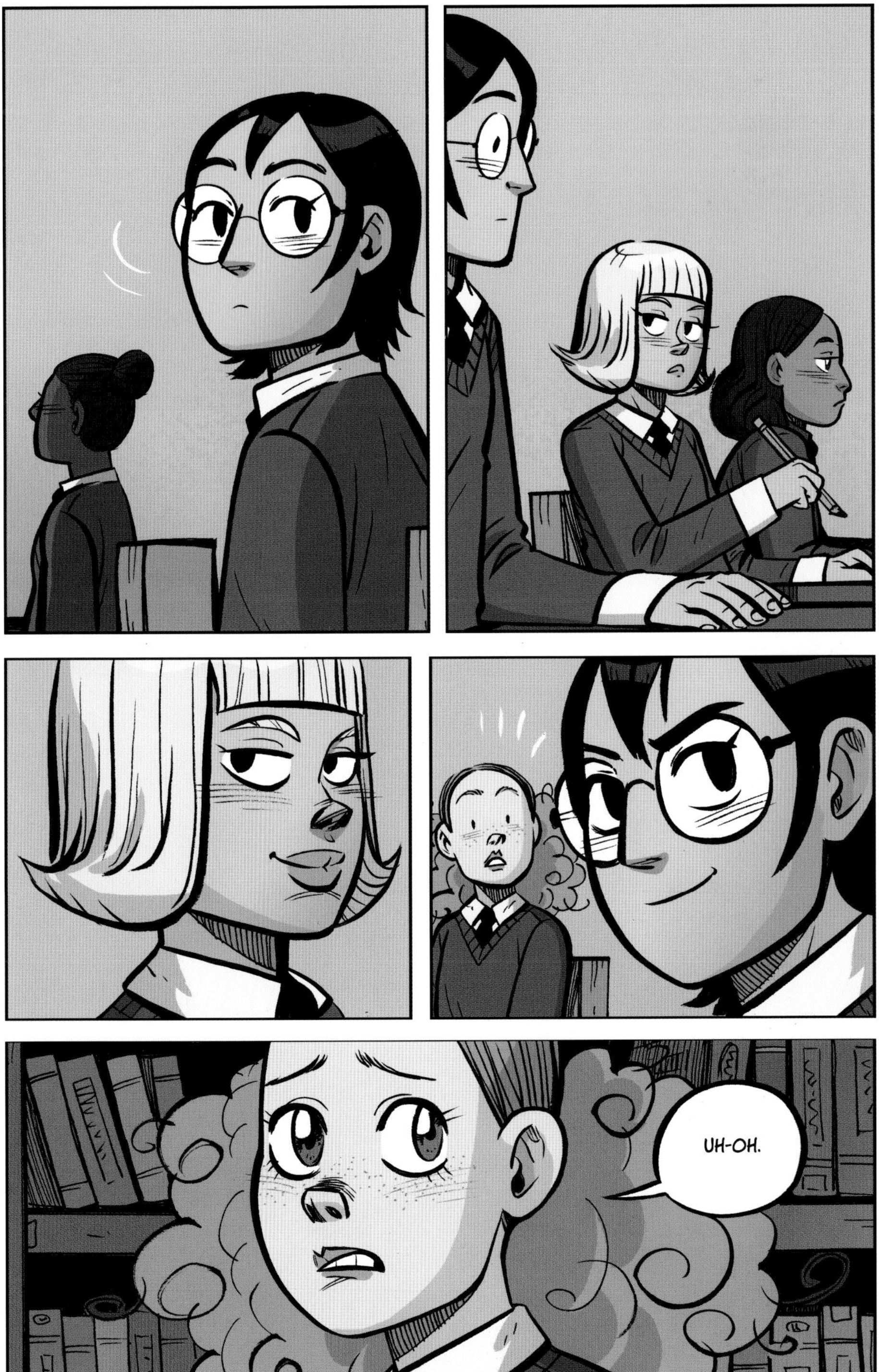
UH-OH.

Chapter Six

Personal Essay
by Juniper

When my dad died

NO.

Personal Essay
by Juniper

When my dad di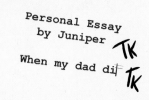

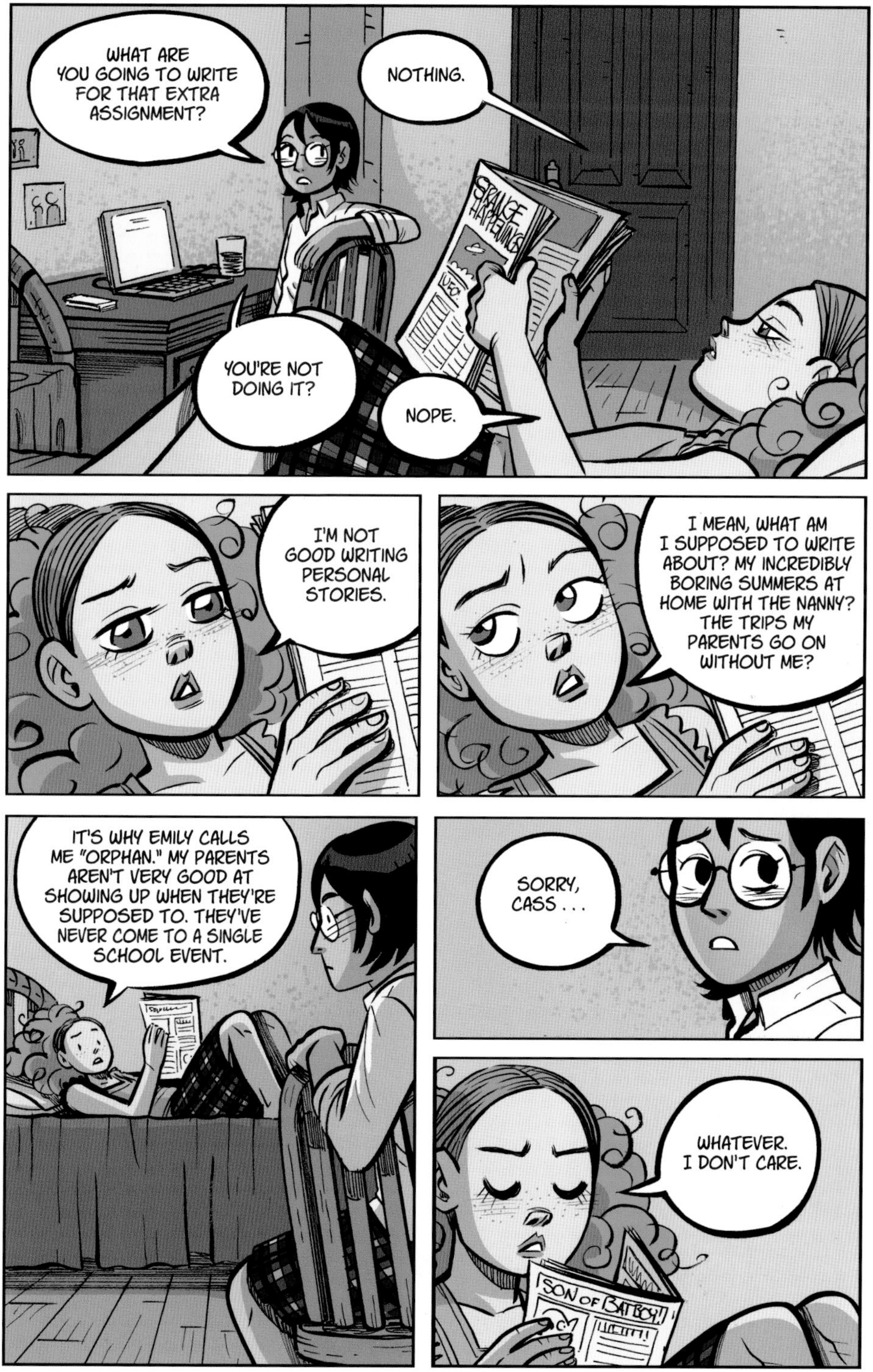
WHAT ARE YOU GOING TO WRITE FOR THAT EXTRA ASSIGNMENT?
NOTHING.
STRANGE HAPPENINGS
YOU'RE NOT DOING IT?
NOPE.
I'M NOT GOOD WRITING PERSONAL STORIES.
I MEAN, WHAT AM I SUPPOSED TO WRITE ABOUT? MY INCREDIBLY BORING SUMMERS AT HOME WITH THE NANNY? THE TRIPS MY PARENTS GO ON WITHOUT ME?
IT'S WHY EMILY CALLS ME "ORPHAN." MY PARENTS AREN'T VERY GOOD AT SHOWING UP WHEN THEY'RE SUPPOSED TO. THEY'VE NEVER COME TO A SINGLE SCHOOL EVENT.
SORRY, CASS . . .
WHATEVER. I DON'T CARE.
SON OF BATBOY!

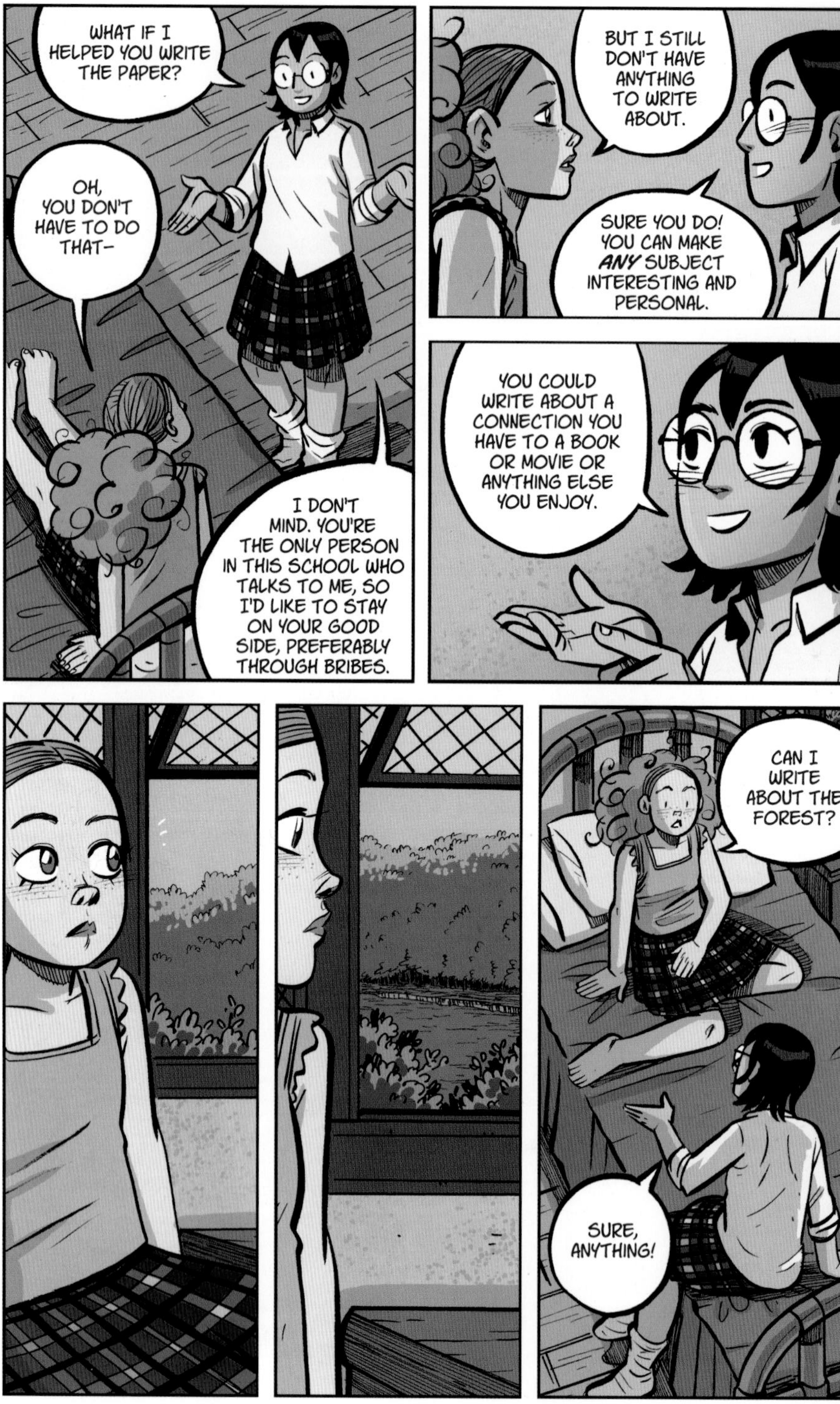
WHAT IF I HELPED YOU WRITE THE PAPER?
OH, YOU DON'T HAVE TO DO THAT–
I DON'T MIND. YOU'RE THE ONLY PERSON IN THIS SCHOOL WHO TALKS TO ME, SO I'D LIKE TO STAY ON YOUR GOOD SIDE, PREFERABLY THROUGH BRIBES.
BUT I STILL DON'T HAVE ANYTHING TO WRITE ABOUT.
SURE YOU DO! YOU CAN MAKE *ANY* SUBJECT INTERESTING AND PERSONAL.
YOU COULD WRITE ABOUT A CONNECTION YOU HAVE TO A BOOK OR MOVIE OR ANYTHING ELSE YOU ENJOY.
CAN I WRITE ABOUT THE FOREST?
SURE, ANYTHING!

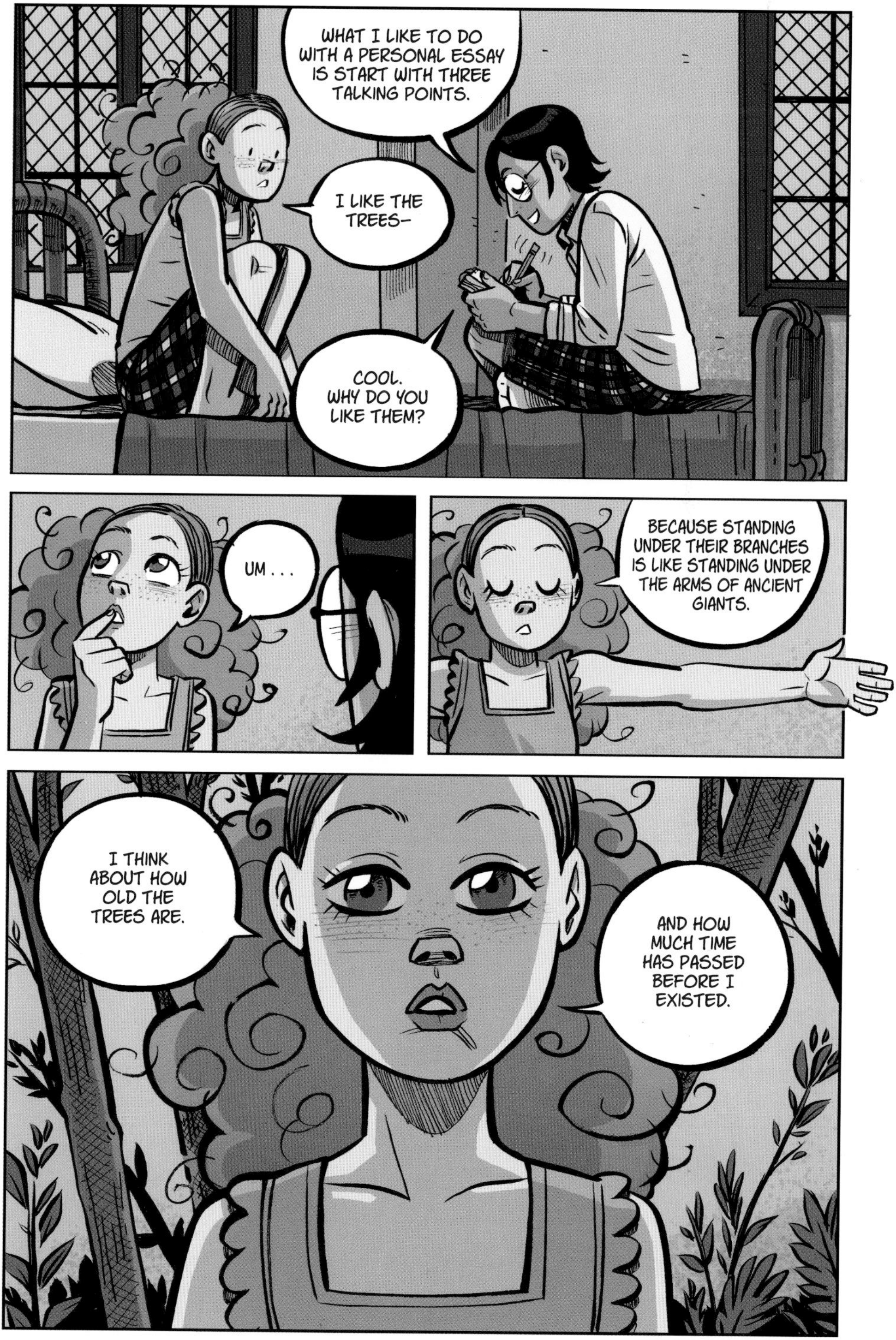
WHAT I LIKE TO DO WITH A PERSONAL ESSAY IS START WITH THREE TALKING POINTS.
I LIKE THE TREES–
COOL. WHY DO YOU LIKE THEM?
UM . . .
BECAUSE STANDING UNDER THEIR BRANCHES IS LIKE STANDING UNDER THE ARMS OF ANCIENT GIANTS.
I THINK ABOUT HOW OLD THE TREES ARE.
AND HOW MUCH TIME HAS PASSED BEFORE I EXISTED.

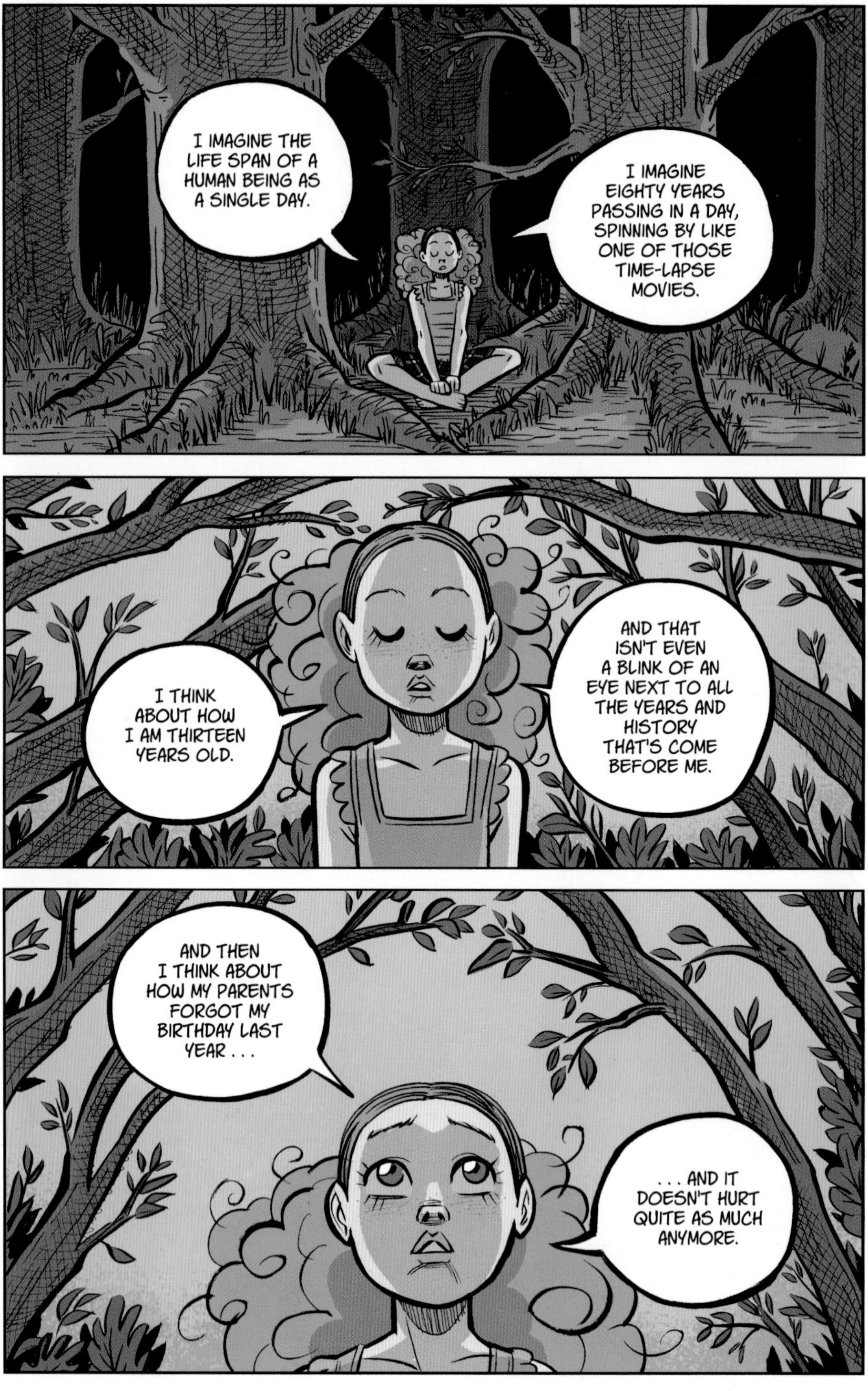
I IMAGINE THE LIFE SPAN OF A HUMAN BEING AS A SINGLE DAY.
I IMAGINE EIGHTY YEARS PASSING IN A DAY, SPINNING BY LIKE ONE OF THOSE TIME-LAPSE MOVIES.
I THINK ABOUT HOW I AM THIRTEEN YEARS OLD.
AND THAT ISN'T EVEN A BLINK OF AN EYE NEXT TO ALL THE YEARS AND HISTORY THAT'S COME BEFORE ME.
AND THEN I THINK ABOUT HOW MY PARENTS FORGOT MY BIRTHDAY LAST YEAR . . .
. . . AND IT DOESN'T HURT QUITE AS MUCH ANYMORE.

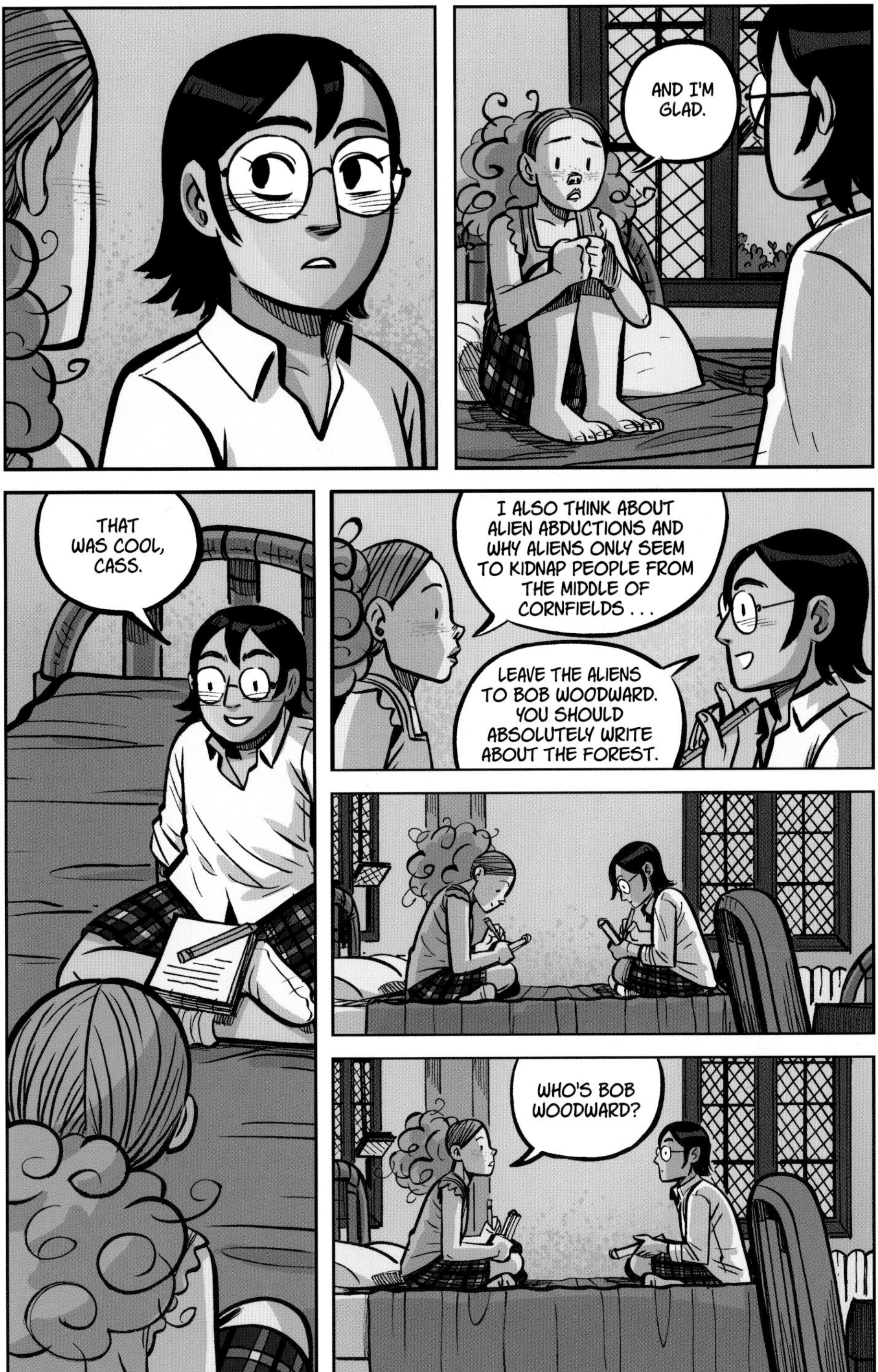
AND I'M GLAD.
THAT WAS COOL, CASS.
I ALSO THINK ABOUT ALIEN ABDUCTIONS AND WHY ALIENS ONLY SEEM TO KIDNAP PEOPLE FROM THE MIDDLE OF CORNFIELDS . . .
LEAVE THE ALIENS TO BOB WOODWARD. YOU SHOULD ABSOLUTELY WRITE ABOUT THE FOREST.
WHO'S BOB WOODWARD?

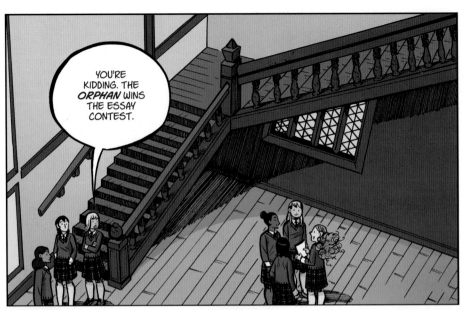

YOU'RE KIDDING. THE *ORPHAN* WINS THE ESSAY CONTEST.

AT LEAST THE PUBLIC SCHOOL PROJECT DIDN'T WIN IT?

NO, THIS IS WORSE. BISHOP'S FAVORITE IMPORT IS HERE TO *CHALLENGE* ME. I *KNOW* HOW TO DEAL WITH HER.

I DON'T THINK—

EVERYONE KNOWS THEIR PLACE AT ELLSMERE, AND THIS IS MESSING WITH HOW THINGS ARE SUPPOSED TO BE.

THE *ORPHAN* ISN'T SUPPOSED TO WIN ESSAY CONTESTS— SHE NEVER GETS GOOD GRADES. SHE ISN'T *SUPPOSED* TO BE A THREAT.

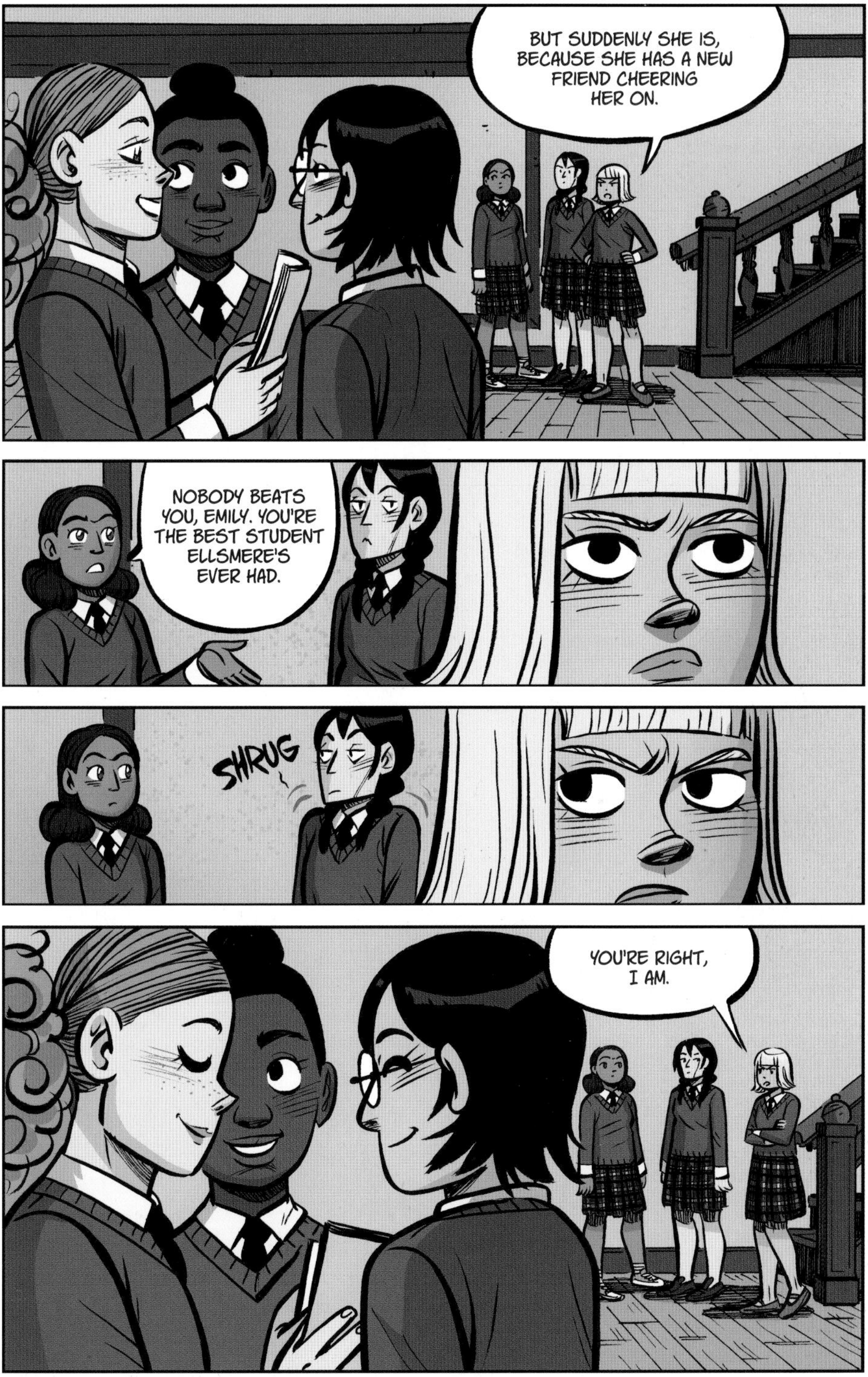
BUT SUDDENLY SHE IS, BECAUSE SHE HAS A NEW FRIEND CHEERING HER ON.
NOBODY BEATS YOU, EMILY. YOU'RE THE BEST STUDENT ELLSMERE'S EVER HAD.
SHRUG
YOU'RE RIGHT, I AM.

Chapter Seven

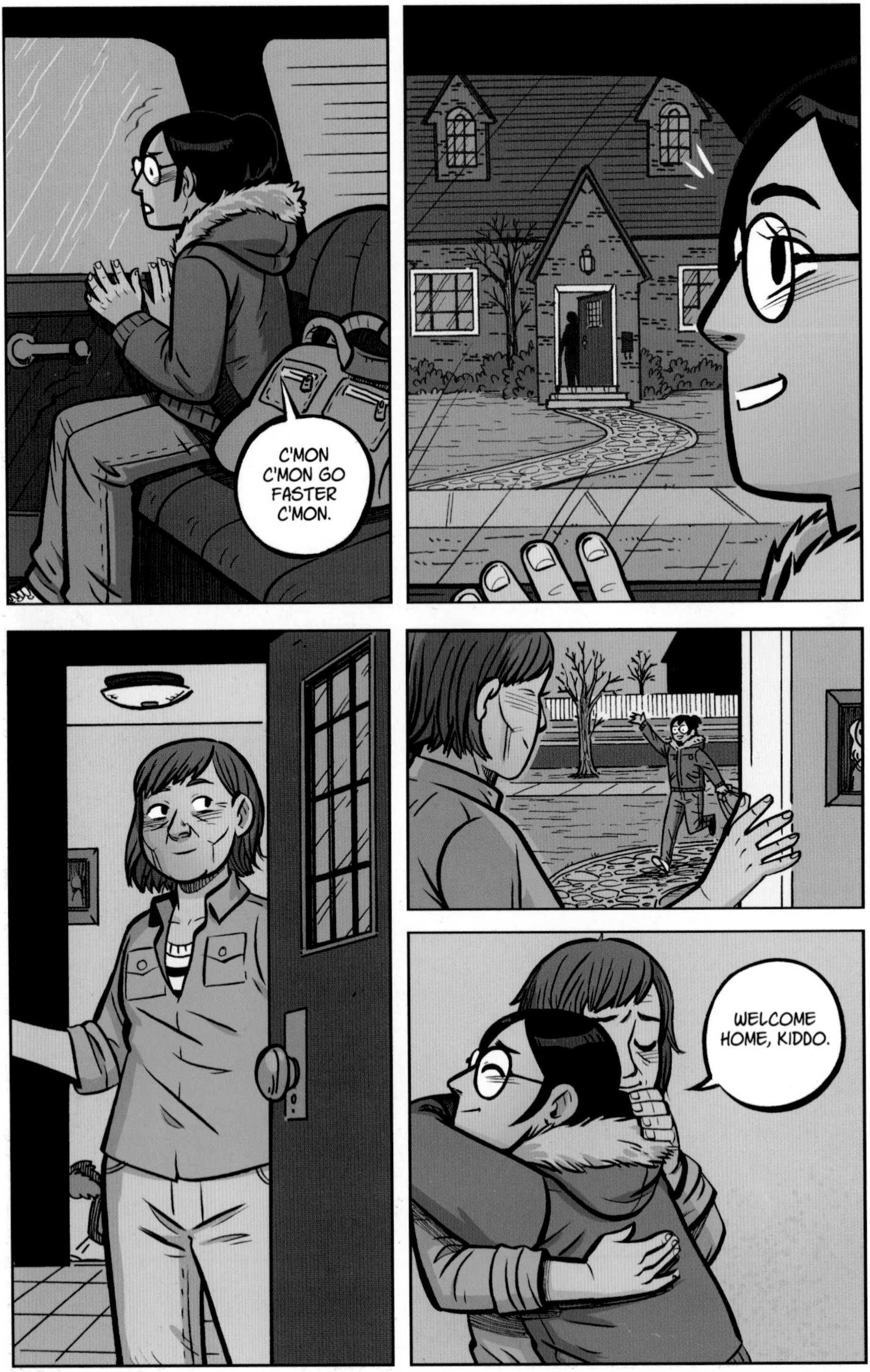
C'MON C'MON GO FASTER C'MON.
WELCOME HOME, KIDDO.

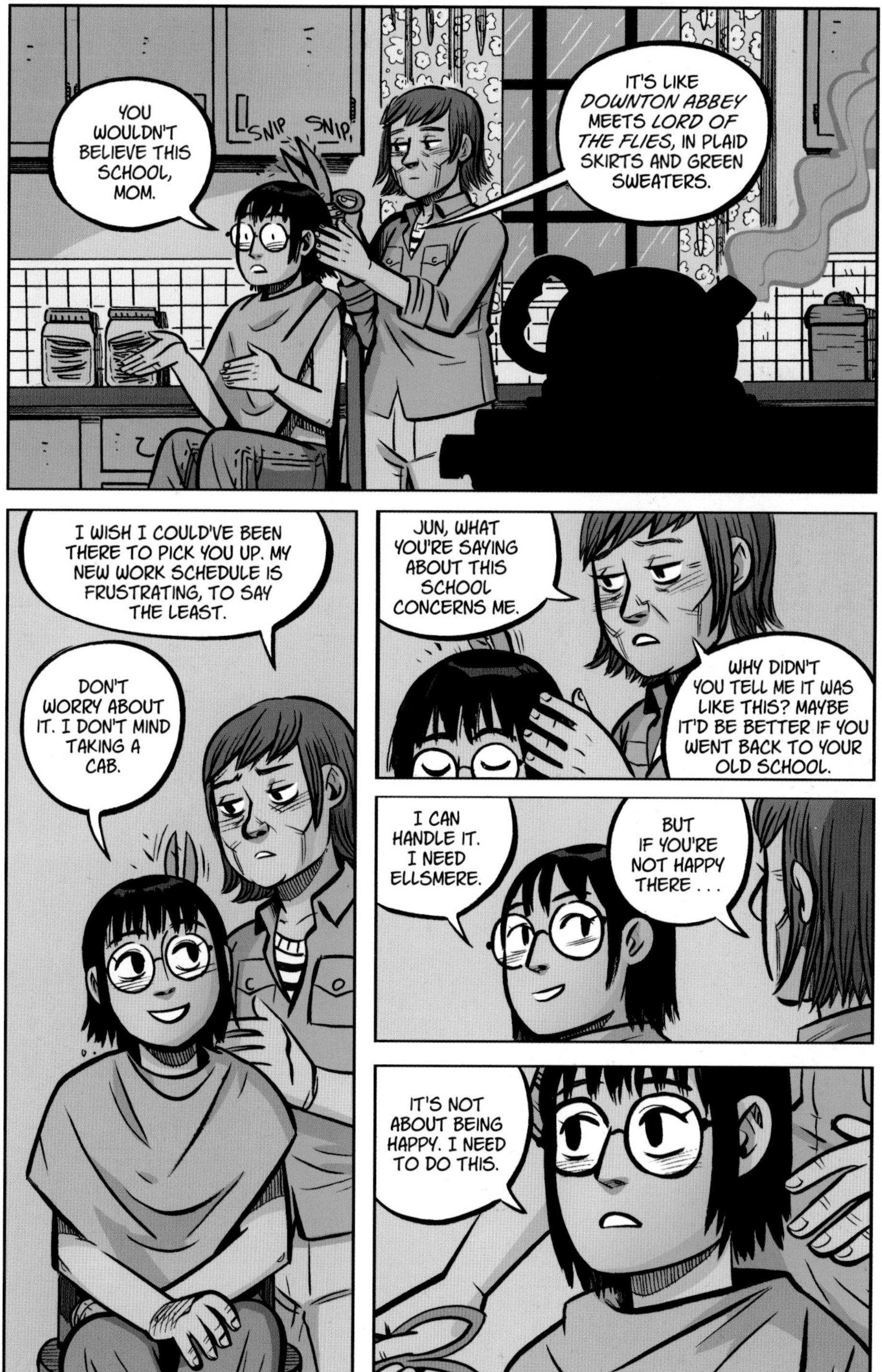
YOU WOULDN'T BELIEVE THIS SCHOOL, MOM.
SNIP SNIP
IT'S LIKE *DOWNTON ABBEY* MEETS *LORD OF THE FLIES*, IN PLAID SKIRTS AND GREEN SWEATERS.
I WISH I COULD'VE BEEN THERE TO PICK YOU UP. MY NEW WORK SCHEDULE IS FRUSTRATING, TO SAY THE LEAST.
DON'T WORRY ABOUT IT. I DON'T MIND TAKING A CAB.
JUN, WHAT YOU'RE SAYING ABOUT THIS SCHOOL CONCERNS ME.
WHY DIDN'T YOU TELL ME IT WAS LIKE THIS? MAYBE IT'D BE BETTER IF YOU WENT BACK TO YOUR OLD SCHOOL.
I CAN HANDLE IT. I NEED ELLSMERE.
BUT IF YOU'RE NOT HAPPY THERE . . .
IT'S NOT ABOUT BEING HAPPY. I NEED TO DO THIS.

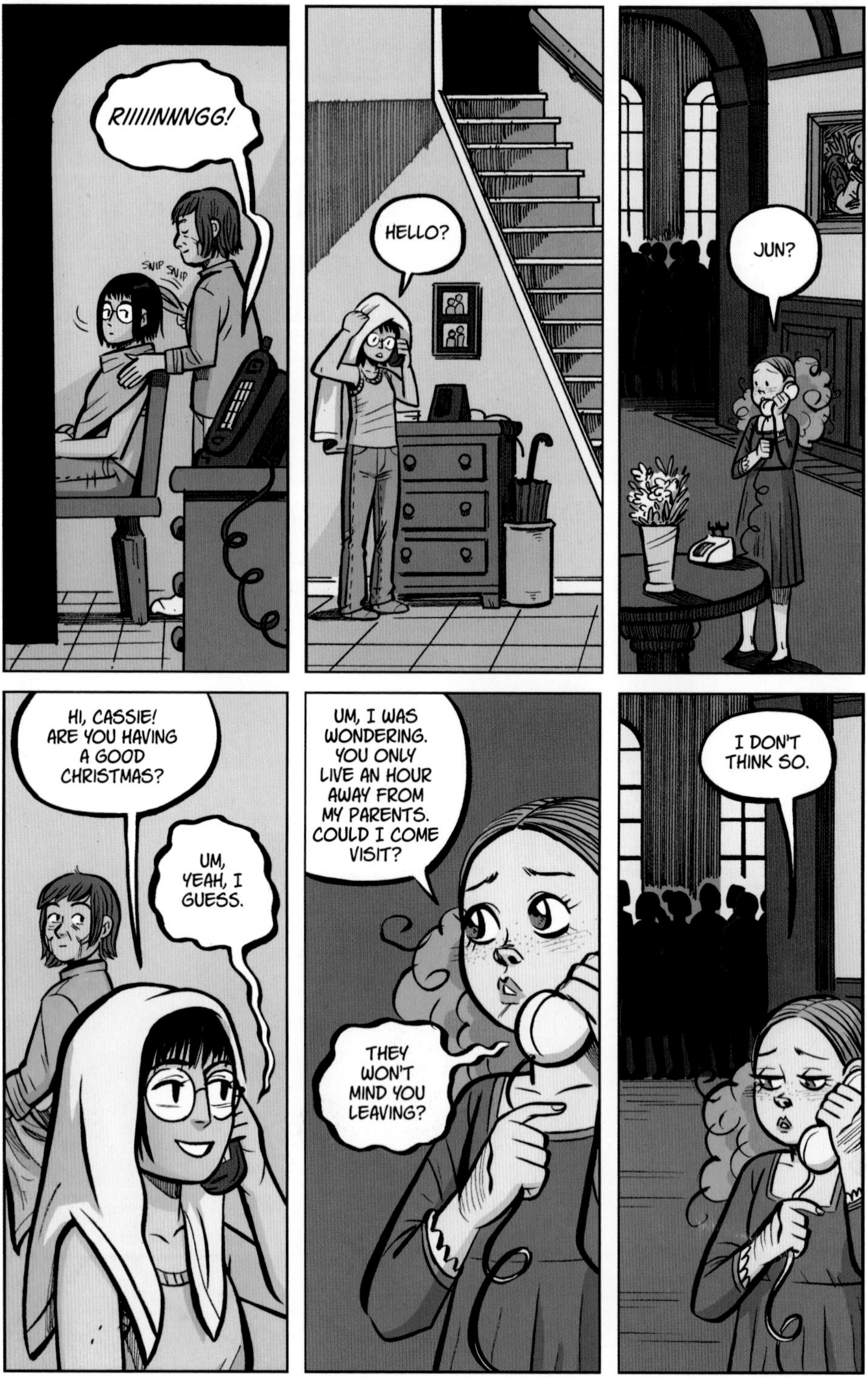
RIIIIINNNGG!
SNIP SNIP
HELLO?
JUN?
HI, CASSIE! ARE YOU HAVING A GOOD CHRISTMAS?
UM, YEAH, I GUESS.
UM, I WAS WONDERING. YOU ONLY LIVE AN HOUR AWAY FROM MY PARENTS. COULD I COME VISIT?
THEY WON'T MIND YOU LEAVING?
I DON'T THINK SO.

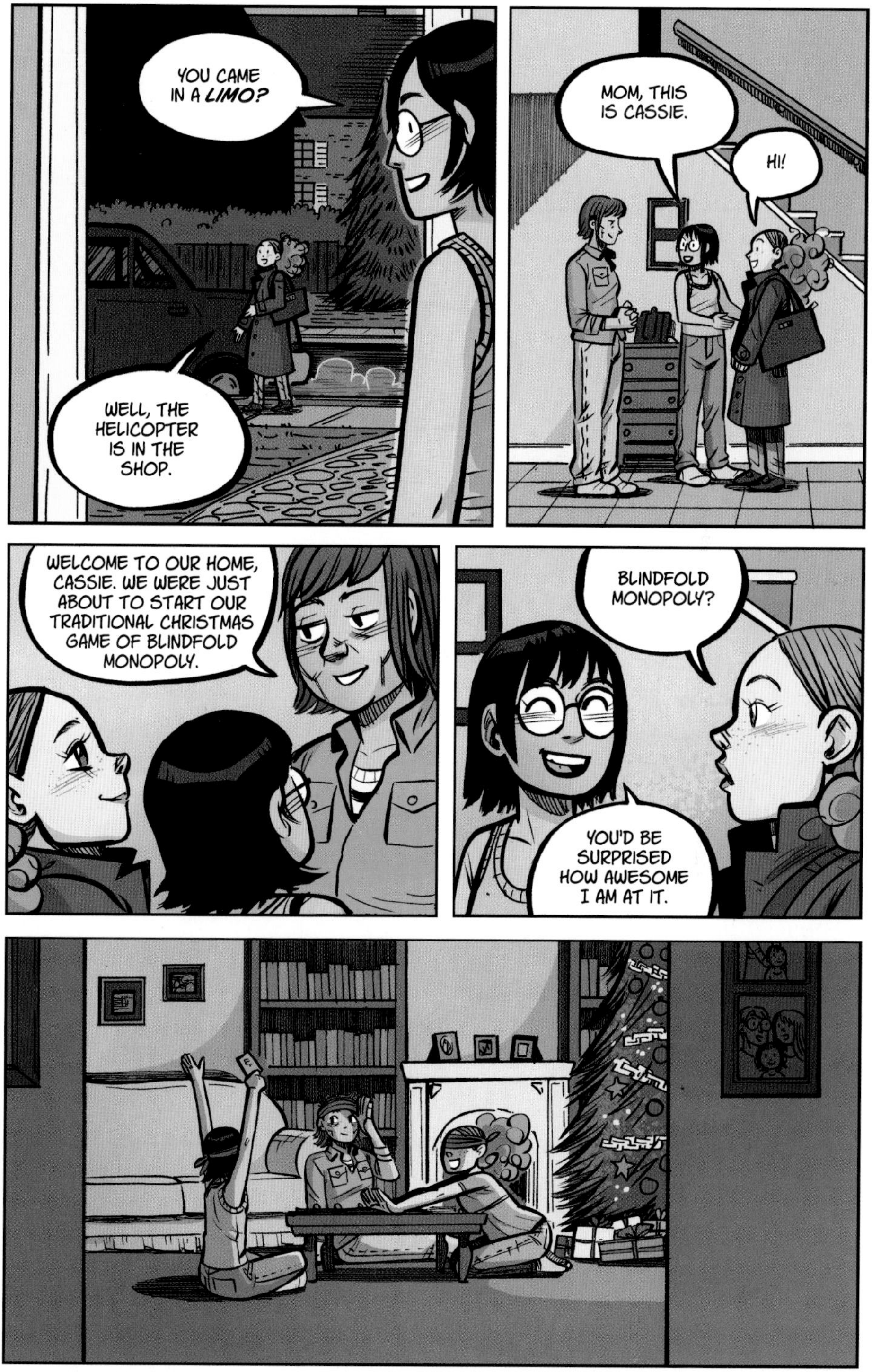
YOU CAME IN A *LIMO?*
WELL, THE HELICOPTER IS IN THE SHOP.
MOM, THIS IS CASSIE.
HI!
WELCOME TO OUR HOME, CASSIE. WE WERE JUST ABOUT TO START OUR TRADITIONAL CHRISTMAS GAME OF BLINDFOLD MONOPOLY.
BLINDFOLD MONOPOLY?
YOU'D BE SURPRISED HOW AWESOME I AM AT IT.

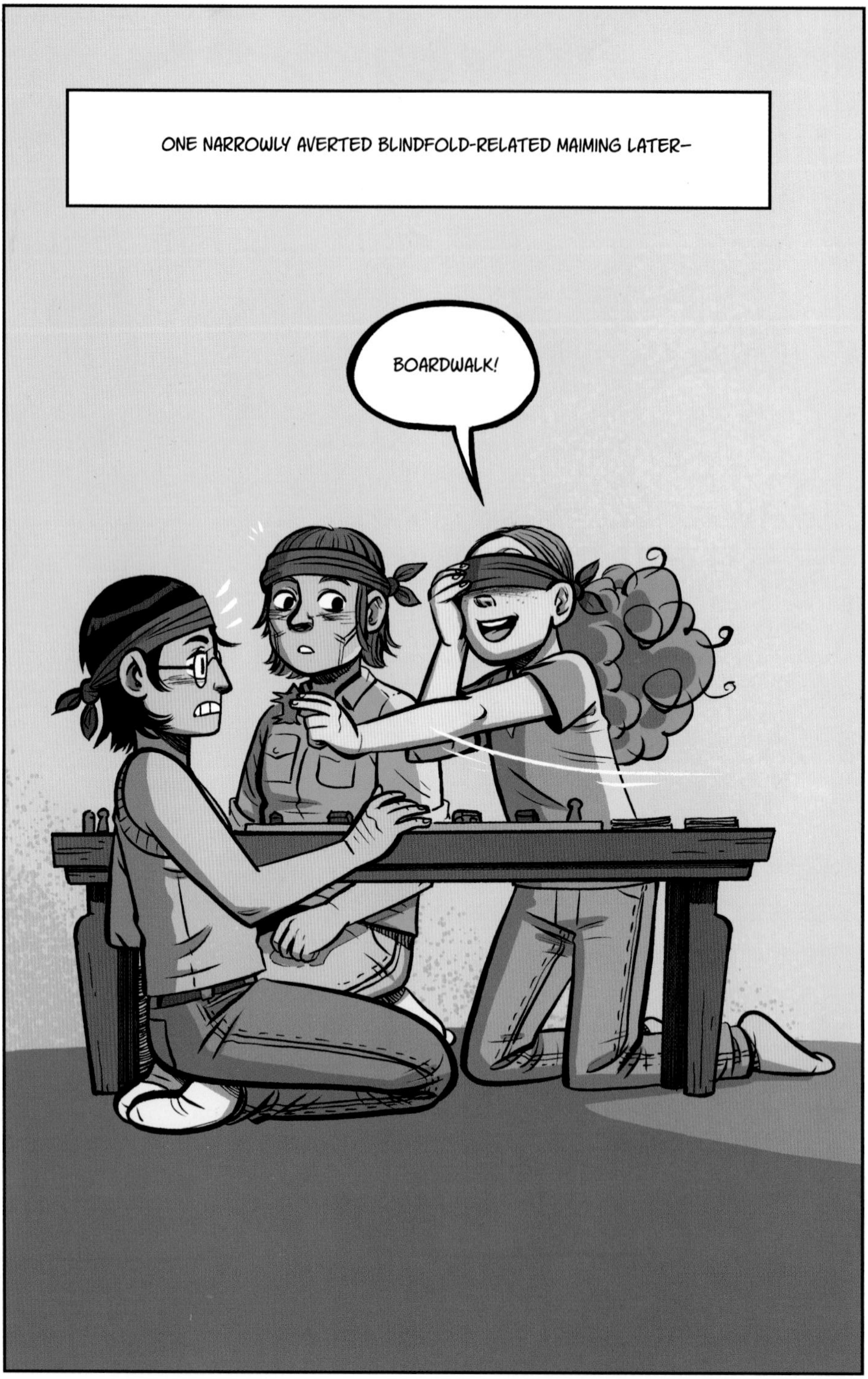
ONE NARROWLY AVERTED BLINDFOLD-RELATED MAIMING LATER–
BOARDWALK!

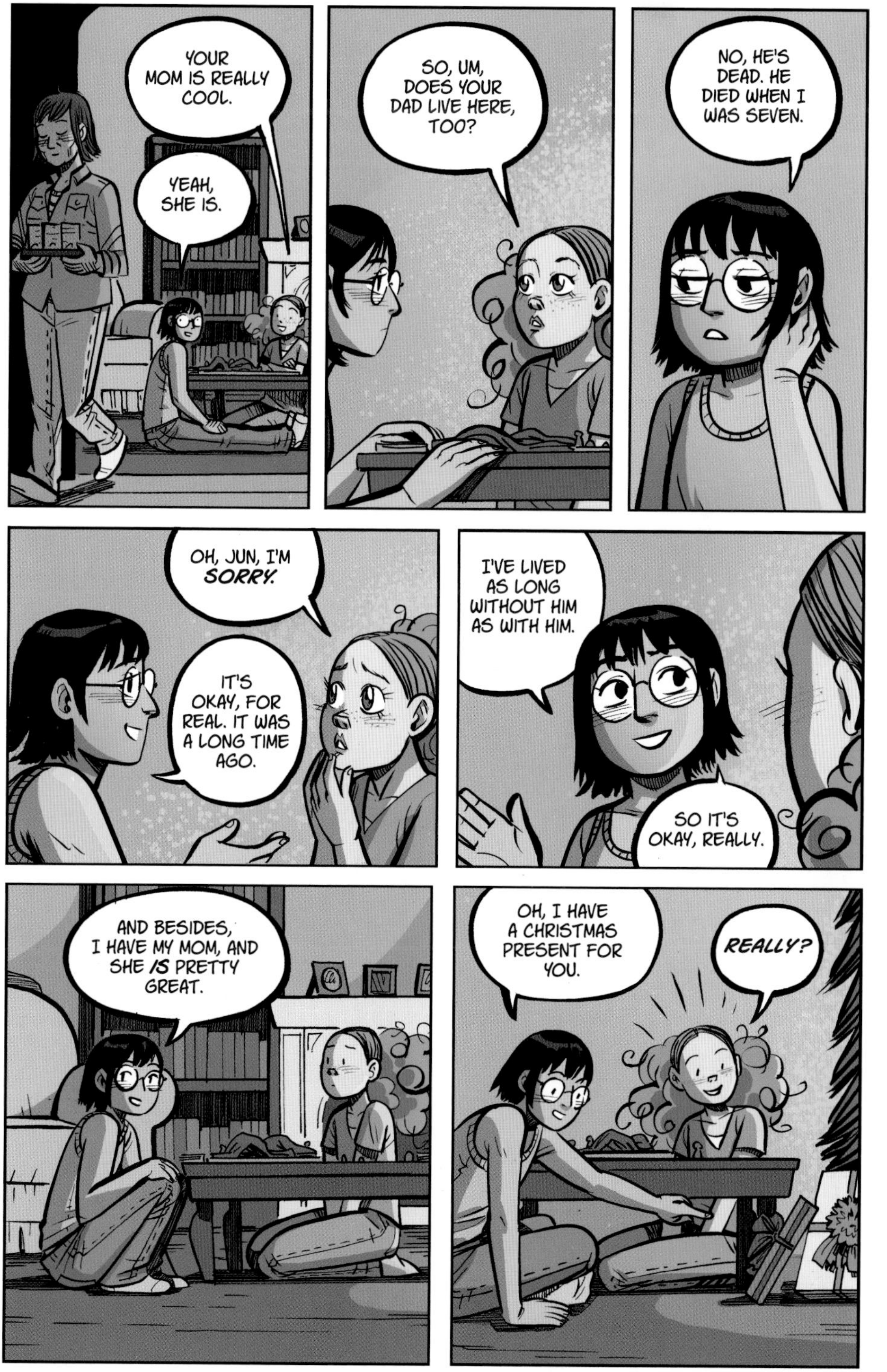
YOUR MOM IS REALLY COOL.
YEAH, SHE IS.
SO, UM, DOES YOUR DAD LIVE HERE, TOO?
NO, HE'S DEAD. HE DIED WHEN I WAS SEVEN.
OH, JUN, I'M *SORRY.*
IT'S OKAY, FOR REAL. IT WAS A LONG TIME AGO.
I'VE LIVED AS LONG WITHOUT HIM AS WITH HIM.
SO IT'S OKAY, REALLY.
AND BESIDES, I HAVE MY MOM, AND SHE *IS* PRETTY GREAT.
OH, I HAVE A CHRISTMAS PRESENT FOR YOU.
REALLY?

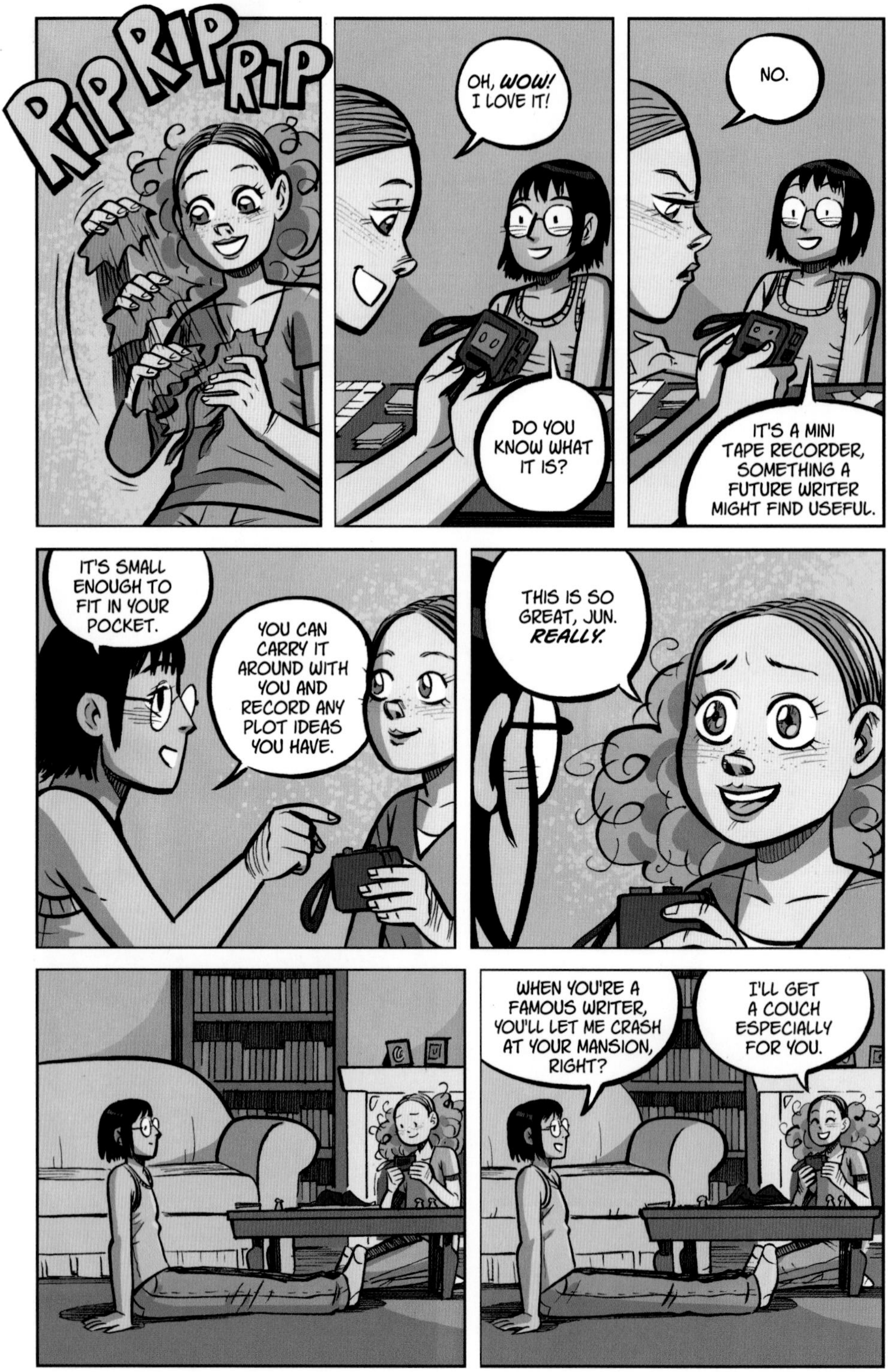
RIP RIP RIP RIP
OH, WOW! I LOVE IT!
DO YOU KNOW WHAT IT IS?
NO.
IT'S A MINI TAPE RECORDER, SOMETHING A FUTURE WRITER MIGHT FIND USEFUL.
IT'S SMALL ENOUGH TO FIT IN YOUR POCKET.
YOU CAN CARRY IT AROUND WITH YOU AND RECORD ANY PLOT IDEAS YOU HAVE.
THIS IS SO GREAT, JUN. REALLY.
WHEN YOU'RE A FAMOUS WRITER, YOU'LL LET ME CRASH AT YOUR MANSION, RIGHT?
I'LL GET A COUCH ESPECIALLY FOR YOU.

Chapter Eight

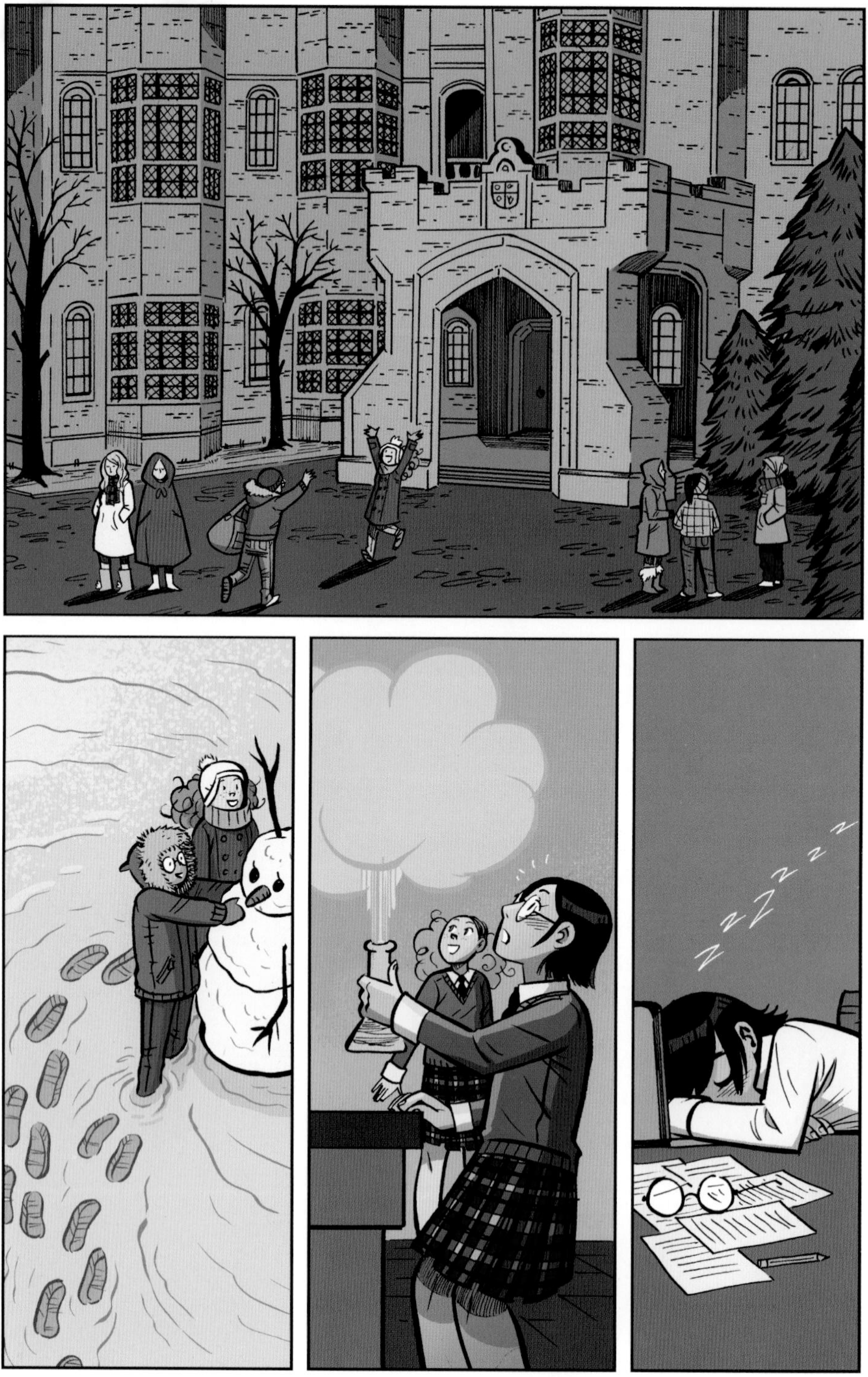

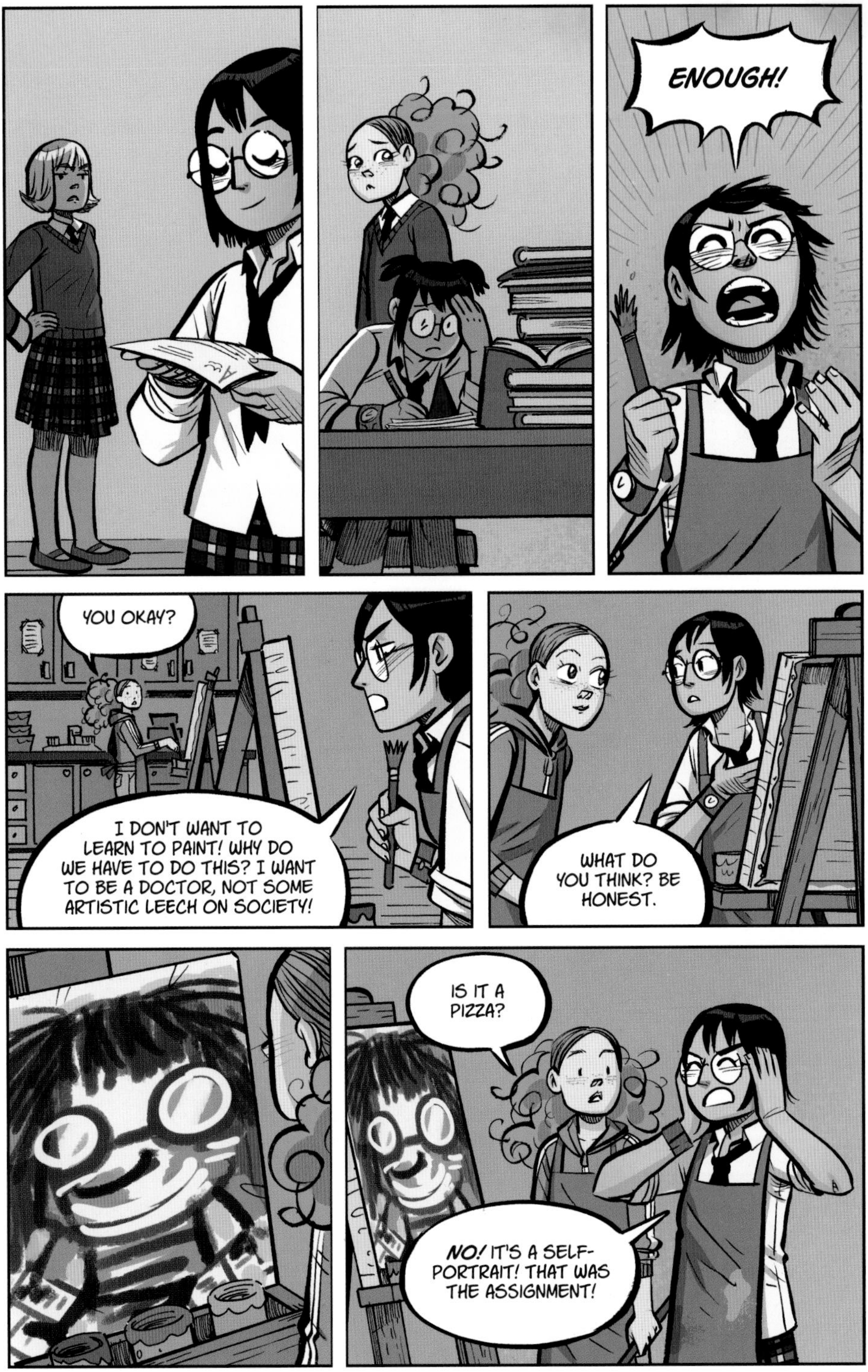
ENOUGH!
YOU OKAY?
I DON'T WANT TO LEARN TO PAINT! WHY DO WE HAVE TO DO THIS? I WANT TO BE A DOCTOR, NOT SOME ARTISTIC LEECH ON SOCIETY!
WHAT DO YOU THINK? BE HONEST.
IS IT A PIZZA?
NO! IT'S A SELF-PORTRAIT! THAT WAS THE ASSIGNMENT!

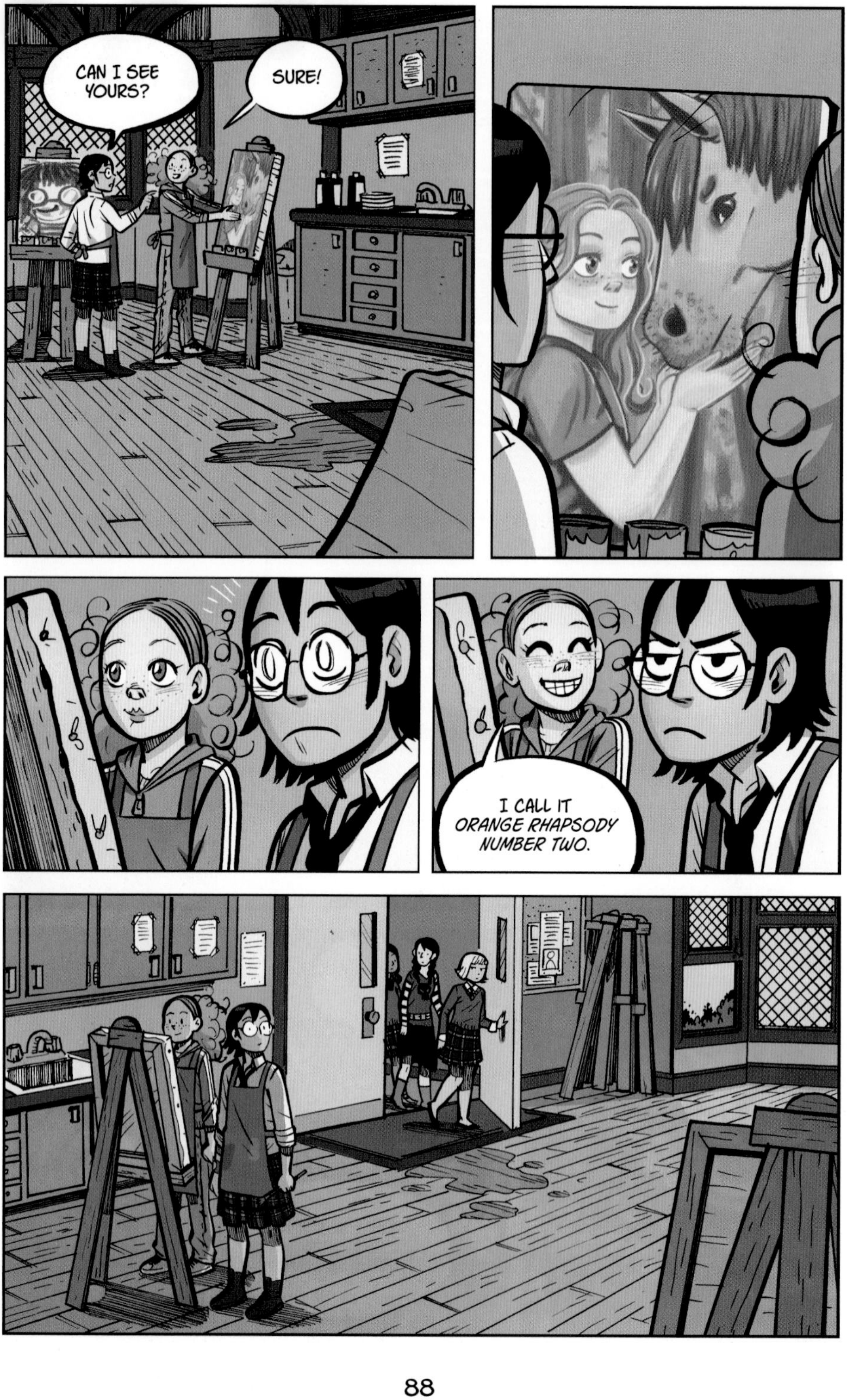
CAN I SEE YOURS?
SURE!
I CALL IT ORANGE RHAPSODY NUMBER TWO.

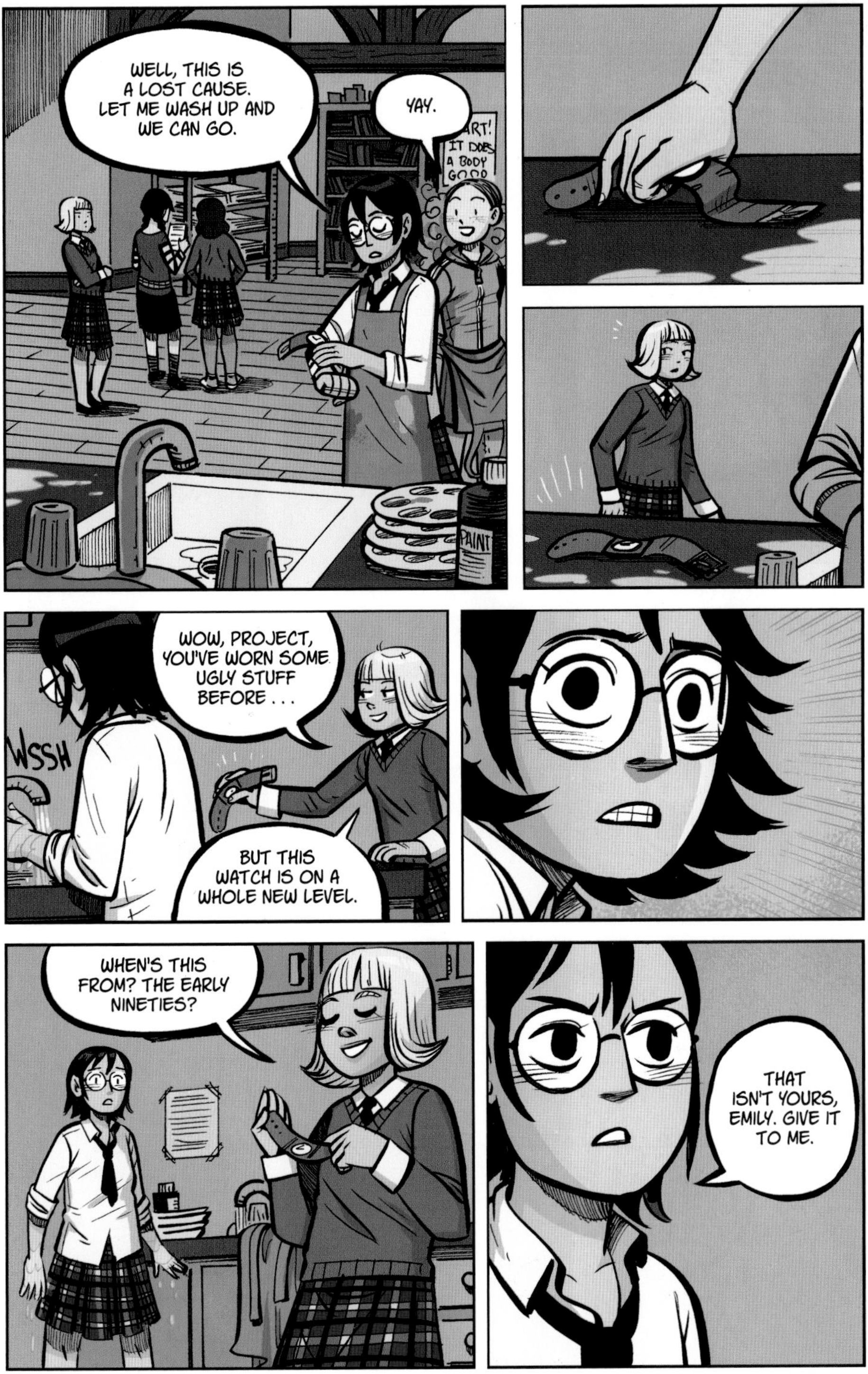
WELL, THIS IS A LOST CAUSE. LET ME WASH UP AND WE CAN GO.
YAY.
ART! IT DOES A BODY GOOD
PAINT
WOW, PROJECT, YOU'VE WORN SOME UGLY STUFF BEFORE . . .
WSSH
BUT THIS WATCH IS ON A WHOLE NEW LEVEL.
WHEN'S THIS FROM? THE EARLY NINETIES?
THAT ISN'T YOURS, EMILY. GIVE IT TO ME.

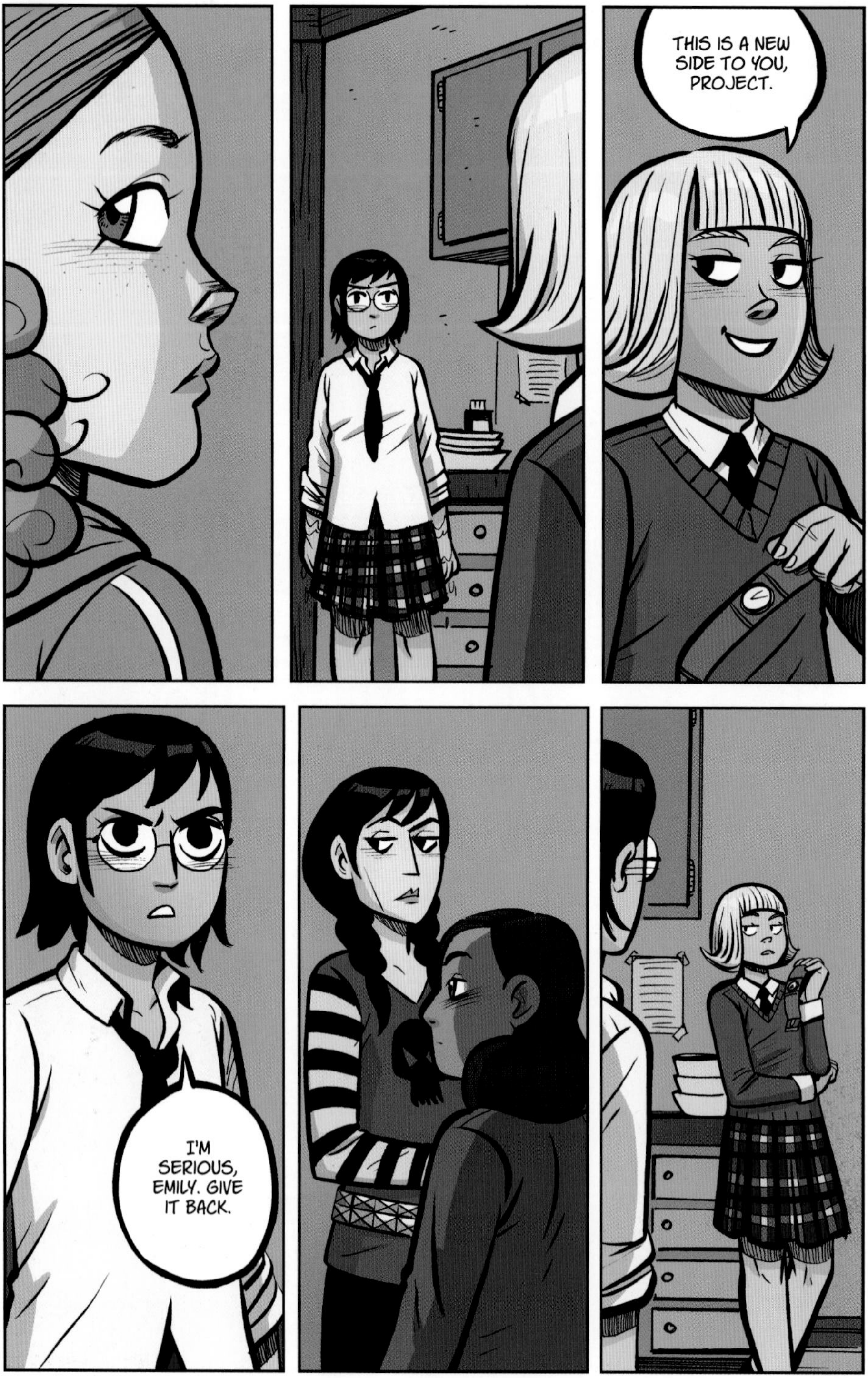
THIS IS A NEW SIDE TO YOU, PROJECT.
I'M SERIOUS, EMILY. GIVE IT BACK.

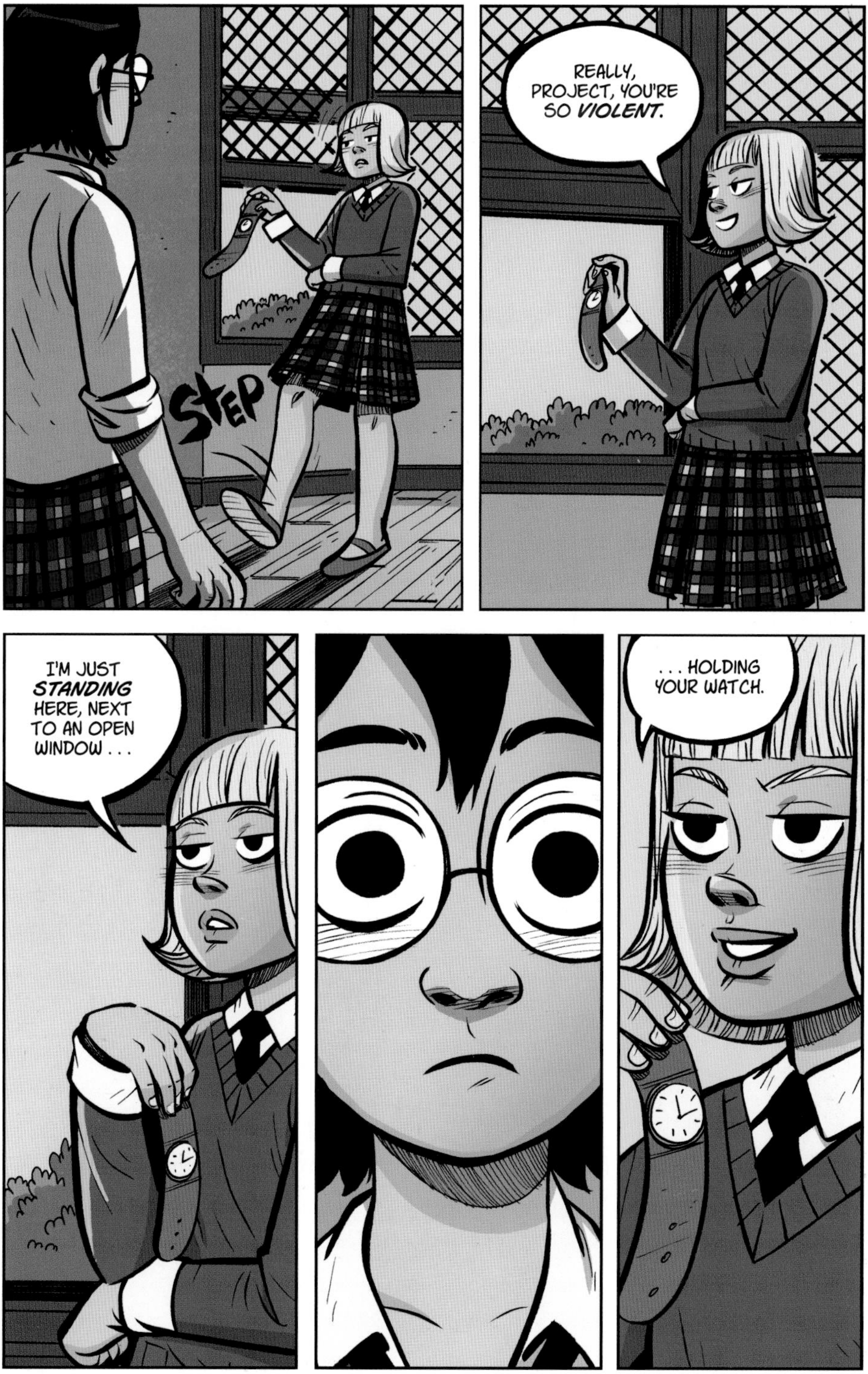
STEP
REALLY, PROJECT, YOU'RE SO VIOLENT.
I'M JUST STANDING HERE, NEXT TO AN OPEN WINDOW . . .
. . . HOLDING YOUR WATCH.

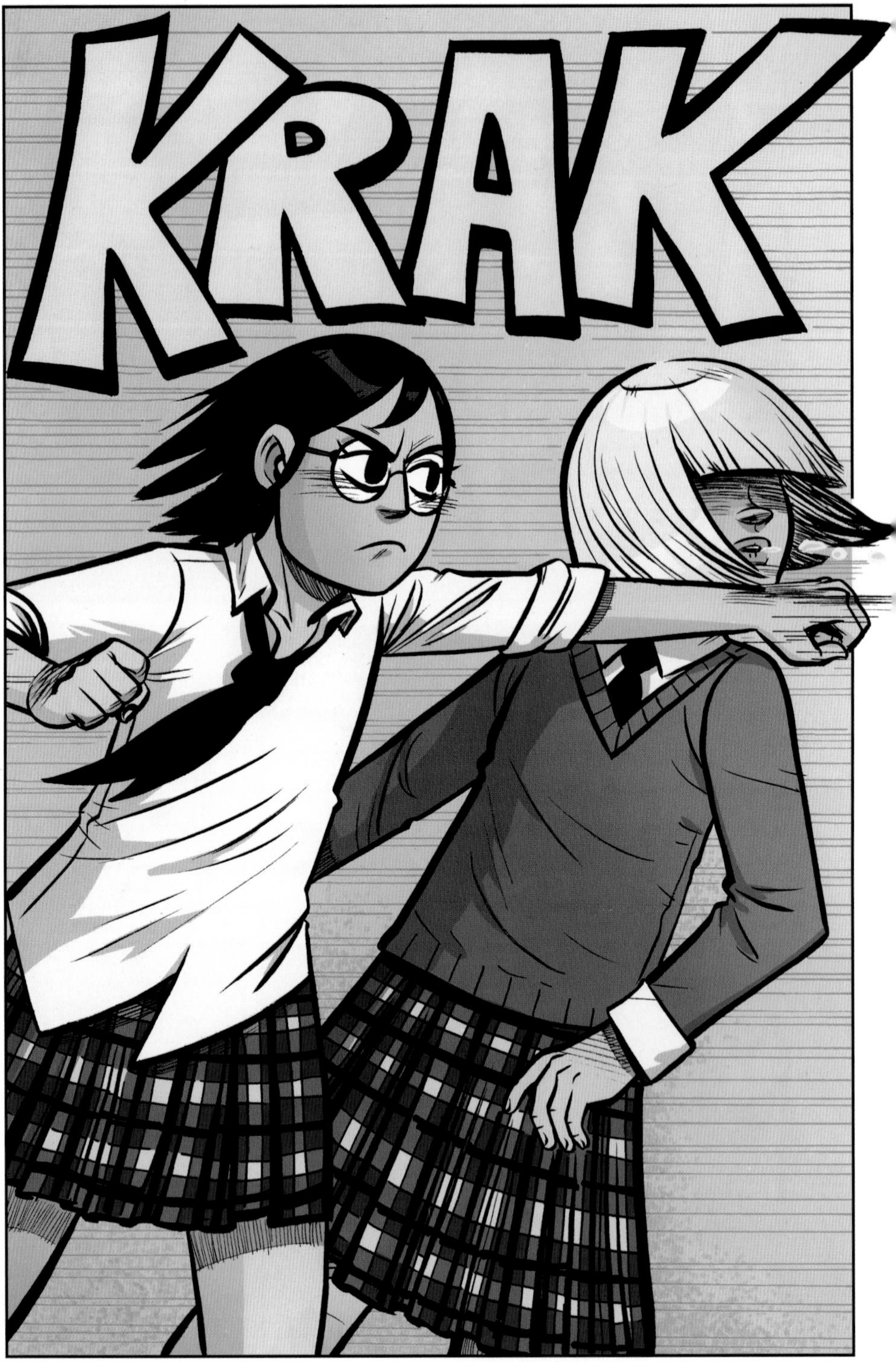
KRAK

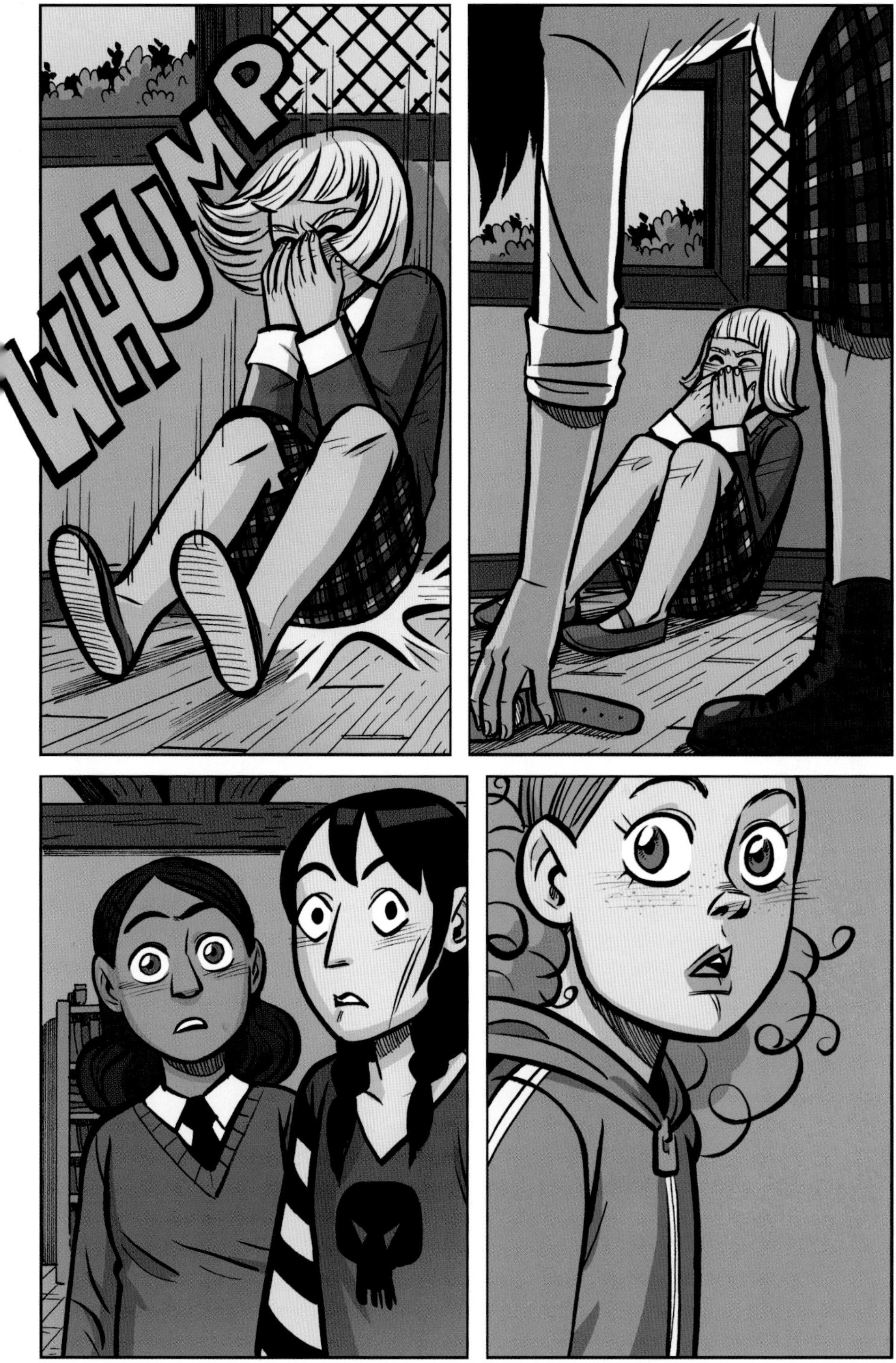
WHUMP

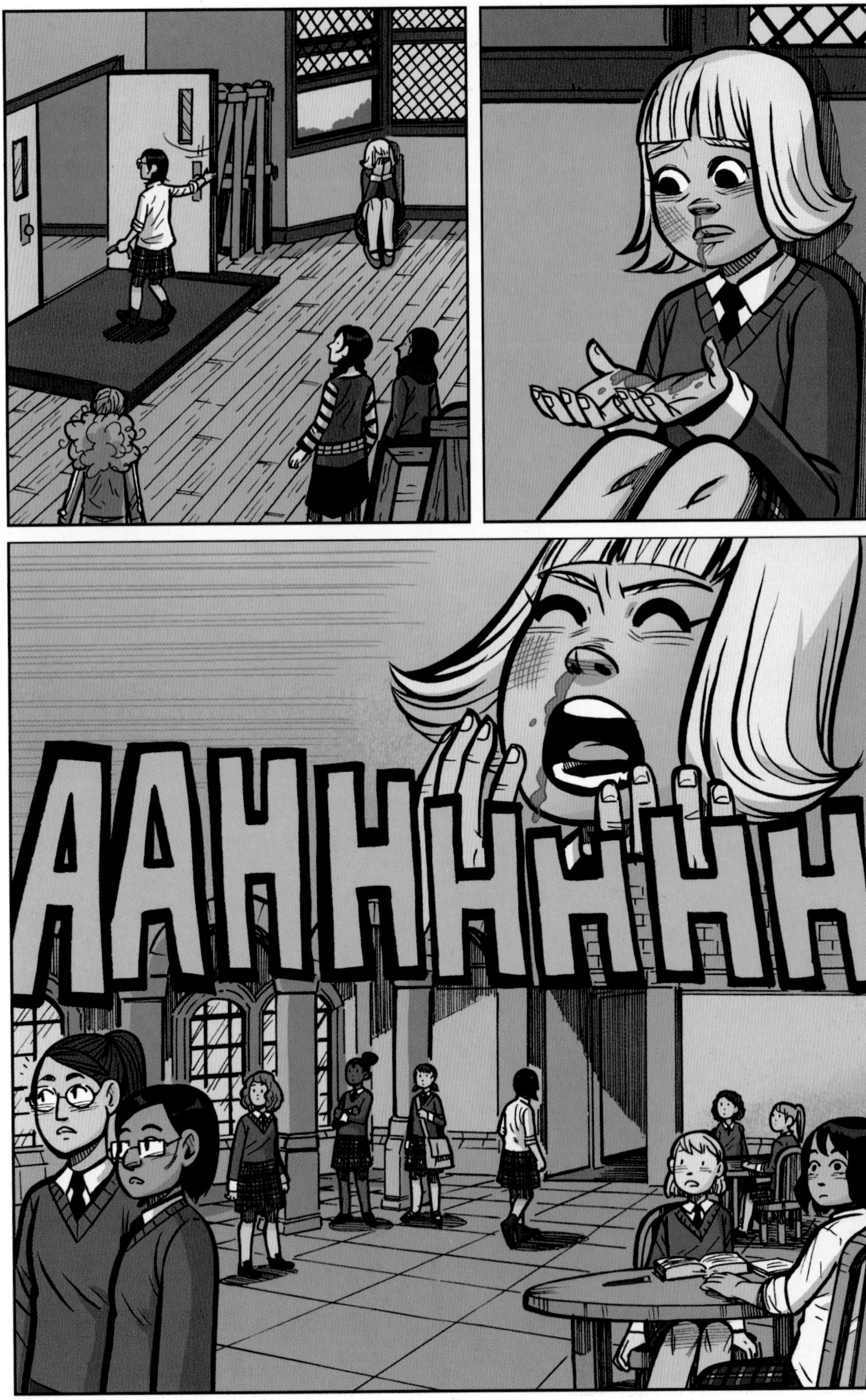
AAHHHHHHH

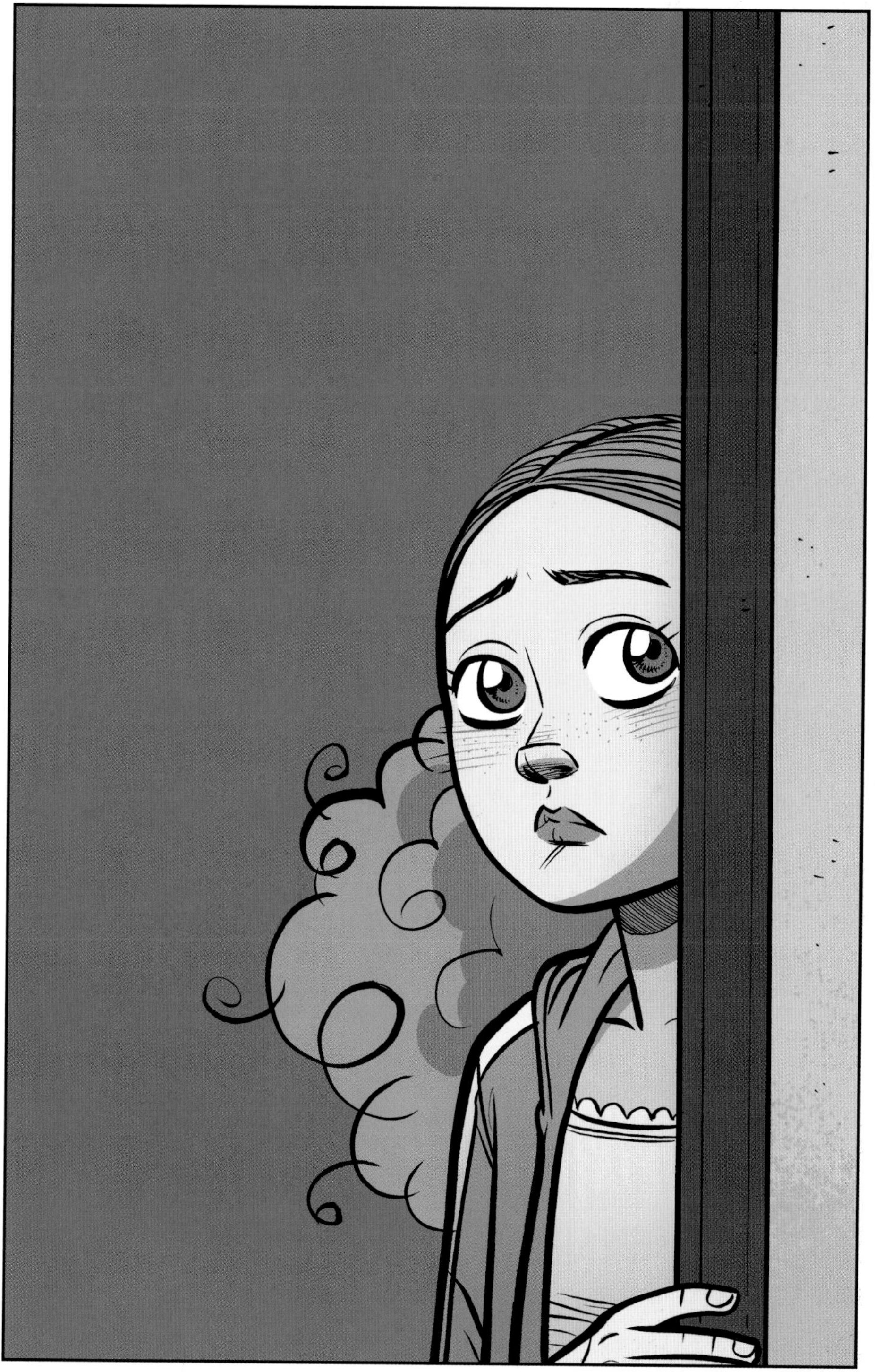

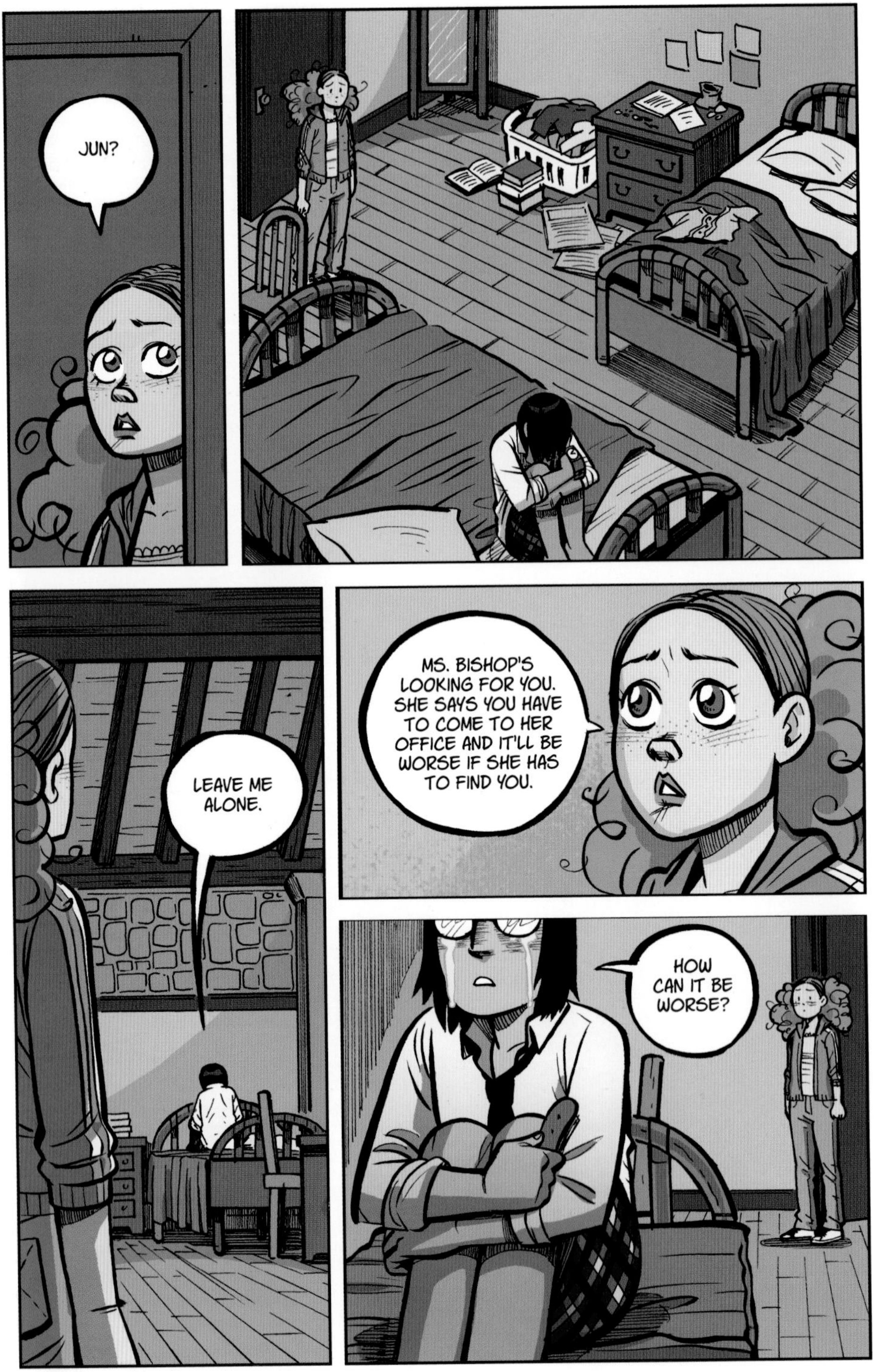
JUN?
LEAVE ME ALONE.
MS. BISHOP'S LOOKING FOR YOU. SHE SAYS YOU HAVE TO COME TO HER OFFICE AND IT'LL BE WORSE IF SHE HAS TO FIND YOU.
HOW CAN IT BE WORSE?

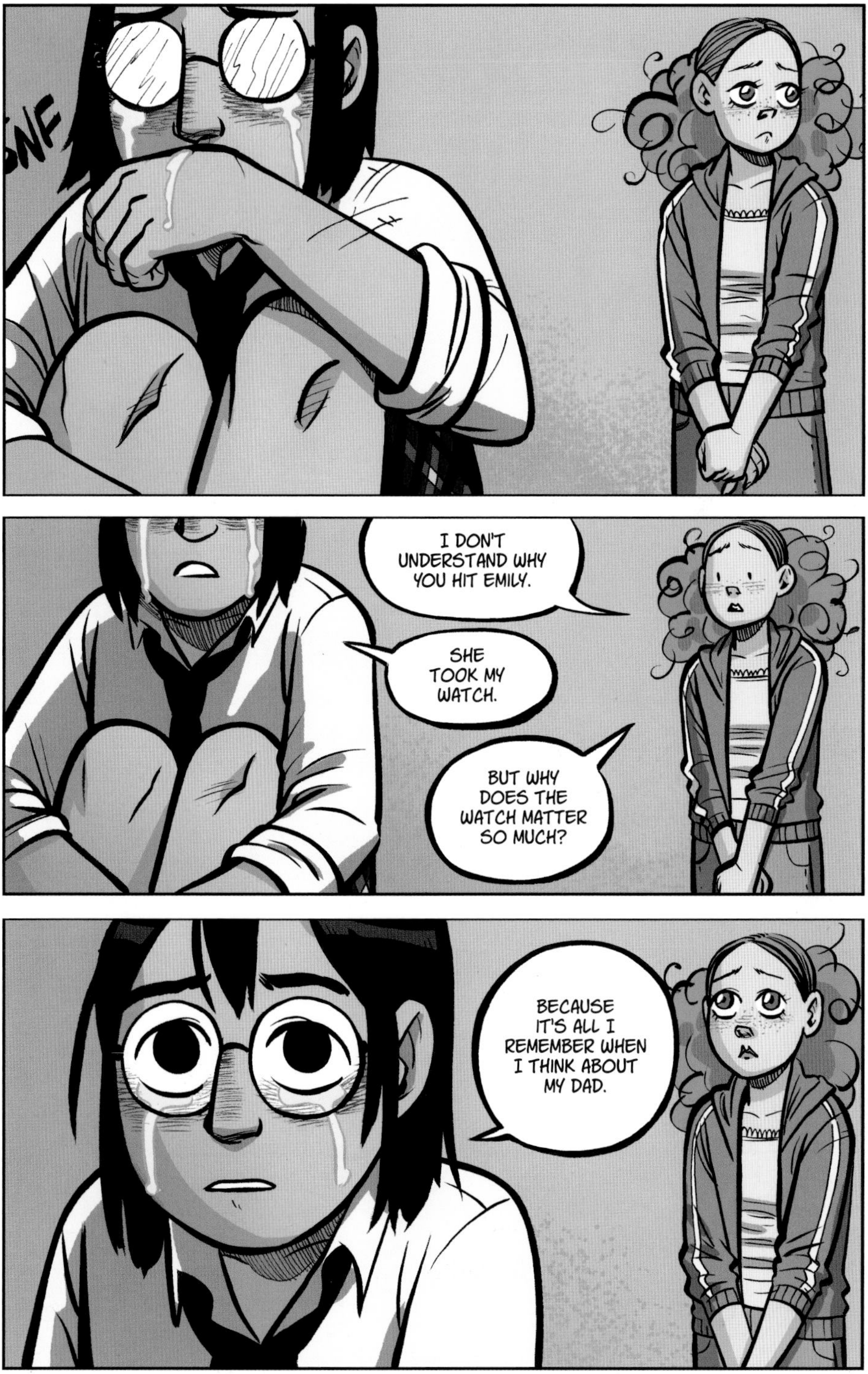
SNF
I DON'T UNDERSTAND WHY YOU HIT EMILY.
SHE TOOK MY WATCH.
BUT WHY DOES THE WATCH MATTER SO MUCH?
BECAUSE IT'S ALL I REMEMBER WHEN I THINK ABOUT MY DAD.

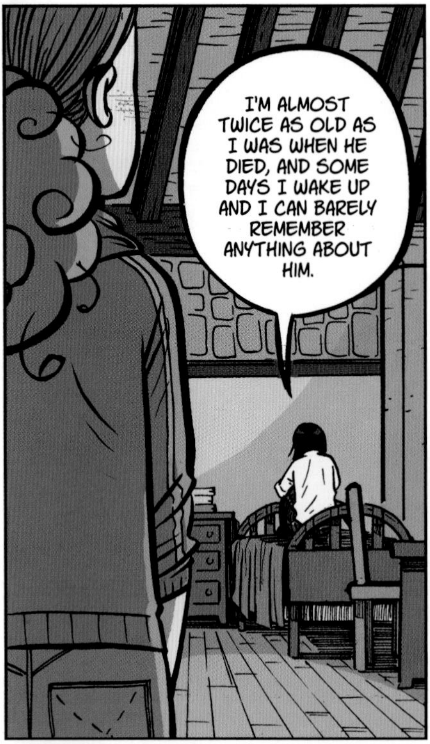
I'M ALMOST TWICE AS OLD AS I WAS WHEN HE DIED, AND SOME DAYS I WAKE UP AND I CAN BARELY REMEMBER ANYTHING ABOUT HIM.

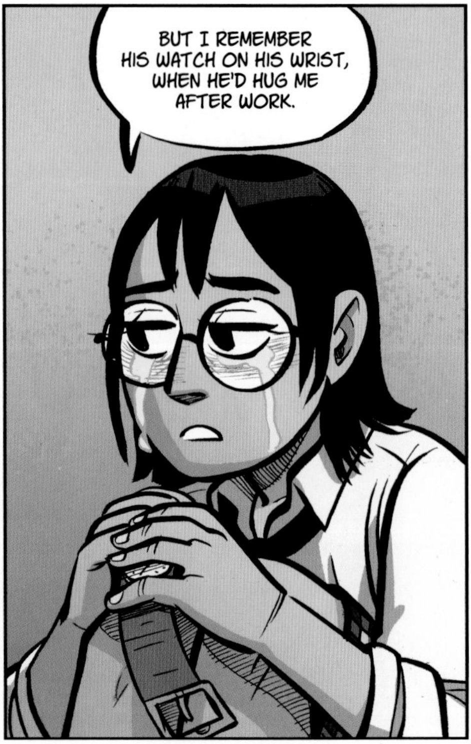
BUT I REMEMBER HIS WATCH ON HIS WRIST, WHEN HE'D HUG ME AFTER WORK.

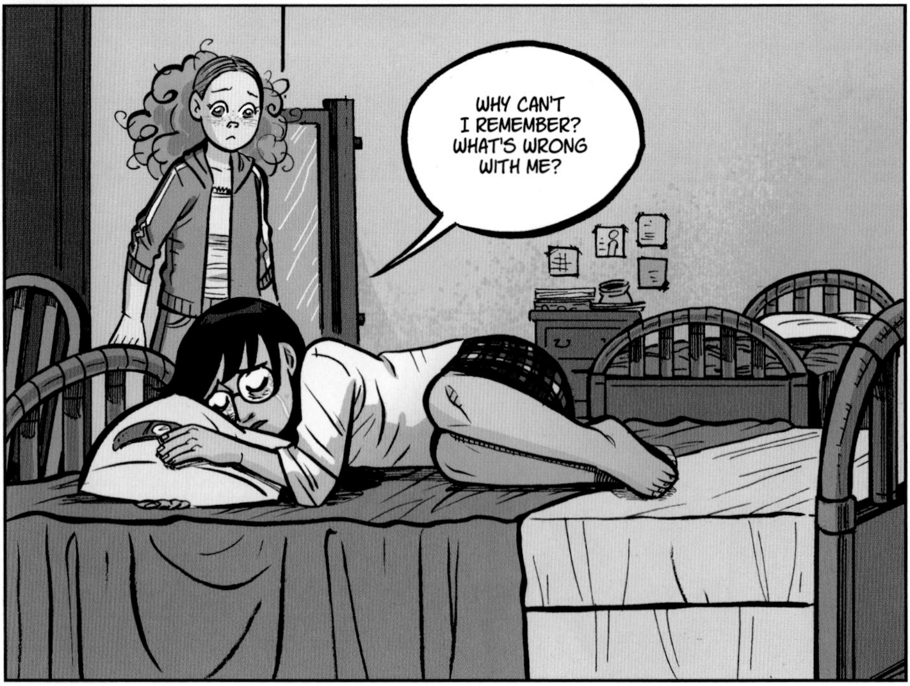
WHY CAN'T I REMEMBER? WHAT'S WRONG WITH ME?

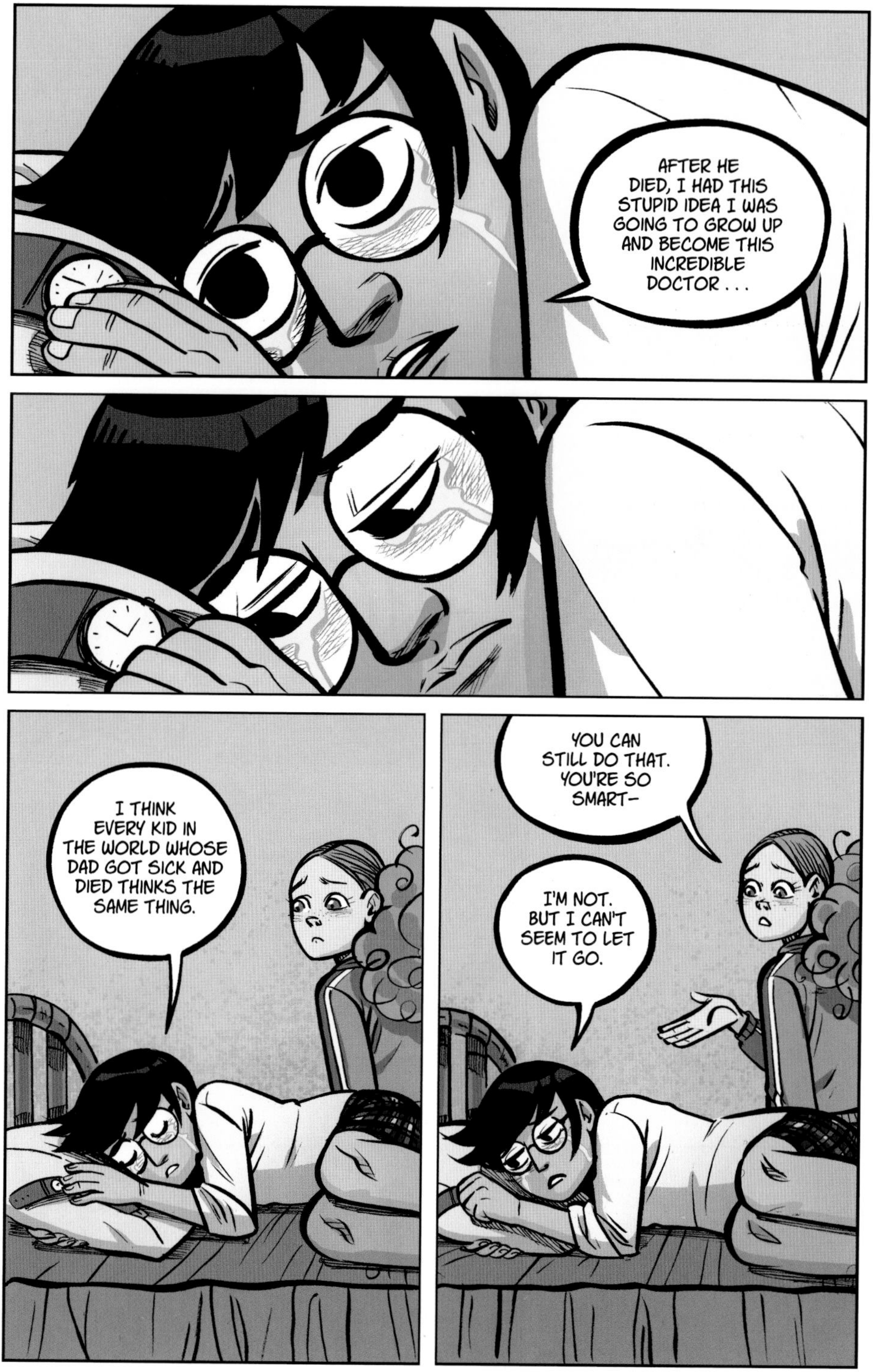
AFTER HE DIED, I HAD THIS STUPID IDEA I WAS GOING TO GROW UP AND BECOME THIS INCREDIBLE DOCTOR . . .
I THINK EVERY KID IN THE WORLD WHOSE DAD GOT SICK AND DIED THINKS THE SAME THING.
YOU CAN STILL DO THAT. YOU'RE SO SMART–
I'M NOT. BUT I CAN'T SEEM TO LET IT GO.

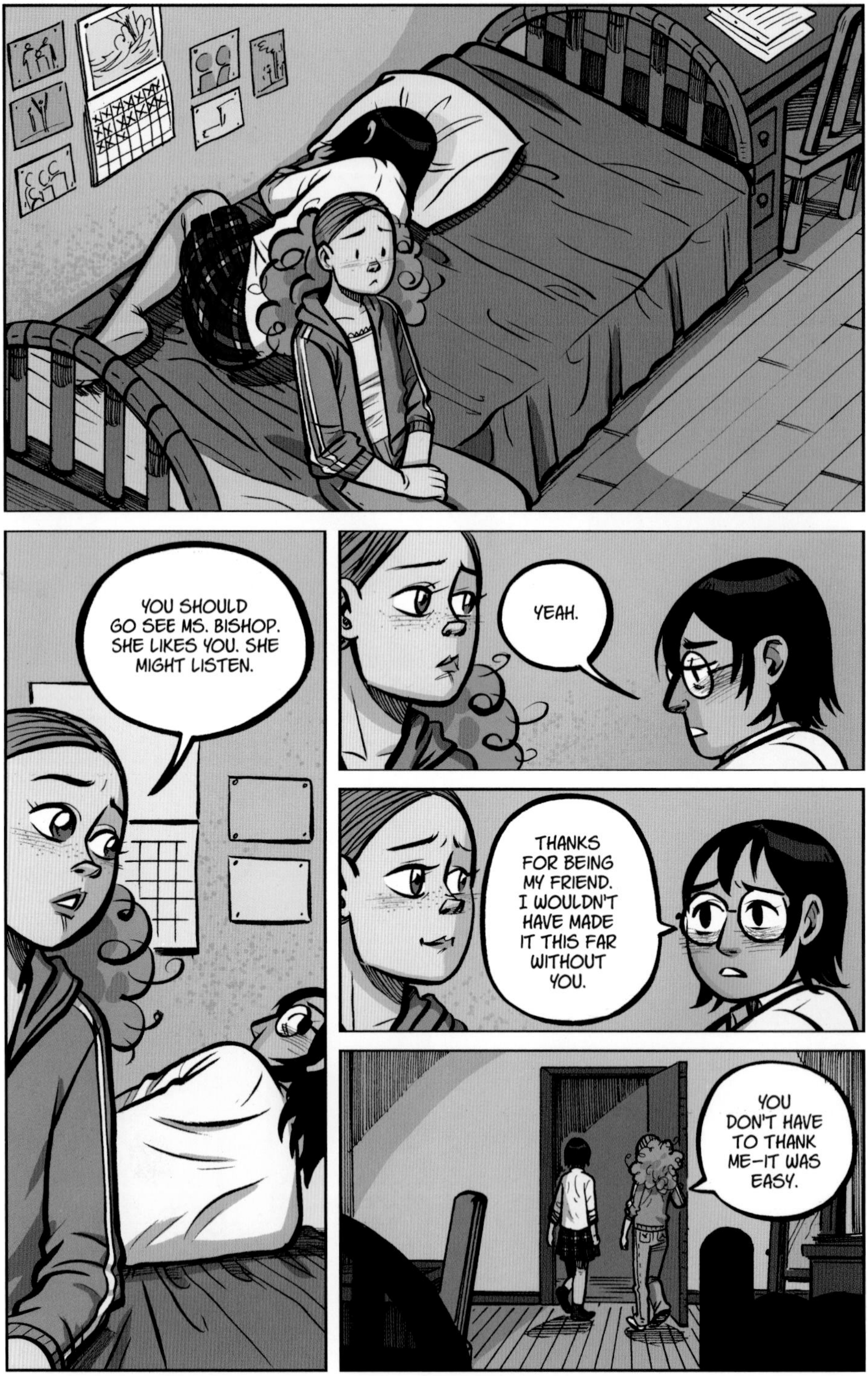
YOU SHOULD GO SEE MS. BISHOP. SHE LIKES YOU. SHE MIGHT LISTEN.
YEAH.
THANKS FOR BEING MY FRIEND. I WOULDN'T HAVE MADE IT THIS FAR WITHOUT YOU.
YOU DON'T HAVE TO THANK ME—IT WAS EASY.

I DON'T UNDERSTAND HOW YOU COULD HAVE LET THIS HAPPEN.

AFTER ALL THE MONEY WE'VE DONATED TO THIS SCHOOL, YOU LET SOME *IMPORT* FROM THE PUBLIC SCHOOL SYSTEM *ASSAULT* MY DAUGHTER?

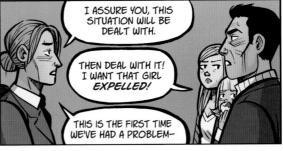

I ASSURE YOU, THIS SITUATION WILL BE DEALT WITH.

THEN DEAL WITH IT! I WANT THAT GIRL *EXPELLED!*

THIS IS THE FIRST TIME WE'VE HAD A PROBLEM—

WHAT DOES THAT MATTER? WHAT MORE DOES THAT VIOLENT CHILD HAVE TO DO? PLAGIARIZE? HIT A *TEACHER?*

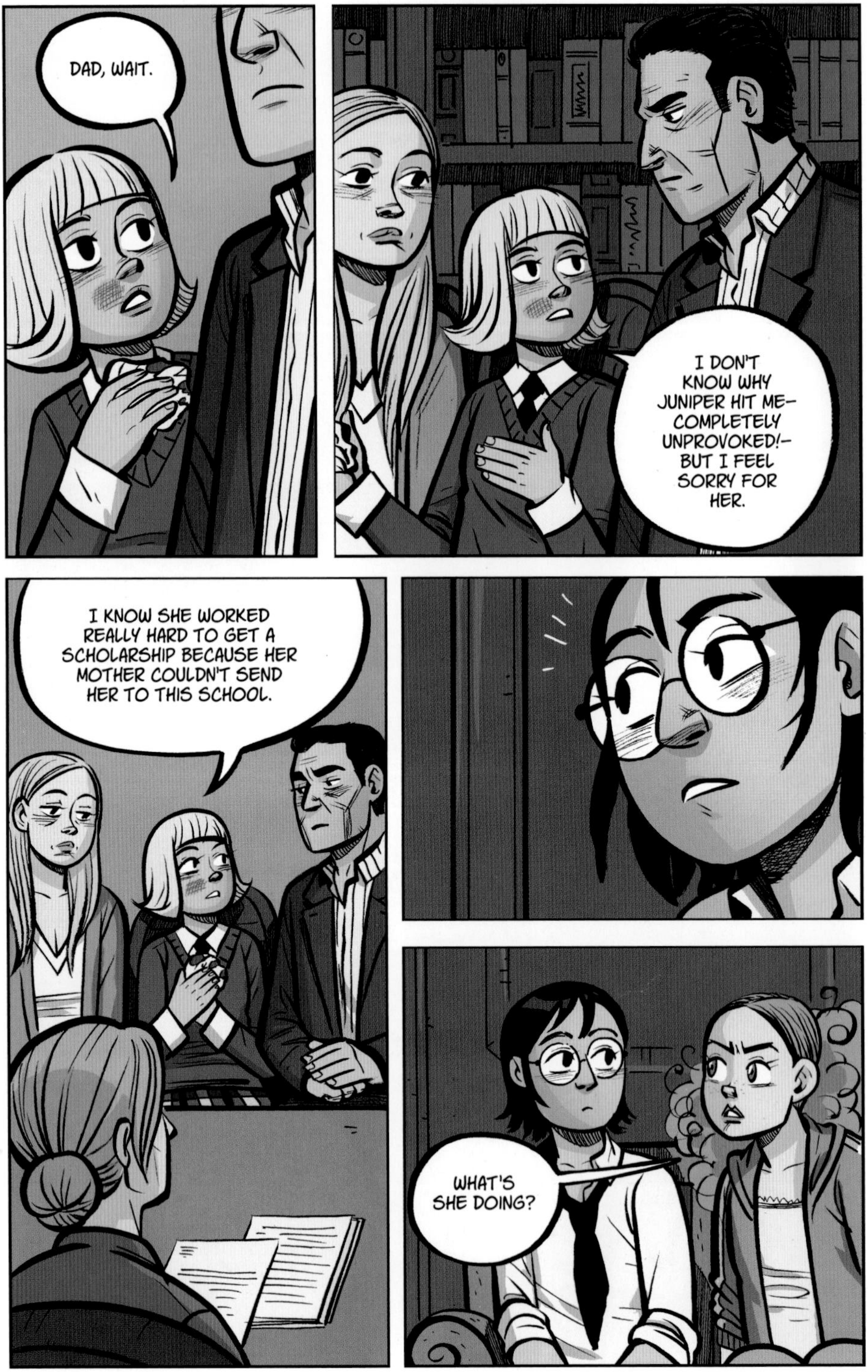
DAD, WAIT.
I DON'T KNOW WHY JUNIPER HIT ME—COMPLETELY UNPROVOKED!—BUT I FEEL SORRY FOR HER.
I KNOW SHE WORKED REALLY HARD TO GET A SCHOLARSHIP BECAUSE HER MOTHER COULDN'T SEND HER TO THIS SCHOOL.
WHAT'S SHE DOING?

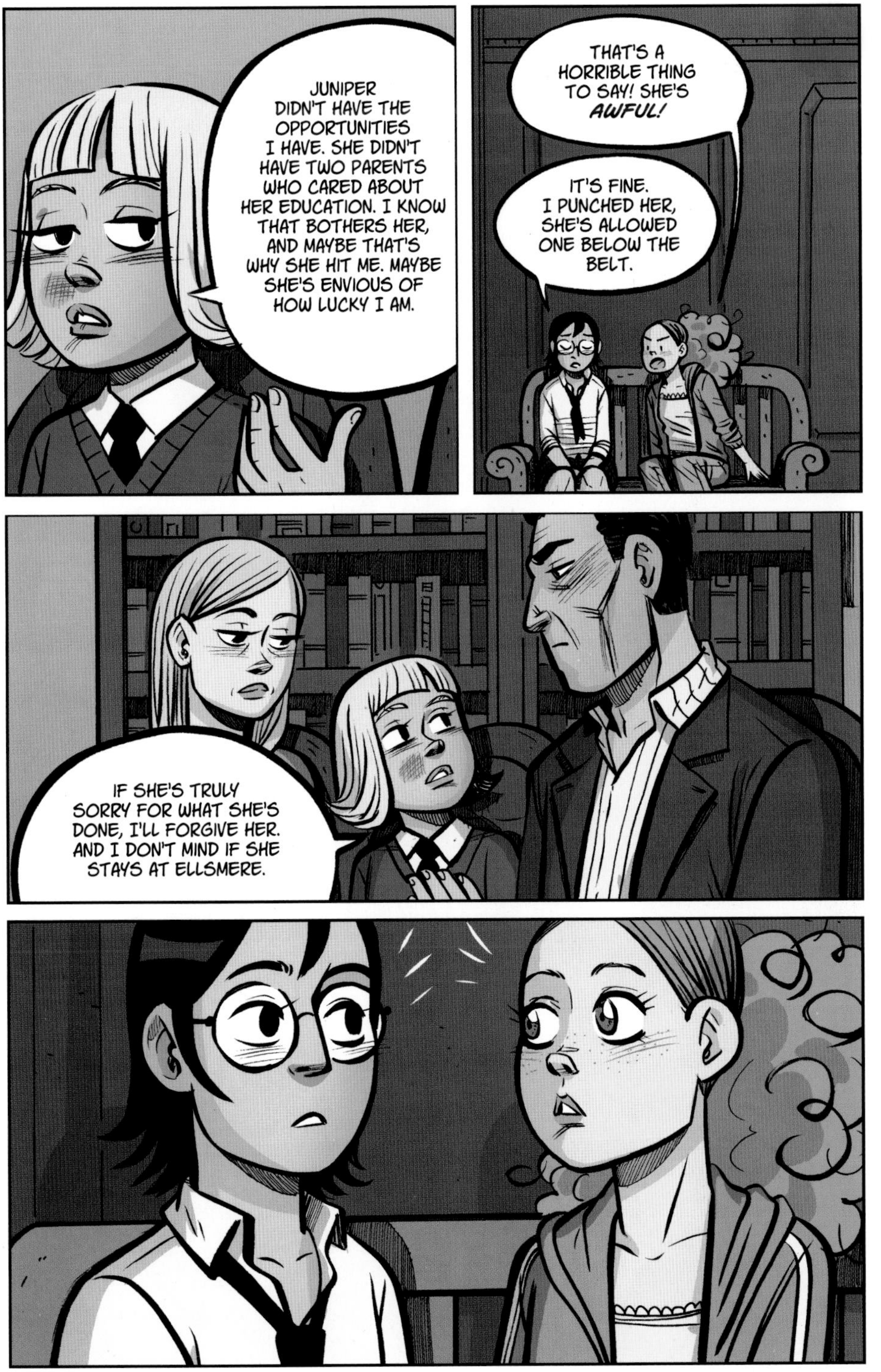
JUNIPER DIDN'T HAVE THE OPPORTUNITIES I HAVE. SHE DIDN'T HAVE TWO PARENTS WHO CARED ABOUT HER EDUCATION. I KNOW THAT BOTHERS HER, AND MAYBE THAT'S WHY SHE HIT ME. MAYBE SHE'S ENVIOUS OF HOW LUCKY I AM.
THAT'S A HORRIBLE THING TO SAY! SHE'S *AWFUL!*
IT'S FINE. I PUNCHED HER, SHE'S ALLOWED ONE BELOW THE BELT.
IF SHE'S TRULY SORRY FOR WHAT SHE'S DONE, I'LL FORGIVE HER. AND I DON'T MIND IF SHE STAYS AT ELLSMERE.

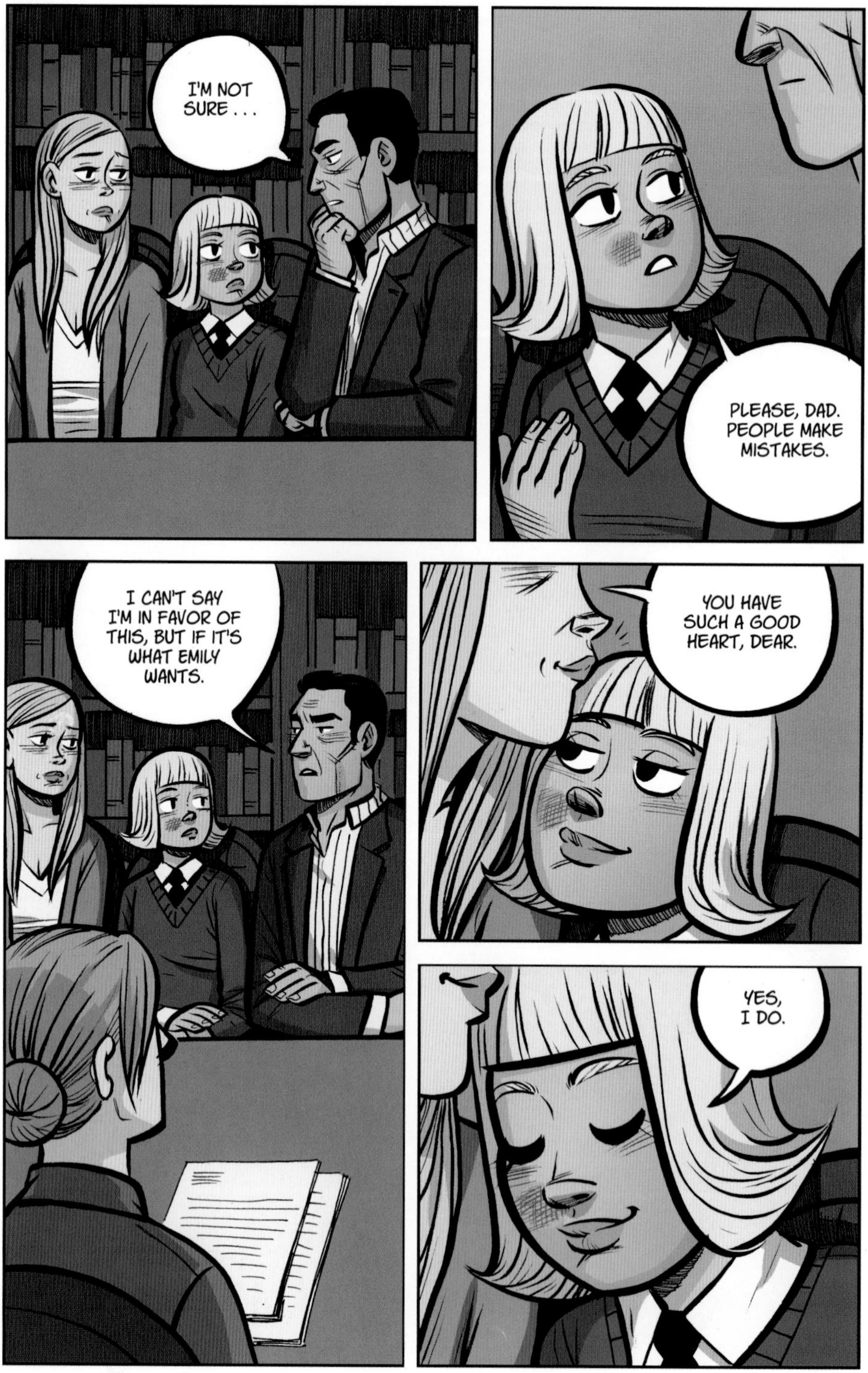
I'M NOT SURE . . .
PLEASE, DAD. PEOPLE MAKE MISTAKES.
I CAN'T SAY I'M IN FAVOR OF THIS, BUT IF IT'S WHAT EMILY WANTS.
YOU HAVE SUCH A GOOD HEART, DEAR.
YES, I DO.

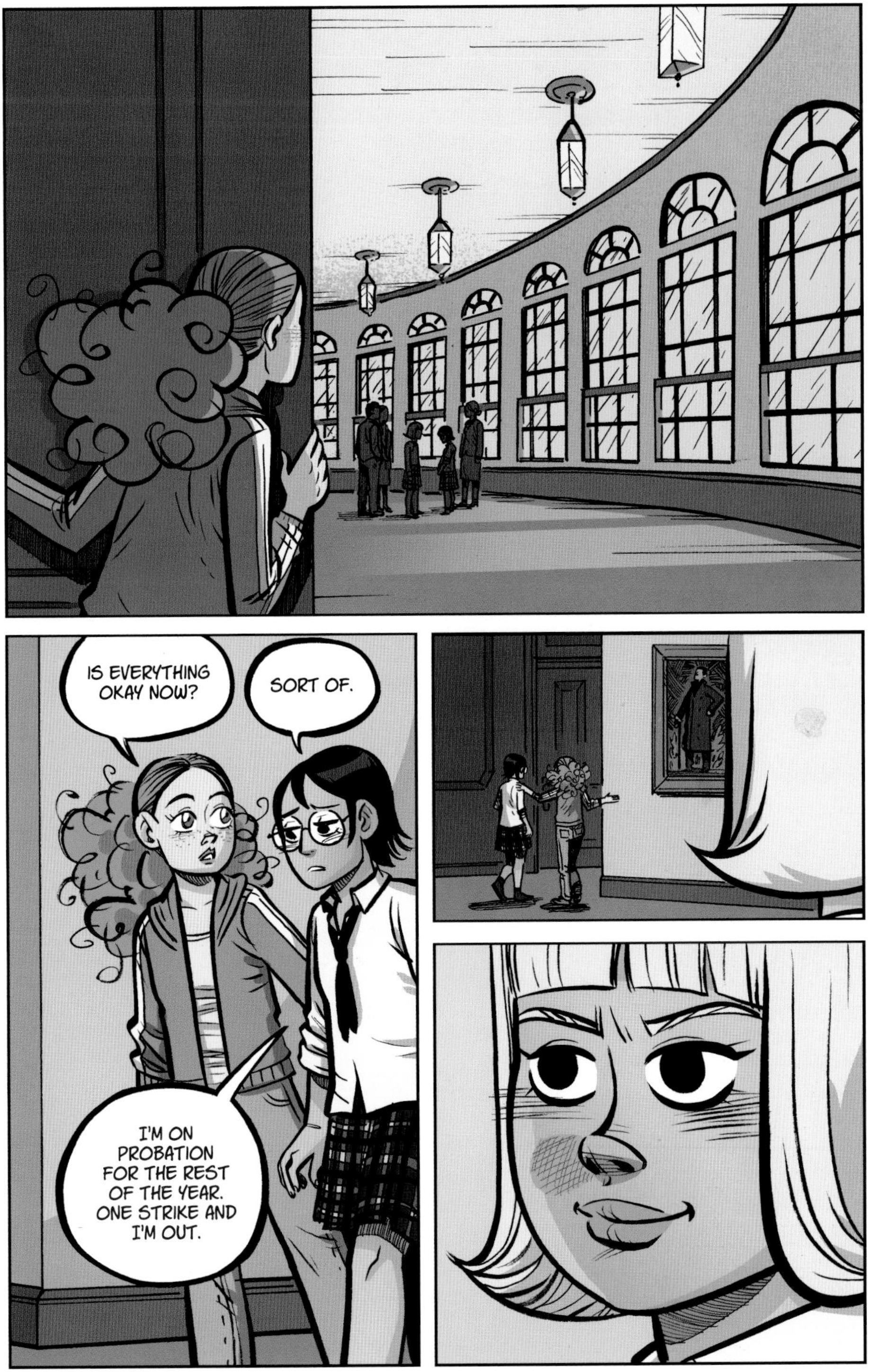
IS EVERYTHING OKAY NOW?
SORT OF.
I'M ON PROBATION FOR THE REST OF THE YEAR. ONE STRIKE AND I'M OUT.

Chapter Nine

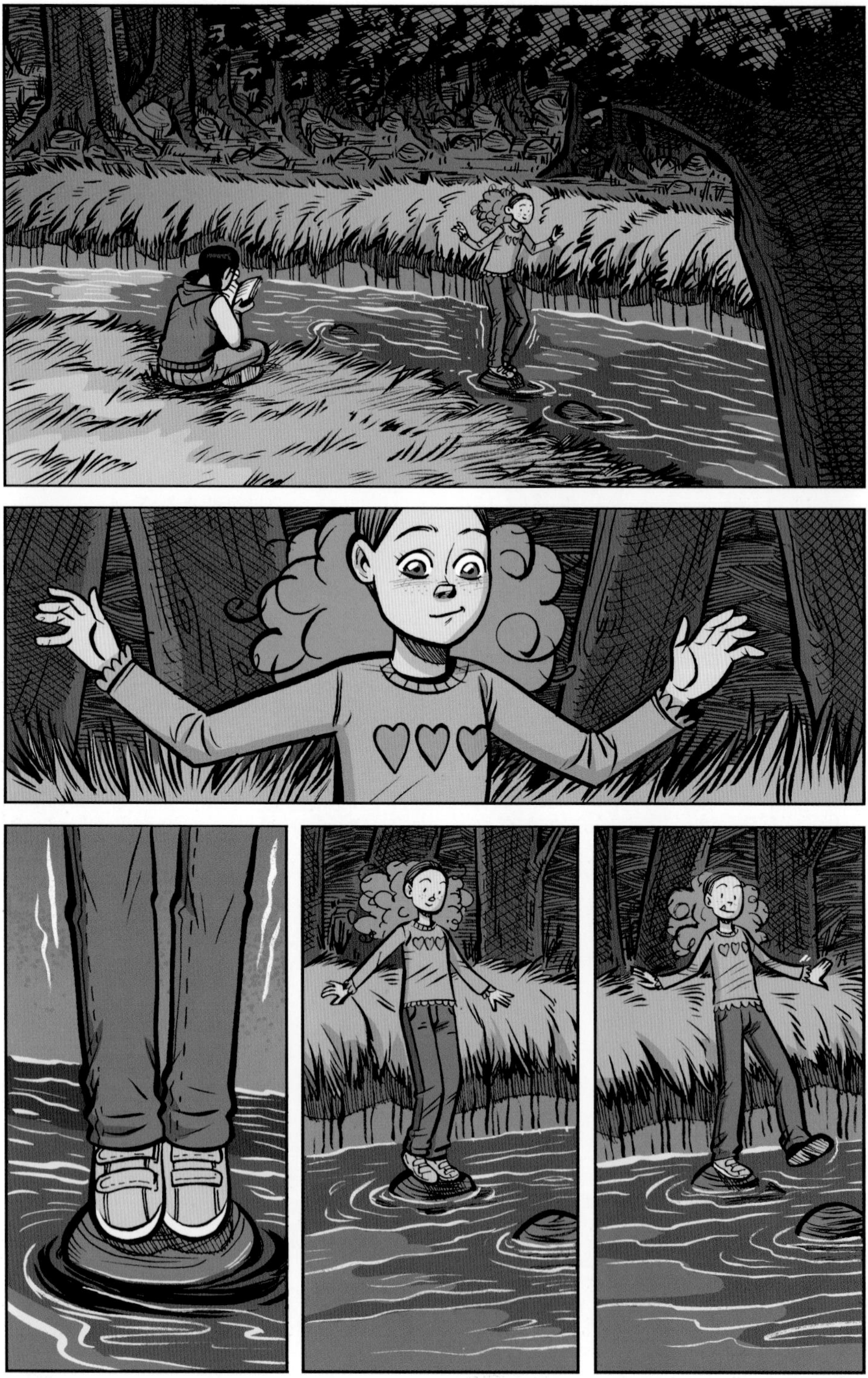

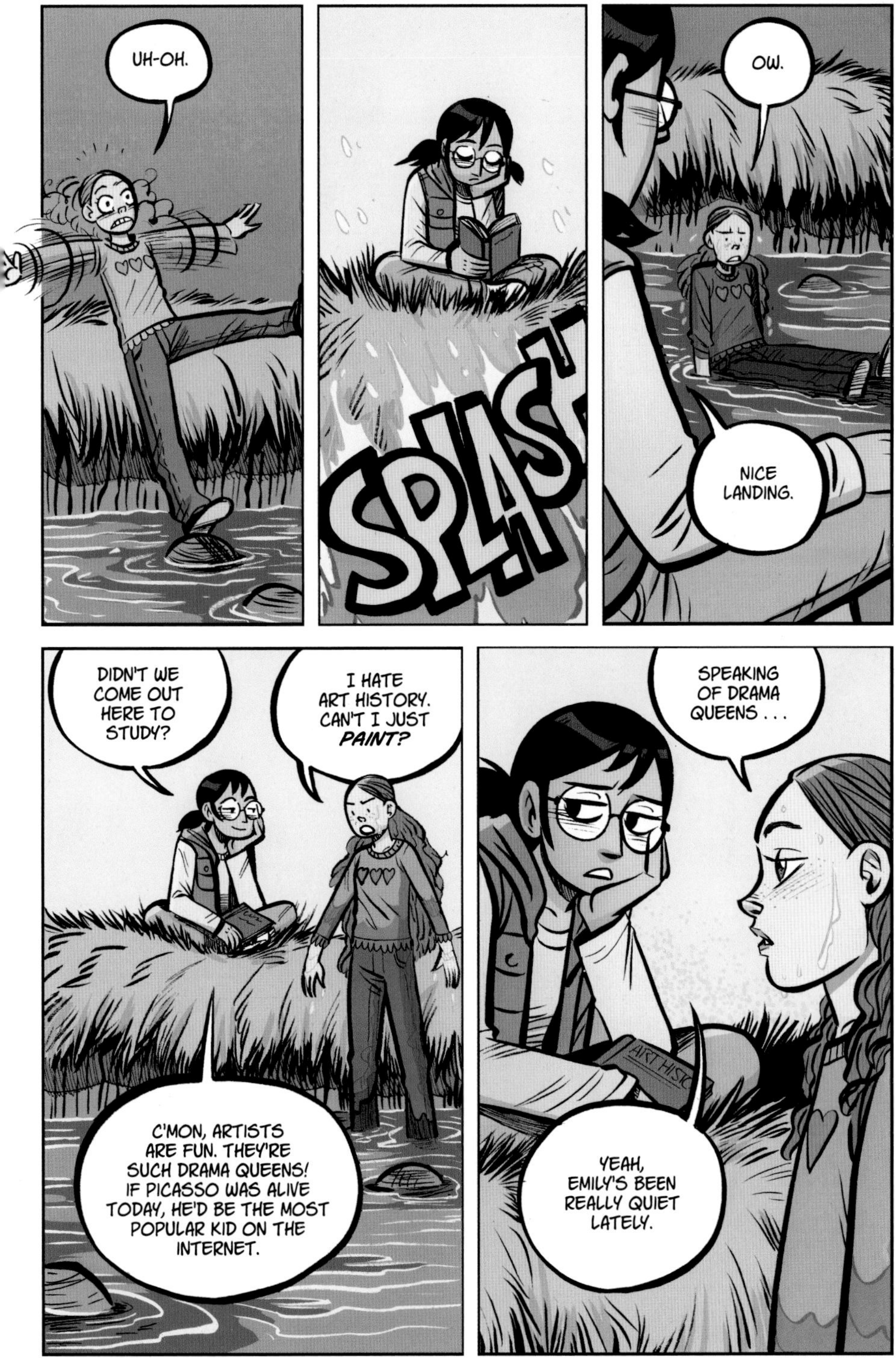
UH-OH.
SPLASH
OW.
NICE LANDING.
DIDN'T WE COME OUT HERE TO STUDY?
I HATE ART HISTORY. CAN'T I JUST *PAINT?*
C'MON, ARTISTS ARE FUN. THEY'RE SUCH DRAMA QUEENS! IF PICASSO WAS ALIVE TODAY, HE'D BE THE MOST POPULAR KID ON THE INTERNET.
SPEAKING OF DRAMA QUEENS . . .
YEAH, EMILY'S BEEN REALLY QUIET LATELY.

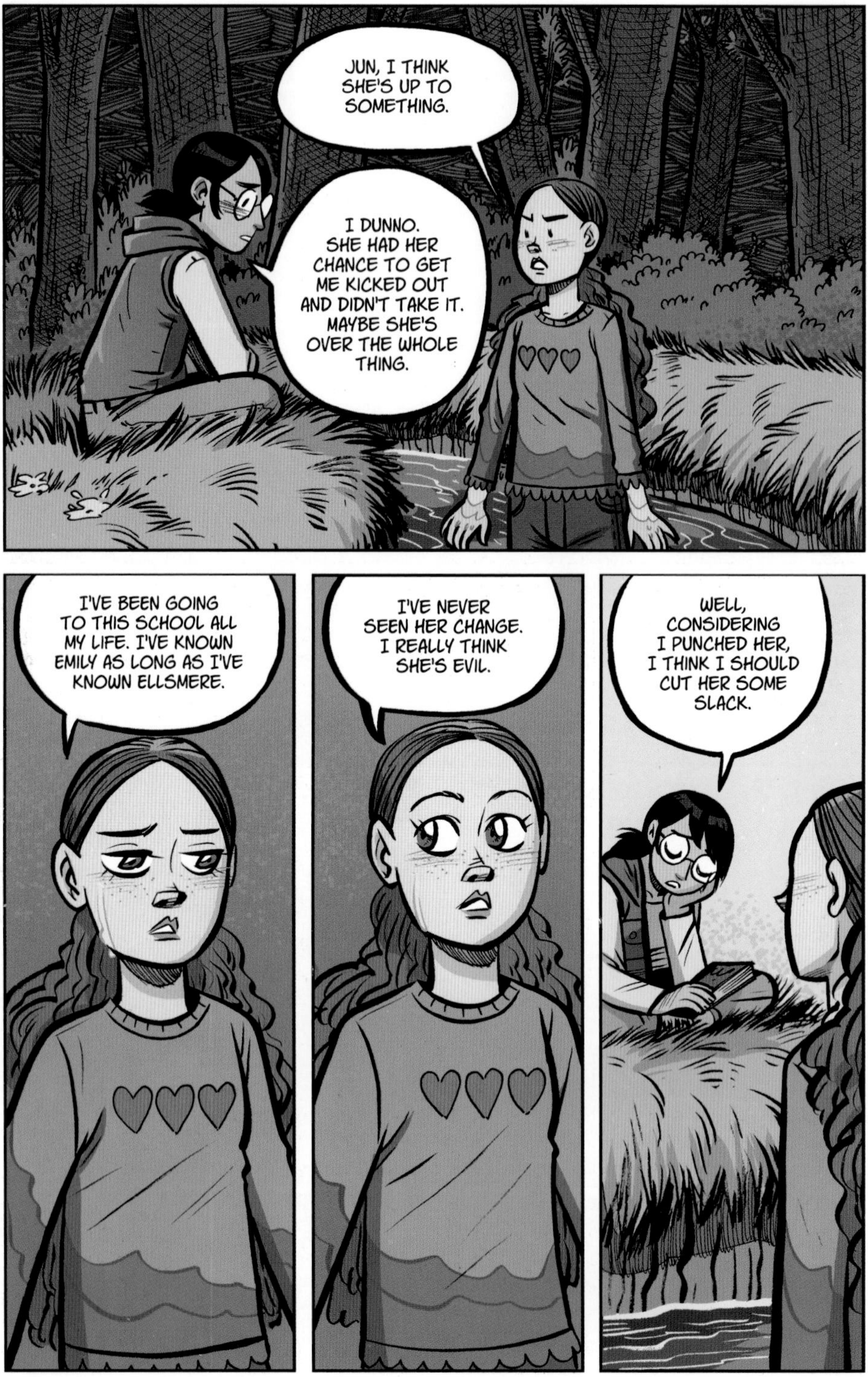
JUN, I THINK SHE'S UP TO SOMETHING.
I DUNNO. SHE HAD HER CHANCE TO GET ME KICKED OUT AND DIDN'T TAKE IT. MAYBE SHE'S OVER THE WHOLE THING.
I'VE BEEN GOING TO THIS SCHOOL ALL MY LIFE. I'VE KNOWN EMILY AS LONG AS I'VE KNOWN ELLSMERE.
I'VE NEVER SEEN HER CHANGE. I REALLY THINK SHE'S EVIL.
WELL, CONSIDERING I PUNCHED HER, I THINK I SHOULD CUT HER SOME SLACK.

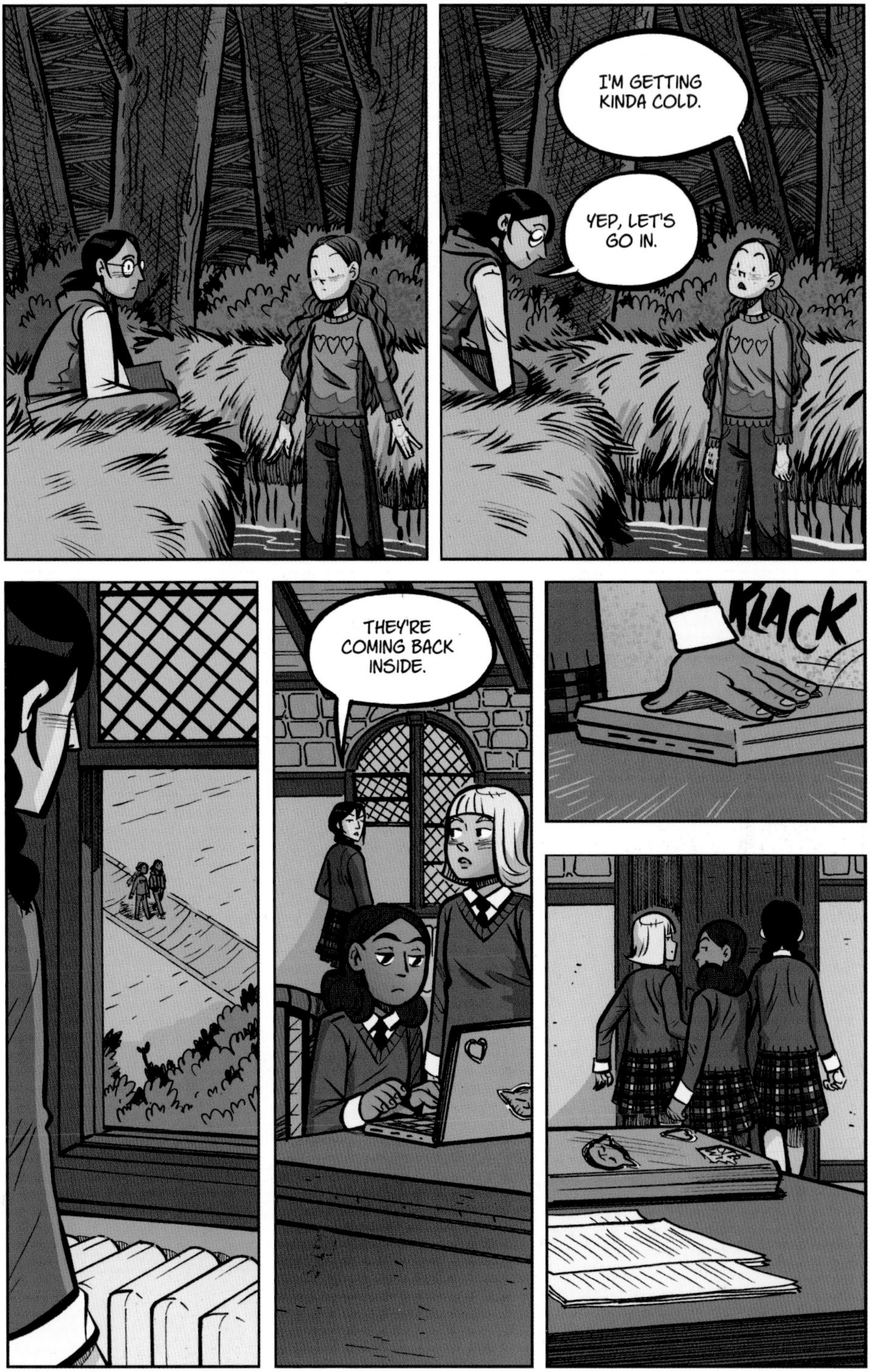
I'M GETTING KINDA COLD.
YEP, LET'S GO IN.
THEY'RE COMING BACK INSIDE.
KLACK

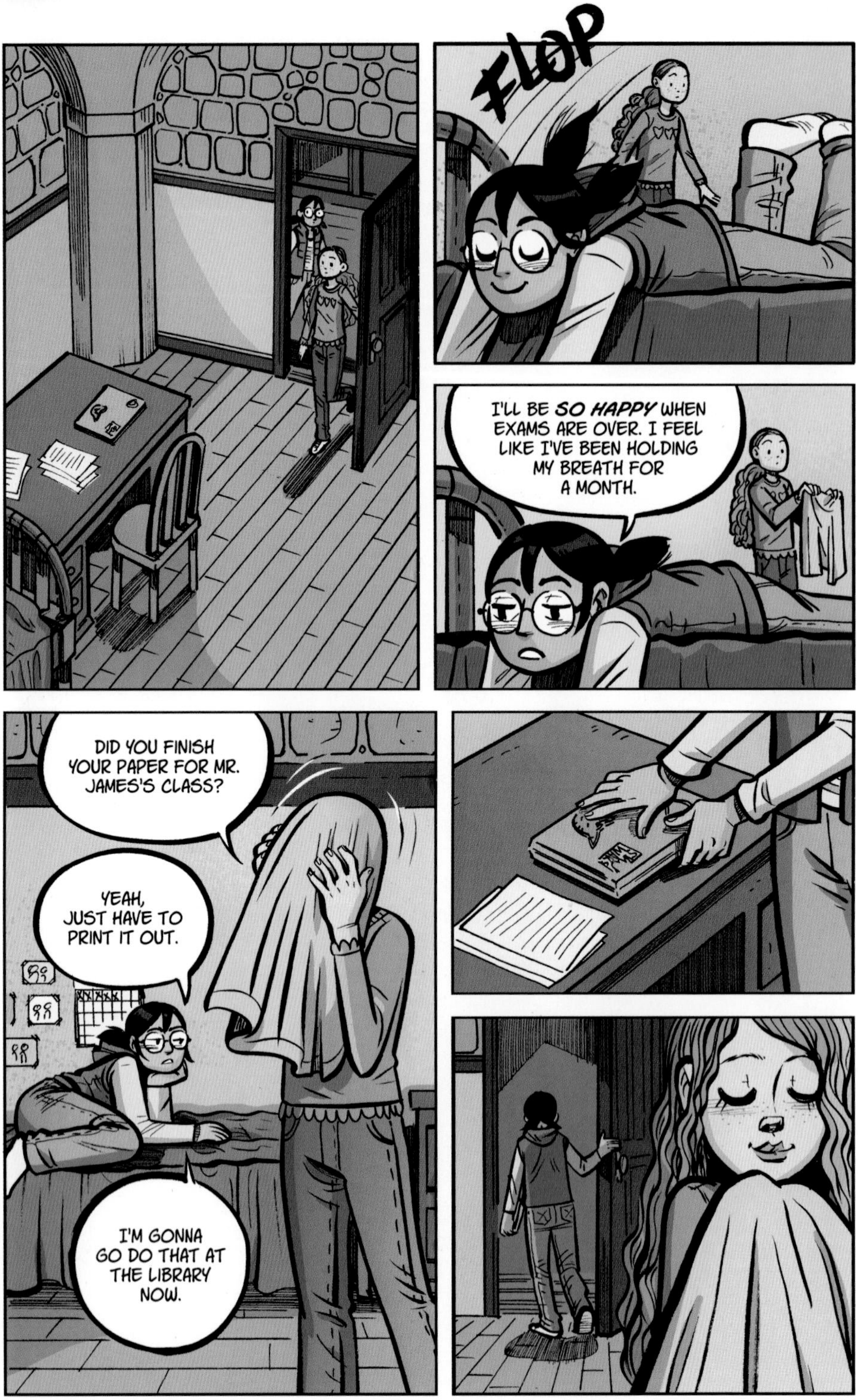
FLOP
I'LL BE SO HAPPY WHEN EXAMS ARE OVER. I FEEL LIKE I'VE BEEN HOLDING MY BREATH FOR A MONTH.
DID YOU FINISH YOUR PAPER FOR MR. JAMES'S CLASS?
YEAH, JUST HAVE TO PRINT IT OUT.
I'M GONNA GO DO THAT AT THE LIBRARY NOW.

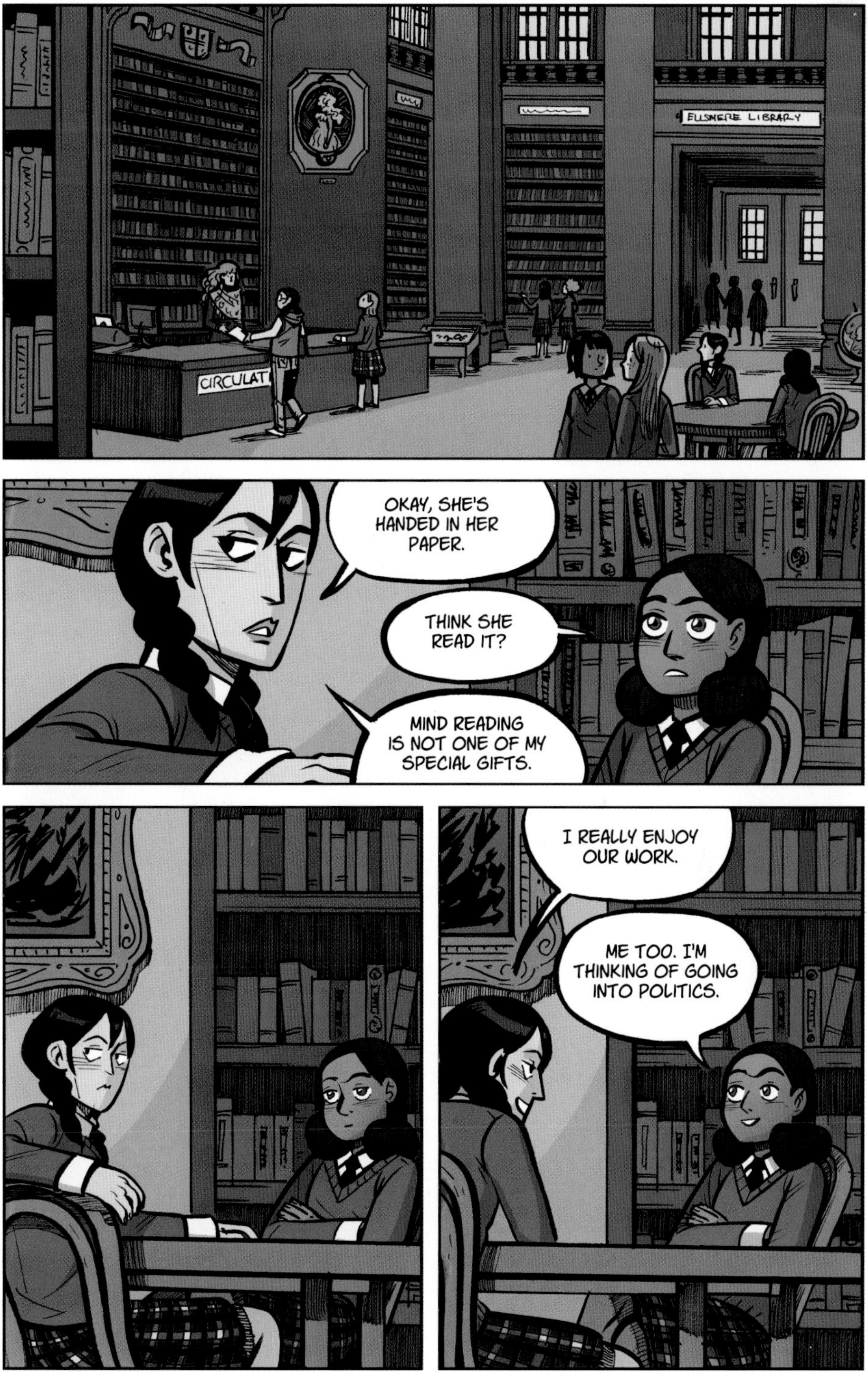
ELLSMERE LIBRARY
CIRCULAT
OKAY, SHE'S HANDED IN HER PAPER.
THINK SHE READ IT?
MIND READING IS NOT ONE OF MY SPECIAL GIFTS.
I REALLY ENJOY OUR WORK.
ME TOO. I'M THINKING OF GOING INTO POLITICS.

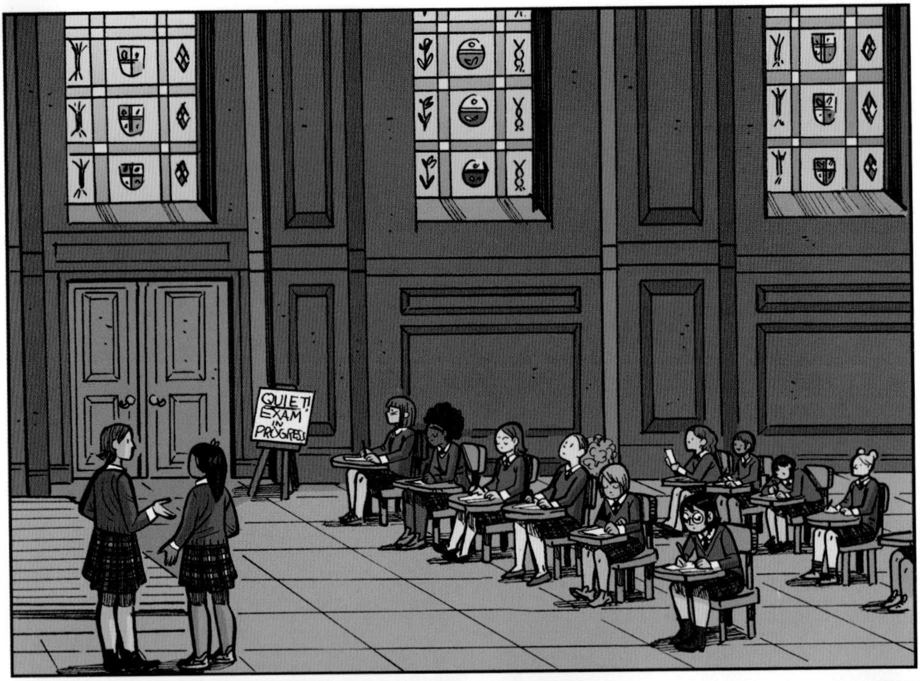
QUIET! EXAM IN PROGRESS

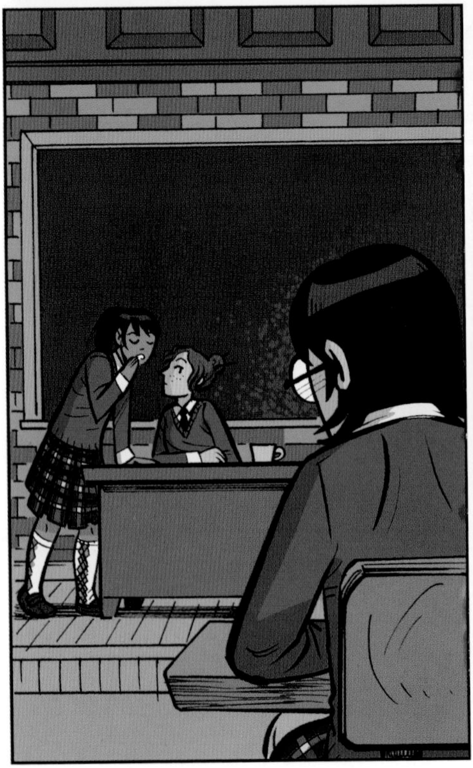

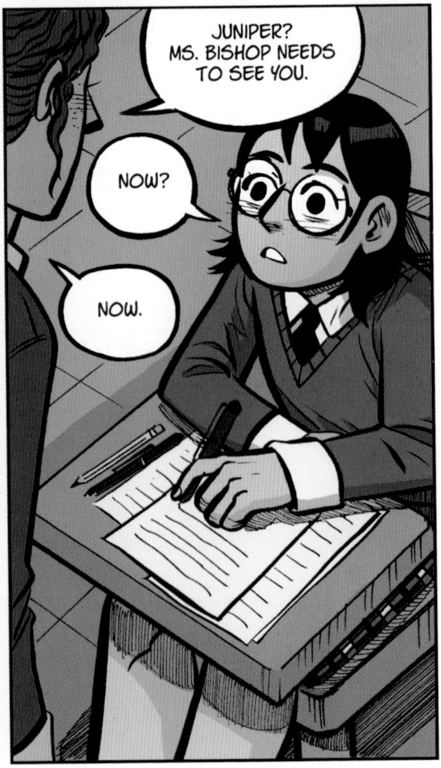
JUNIPER? MS. BISHOP NEEDS TO SEE YOU.
NOW?
NOW.

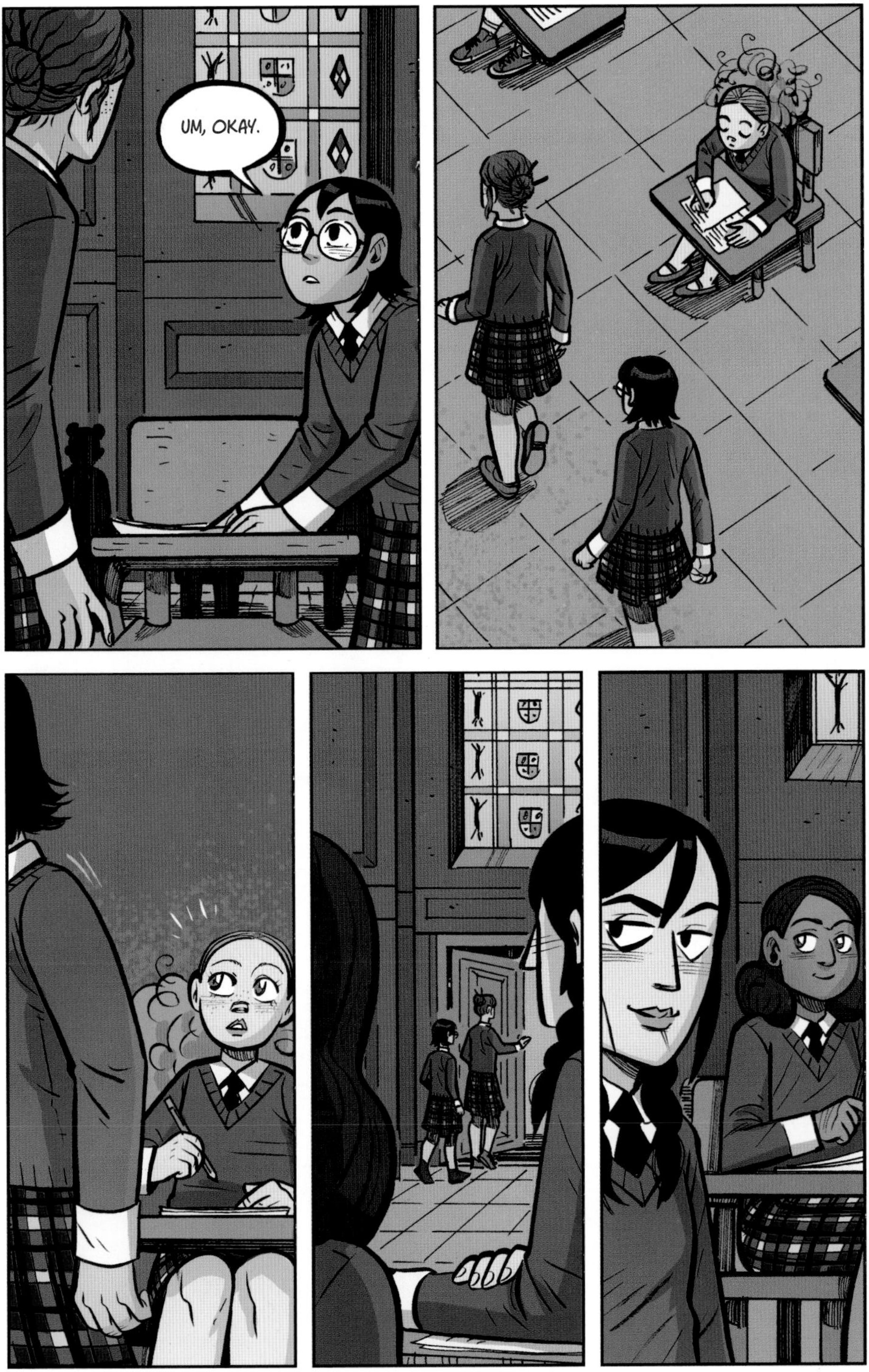
UM, OKAY.

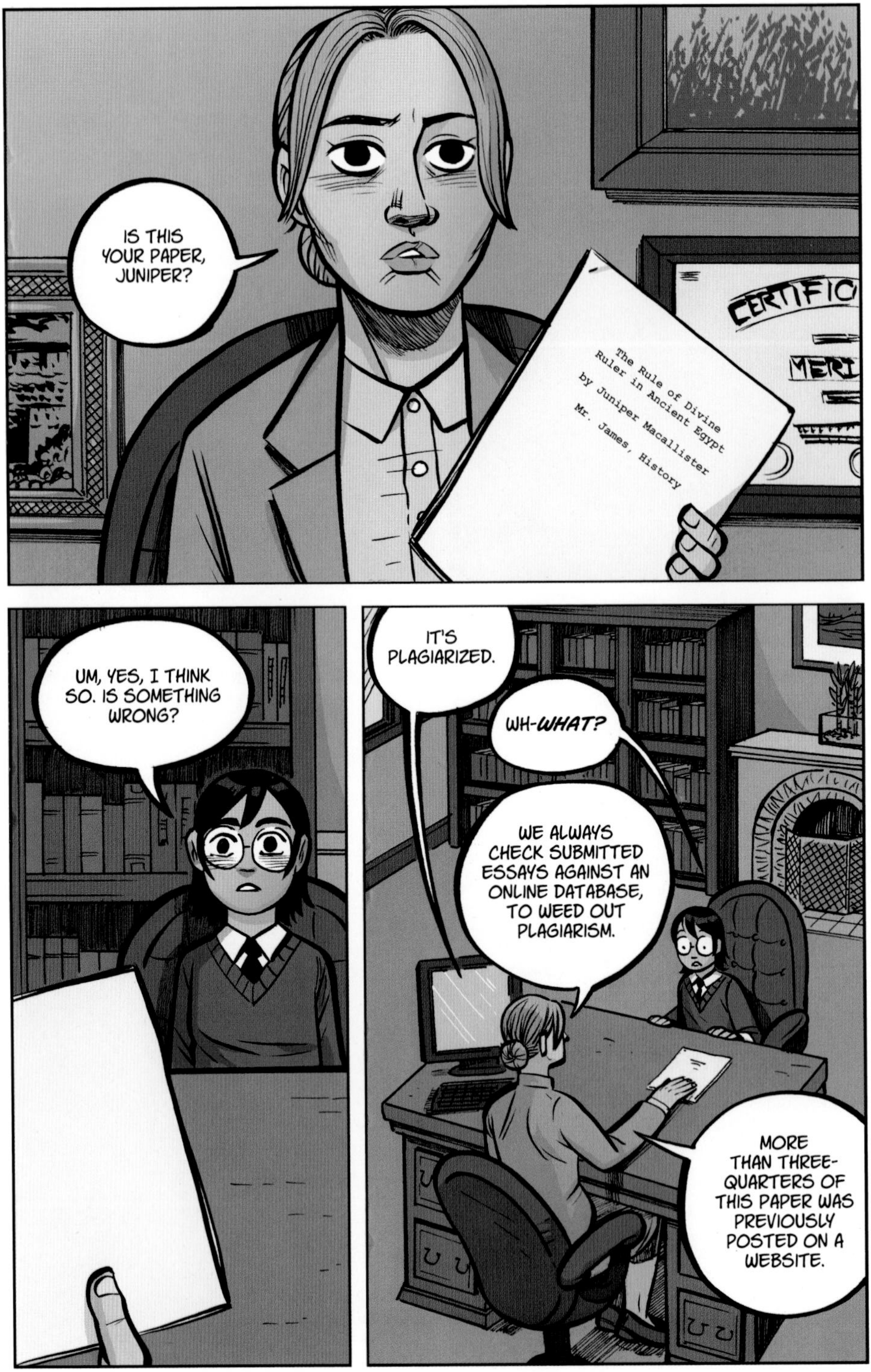
IS THIS YOUR PAPER, JUNIPER?
The Rule of Divine Ruler in Ancient Egypt
by Juniper Macallister
Mr. James, History
CERTIFIC
MERI
UM, YES, I THINK SO. IS SOMETHING WRONG?
IT'S PLAGIARIZED.
WH-*WHAT?*
WE ALWAYS CHECK SUBMITTED ESSAYS AGAINST AN ONLINE DATABASE, TO WEED OUT PLAGIARISM.
MORE THAN THREE-QUARTERS OF THIS PAPER WAS PREVIOUSLY POSTED ON A WEBSITE.

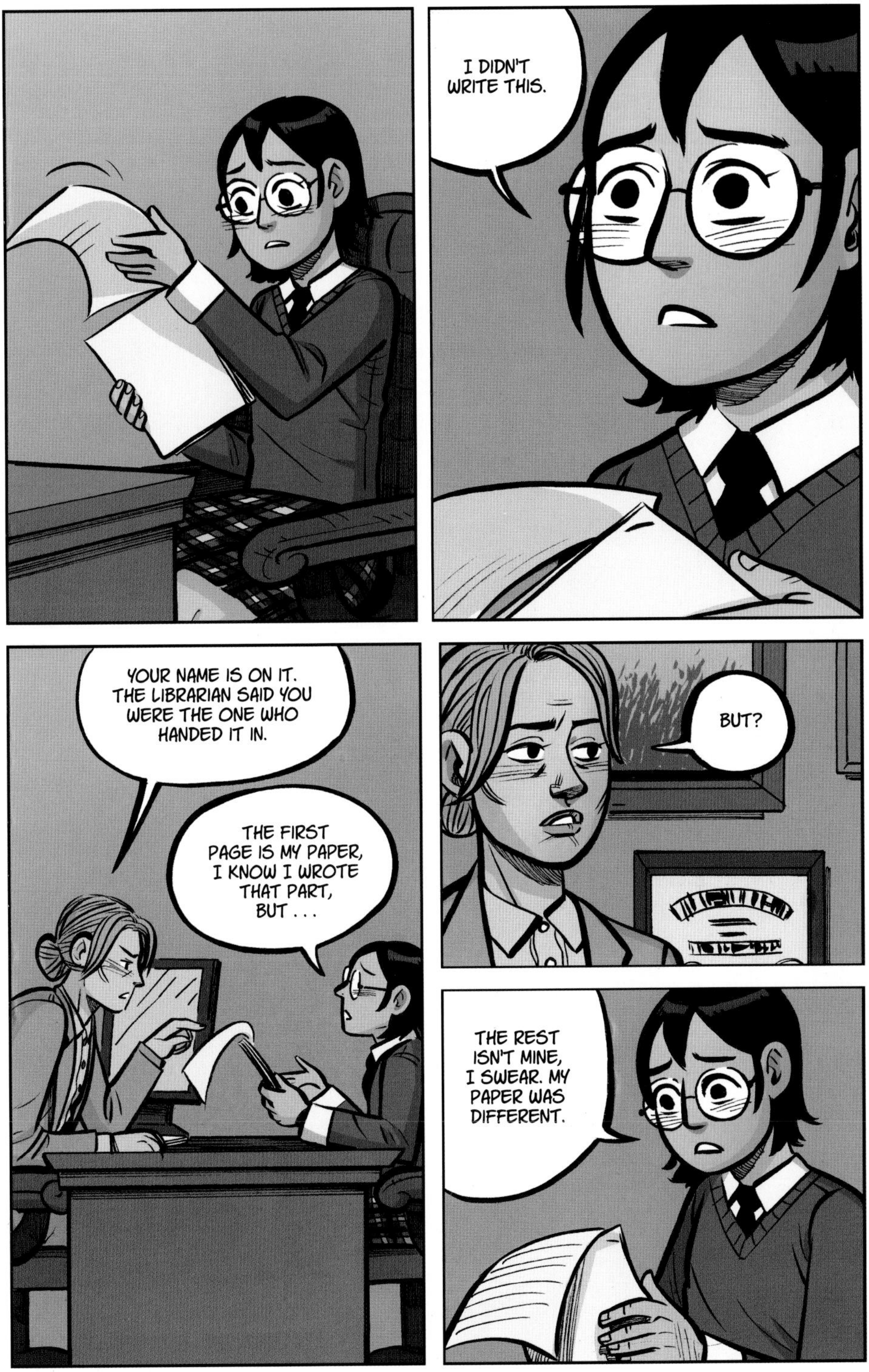
I DIDN'T WRITE THIS.
YOUR NAME IS ON IT. THE LIBRARIAN SAID YOU WERE THE ONE WHO HANDED IT IN.
THE FIRST PAGE IS MY PAPER, I KNOW I WROTE THAT PART, BUT . . .
BUT?
THE REST ISN'T MINE, I SWEAR. MY PAPER WAS DIFFERENT.

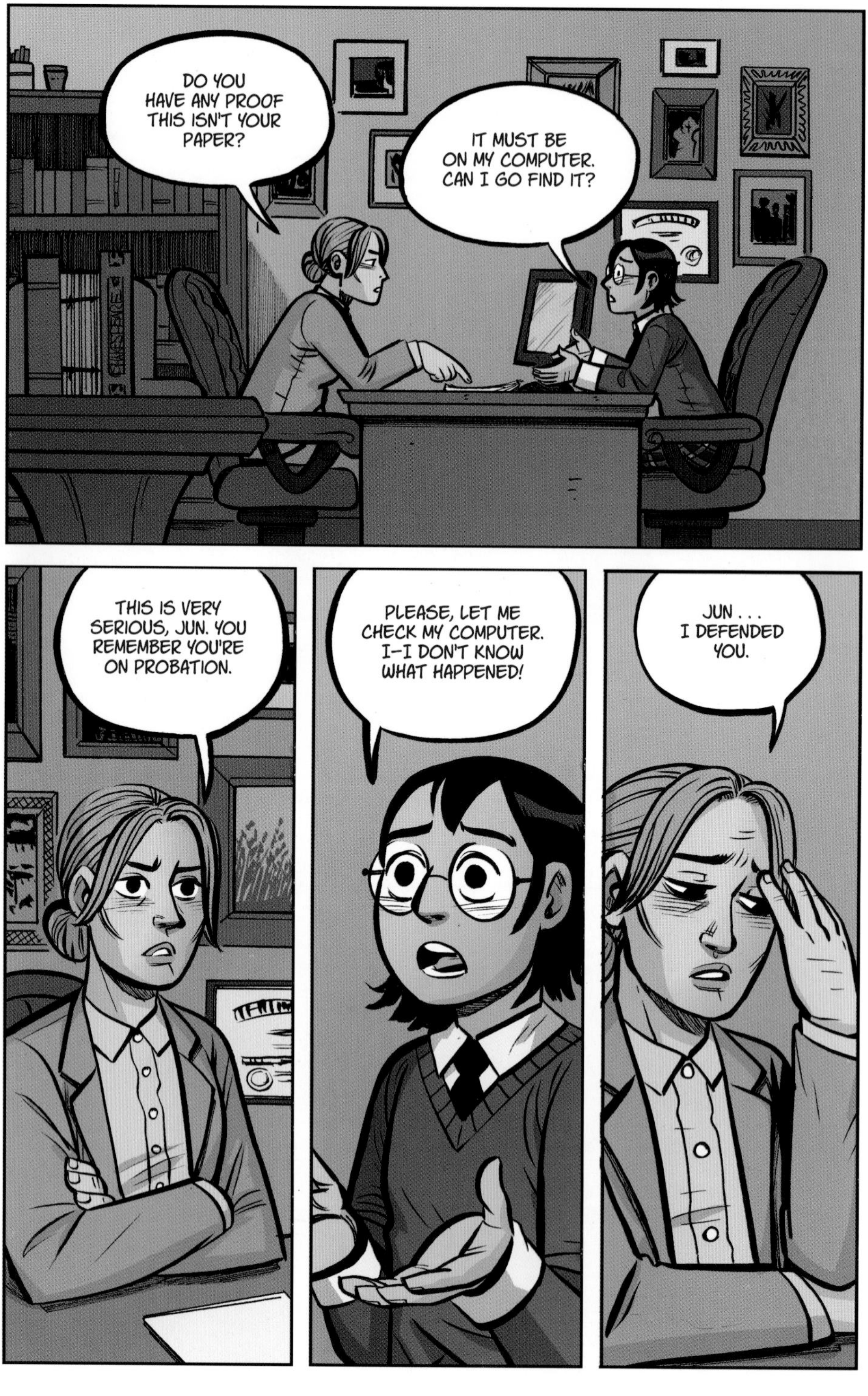
DO YOU HAVE ANY PROOF THIS ISN'T YOUR PAPER?
IT MUST BE ON MY COMPUTER. CAN I GO FIND IT?
THIS IS VERY SERIOUS, JUN. YOU REMEMBER YOU'RE ON PROBATION.
PLEASE, LET ME CHECK MY COMPUTER. I–I DON'T KNOW WHAT HAPPENED!
JUN . . . I DEFENDED YOU.

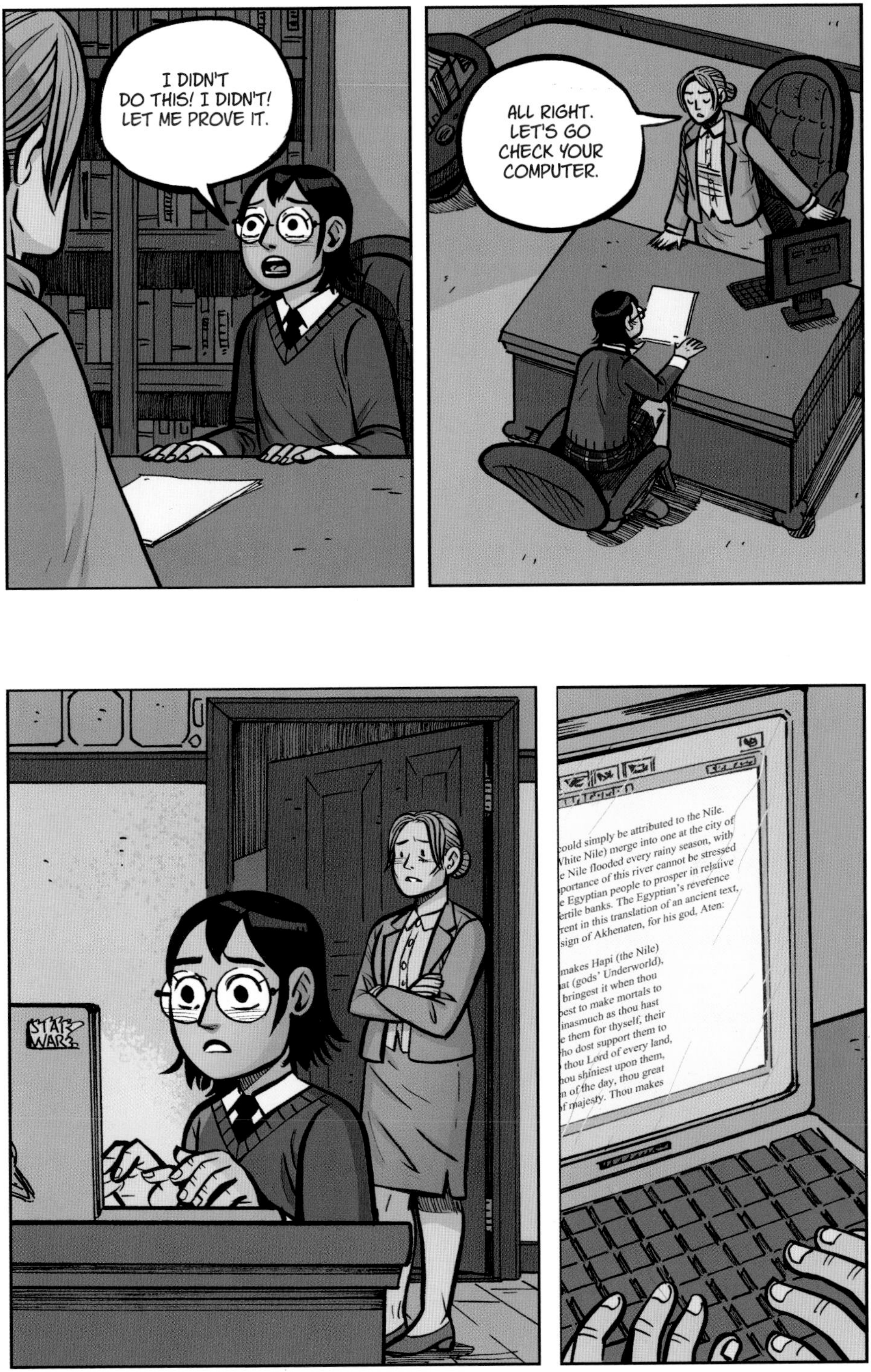
I DIDN'T DO THIS! I DIDN'T! LET ME PROVE IT.
ALL RIGHT. LET'S GO CHECK YOUR COMPUTER.

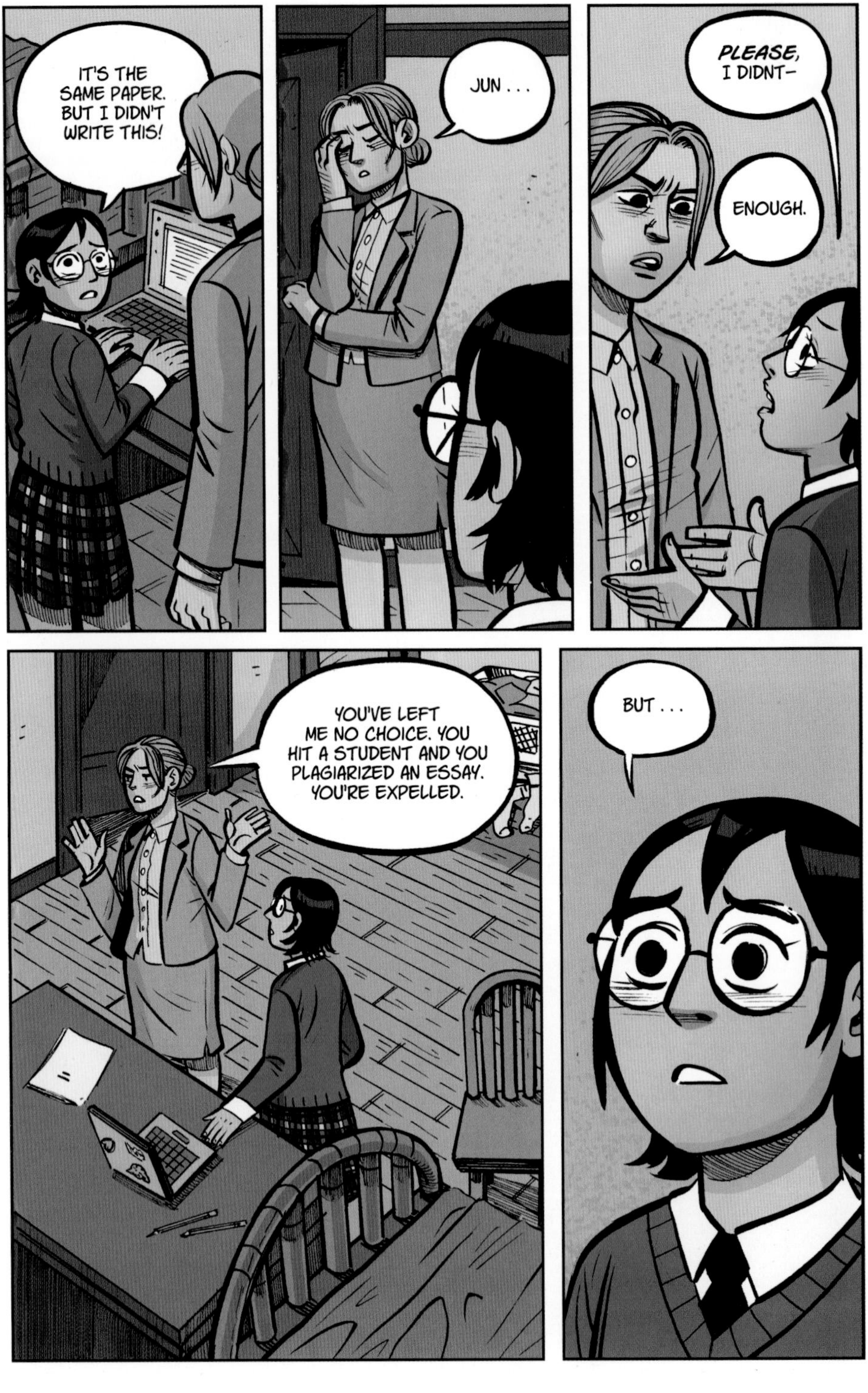
IT'S THE SAME PAPER. BUT I DIDN'T WRITE THIS!
JUN . . .
PLEASE, I DIDNT–
ENOUGH.
YOU'VE LEFT ME NO CHOICE. YOU HIT A STUDENT AND YOU PLAGIARIZED AN ESSAY. YOU'RE EXPELLED.
BUT . . .

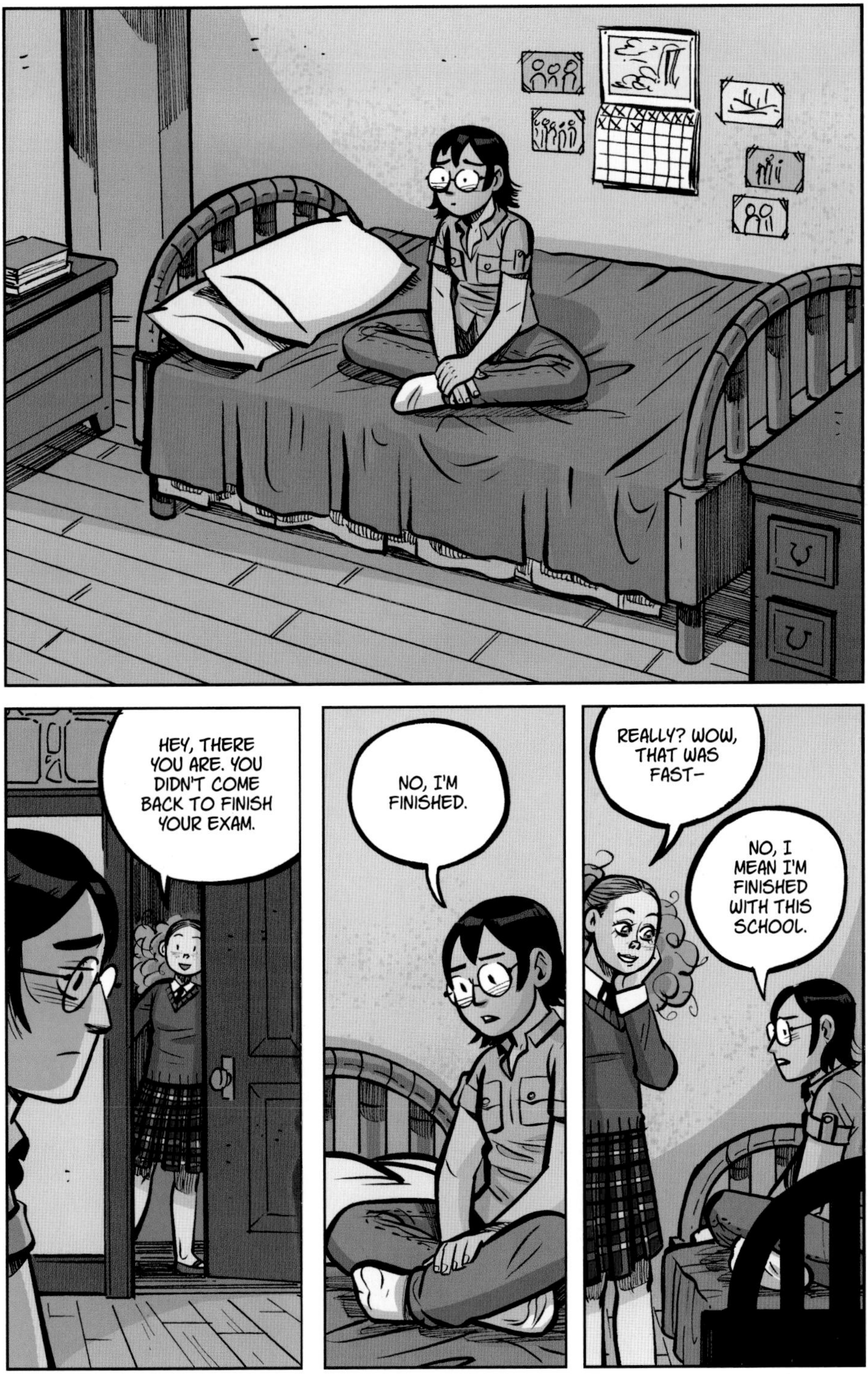
HEY, THERE YOU ARE. YOU DIDN'T COME BACK TO FINISH YOUR EXAM.
NO, I'M FINISHED.
REALLY? WOW, THAT WAS FAST–
NO, I MEAN I'M FINISHED WITH THIS SCHOOL.

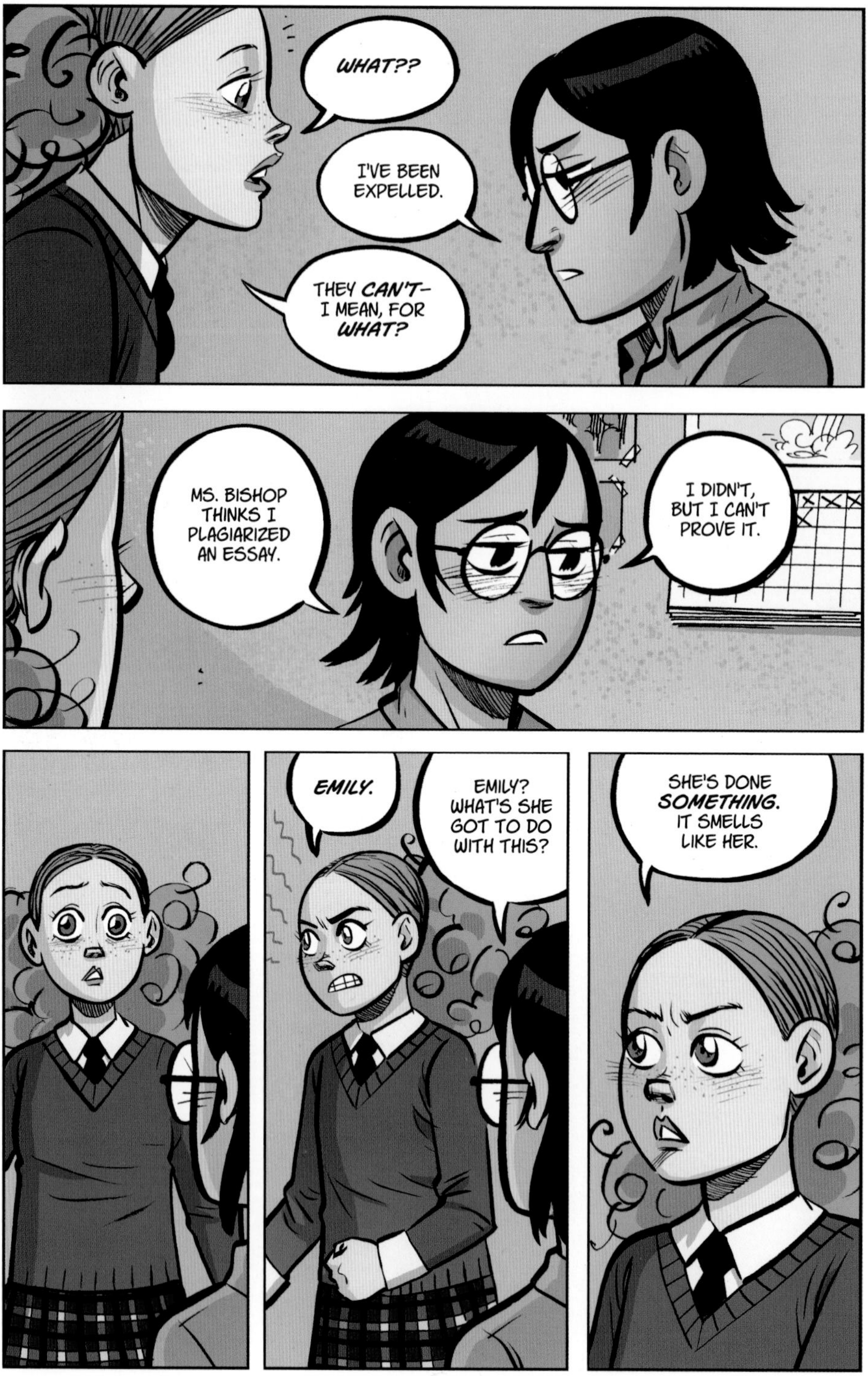
WHAT??
I'VE BEEN EXPELLED.
THEY *CAN'T*— I MEAN, FOR *WHAT?*
MS. BISHOP THINKS I PLAGIARIZED AN ESSAY.
I DIDN'T, BUT I CAN'T PROVE IT.
EMILY.
EMILY? WHAT'S SHE GOT TO DO WITH THIS?
SHE'S DONE *SOMETHING.* IT SMELLS LIKE HER.

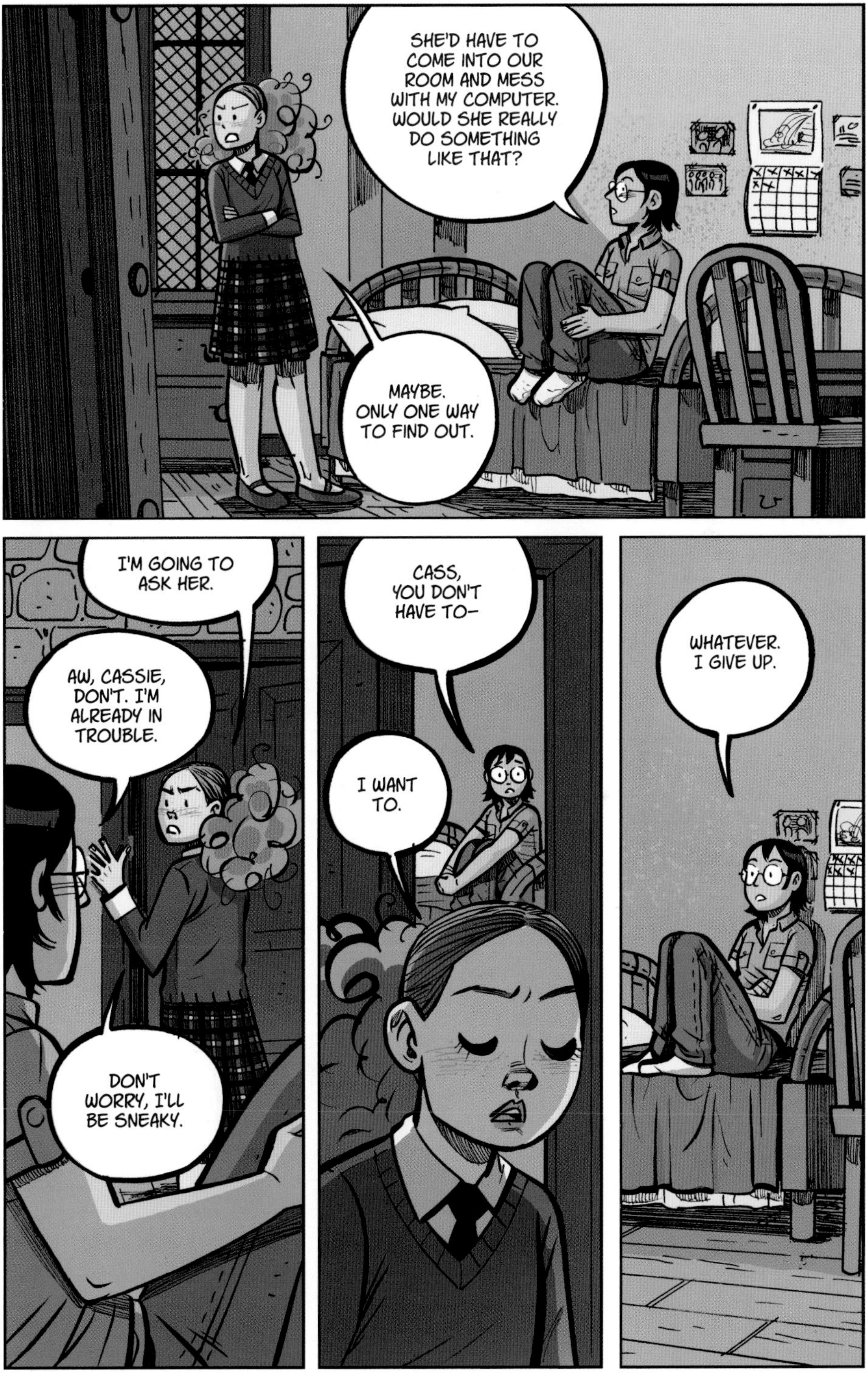
SHE'D HAVE TO COME INTO OUR ROOM AND MESS WITH MY COMPUTER. WOULD SHE REALLY DO SOMETHING LIKE THAT?
MAYBE. ONLY ONE WAY TO FIND OUT.
I'M GOING TO ASK HER.
AW, CASSIE, DON'T. I'M ALREADY IN TROUBLE.
DON'T WORRY, I'LL BE SNEAKY.
CASS, YOU DON'T HAVE TO–
I WANT TO.
WHATEVER. I GIVE UP.

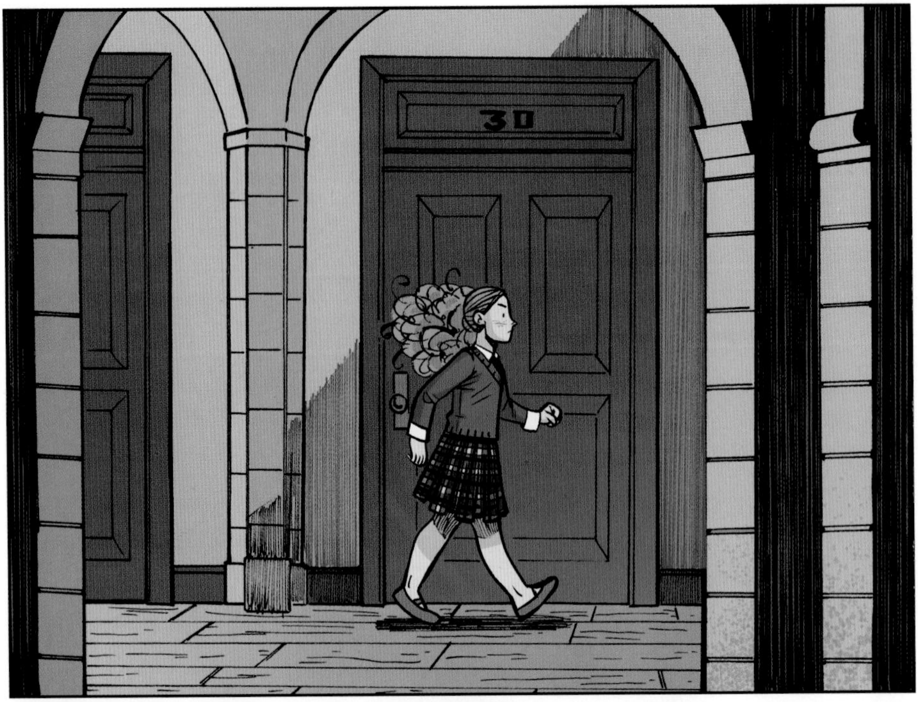
3D

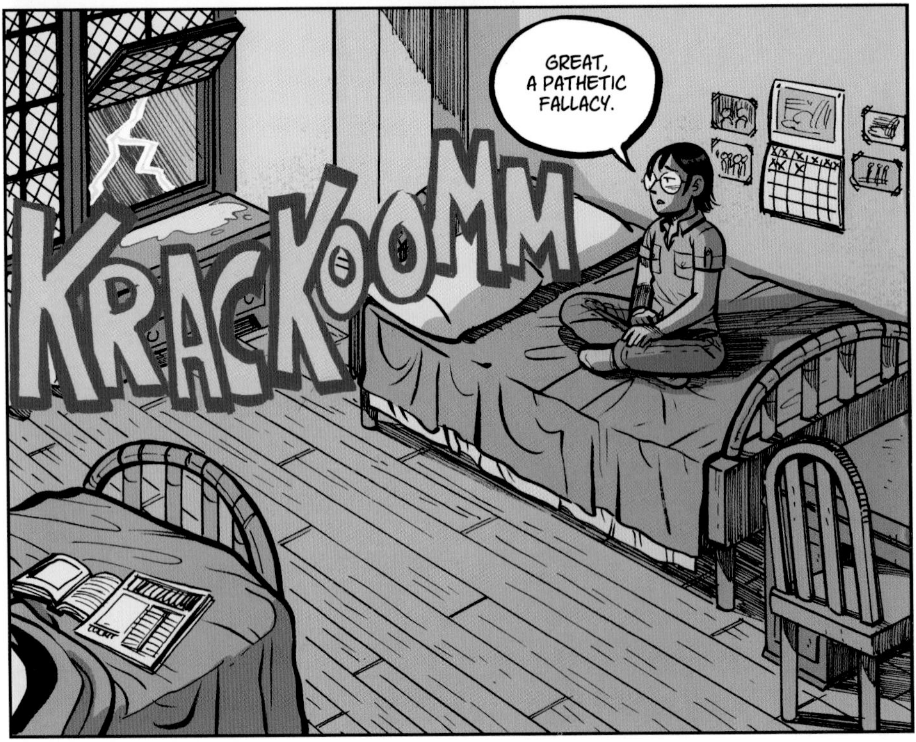
GREAT, A PATHETIC FALLACY.
KRACKOOMM

Chapter Ten

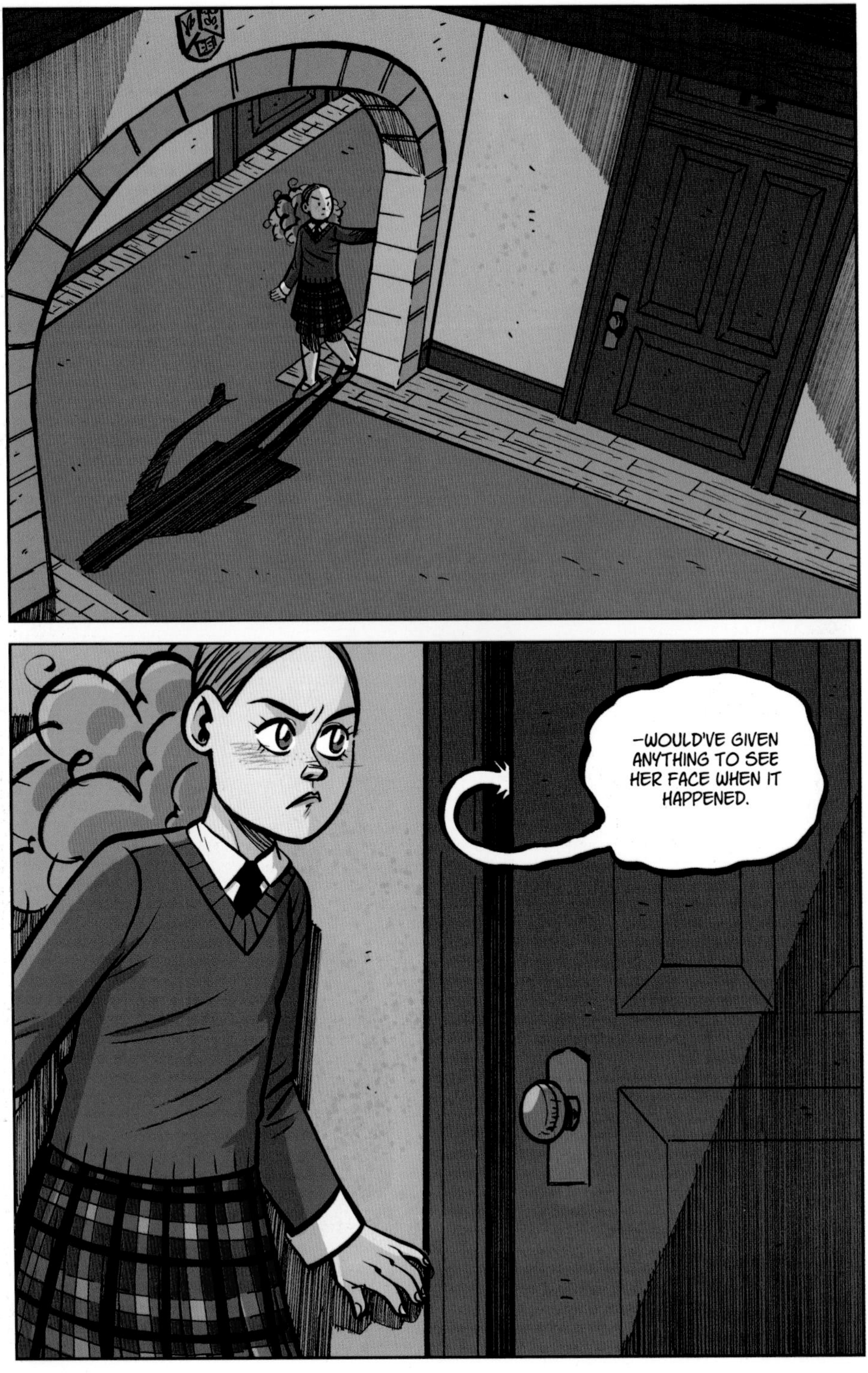
-WOULD'VE GIVEN ANYTHING TO SEE HER FACE WHEN IT HAPPENED.

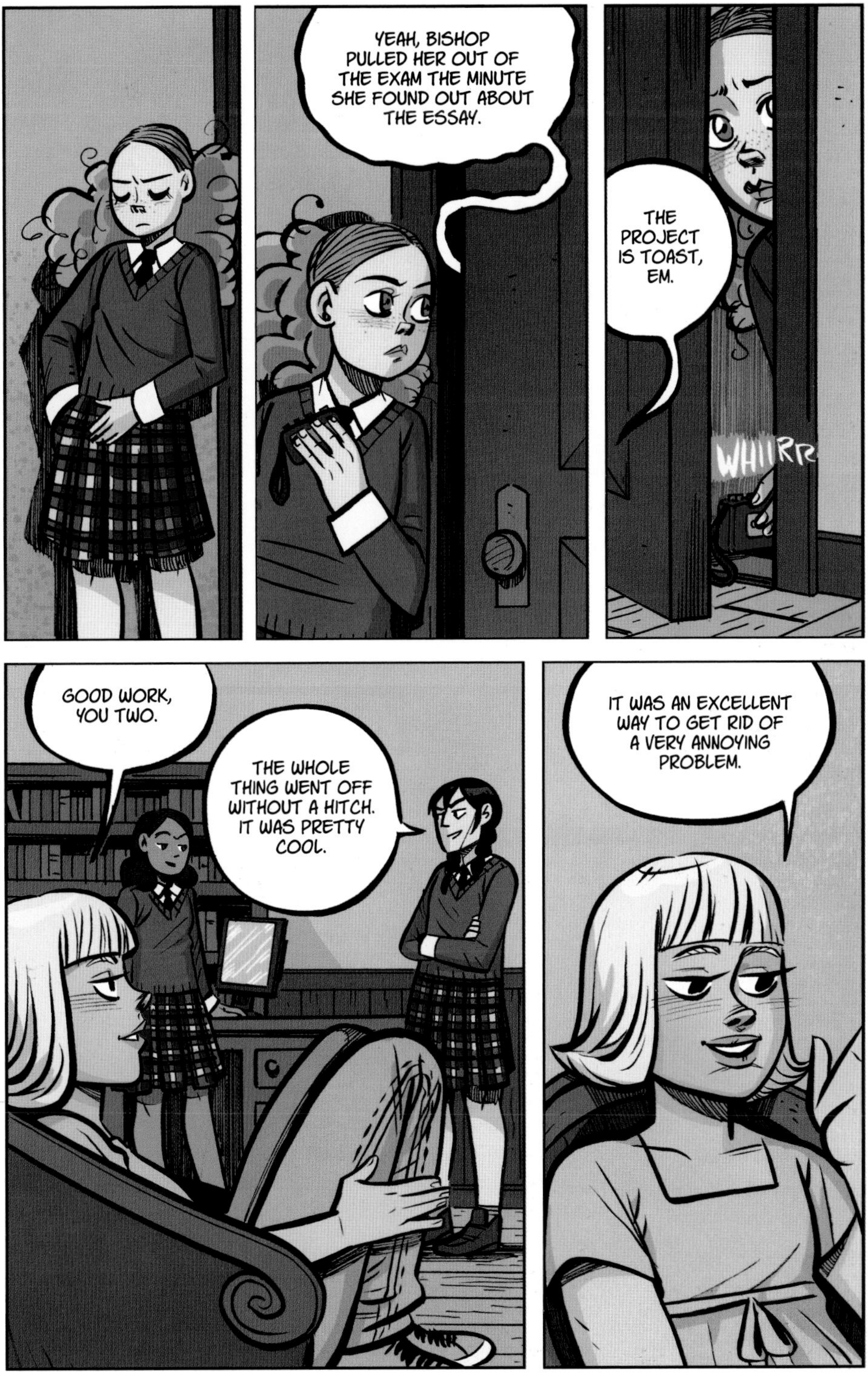
YEAH, BISHOP PULLED HER OUT OF THE EXAM THE MINUTE SHE FOUND OUT ABOUT THE ESSAY.
THE PROJECT IS TOAST, EM.
WHIIRR
GOOD WORK, YOU TWO.
THE WHOLE THING WENT OFF WITHOUT A HITCH. IT WAS PRETTY COOL.
IT WAS AN EXCELLENT WAY TO GET RID OF A VERY ANNOYING PROBLEM.

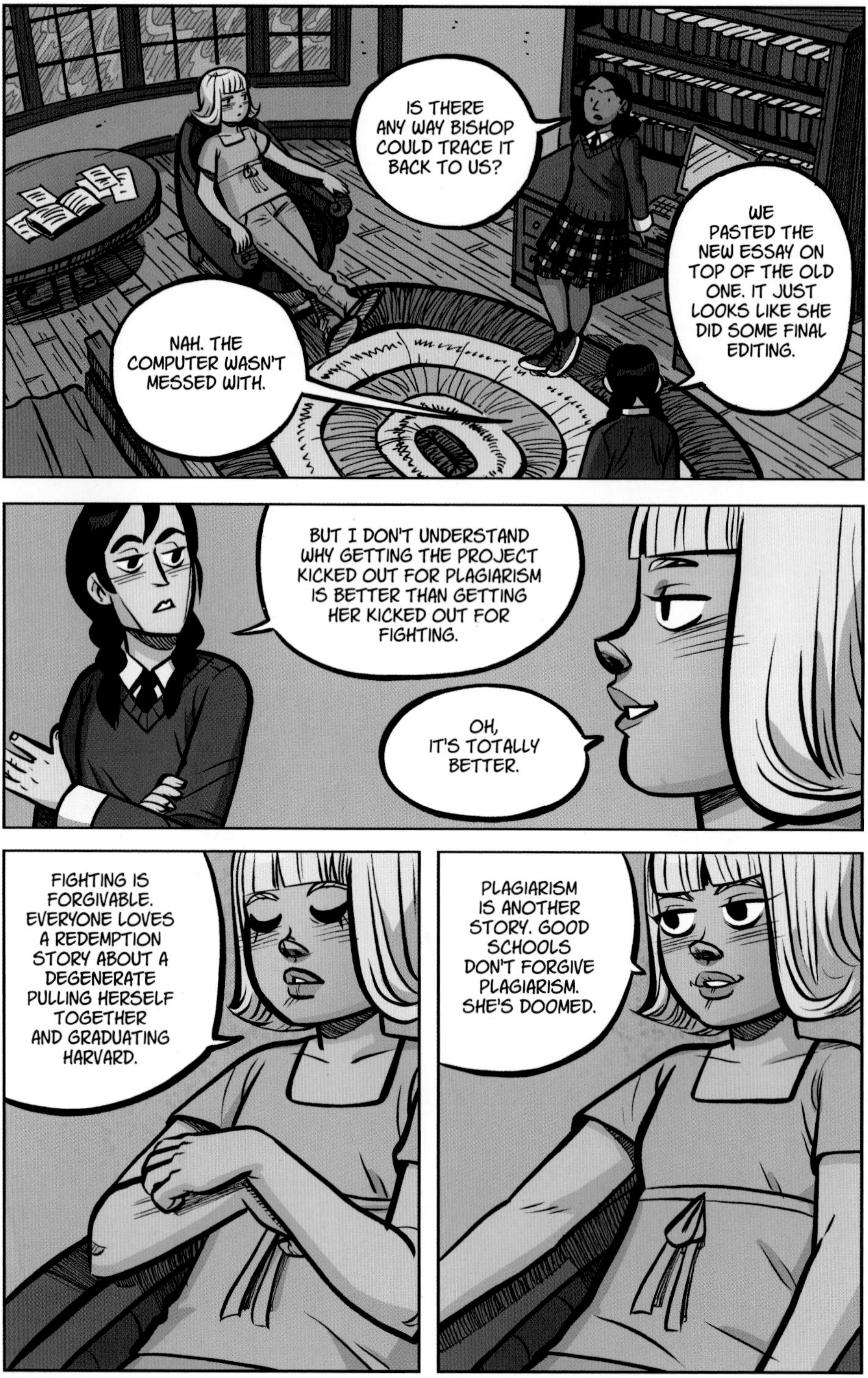
IS THERE ANY WAY BISHOP COULD TRACE IT BACK TO US?
WE PASTED THE NEW ESSAY ON TOP OF THE OLD ONE. IT JUST LOOKS LIKE SHE DID SOME FINAL EDITING.
NAH. THE COMPUTER WASN'T MESSED WITH.
BUT I DON'T UNDERSTAND WHY GETTING THE PROJECT KICKED OUT FOR PLAGIARISM IS BETTER THAN GETTING HER KICKED OUT FOR FIGHTING.
OH, IT'S TOTALLY BETTER.
FIGHTING IS FORGIVABLE. EVERYONE LOVES A REDEMPTION STORY ABOUT A DEGENERATE PULLING HERSELF TOGETHER AND GRADUATING HARVARD.
PLAGIARISM IS ANOTHER STORY. GOOD SCHOOLS DON'T FORGIVE PLAGIARISM. SHE'S DOOMED.

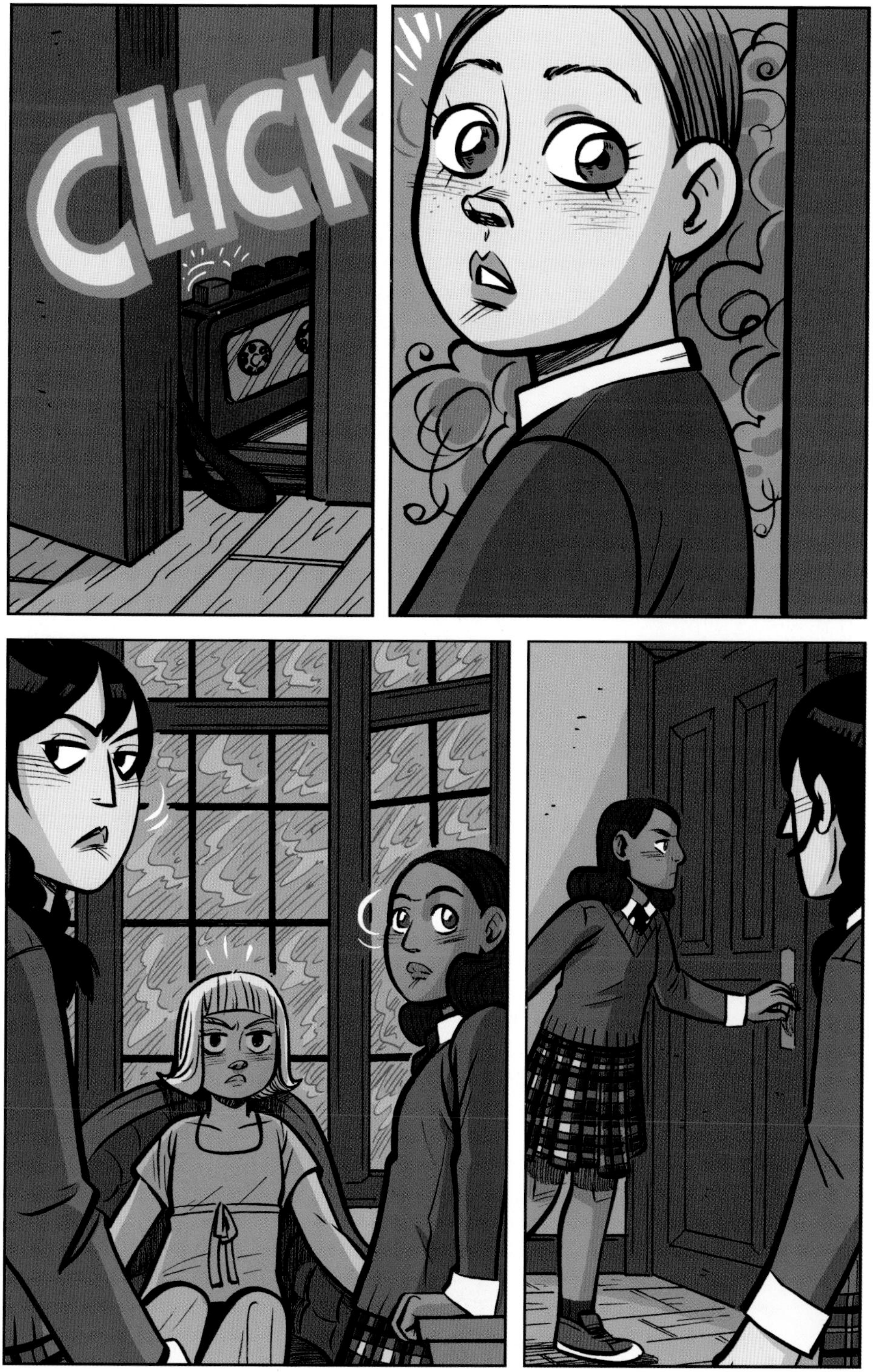
CLICK

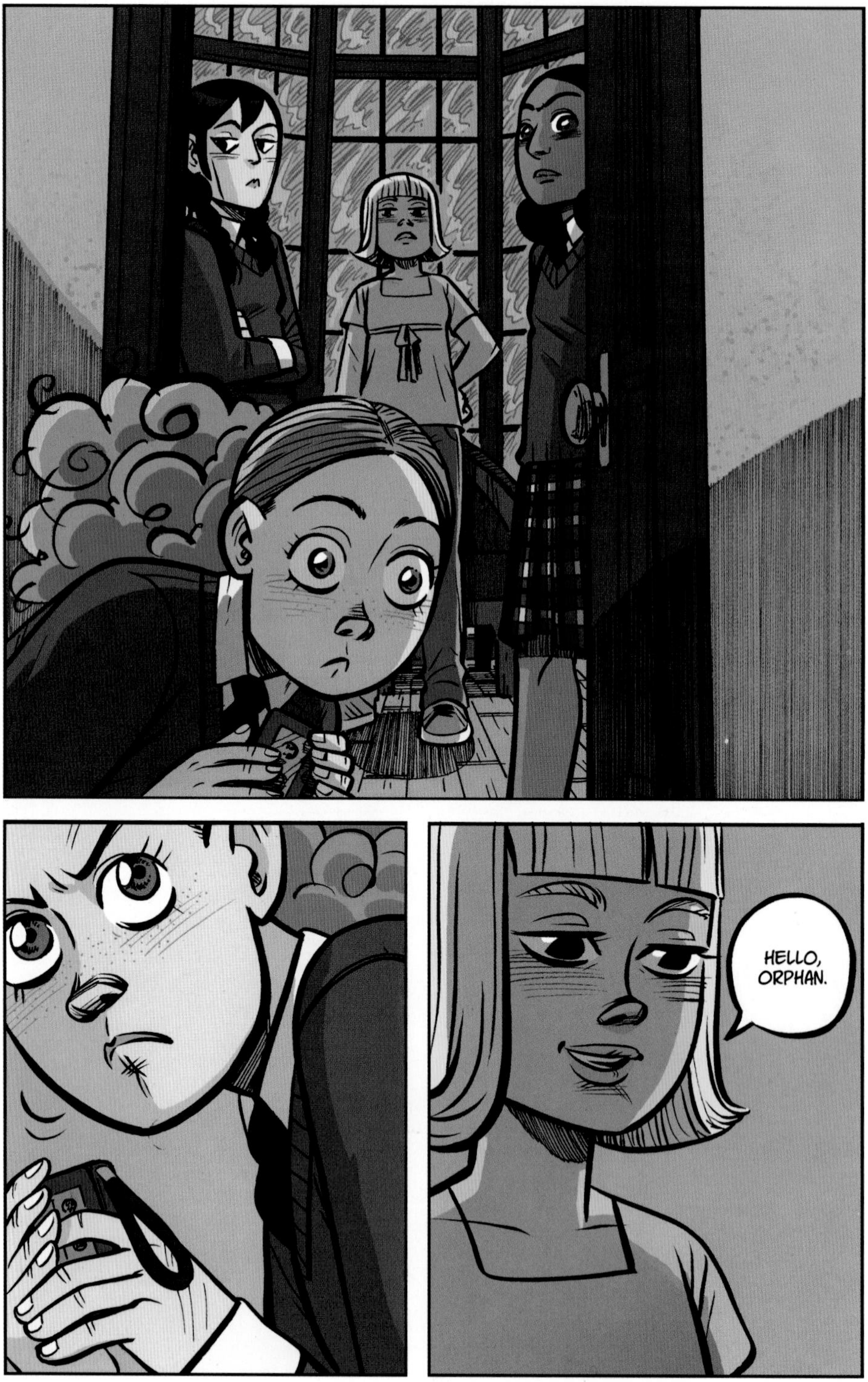
HELLO, ORPHAN.

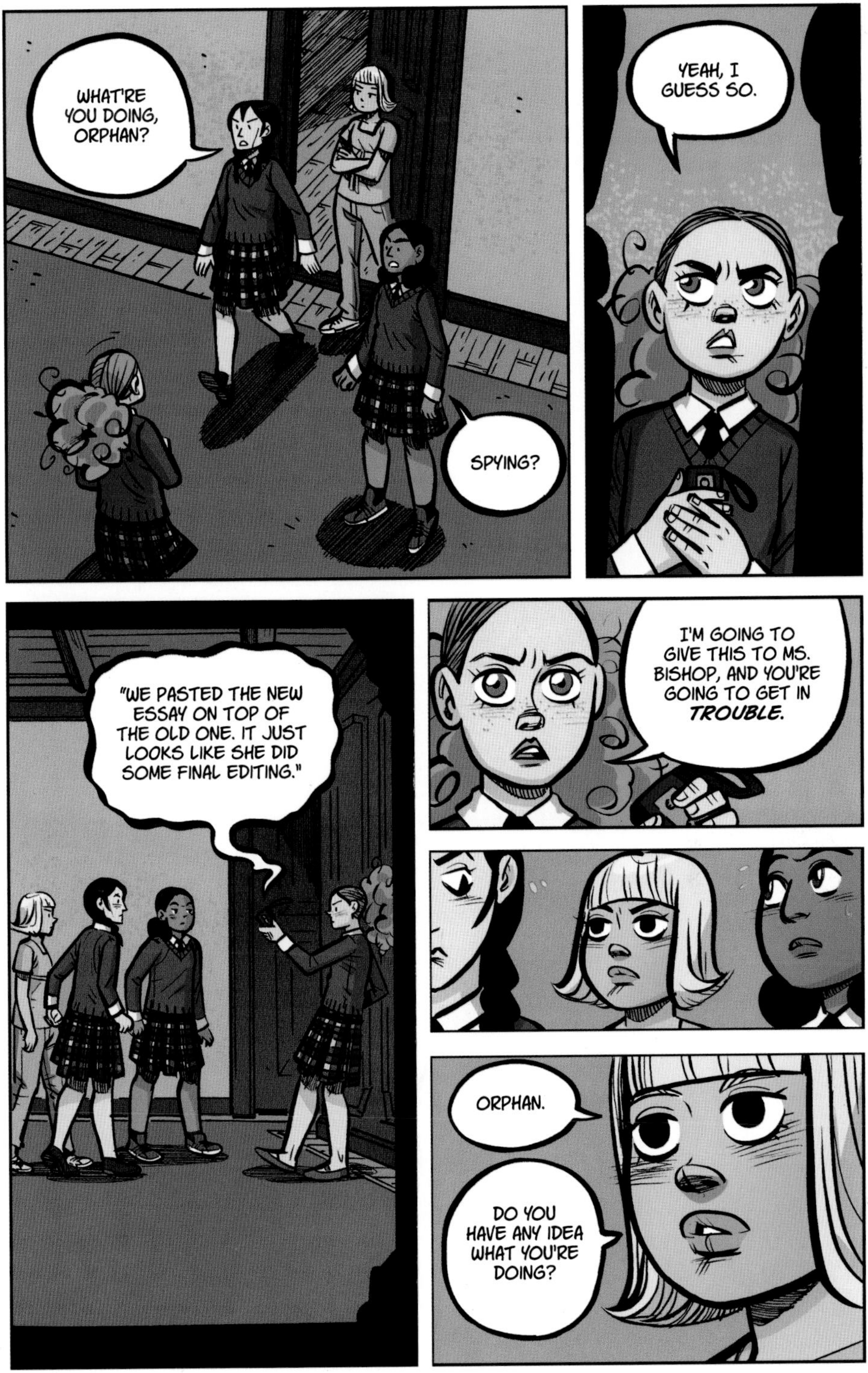
WHAT'RE YOU DOING, ORPHAN?
SPYING?
YEAH, I GUESS SO.
"WE PASTED THE NEW ESSAY ON TOP OF THE OLD ONE. IT JUST LOOKS LIKE SHE DID SOME FINAL EDITING."
I'M GOING TO GIVE THIS TO MS. BISHOP, AND YOU'RE GOING TO GET IN *TROUBLE*.
ORPHAN.
DO YOU HAVE ANY IDEA WHAT YOU'RE DOING?

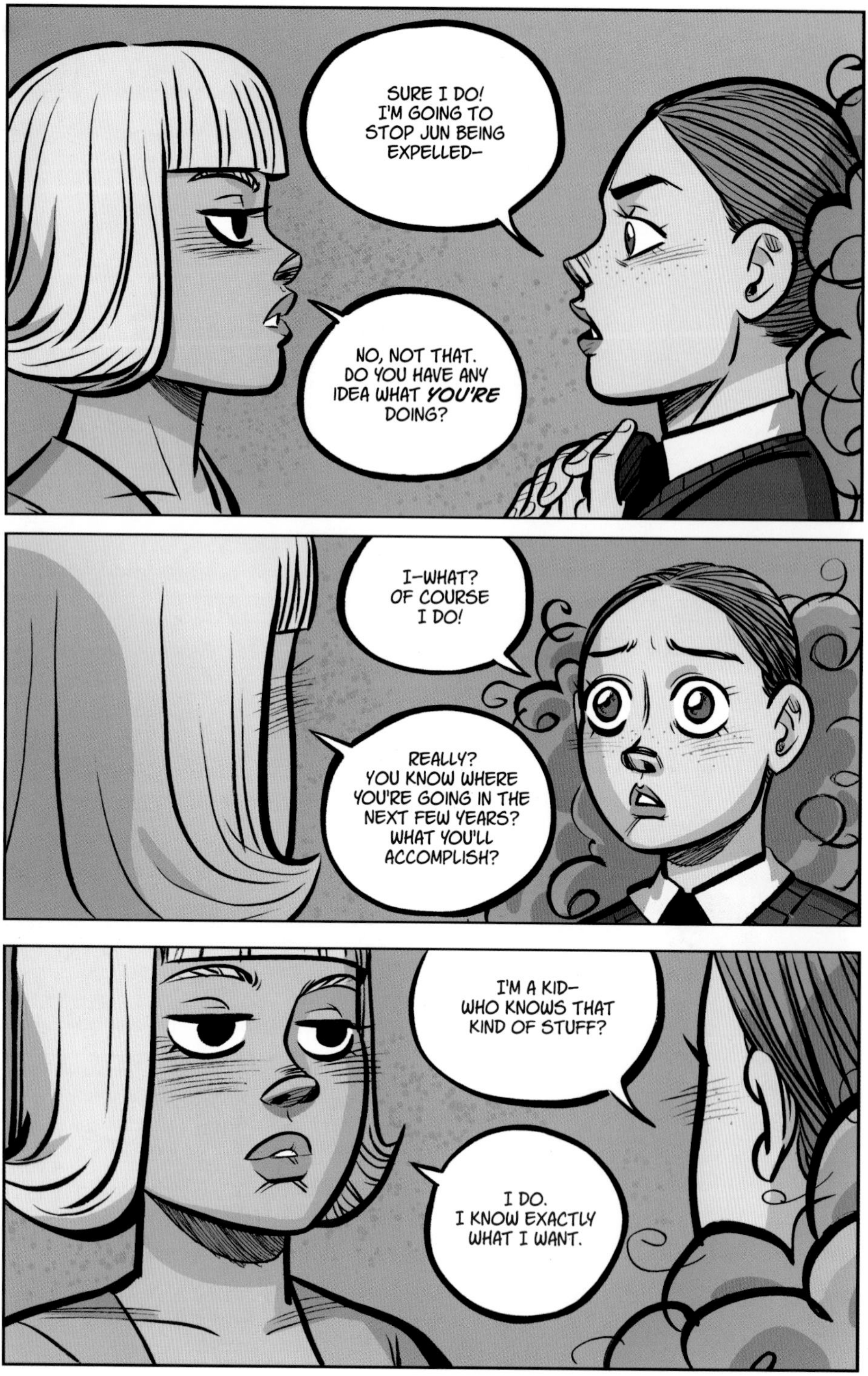
SURE I DO! I'M GOING TO STOP JUN BEING EXPELLED–
NO, NOT THAT. DO YOU HAVE ANY IDEA WHAT *YOU'RE* DOING?
I–WHAT? OF COURSE I DO!
REALLY? YOU KNOW WHERE YOU'RE GOING IN THE NEXT FEW YEARS? WHAT YOU'LL ACCOMPLISH?
I'M A KID– WHO KNOWS THAT KIND OF STUFF?
I DO. I KNOW EXACTLY WHAT I WANT.

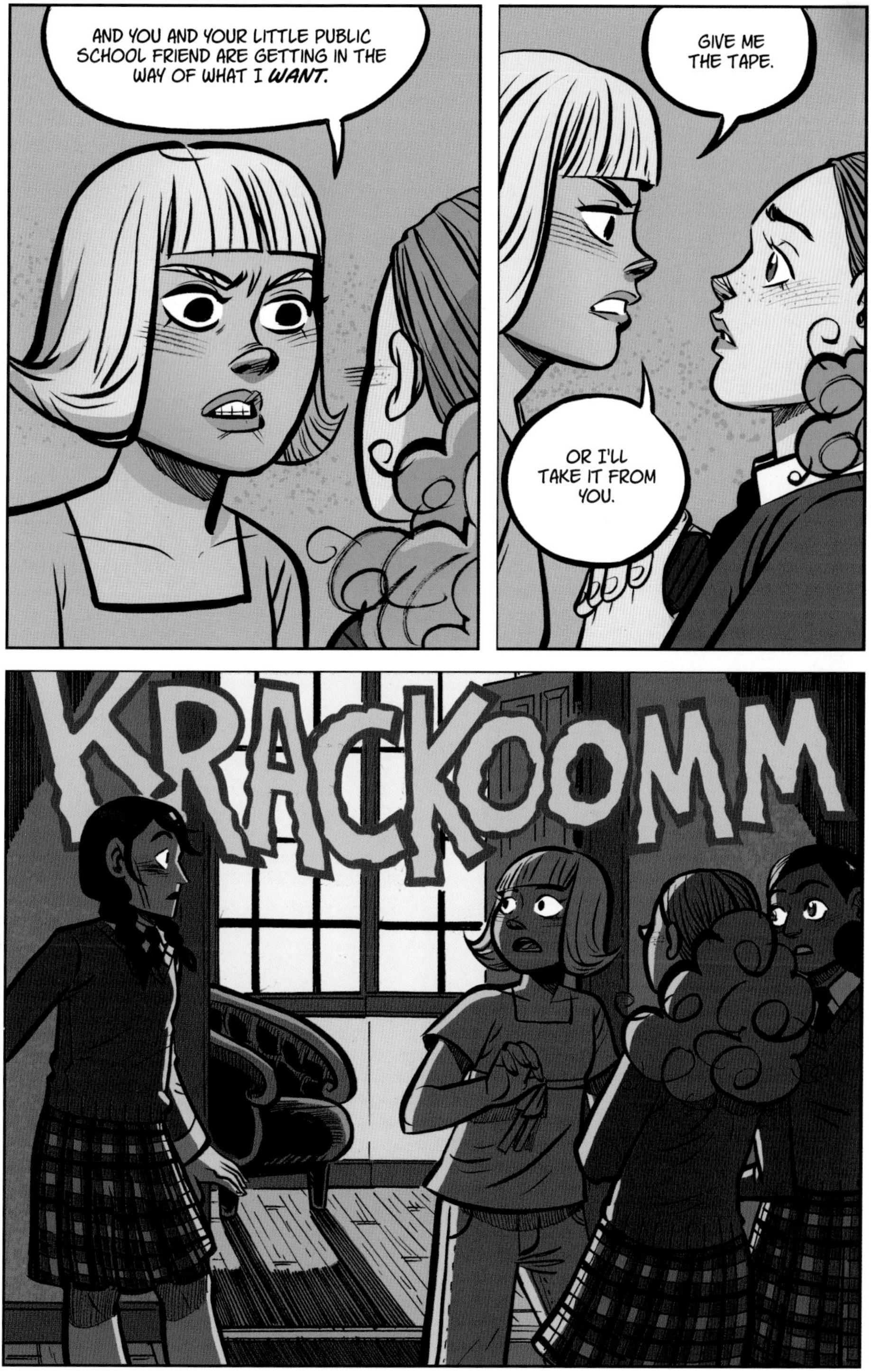

AND YOU AND YOUR LITTLE PUBLIC SCHOOL FRIEND ARE GETTING IN THE WAY OF WHAT I *WANT*.
GIVE ME THE TAPE.
OR I'LL TAKE IT FROM YOU.
KRACKOOMM

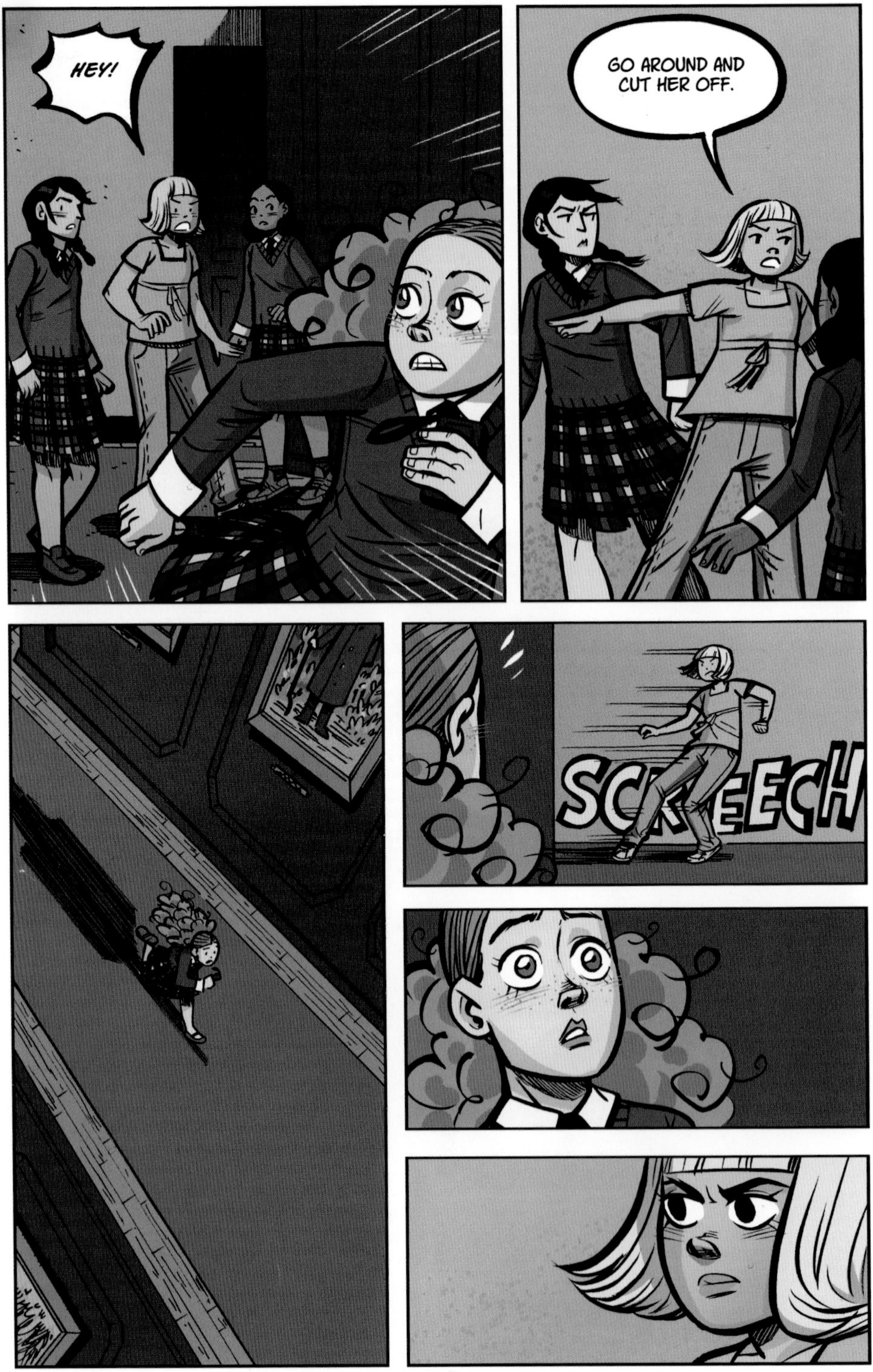
HEY!
GO AROUND AND CUT HER OFF.
SCREECH

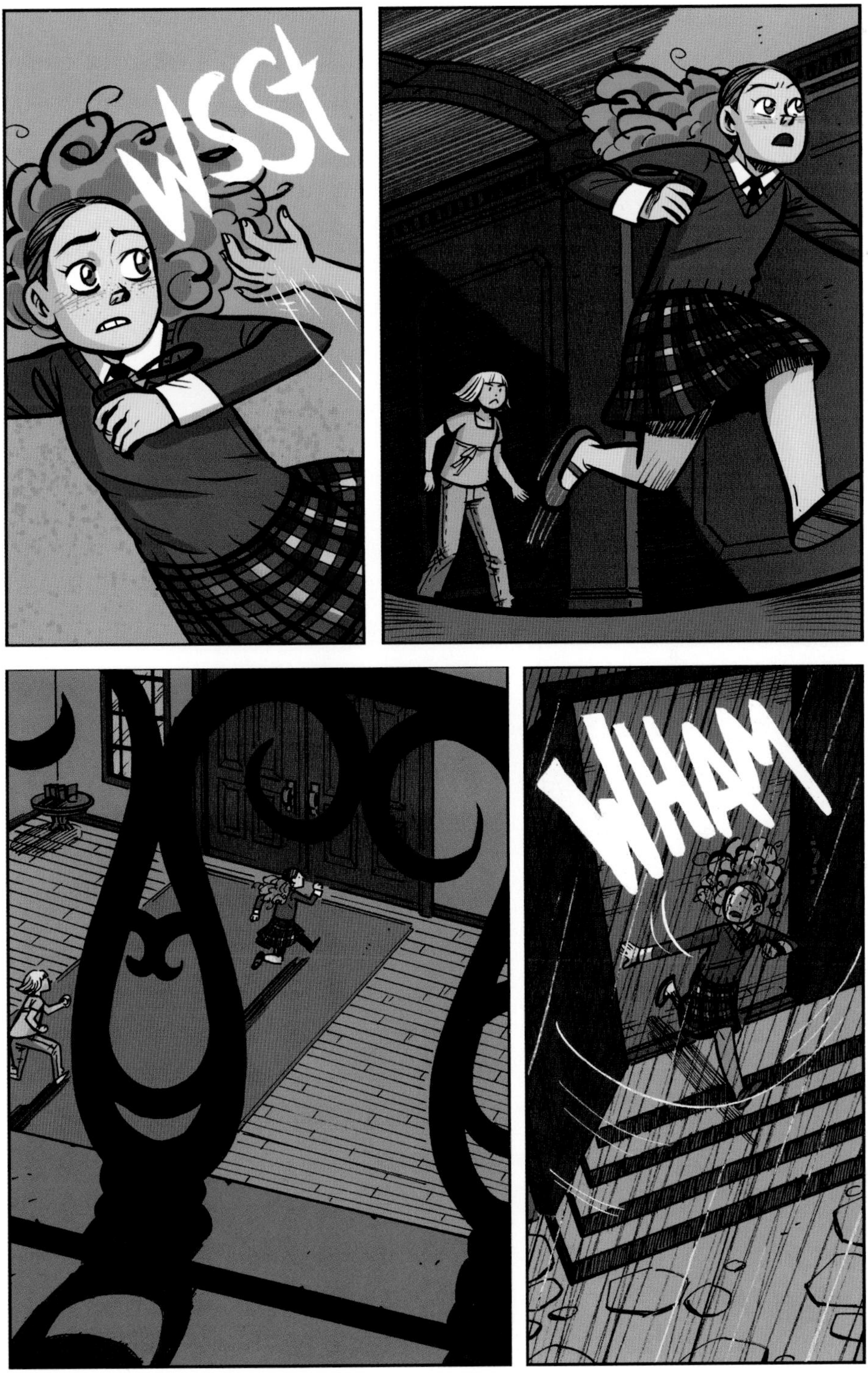
WSST
WHAM

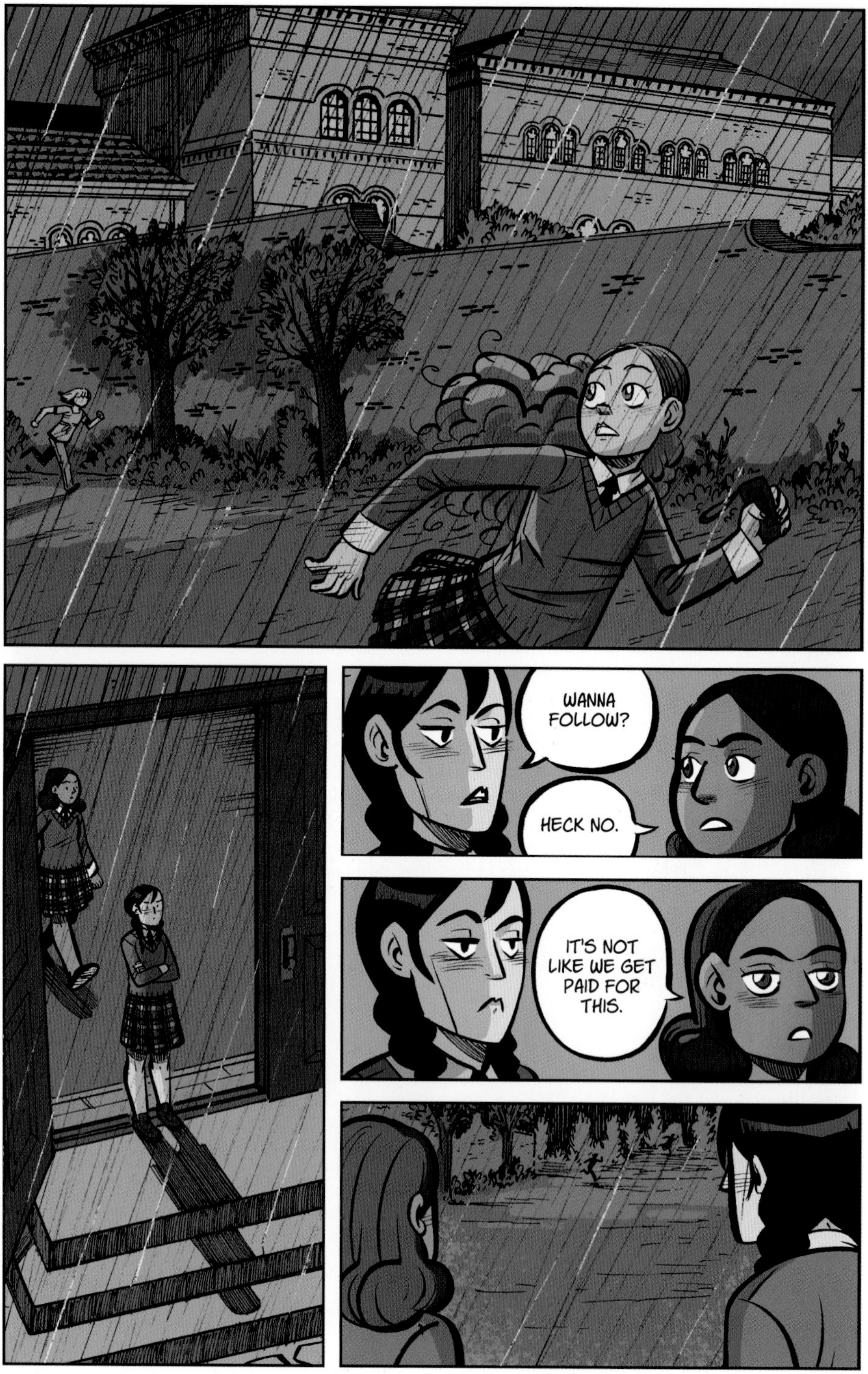
WANNA FOLLOW?
HECK NO.
IT'S NOT LIKE WE GET PAID FOR THIS.

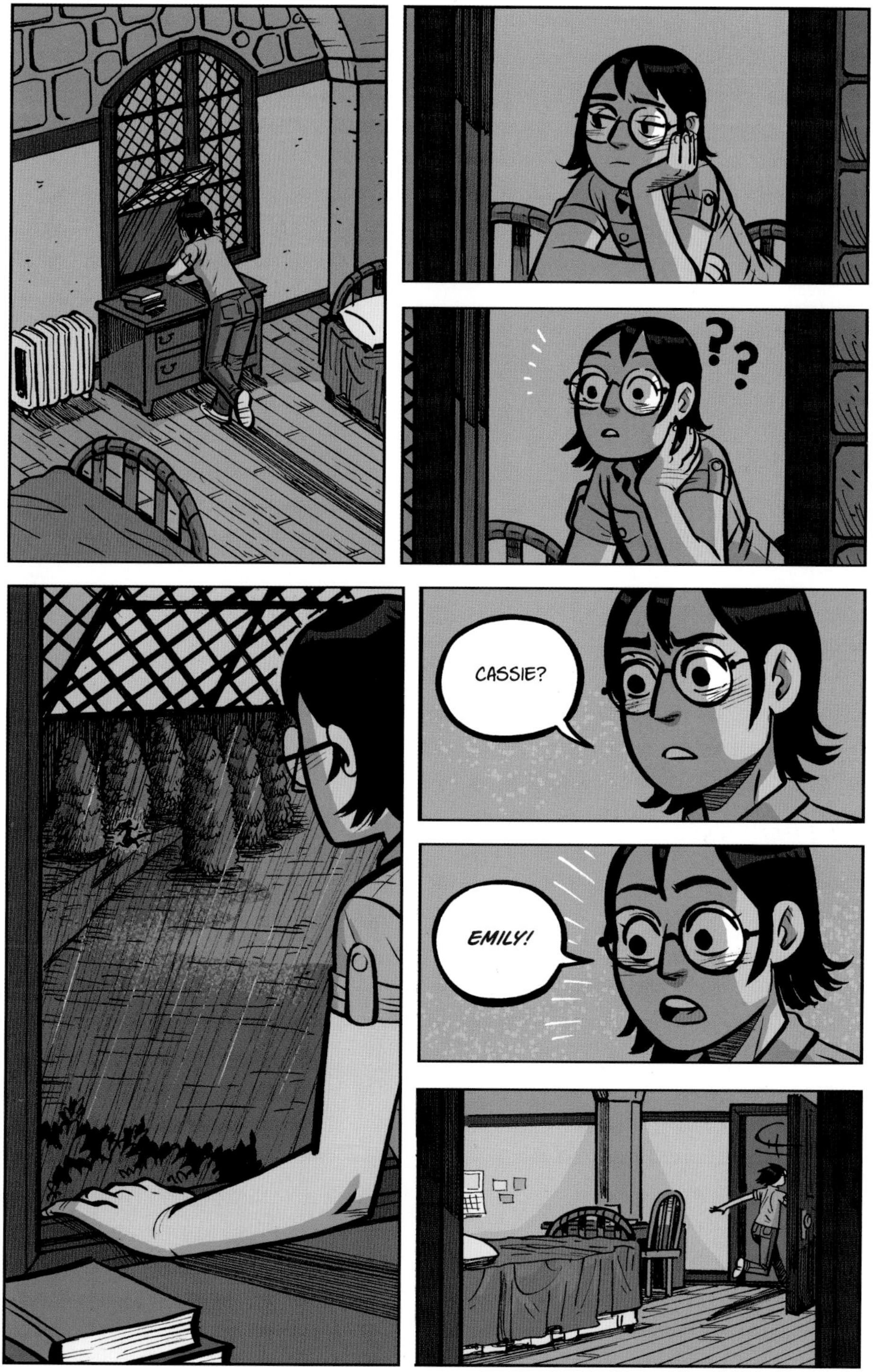
??
CASSIE?
EMILY!

Chapter Eleven

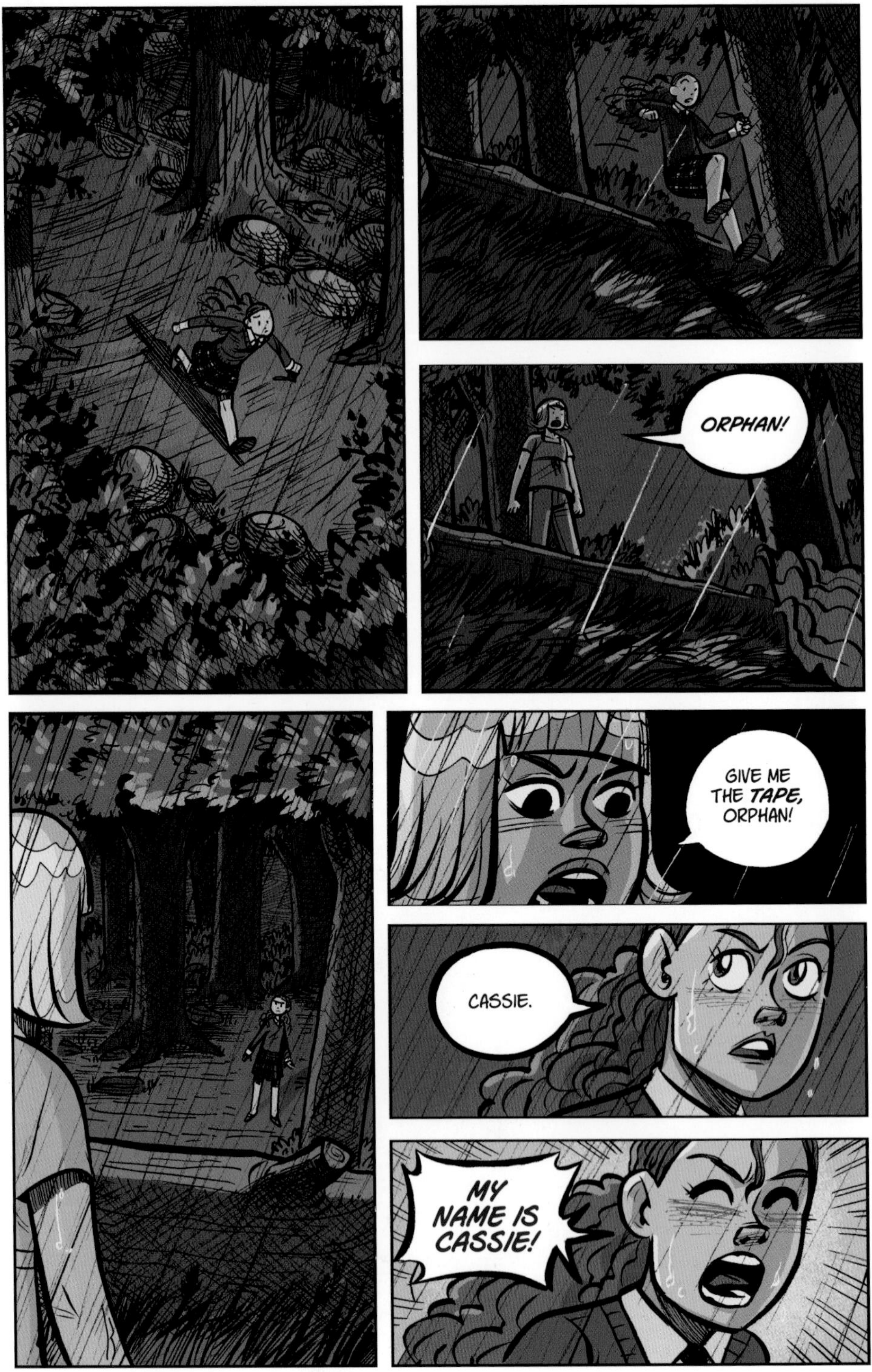
ORPHAN!
GIVE ME THE *TAPE,* ORPHAN!
CASSIE.
MY NAME IS CASSIE!

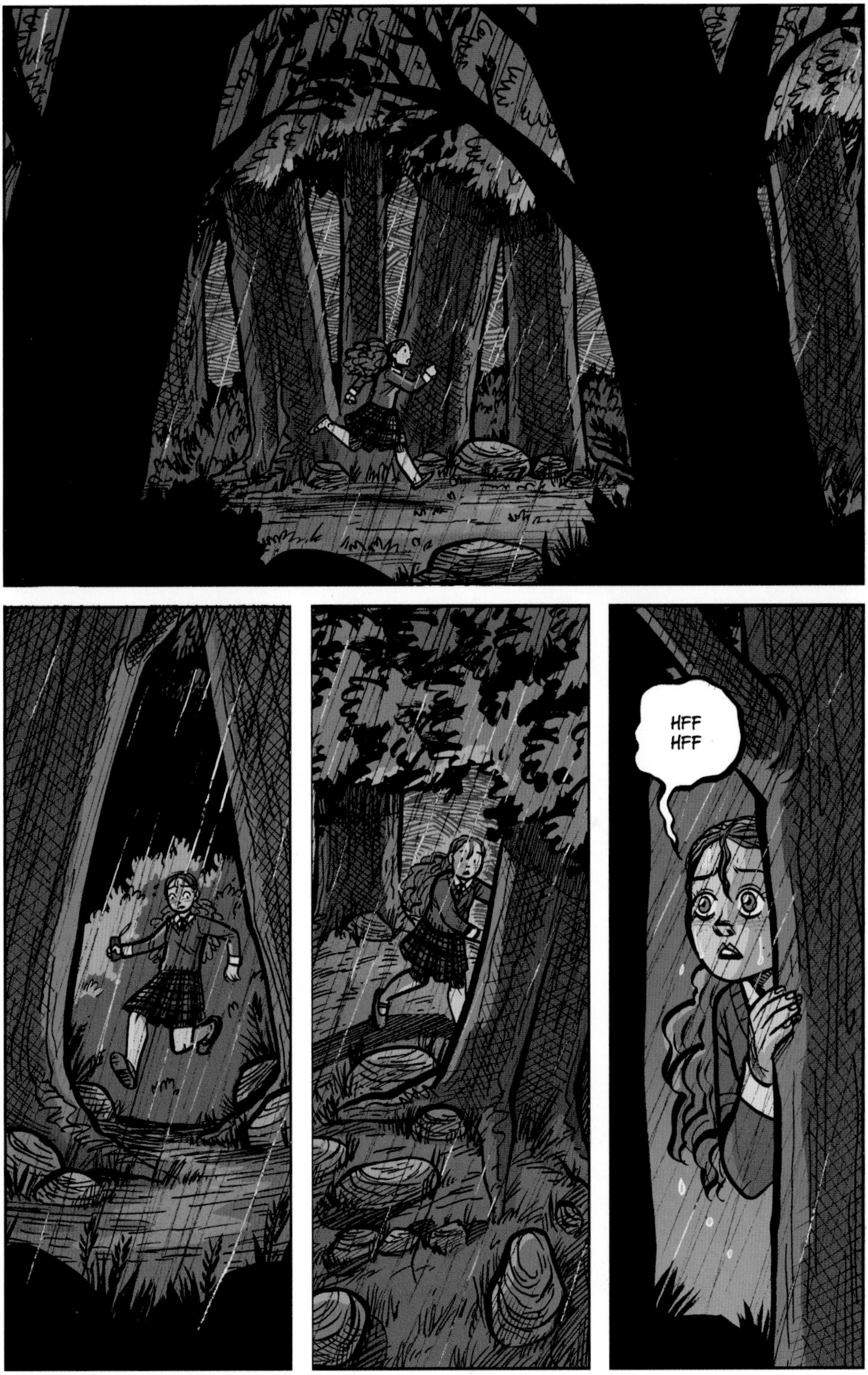
HFF
HFF

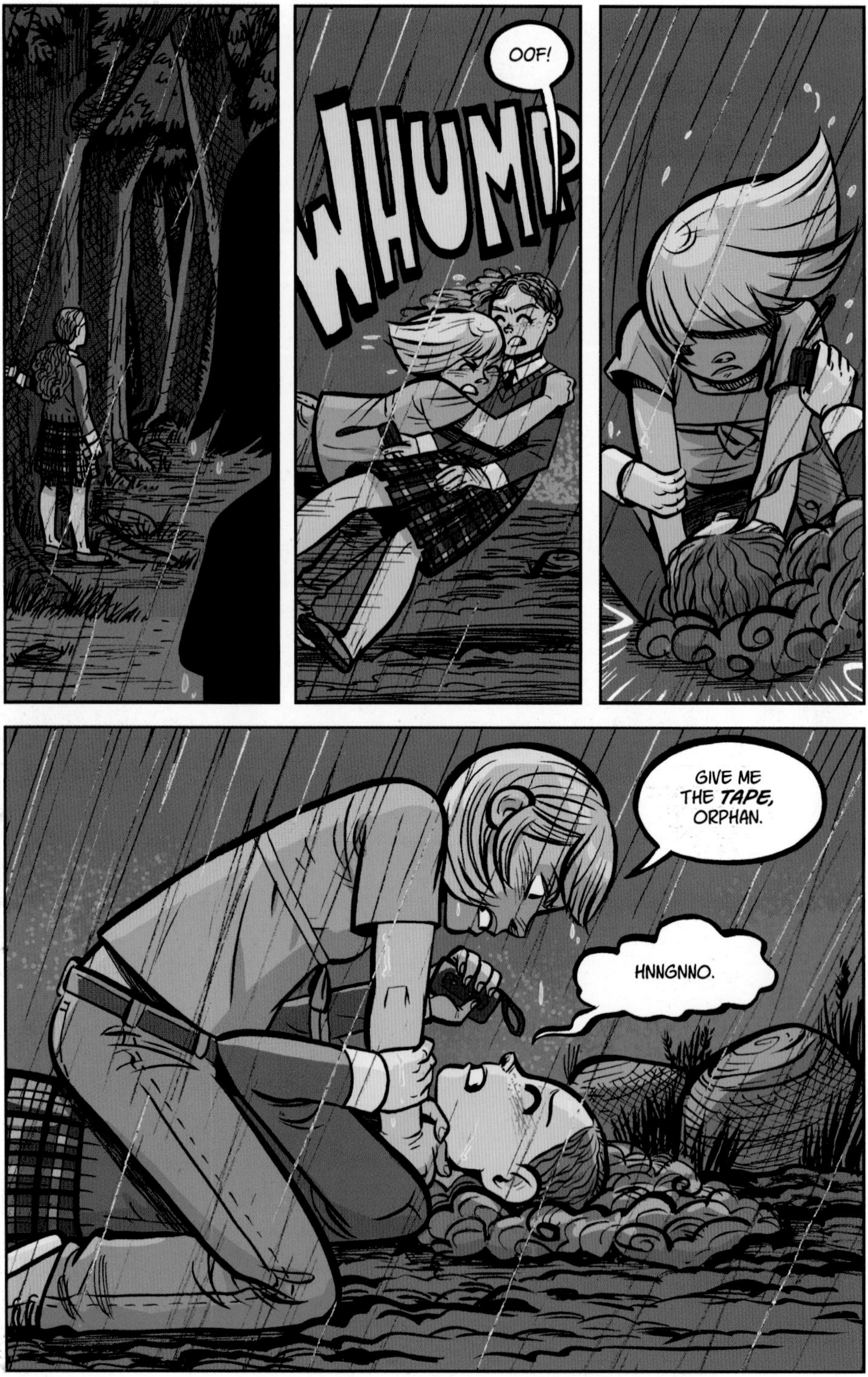
OOF!
WHUMP
GIVE ME THE *TAPE,* ORPHAN.
HNNGNNO.

EMILY!

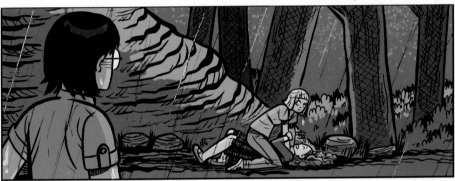

WHAT'S *WRONG* WITH YOU THAT YOU'RE LIKE THIS?

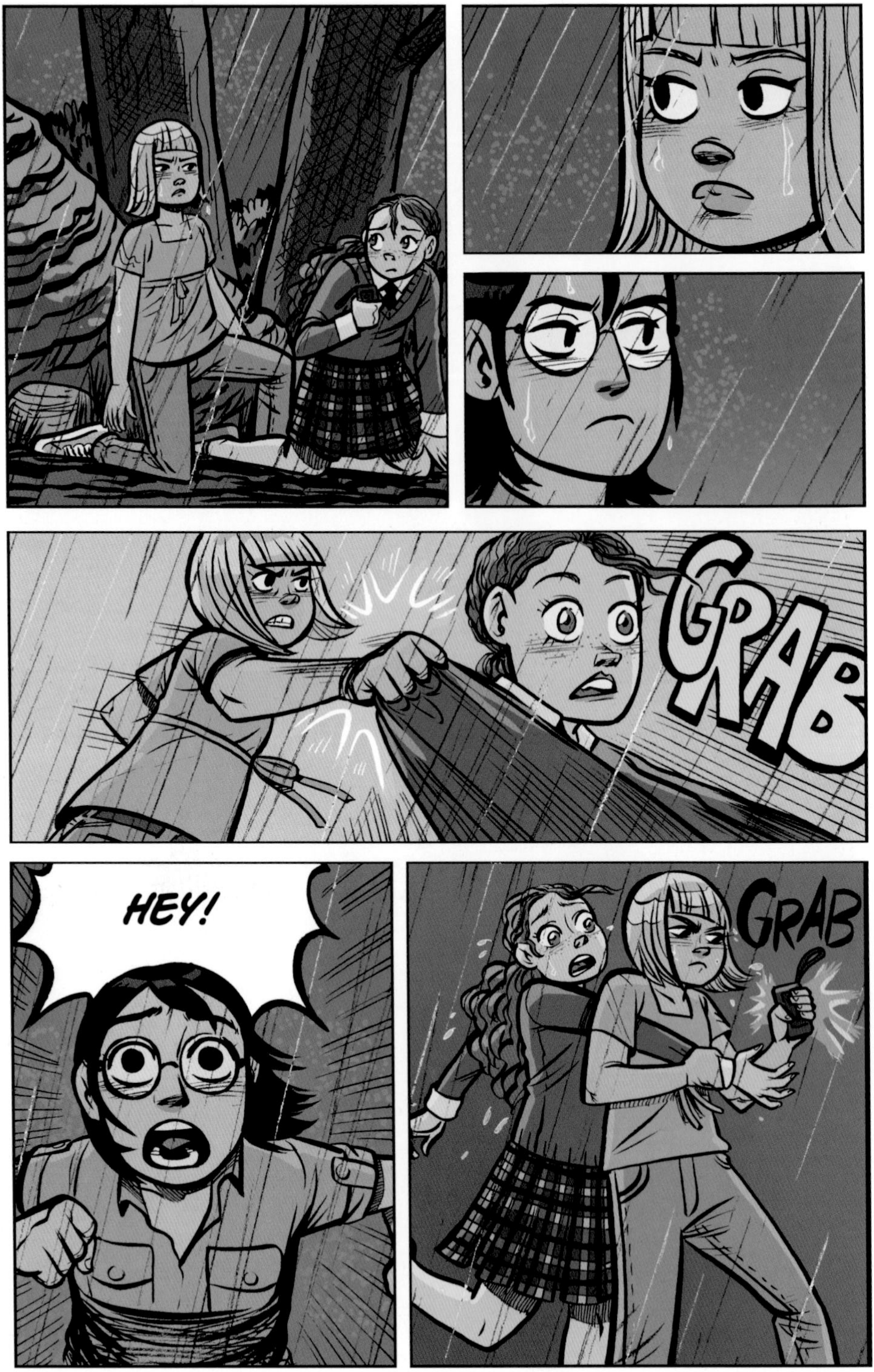
GRAB
HEY!
GRAB

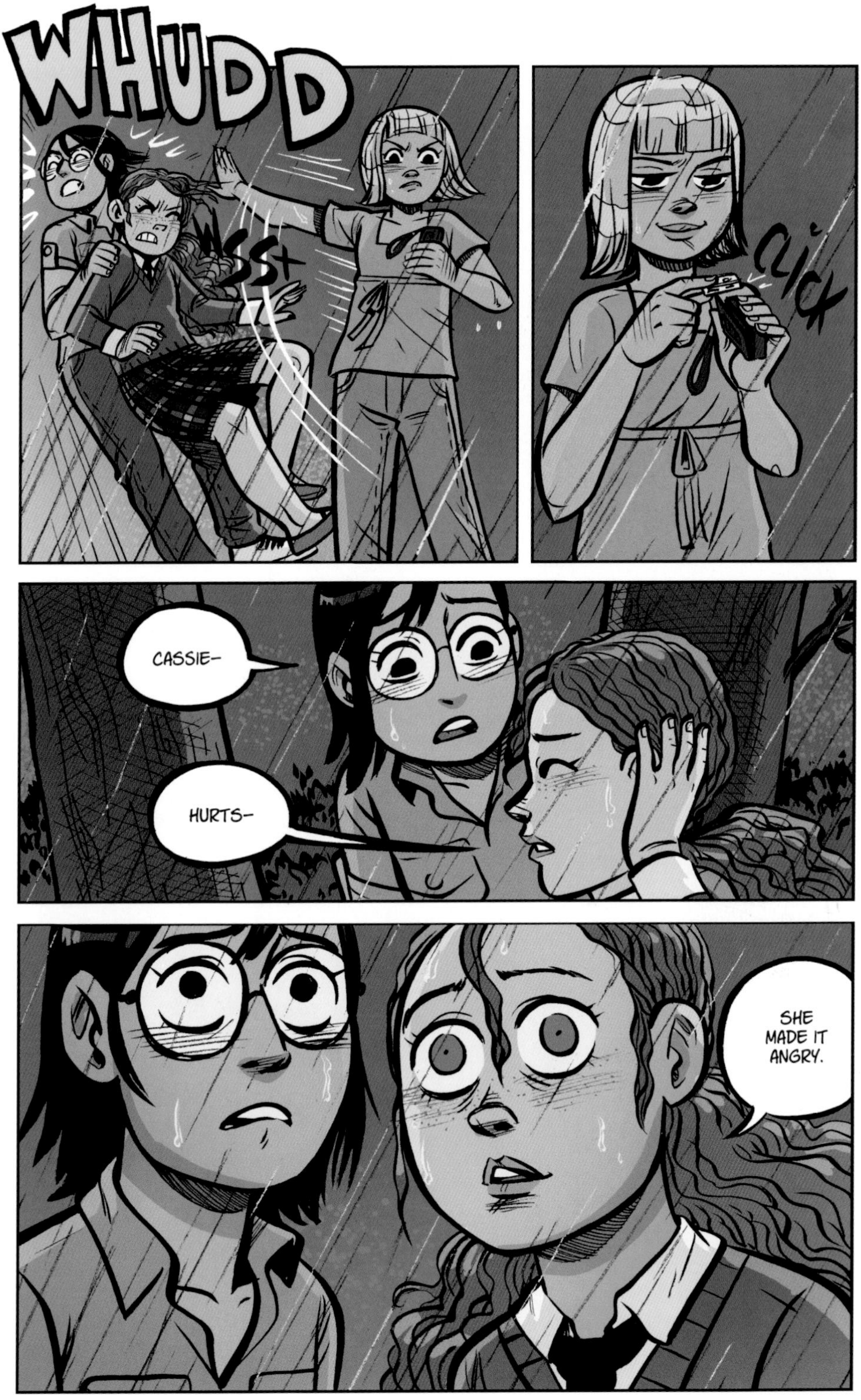
WHUDD
WSST
CLICK
CASSIE-
HURTS-
SHE MADE IT ANGRY.

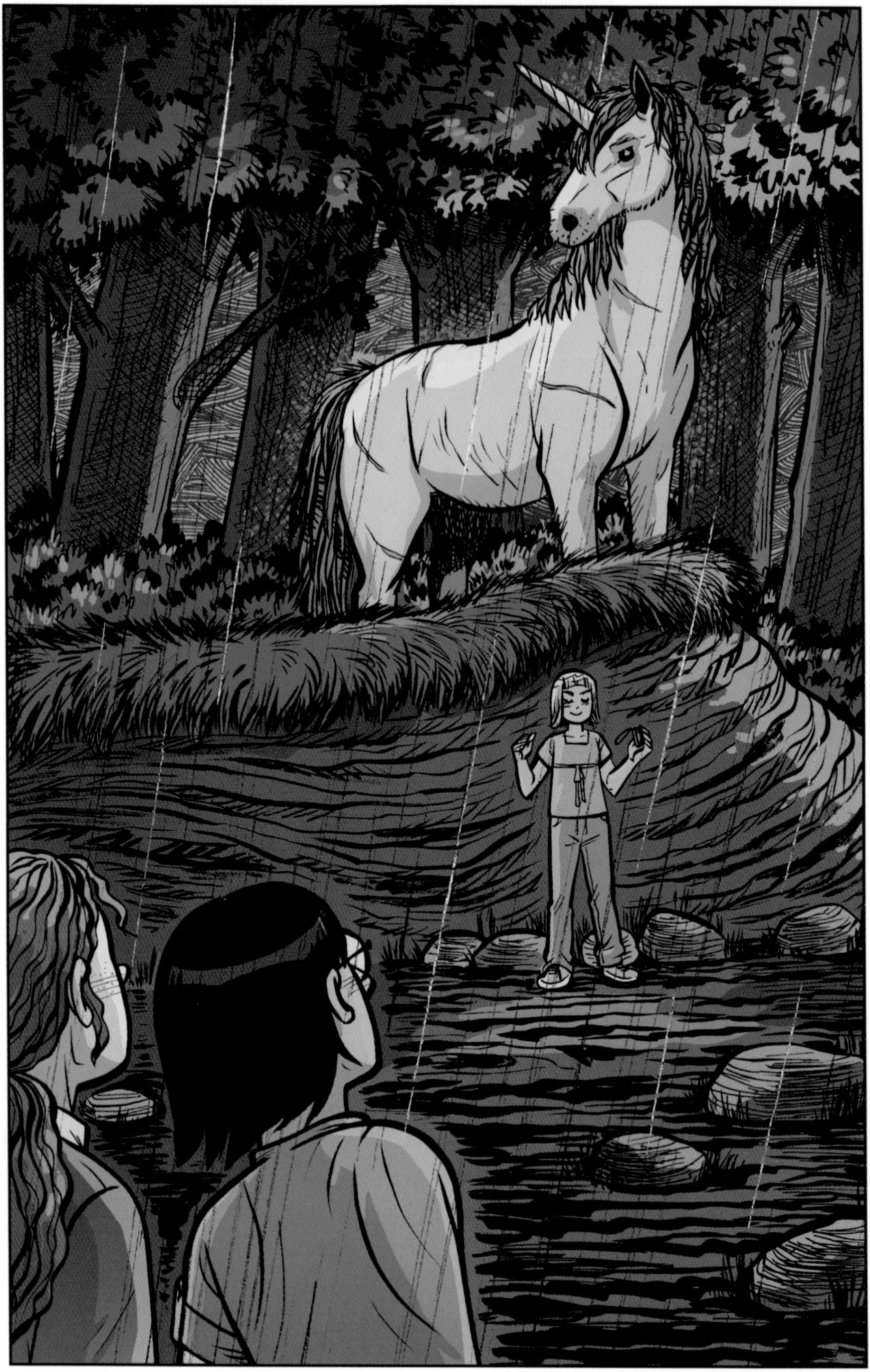

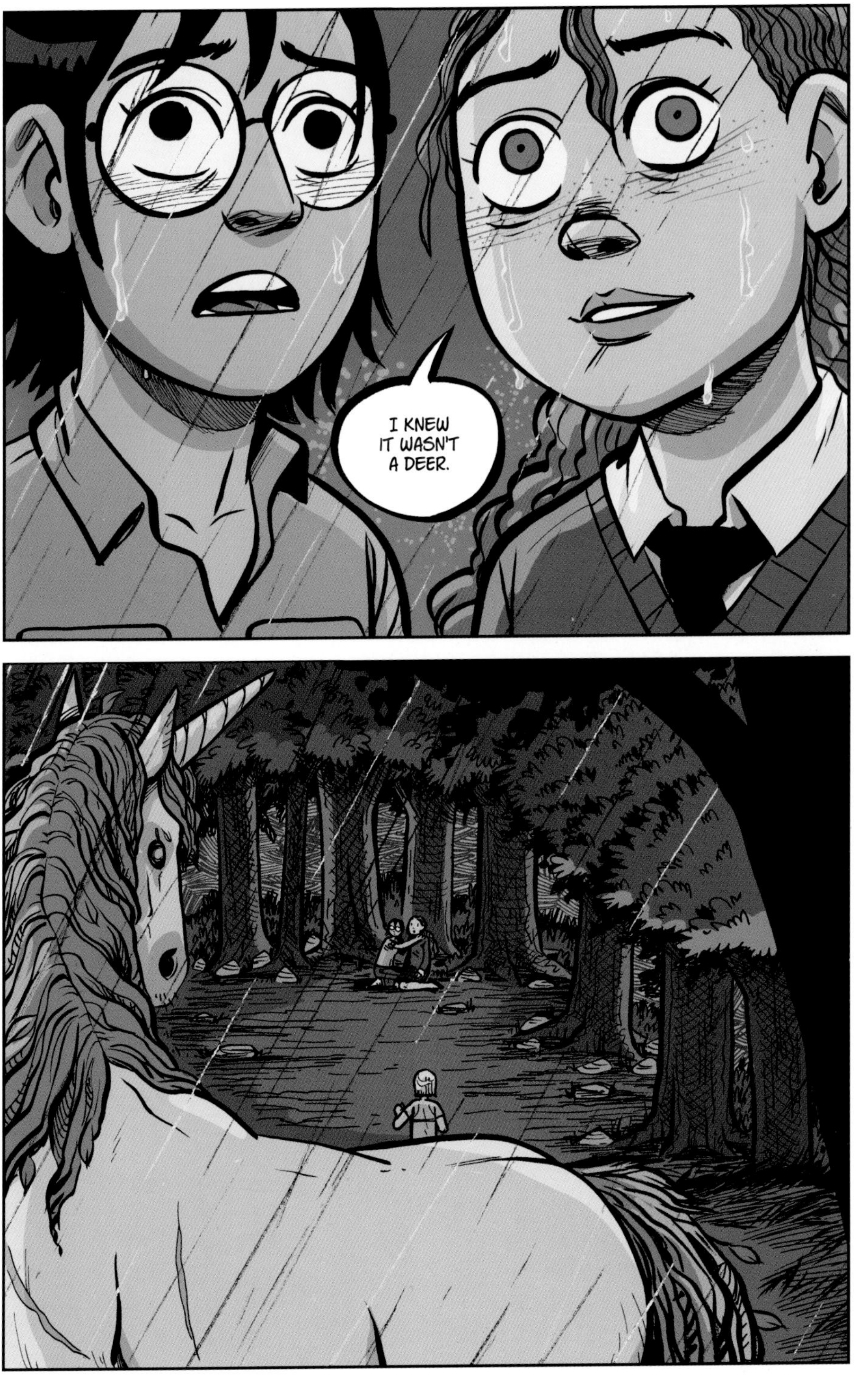
I KNEW IT WASN'T A DEER.

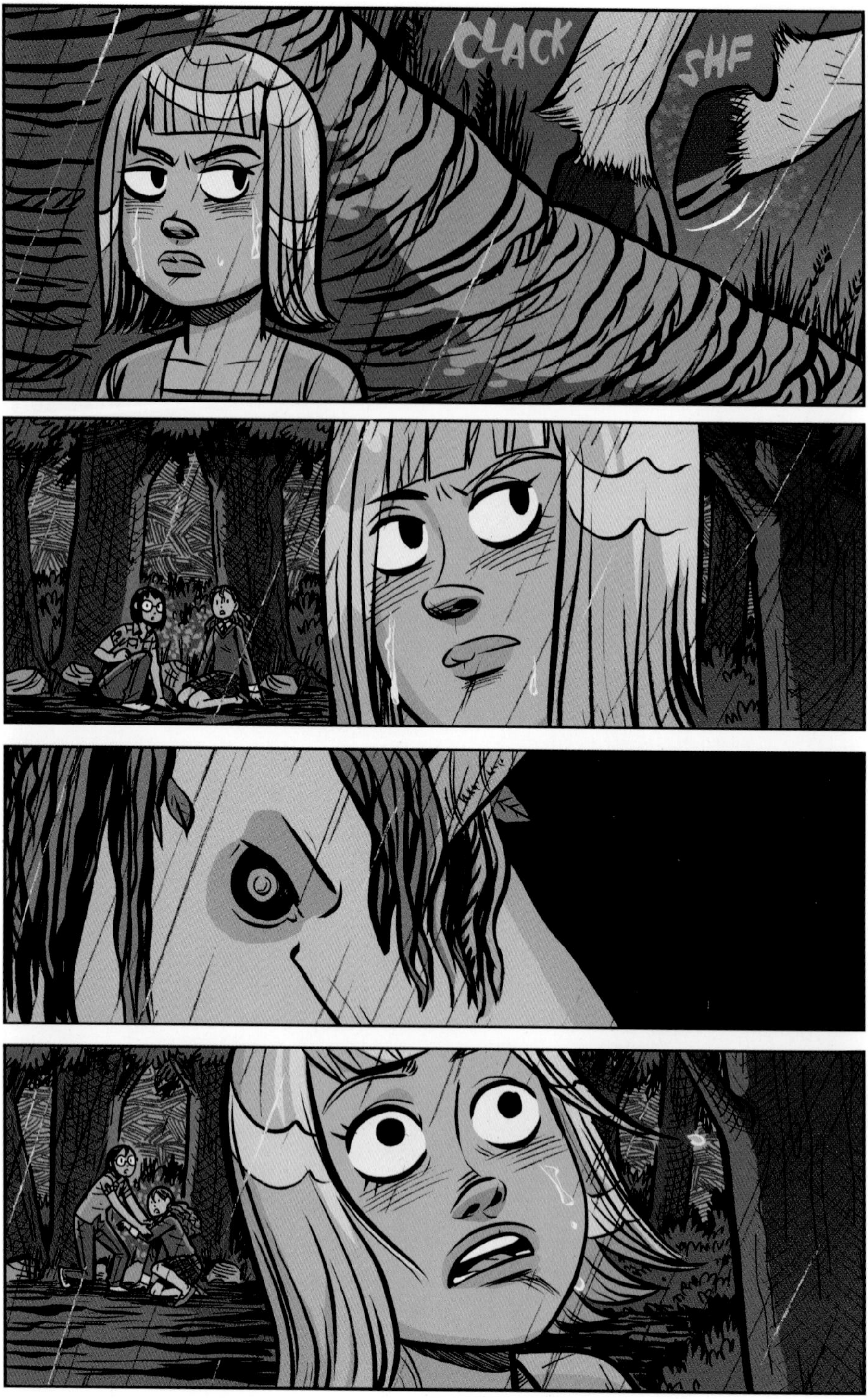
CLACK
SHF

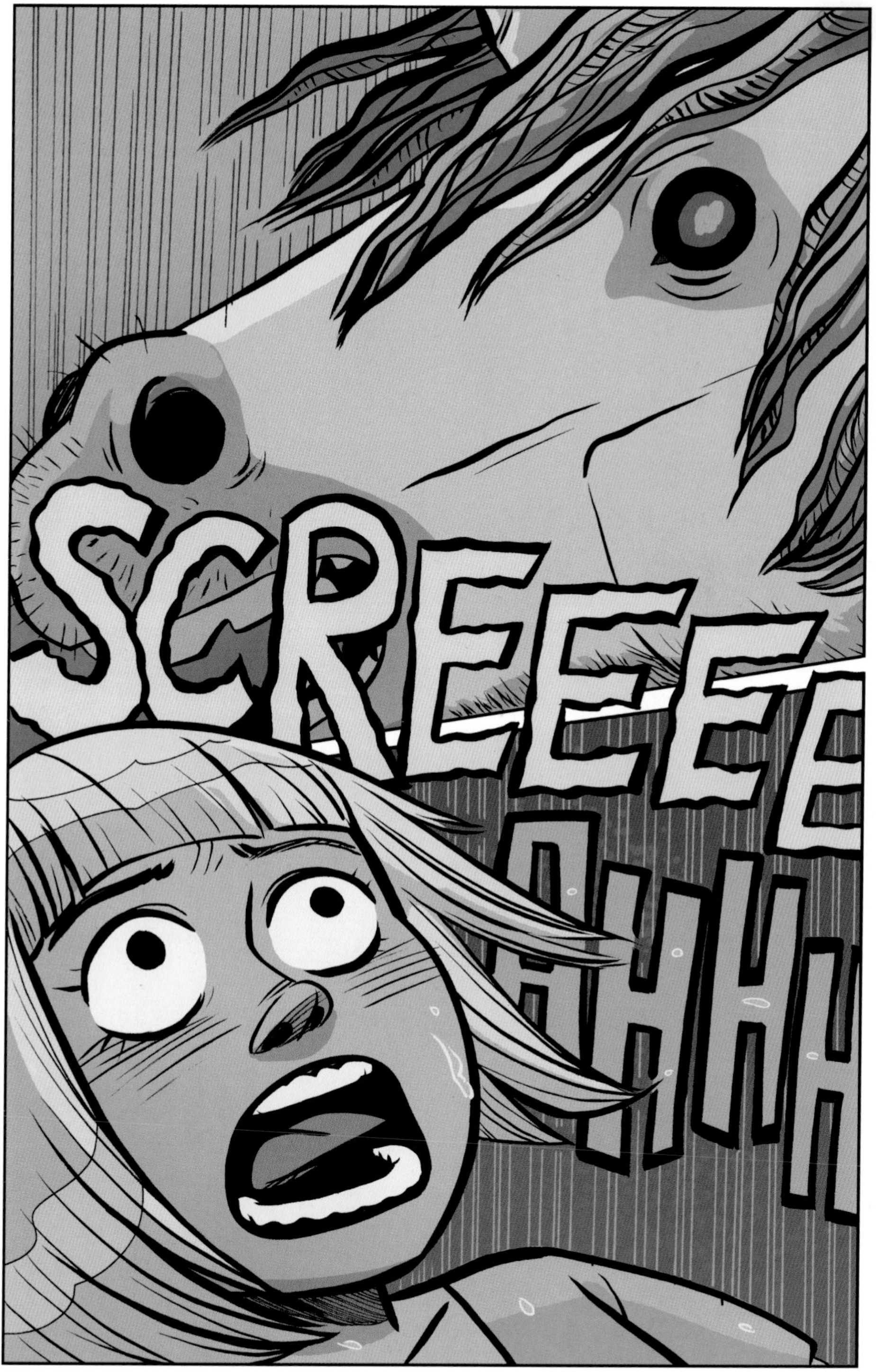
SCREEEEE
AHHH

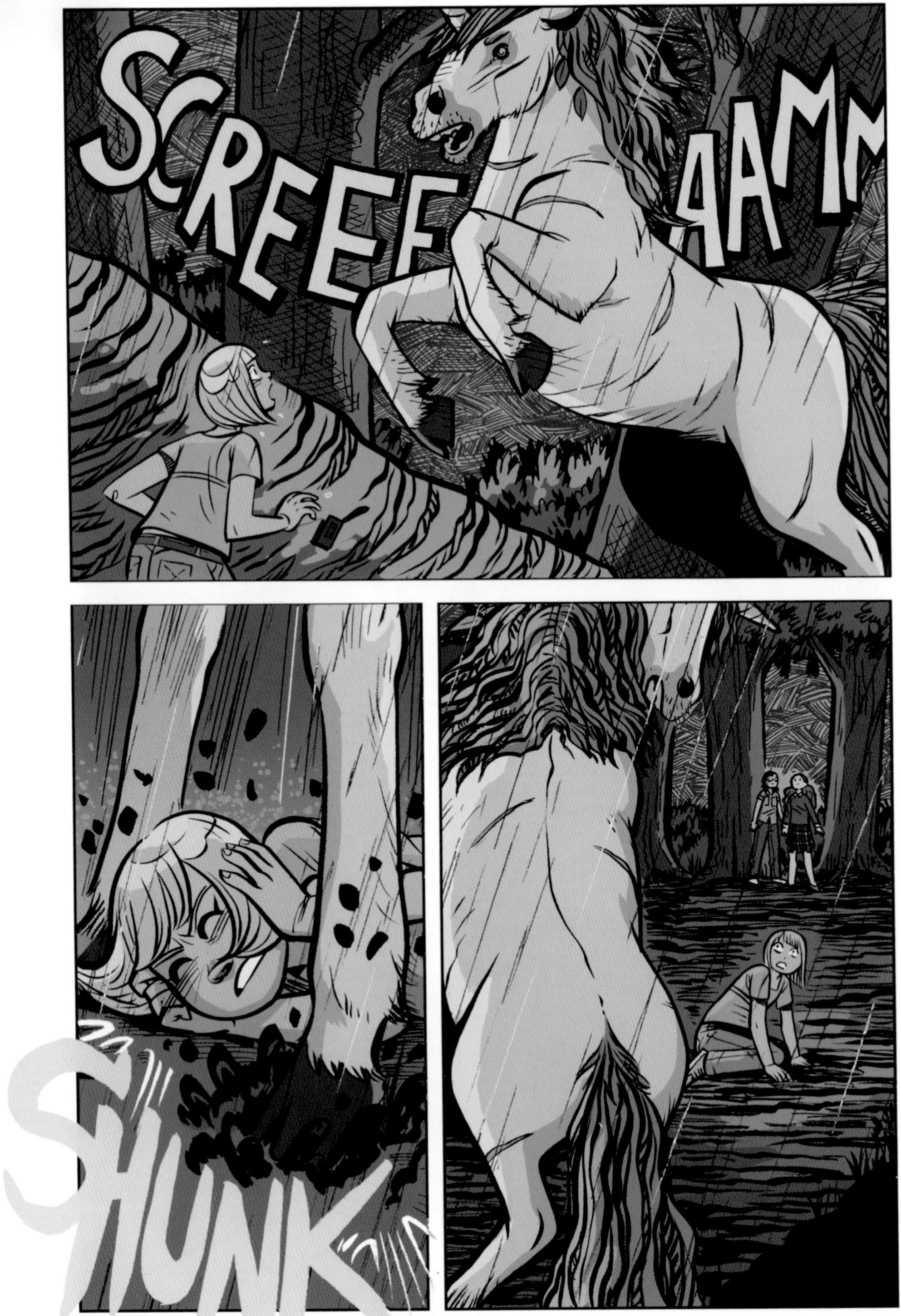
SCREEEAAMM
SHUNK

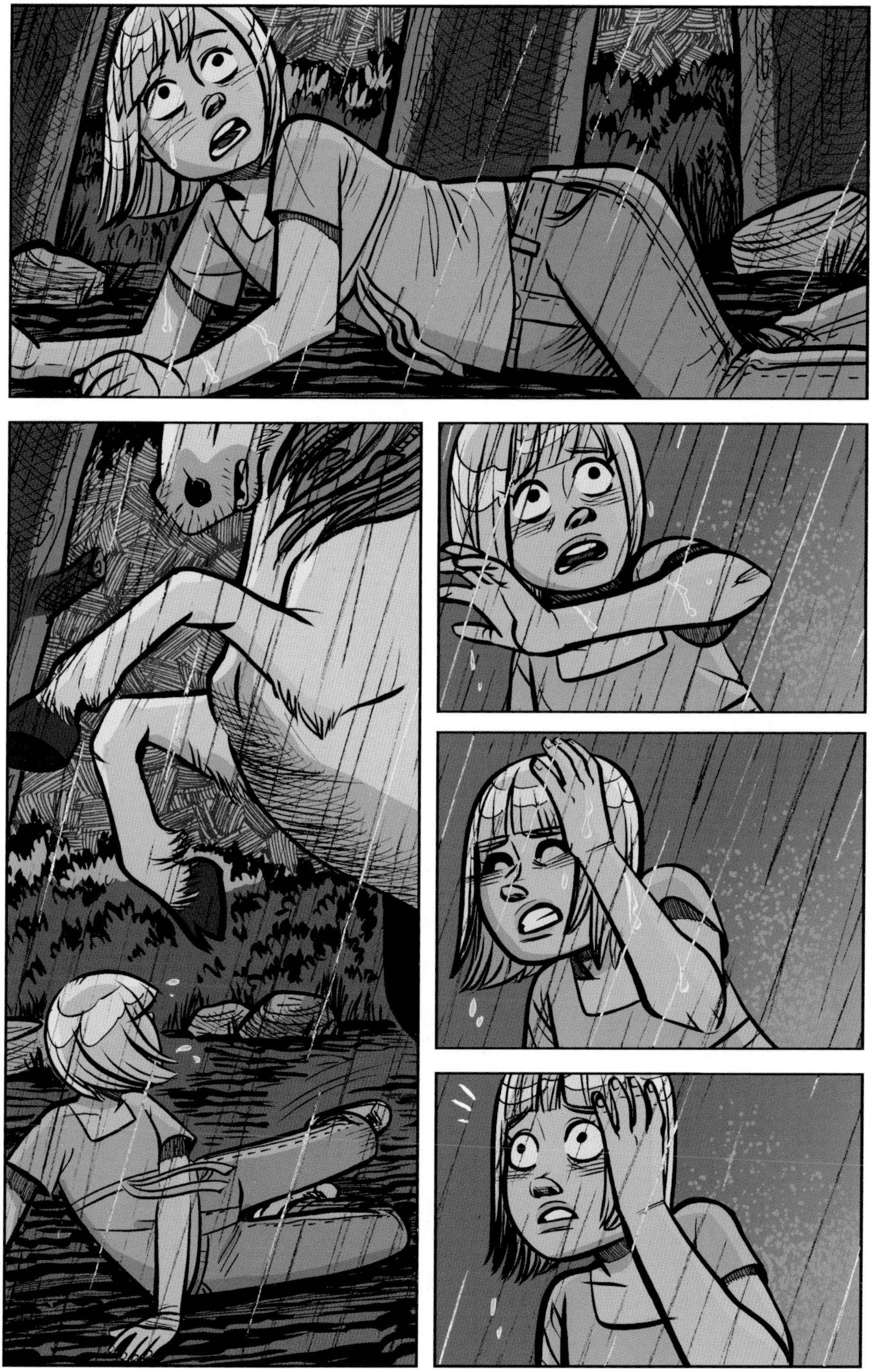

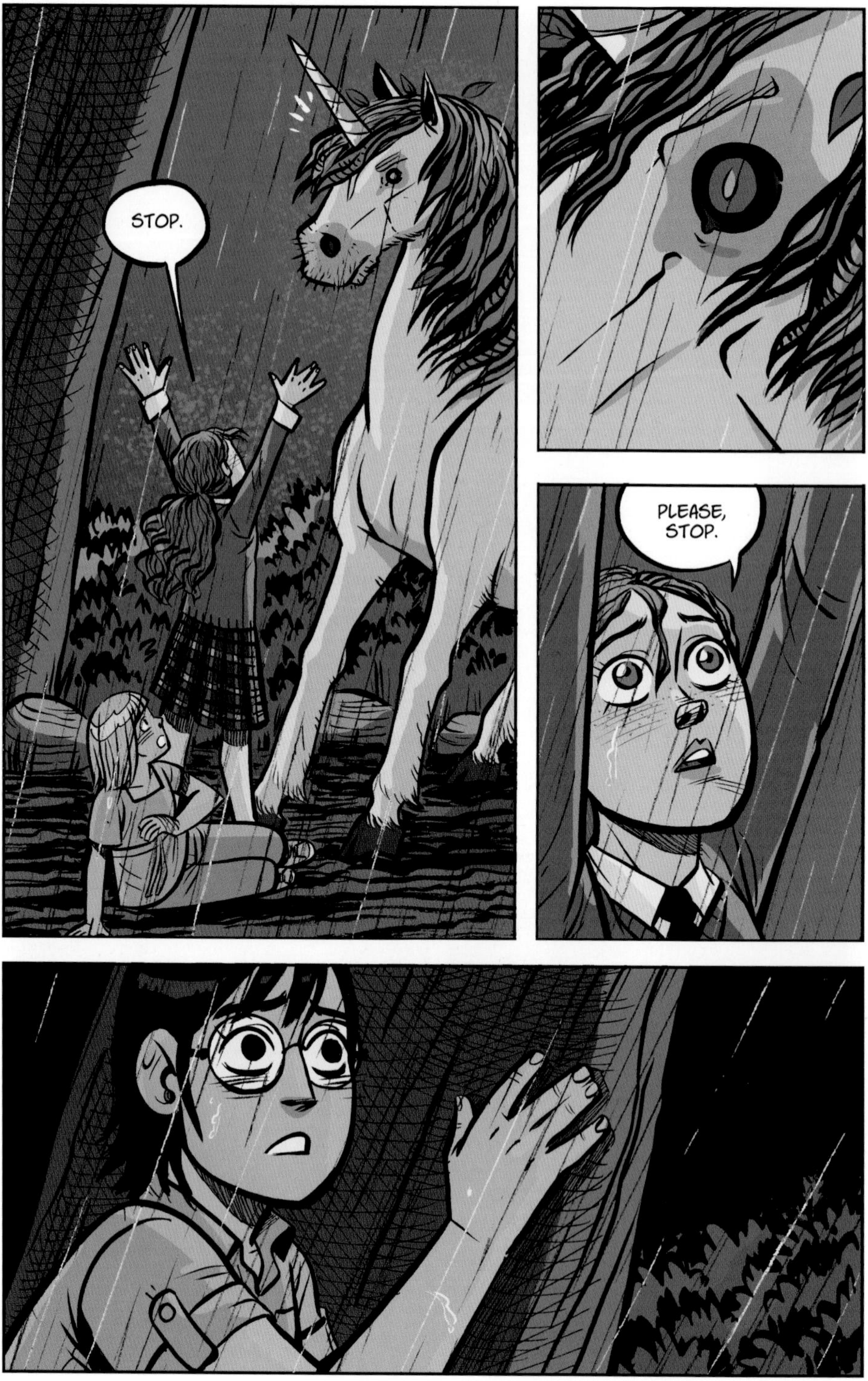
STOP.
PLEASE, STOP.

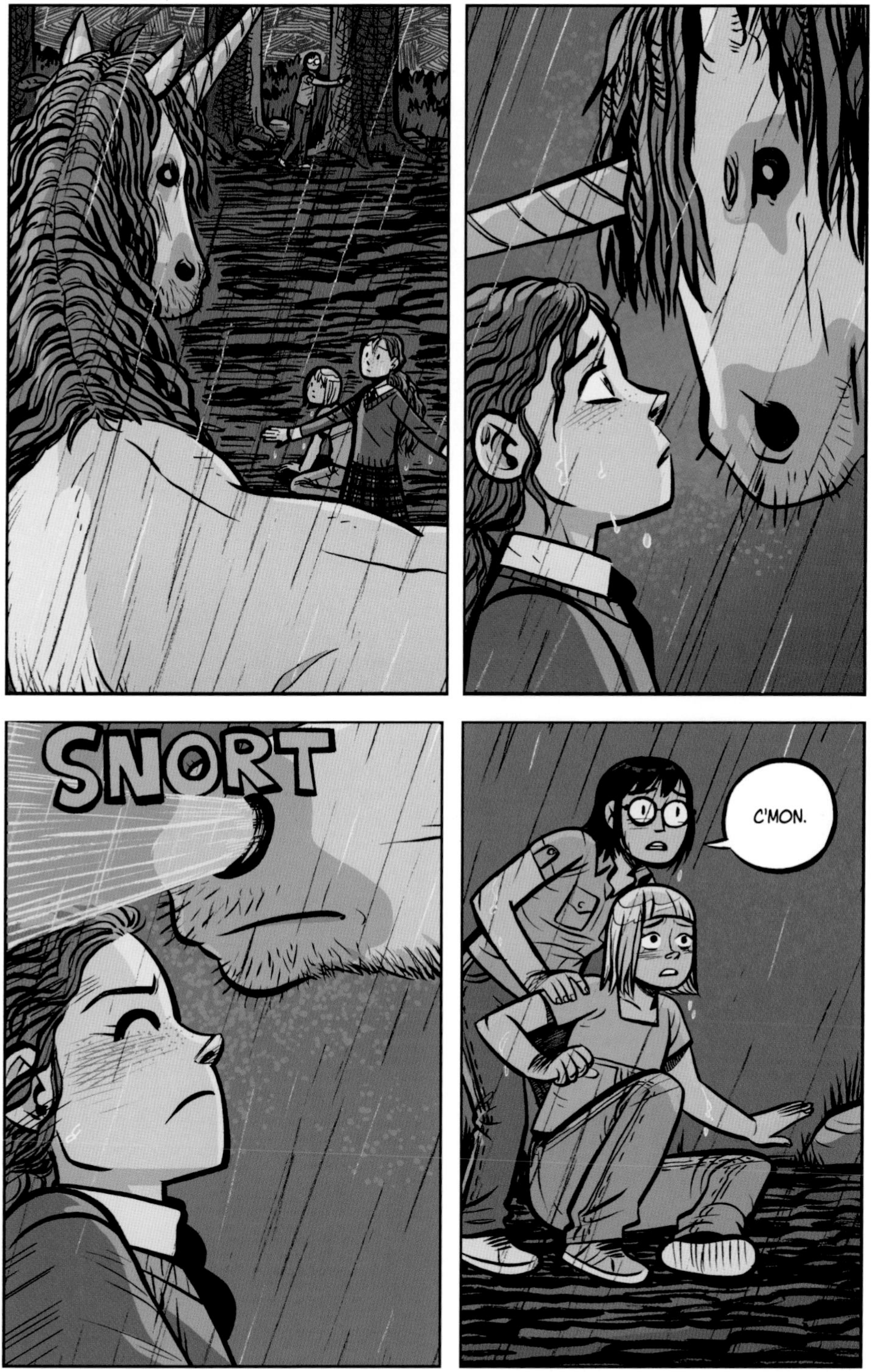
SNORT
C'MON.

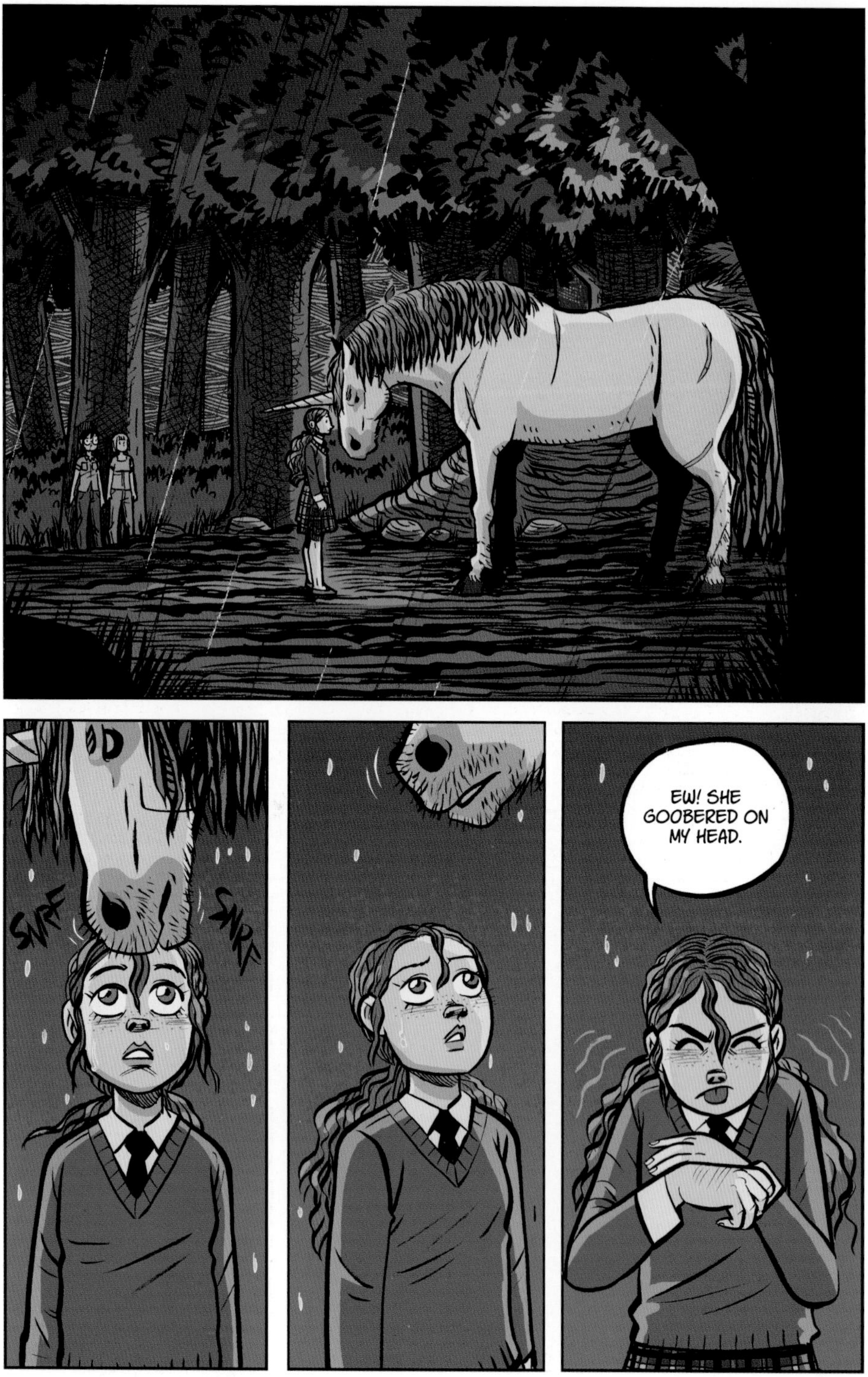
SNRF
SNRF
EW! SHE GOOBERED ON MY HEAD.

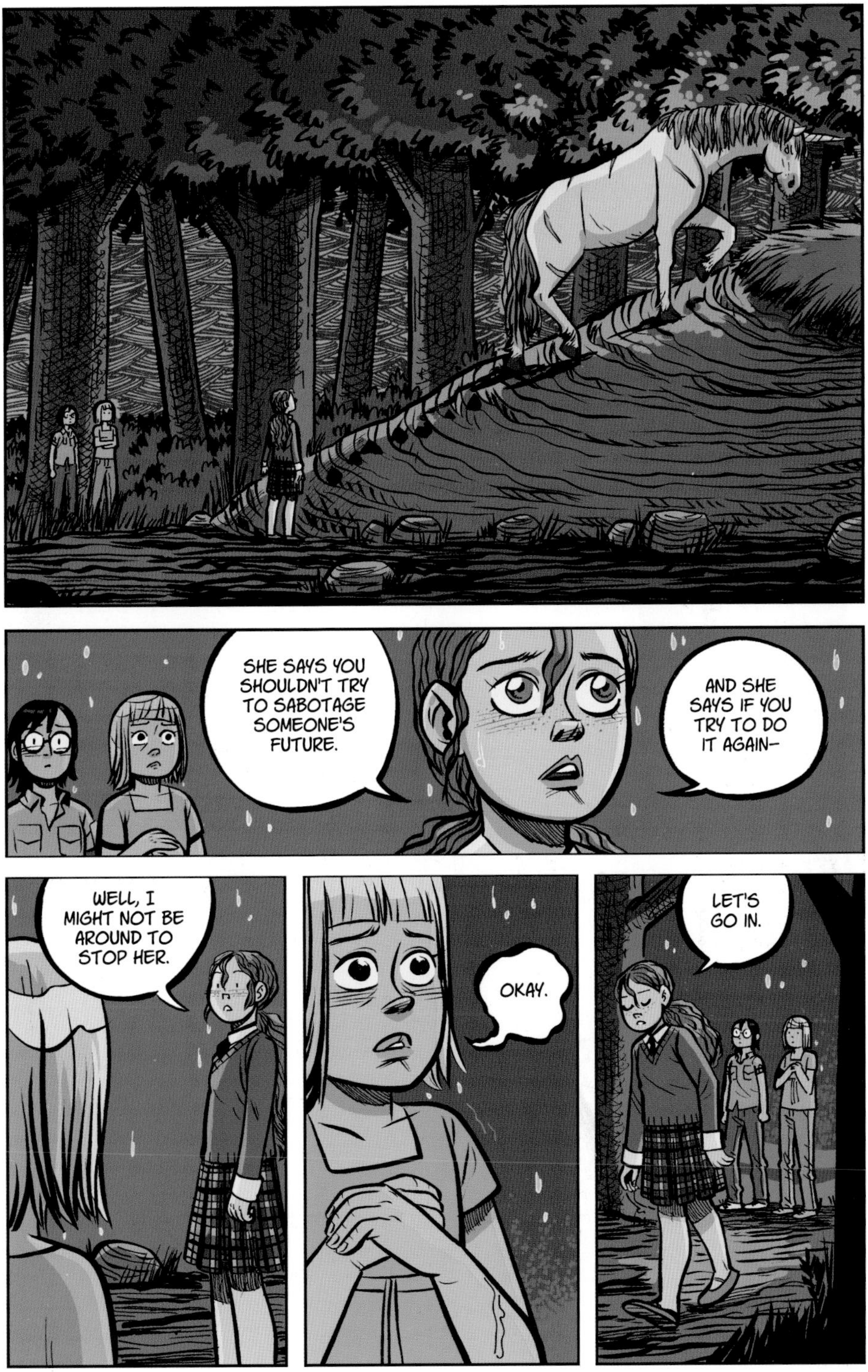
SHE SAYS YOU SHOULDN'T TRY TO SABOTAGE SOMEONE'S FUTURE.
AND SHE SAYS IF YOU TRY TO DO IT AGAIN–
WELL, I MIGHT NOT BE AROUND TO STOP HER.
OKAY.
LET'S GO IN.

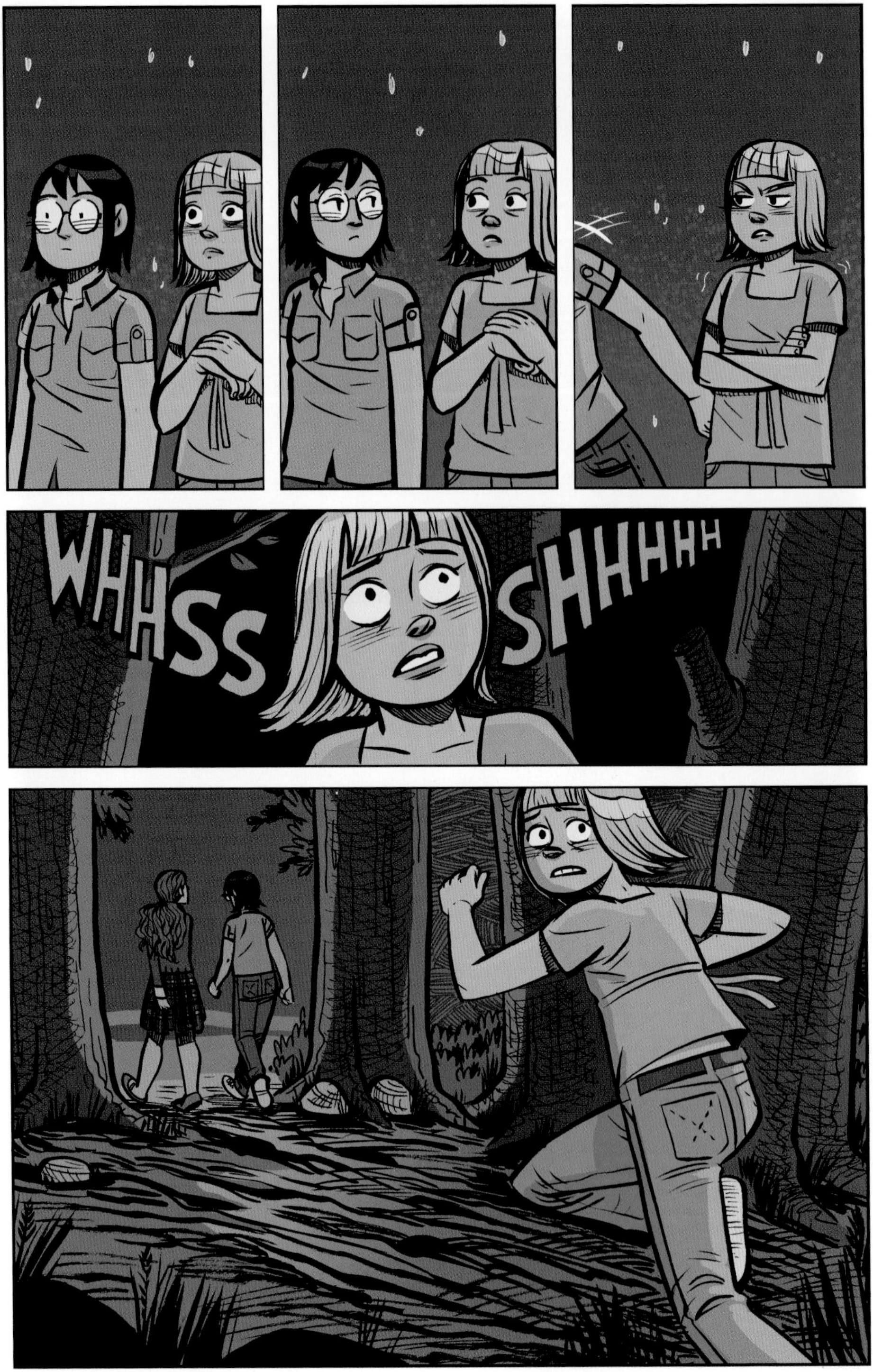
WHHSS
SHHHHH

Chapter Twelve

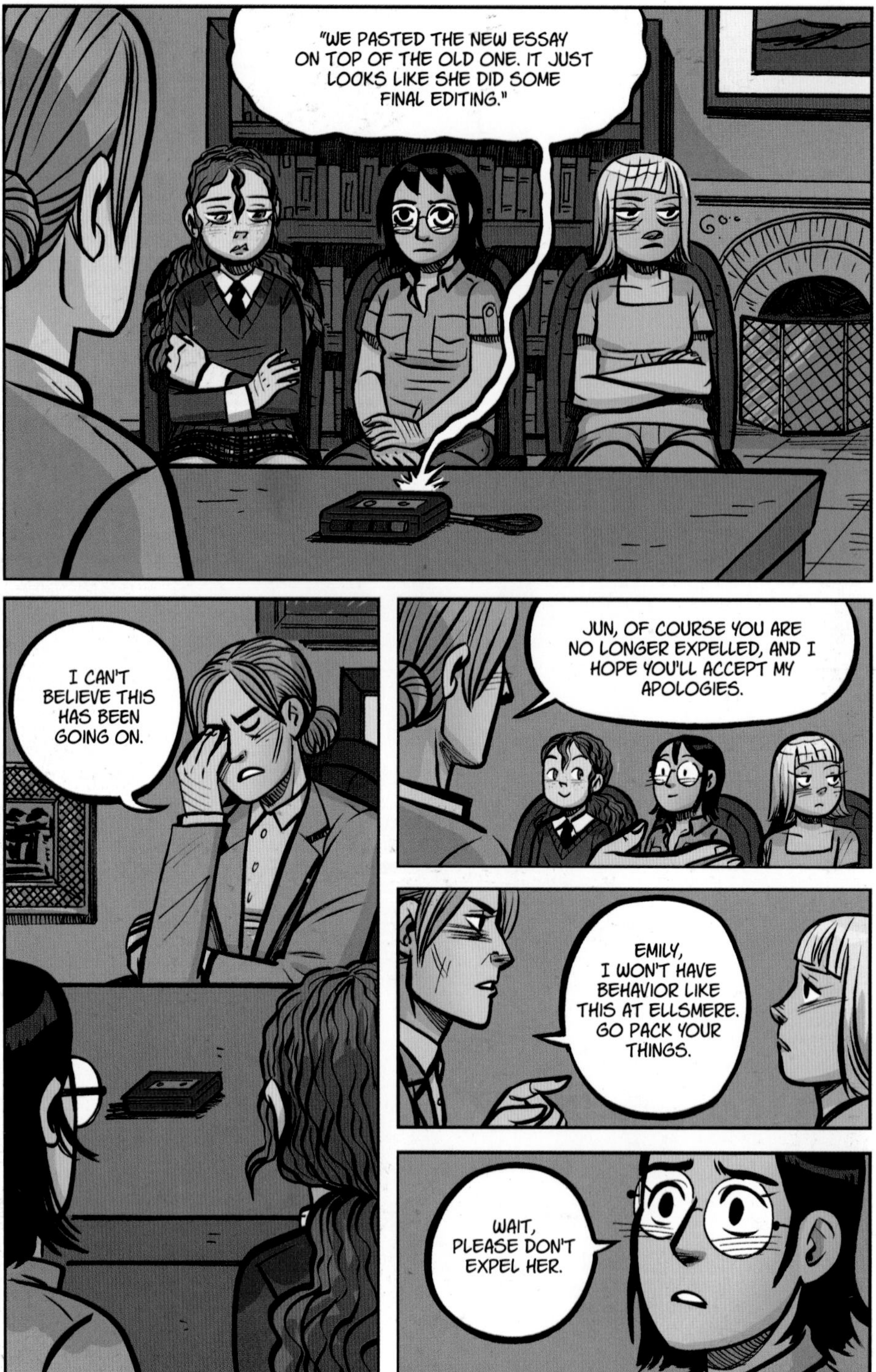
"WE PASTED THE NEW ESSAY ON TOP OF THE OLD ONE. IT JUST LOOKS LIKE SHE DID SOME FINAL EDITING."
I CAN'T BELIEVE THIS HAS BEEN GOING ON.
JUN, OF COURSE YOU ARE NO LONGER EXPELLED, AND I HOPE YOU'LL ACCEPT MY APOLOGIES.
EMILY, I WON'T HAVE BEHAVIOR LIKE THIS AT ELLSMERE. GO PACK YOUR THINGS.
WAIT, PLEASE DON'T EXPEL HER.

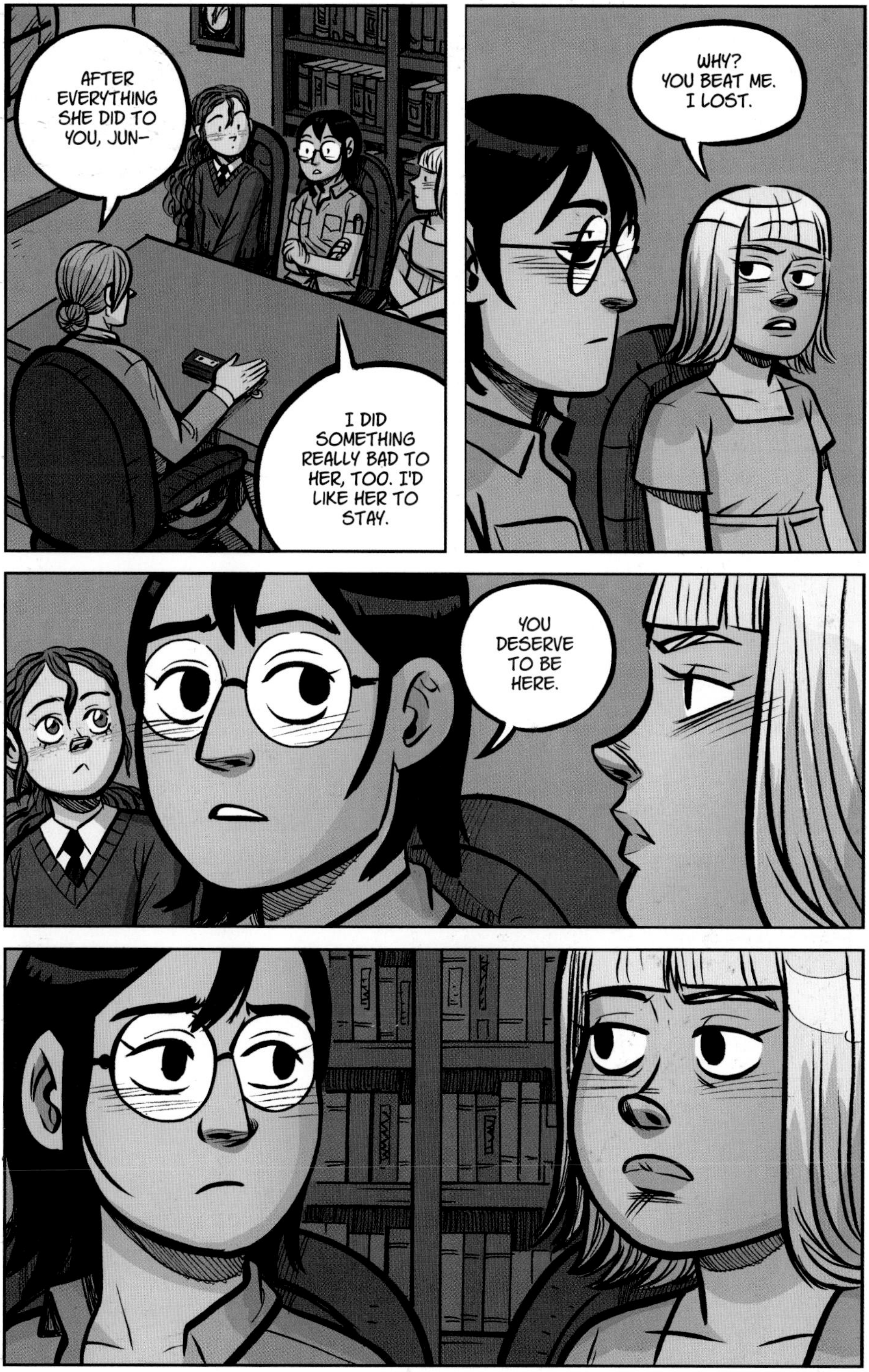
AFTER EVERYTHING SHE DID TO YOU, JUN-
I DID SOMETHING REALLY BAD TO HER, TOO. I'D LIKE HER TO STAY.
WHY? YOU BEAT ME. I LOST.
YOU DESERVE TO BE HERE.

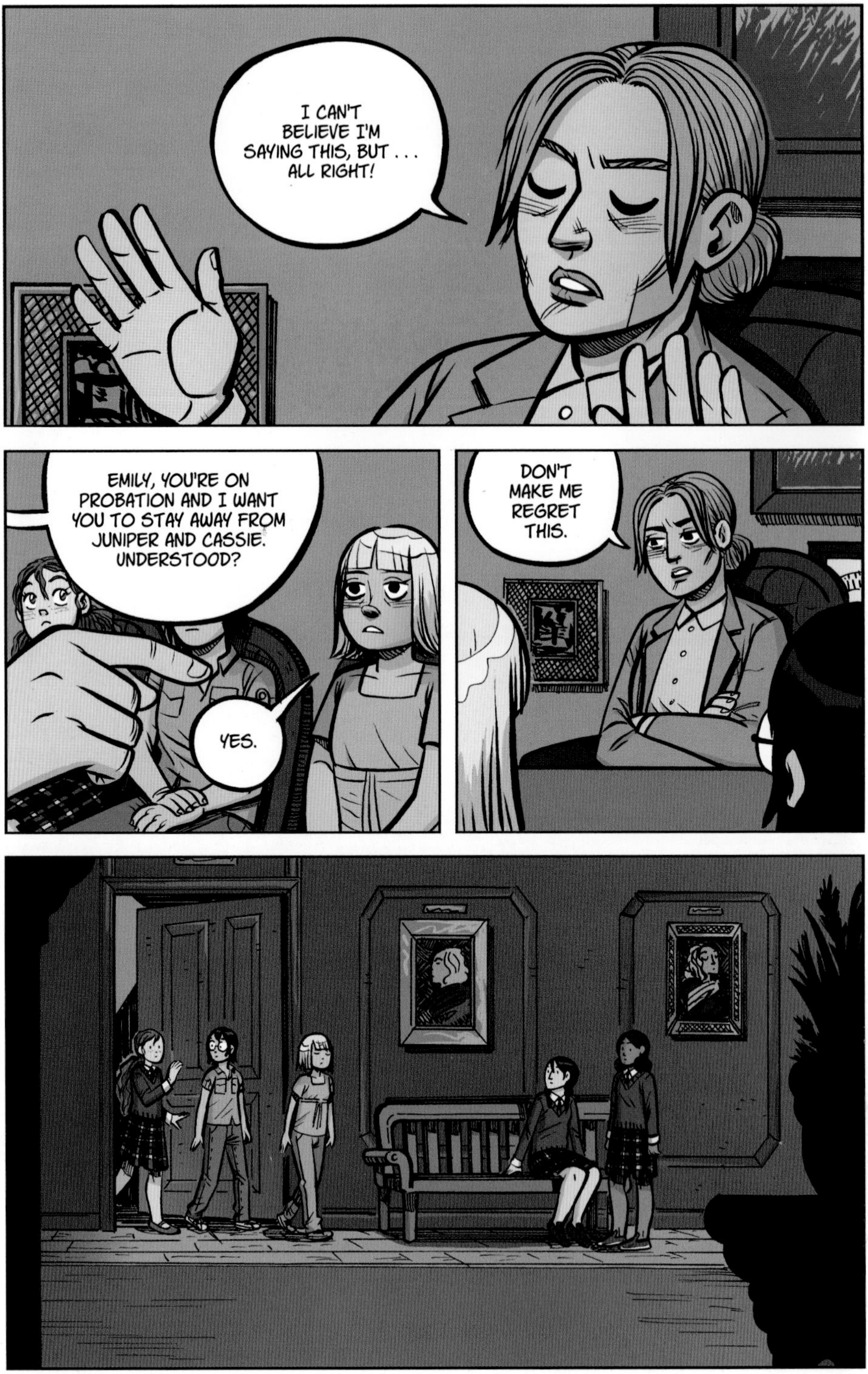
I CAN'T BELIEVE I'M SAYING THIS, BUT . . . ALL RIGHT!
EMILY, YOU'RE ON PROBATION AND I WANT YOU TO STAY AWAY FROM JUNIPER AND CASSIE. UNDERSTOOD?
YES.
DON'T MAKE ME REGRET THIS.

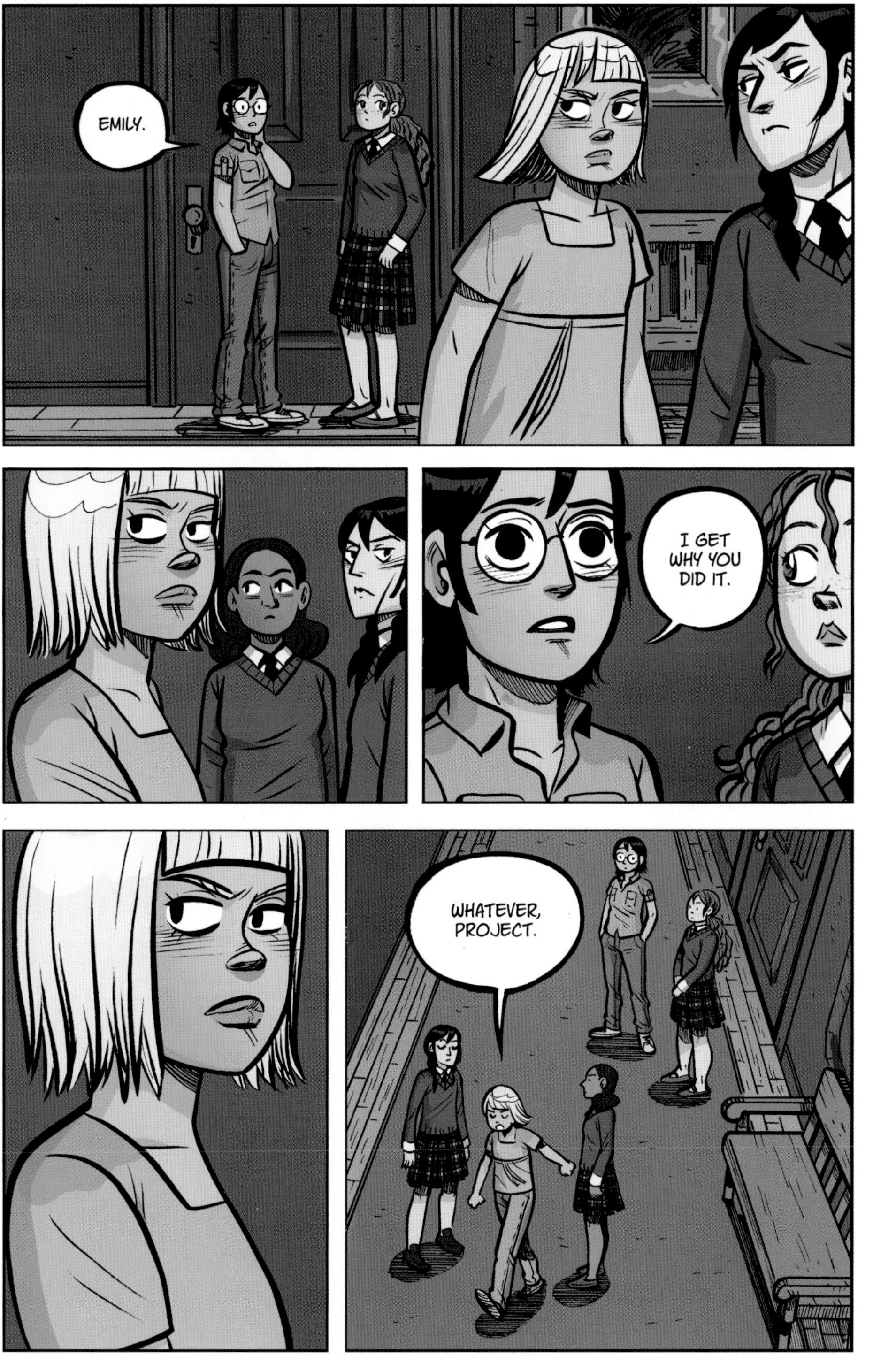
EMILY.
I GET WHY YOU DID IT.
WHATEVER, PROJECT.

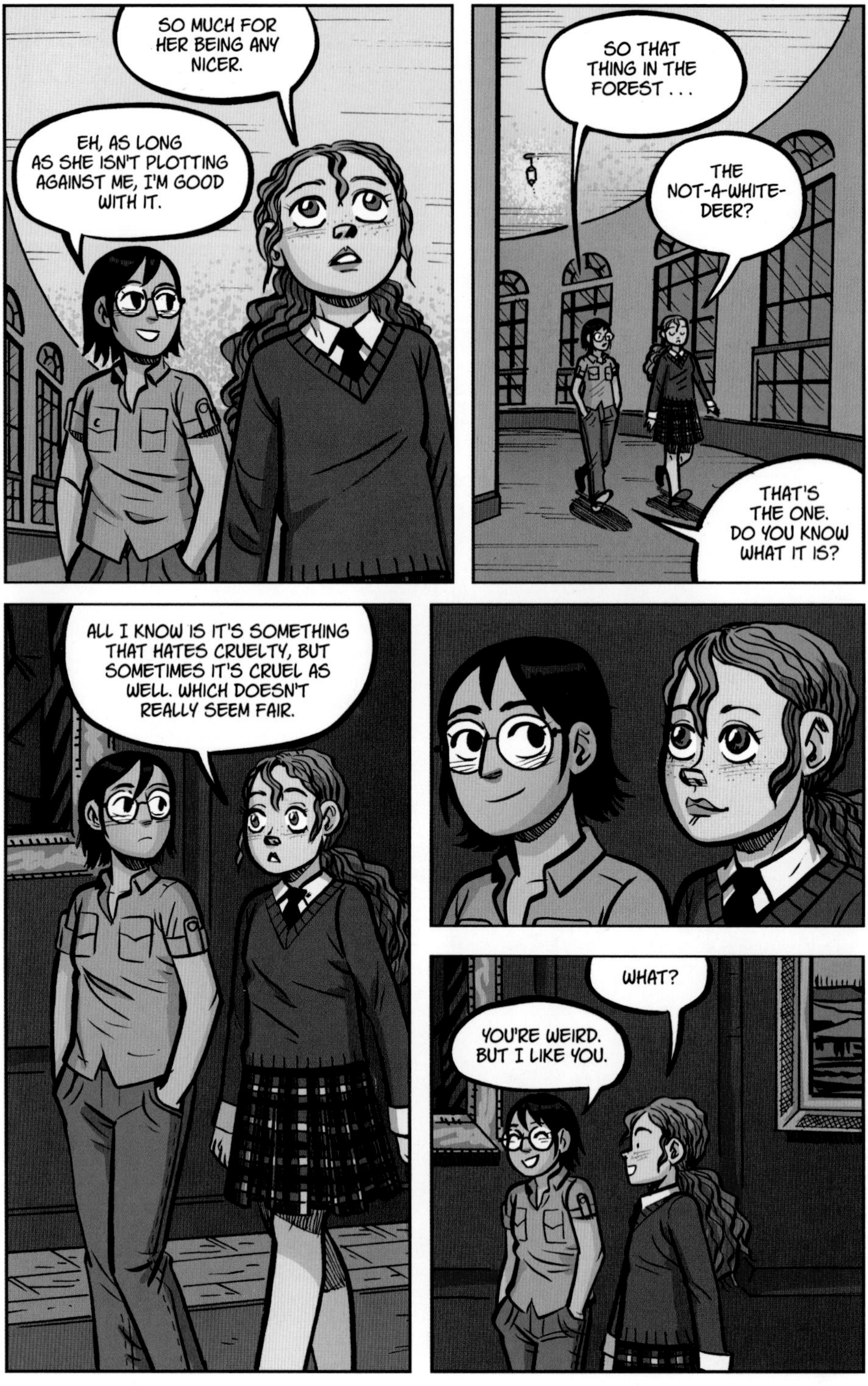
SO MUCH FOR HER BEING ANY NICER.
EH, AS LONG AS SHE ISN'T PLOTTING AGAINST ME, I'M GOOD WITH IT.
SO THAT THING IN THE FOREST . . .
THE NOT-A-WHITE-DEER?
THAT'S THE ONE. DO YOU KNOW WHAT IT IS?
ALL I KNOW IS IT'S SOMETHING THAT HATES CRUELTY, BUT SOMETIMES IT'S CRUEL AS WELL. WHICH DOESN'T REALLY SEEM FAIR.
WHAT?
YOU'RE WEIRD. BUT I LIKE YOU.

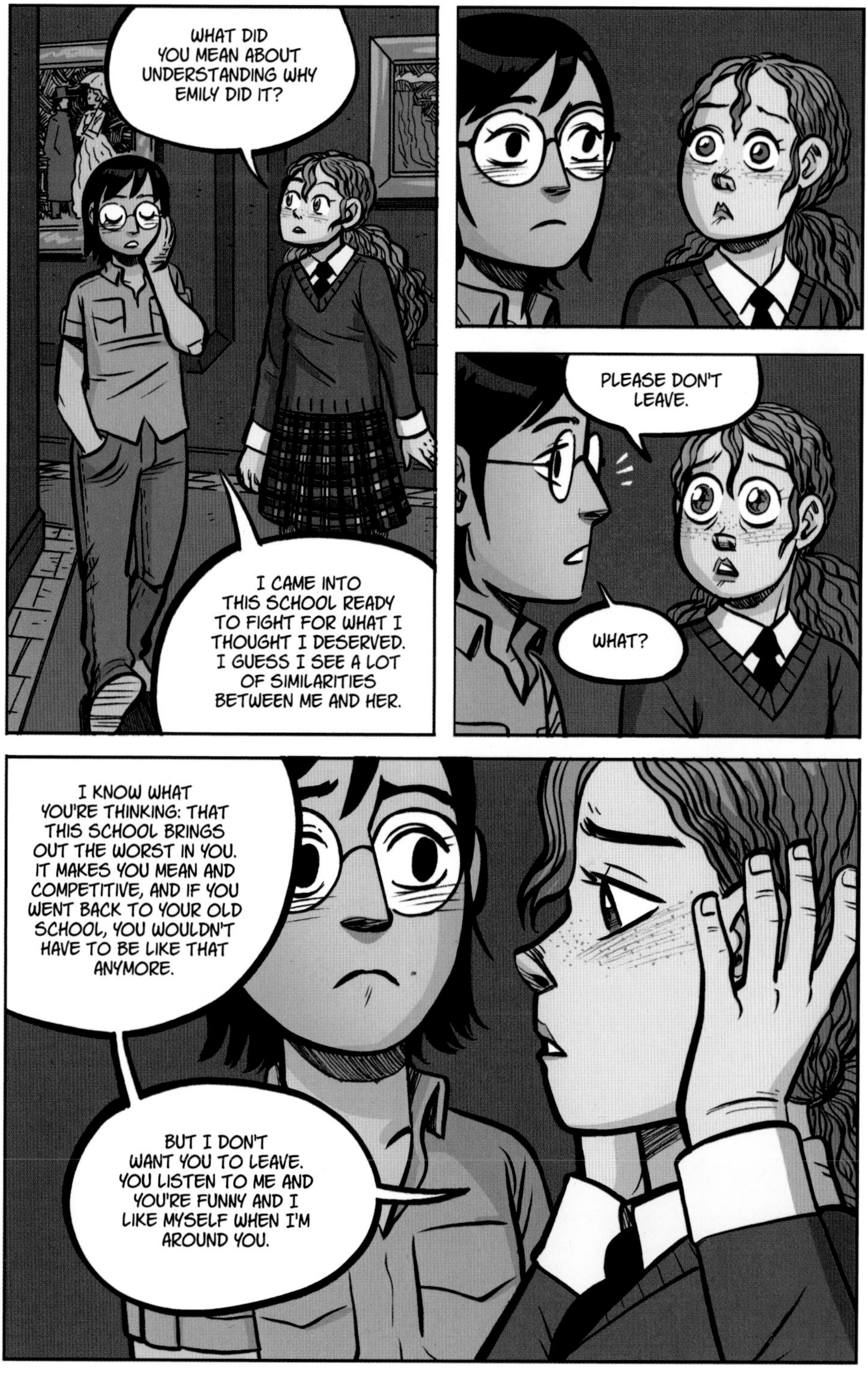
WHAT DID YOU MEAN ABOUT UNDERSTANDING WHY EMILY DID IT?
I CAME INTO THIS SCHOOL READY TO FIGHT FOR WHAT I THOUGHT I DESERVED. I GUESS I SEE A LOT OF SIMILARITIES BETWEEN ME AND HER.
PLEASE DON'T LEAVE.
WHAT?
I KNOW WHAT YOU'RE THINKING: THAT THIS SCHOOL BRINGS OUT THE WORST IN YOU. IT MAKES YOU MEAN AND COMPETITIVE, AND IF YOU WENT BACK TO YOUR OLD SCHOOL, YOU WOULDN'T HAVE TO BE LIKE THAT ANYMORE.
BUT I DON'T WANT YOU TO LEAVE. YOU LISTEN TO ME AND YOU'RE FUNNY AND I LIKE MYSELF WHEN I'M AROUND YOU.

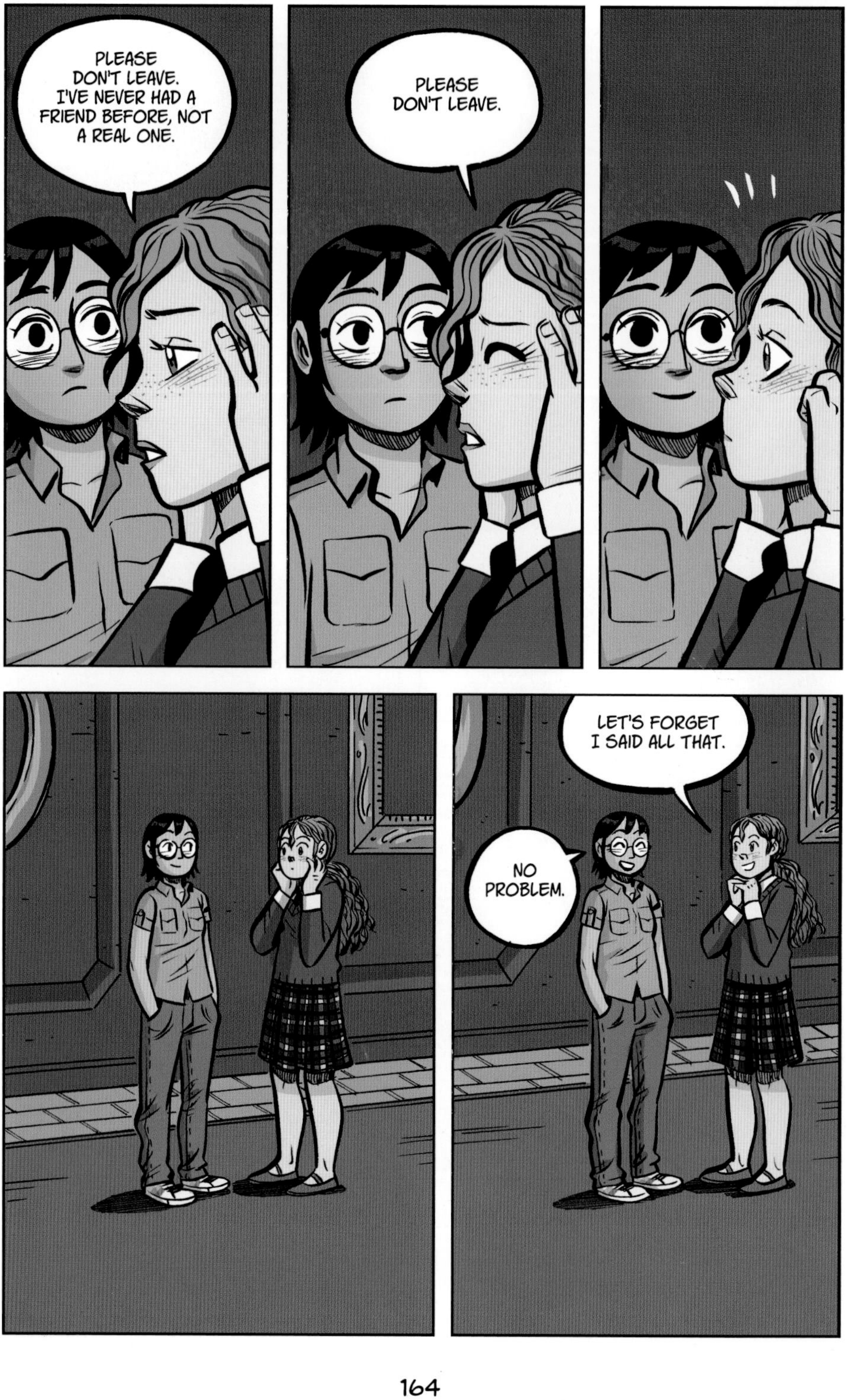
PLEASE DON'T LEAVE. I'VE NEVER HAD A FRIEND BEFORE, NOT A REAL ONE.
PLEASE DON'T LEAVE.
LET'S FORGET I SAID ALL THAT.
NO PROBLEM.

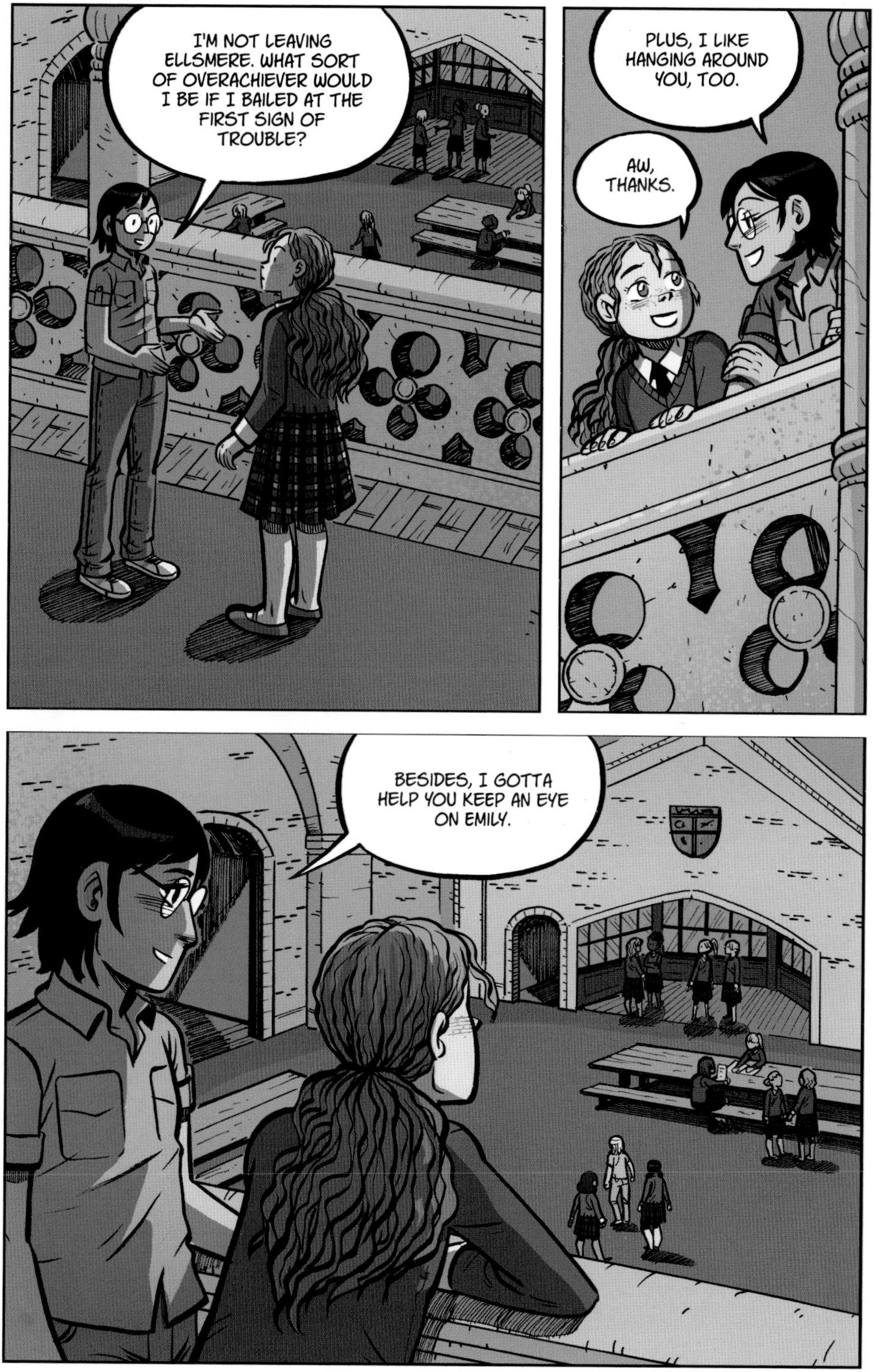
I'M NOT LEAVING ELLSMERE. WHAT SORT OF OVERACHIEVER WOULD I BE IF I BAILED AT THE FIRST SIGN OF TROUBLE?
PLUS, I LIKE HANGING AROUND YOU, TOO.
AW, THANKS.
BESIDES, I GOTTA HELP YOU KEEP AN EYE ON EMILY.

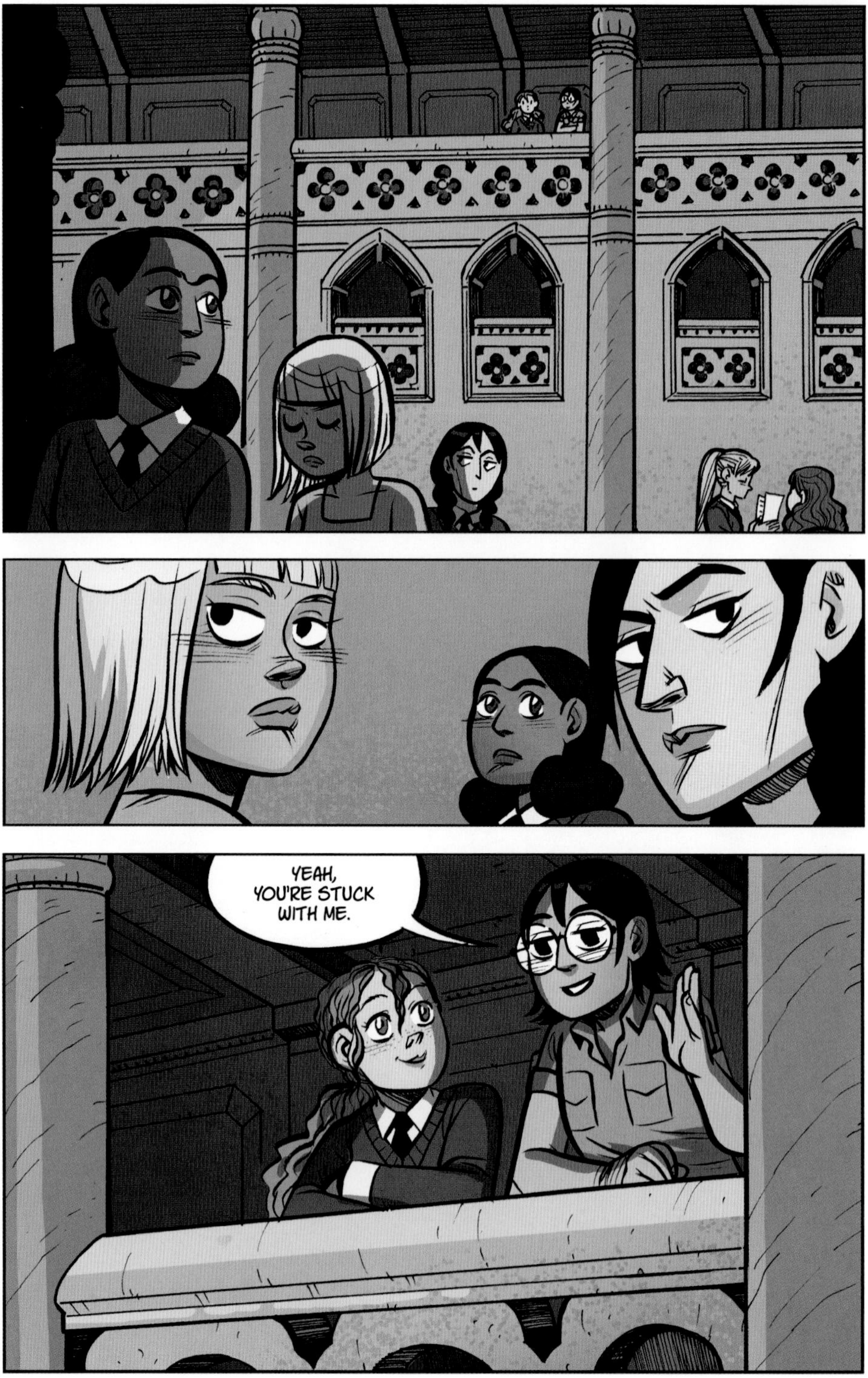
YEAH,
YOU'RE STUCK
WITH ME.

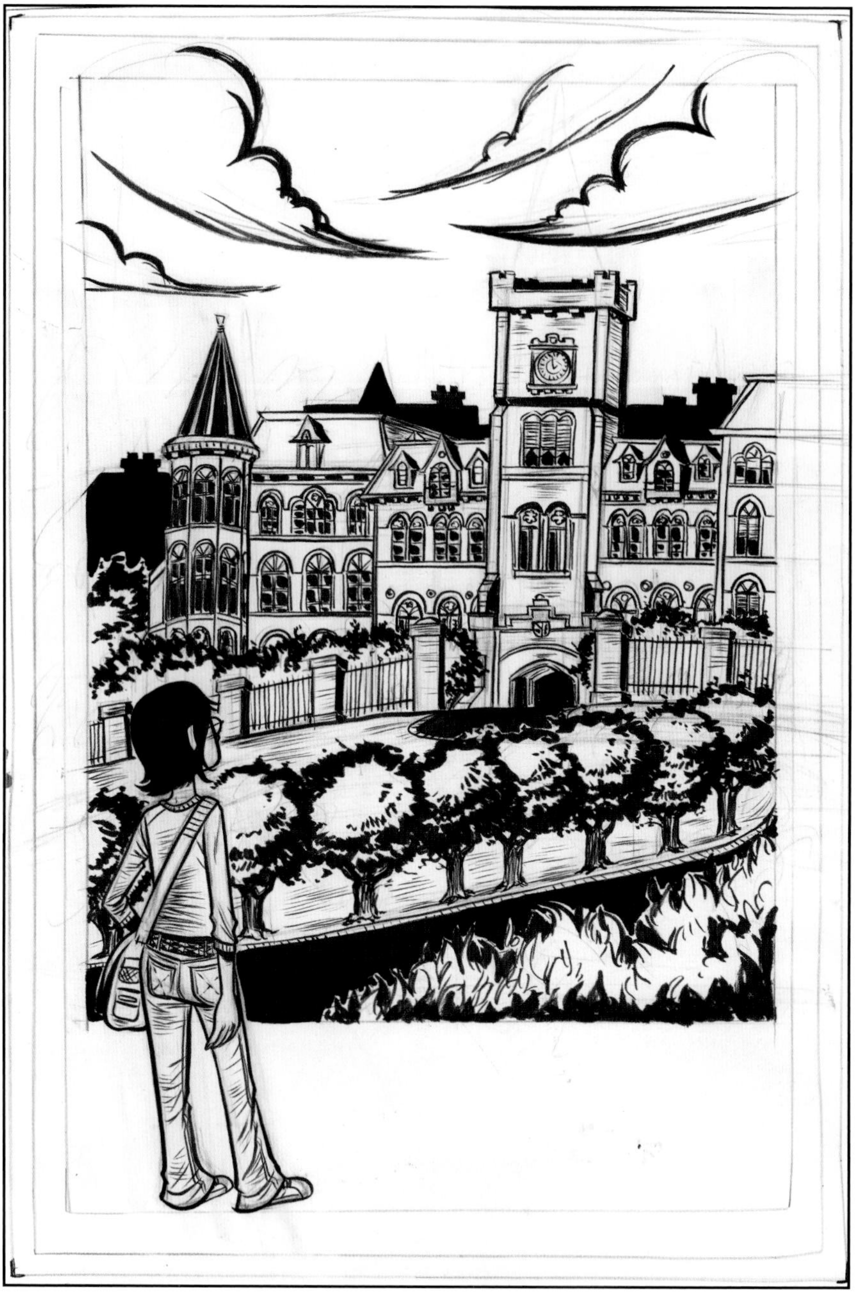

Here is the original page 1 of Ellsmere, which I dug out of storage. I decided I wanted to re-ink the entire book, so I started by scanning the old pages into my computers.

Using Adobe Photoshop, I turned the line art blue so it was ready for editing. The reason I use blue for line art is that the blue is too light for my scanner to pick up when I scan the inked page back into the computer. No worries about erasing or stray pencil lines messing up my inks!

I did some edits to the drawing of Juniper using my Wacom Cintiq (a monitor you can draw on), but left the background as it was originally. This is what I did throughout the editing process: I often redrew or corrected the character drawings, but left the backgrounds alone.

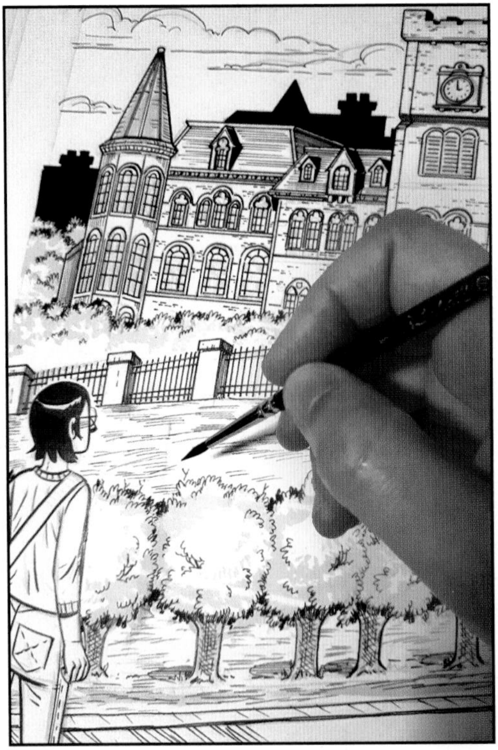

Then I printed out the pages onto sheets of Bristol paper, and inked them with a watercolor brush. This is how I make my comics normally, penciling digitally and inking traditionally.

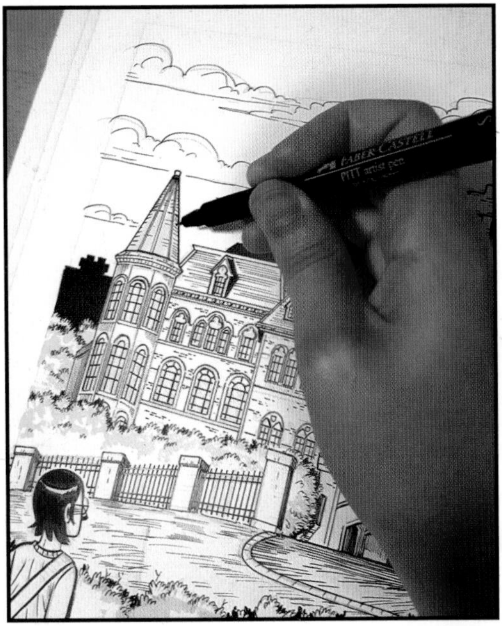
FABER-CASTELL
PITT artist pen

For any inking that required a ruler (like buildings), I used a Faber-Castell pen.

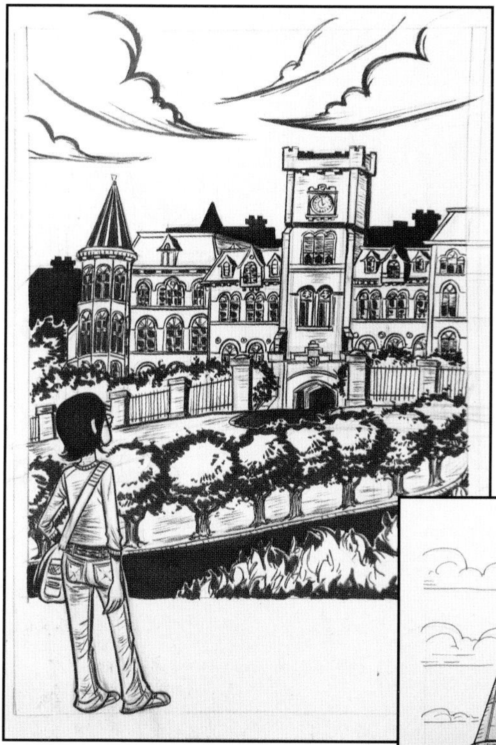

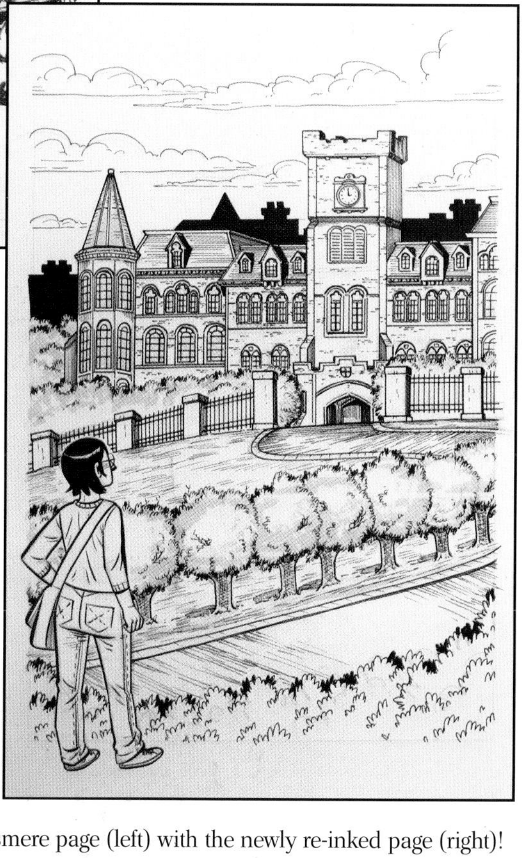

Here's a comparison of the original Ellsmere page (left) with the newly re-inked page (right)! They look a lot different, don't they? I'm very happy I was able to give this comic a spiffy new look. I think it turned out great!

ELLSMERE ACADEMY FOR GIRLS

First Second

Copyright © 2020 by Faith Erin Hicks
Published by First Second
First Second is an imprint of Roaring Brook Press,
a division of Holtzbrinck Publishing Holdings Limited Partnership
120 Broadway, New York, NY 10271

Previously published in Canada in 2008 by SLG Publishing as *The War at Ellsmere*.

Don't miss your next favorite book from First Second!
For the latest updates go to firstsecondnewsletter.com and sign up for our enewsletter.

Library of Congress Control Number: 2019903650
Paperback ISBN: 978-1-250-21910-7
Hardcover ISBN: 978-1-250-21909-1

Our books may be purchased in bulk for promotional, educational, or business use.
Please contact your local bookseller or the Macmillan Corporate and Premium Sales Department
at (800) 221-7945 ext. 5442 or by email at MacmillanSpecialMarkets@macmillan.com.

First Second edition edited by Calista Brill and Kiara Valdez
Cover design by Colleen AF Venable
Interior book design by Rob Steen and Molly Johanson
Color by Shelli Paroline

Originally drawn in 2008 on Bristol paper with a Col-Erase blue pencil, inked with a Pentel
brush pen. Redrawn in 2019 on a Wacom Cintiq in Manga Studio, inked with a
Raphael Kolinsky watercolor brush, size 1.

Printed in China by 1010 Printing International Limited, North Point, Hong Kong

Paperback: 10 9 8 7 6 5 4 3 2 1
Hardcover: 10 9 8 7 6 5 4 3 2 1